MAIN
KANSAS CITY KANSAS
PUBLIC LIBRARY

BOUNDARY CROSSED

D1248385

By Melissa F. Olson

Scarlett Bernard novels

Dead Spots
Trail of Dead
Hunter's Trail

Short Fiction

Sell-By Date: An Old World Short Story
Bloodsick: An Old World Novella

Lena Dane mysteries

The Big Keep

BOUNDARY CROSSED

A NOVEL OF THE OLD WORLD

MELISSA F. OLSON

47N⬦RTH

This is a work of fiction. Names, characters, organizations, places, events, and incidents are either products of the author's imagination or are used fictitiously.

Text copyright © 2015 Melissa F. Olson
All rights reserved.

No part of this book may be reproduced, or stored in a retrieval system, or transmitted in any form or by any means, electronic, mechanical, photocopying, recording, or otherwise, without express written permission of the publisher.

Published by 47North, Seattle

www.apub.com

Amazon, the Amazon logo, and 47North are trademarks of Amazon.com, Inc., or its affiliates.

ISBN-10: 1477849432
ISBN-13: 9781477849439

Cover Design by Jason Blackburn
Cover Image by Mae I Design

Library of Congress Control Number: 1477849432

Printed in the United States of America

For Beth, Stephi, and Chris: each of you has sculpted a part of me.

Chapter 1

The third time I died was early on a Monday morning, a week after Labor Day.

I was working third shift at the Flatiron Depot on Arapahoe Ave, one of a small chain of twenty-four-hour convenience stores in my hometown of Boulder, Colorado. It was just after three in the morning, and I had spent the last two hours building an elaborate promotional display out of twelve-packs of soda, pushing the boxes in or out to spell the word "Welcome." I'd used brands of soda that came in black, silver, and gold for the lettering. The whole thing was a not-so-subtle attempt to kiss the asses of the incoming University of Colorado students, who would be stopping in for school supplies and all the weird little objects you find yourself needing whenever you move: box cutters and screwdrivers and lots and lots of chargers for assorted electronic devices. We've got it all at the Flatiron Depot, or at least that's what my boss makes me say when I answer the phone.

I was just standing back to admire my work, hands on my hips, a little sweaty from hauling the twelve-packs around, when I heard two people bickering in the baby aisle.

"Why would I have any idea what brand to get?" a female voice whined. "You think just because I've got tits, I know everything about diapers?"

I winced at the florid use of the word "tits" at such high volume, although it wasn't like there were a lot of minors in the store in the middle of the night. An exasperated male voice replied, "I dunno, let's just get the generic, then. What size do you think she needs?" Their accents sounded East Coast to me. Tourists, probably.

"She's what, like a year old? Is there a one-year-old size?" she said, frustrated.

No, there is not. I sighed as I left the soda display and trudged toward the voices. How do you have a one-year-old baby without knowing what size diapers to buy? They were probably used to using cloth diapers or something, I decided.

I was still an aisle away when the male voice said, "Look, it goes by weight. How much does she weigh?"

"Um . . . maybe like twenty-five pounds?"

I rounded an endcap display of neck pillows and saw them: a huge man and a woman about my size, both of them a couple of years younger than my thirty-one. They were huddled around a box of diapers, and sure enough, there was something distinctly non-Boulder about them. If cities were high schoolers, Boulder would sit at the trendy-hippie table in the cafeteria, along with Madison, Berkeley, and Portland. But the people in front of me were dressed in expensive jeans, black leather jackets, and leather boots. The woman's golden hair was highlighted six ways to Sunday, and the man had a tighter buzz cut than I'd seen since I was discharged from the army. Yes, they definitely looked new to Boulder.

Behind the man's legs I spotted a baby carrier, the kind that clips into a base that you leave in the car. They'd set it sideways so the baby was facing the wall of diapers too, which I found kind of funny, like they were hoping he or she might recommend a brand.

"Can I help you?" I said, keeping my tone polite.

The couple looked up, both with startled expressions on their faces like I'd conjured myself out of the air. "We're fine, lady," the woman said sullenly, at the exact same time as the guy said, "We don't usually buy diapers, is all . . ."

"No problem," I said, glancing between them. I was trying to sound sympathetic. My manager, Big Scott, had recently criticized my "approachability," suggesting that in the last ten months I had begun to give off a "hermit vibe." "Cloth diapers can be great," I continued, "but it's definitely worth it to have a couple of disposables on hand too, for emergencies." I stepped closer. "Do you know how much your son or daughter—" I automatically glanced down into the baby carrier, and just like that there was a pained roaring in my ears, as though everything in the store had been suddenly sucked into my chest. The baby in the car seat was about a year and a half old, dressed in warm fleece pajamas, and covered with a light cotton swaddling blanket. Uneven tufts of dark brown hair stuck out in funny whorls all over her head, which was crooked to one side, practically resting on her left shoulder. Her eyes were closed, but I knew they would be bright blue.

Just like her mother's. And just like mine.

"That's not your baby," I said almost absently, taking an unconscious step closer. Was I nuts? *It can't be Charlotte*, I told myself. That was just stupid. My niece was two miles away, fast asleep at her father's house. I had to be imagining the resemblance. Lots of babies look alike, don't they?

But even though it seemed impossible, I knew I was right. I had bought her those pajamas myself, and the swaddling blanket had a purple stain from when my mother had given her grape juice. I remembered myself and stood up straighter, glaring at the couple. "That's not your baby," I said, iron in my voice now.

"Of course it is," the woman insisted. "This is our daughter, Sally."

"*No.*" Currents of fear for my niece were racing through my body like rats in a maze with no exit. There was so much space between them and me, and no space at all between them and Charlie. Without realizing it, I had loosened my stance, readying myself for a fight. "Her name is Charlotte Allison Wheaton, and she's my niece. Turn around and walk away from her. *Now.*"

They both stared at me with empty, alien eyes. They didn't look outraged by my kidnapping accusation, or even all that concerned. Instead, they gazed at me with cold, distant curiosity, like I'd just performed an interesting card trick.

"Bettina!" I hollered, loud enough for my coworker at the cash registers to hear. "Call 911!"

"Um . . . really?" came a small voice from the front. Bettina is a twenty-five-year-old single mother of two. She's so passive that our store manager forbids her from working on Black Friday, for fear of a riot.

"*NOW!*" I screamed.

The couple exchanged a glance. The man nodded, and the woman took a few steps backward, slinking away. Then she abruptly *vanished.* It was startling, but I didn't bother to process it. I kept my eyes trained on the baby. On Charlie. My scream had caused her to stir a little, but she was still mostly asleep. I edged closer.

The man reached toward me quickly, and I braced myself, ready to flip him on his ass. Instead of striking me or restraining me, however, he curled one hand around the back of my neck, bringing me in close, as if for a kiss. That surprised me enough that I was off balance when he tangled his fingers in my hair and dragged me backward, farther away from the baby.

Yelping with pain, I instinctively raised my hands to where he was gripping me. Then I remembered my combat training and relaxed my arms, trying to ignore the pain so I could pull together a strike to his solar plexus. Anticipating the movement, he gave my head a little jerk and arched it up so I would meet his eyes. He was handsome in a hawkish, angular kind of way.

"You never saw us," he whispered, his voice suddenly a soothing arc of honey and promises. "We were never here, and neither was the kid."

He was giving me the weirdest look, which I can only describe as *significant*, like he was trying to imply something I wasn't getting. Acting on some instinct I didn't really understand, I let myself slacken in his grip, my eyes unfocusing, my face relaxing. A small smile played at the corners of his mouth.

And then I kneed him as hard as I could in the testicles.

The blow should have floored him, but he just released me and bent over a little, wincing. *Fine.* I pulled back my leg to knee him in the face, but before I could do more than shift my weight, he looked up at me and snarled. I almost fell over at the sight.

His face wasn't human.

I don't know how else to describe it; it was like all the life had fled his face, replaced by a monster that now glared at me through the thin barrier of his eyes. I didn't really register his moving, but suddenly my back was smacking into the linoleum floor, and the guy had my wrists pinned on either side of my head. He straddled me, snarling again, and all of a sudden I felt split in two: part of me was so frightened I couldn't feel my limbs, while another part of me was oddly pleased. The more this guy focused on me, the less attention he could pay to Charlie.

But now the woman had returned, abruptly appearing behind the guy with an impatient look on her face. "Hurry *up*, Victor," she complained, as though he was lingering over coffee. "We gotta get out of here before someone else shows up."

"She won't press," Victor growled, keeping his eyes on me. I tried wiggling my wrist, hoping to break his hold, but his grip was like a piece of steel rebar bent around my limbs. Even for a big guy, he was freakishly strong.

"Then just kill her," the woman said in a bored voice. "We're leaving this shithole anyway."

Victor darted his head down toward me, moving faster than should be possible, but the woman broke in. "No! It should look like a robbery or something. We'll get the other one on the way out."

I understood that "the other one" was Bettina. They were going to kill her too.

"Right," Victor grunted. He released my left hand to reach into his pocket, pulling out a wicked, very illegal switchblade. He hit the button to release the weapon.

But now my left arm was free. And I happen to be left-handed. I reached toward the shelf next to me and grabbed a thick glass jar of baby food, swinging it as hard as I could to brain him in the temple. The jar cracked in my hand, sending liquid peas spurting through my fingers. Victor dropped the knife and recoiled slightly, but then he just gave his head a little shake and batted the ruined container from my hand with an easy swipe. He collected my wrist with another snap of movement, like grabbing a fly out of the air. I stared in surprise. That had been a perfect shot; it should have dented his skull and maybe even knocked him out. Who . . . or *what* . . . was this guy?

"Stop fucking around, Victor!" the woman said sharply. I risked a glance and registered that she'd been thrusting her hand into various boxes of diapers, taking handfuls and shoving them into her purse. "Kill her and let's go."

Her raised voice finally woke baby Charlie, who began to squall in her car seat. Both Victor and the woman turned to glance behind them at the baby, and I saw my opportunity: I twisted my wrist toward the weakest part of the guy's grip, where his thumb and forefinger met, and managed to slip my right wrist out of his iron hold. His head snapped back around toward me, irritation in his eyes. Moving as fast as I could before he grabbed me again, I held my first two fingers as rigid as possible and thrust them into his eye sockets. I don't care how hard your skull is: everybody has eyeballs, and nobody's eyeballs are made of granite.

I jammed my fingers, spraining the joint with the force of the strike. It worked, though: Victor screamed and scrambled back, toward the baby. Then he screamed anew, like being near her had somehow wounded him further. He lurched back farther, toward the woman, wailing in pain.

I ignored both of them and scooted as fast as I could toward baby Charlie, keeping my injured left fingers off the ground. "It's okay, pumpkin," I crooned to her over her crying. She gave a startled hiccup and looked up at me, recognizing my voice. "It's Aunt Lex, babe. Let's get you out of there," I whispered. I undid her car seat straps with my working fingers, which was easier than it sounds because I knew exactly where the buttons were and how they worked. They'd kidnapped Charlie in her own goddamned car seat.

The couple had disappeared around the corner of the aisle, but I couldn't hear their footsteps over the whimpering baby. I picked Charlie up and gathered her to my chest—and then I felt the thrust of the knife into my back. It was followed by another. And another.

I screamed, upsetting the baby all over again, and turned my head just enough to see my attacker. The woman had circled the aisle and crept up behind me, picking up the knife on her way. She shot me a wicked, triumphant smile as she flicked my blood off the blade.

Shock kicked in, dulling the pain. I could still move my right arm, but the left felt damaged. She'd sliced some tendons, and definitely punctured at least one lung—my breath was coming in hard-earned jags. I fought just to keep breathing. The woman was screaming something at me, and there was movement in my peripheral vision—the man?—but my whole world narrowed to the baby in my arms. I hugged Charlie to my chest, whispering nonsense into her hair and ignoring the fingers that tried to pry her away from me. I felt the warm blood running down my back, into my khaki work pants, but I ignored it.

I was gonna die. For good, this time.

The knowledge filled me with a creeping, acidic calm, but it was replaced by fear for my niece. When I was dead, they could just take her from me. I had no idea what they wanted with Charlie, but it couldn't be anything good. And I couldn't save her.

Then I heard the sirens.

Bettina must have hit the alarm button before the woman got to her, bless her passive little heart. Behind me, the woman cursed loudly. The man had stumbled away from Charlie and me, and I heard him say something to her from fifteen feet behind us, calling her Darcy. I didn't bother trying to fight anymore. I didn't have to beat them; I didn't even have to live. All I had to do was keep Charlie safe until those sirens got here. I locked my arms around the baby without squeezing, curling my body to cover as much of her as possible. It probably should have hurt, but my body was in shock by then, and I didn't notice any pain. All that mattered was Charlie.

I slumped sideways, managing to control my fall enough to keep the panicking baby from hitting her head on the floor. Out of the corner of my eye, I could see the couple arguing. As Victor spoke, the woman held the knife up to her lips and absently *licked the blood* that had run down her hand. My blood. She looked at the hand for a moment, then back up at me with confused surprise.

The last thing I registered before passing out was that although there were streaks of blood and other fluids running down his cheeks, Victor's eyes had almost completely healed.

Chapter 2

I knew I was in the hospital long before I managed to open my eyes. I'd spent a lot of time in a German hospital after Iraq, and they smell the same everywhere.

I shifted my weight experimentally, and realized I was lying on my stomach, my head turned to the left, my upper back swathed in something with sticky, itchy edges. I was covered by a light blanket that went to my shoulders. My thoughts were fuzzy, and there was a distant sense of pain that I was certain was being smothered by some pretty delicious painkillers. I automatically tried to swallow and discovered that I had a chest tube. And a catheter. Great. Straining with effort, I finally managed to drag up my eyelids.

The first thing I saw was Charlie's father, John. My brother-in-law was sitting in an uncomfortable-looking chair next to my bed, with his long legs stretched out in front of him and his head propped up on one hand. He wore jeans and a wrinkled canvas shirt with *Luther Shoes*, the name of my father's company, embroidered on the chest. John's eyes were closed, and I studied him for a moment. John was half Arapaho Indian, which is where he got his tawny skin and the black hair that was currently sticking up in uneven tufts, just like Charlie's did when she slept. He looked haggard and pale, as though he'd been indoors for months.

I hoped it hadn't actually been months.

The clock on the wall said six o'clock, and dim early-morning light was streaming in through the window. I made a noise in the back of my throat, and John started awake, his dark eyes pinning me to the bed. He leaned forward, looking at my face gratefully for a long moment. "I thought I'd lost you," he whispered, pushing back a strand of hair that had fallen into my eyes. "I thought I'd lost you, too."

I made the noise again. "Charlie's fine," he assured me, relief in his voice. John was always good at knowing what I needed, often before I did. "I got her checked out; there wasn't a scratch on her. She's with your parents now. Elise is there too. We've been taking turns here."

My cousin Elise was a patrol officer with Boulder PD. I relaxed and managed a teeny nod. Then I was struck by a horrible thought: What if Victor and Darcy hadn't decided to stop for diapers? What if they'd stopped anywhere but the Depot? I winced around my chest tube. We'd gotten lucky.

My left hand was curled up by my cheek, and I raised it and made a scribbling motion. John nodded and took a small pad of paper and a pen off one of those wheeled tray tables. He placed the pad under my left hand and put the pen between my swollen fingers. It didn't hurt, and I upped my assessment of the painkillers. *What happened after?* I wrote laboriously.

"After you saved Charlie?" John finished for me, a tiny smile on his face. "I don't know how much you remember, but you wouldn't let go of her. The paramedics called me, and I drove to the store—" He paused, the echoes of terror etching lines on his face. John's house is only five minutes away from my store, but I couldn't imagine what that drive must have been like. "You handed the baby to me, and . . . and you *died*, Allie. They said your heart stopped. You looked . . ." He trailed off, shaking his head in wonder.

I scribbled on the pad again, and he read it out loud. "'Don't call me Allie.'" He gave me a brief smile. "Right. Sorry."

I wrote, *Bettina?*

"Your coworker? She's fine." A strange look passed over his face, so swiftly that my addled brain couldn't decipher its meaning. "Actually . . . she has no memory of any of it. She doesn't even remember pushing the panic button."

I blinked, surprised. The panic button is a big deal at my store: once a year our store manager holds a special meeting just to go over the rules of when to push it. How could you not remember doing something like that?

John fumbled for the little remote thingy attached to my hospital bed. "Speaking of buttons, we should let them know you're up." Before I could ask, he added, "It's Wednesday, by the way. You spent most of yesterday in surgery." He pressed the button for the nurse, who promised to send the surgeon in to speak with me right away.

I was getting tired already. It's amazing how in a couple of days your body can go from perfect health to getting exhausted by two minutes of conversation. All it took was a little thing like your heart stopping.

While we waited for the doctor, I wrote on the pad again. *The couple—I think names were Darcy and Victor.*

John's face darkened with rage. "I'll tell the police that, but . . . they got away." He looked away from me, and I saw the shame in his eyes. "I didn't hear a *thing*, Lex. They came into my house and took my child, and I didn't even wake up. How is that possible?"

Not your fault, I wrote. I remembered the strange way the couple had moved, how the man had shaken off my blow with the baby food jar like it was nothing. *There was something weird about them.*

John read the message. "What do you mean?" he asked.

Before I could respond, a petite Asian woman in a white lab coat bustled in, eyes glued to a clipboard in front of her. "Good morning, Miss Luther." She looked up, her eyes taking us in. "And Mr. Luther?"

"No, we're not together," John said quietly, not looking at me. "I'm her brother-in-law."

"Oh, sorry," the doctor said with a shrug. "But I need to talk to Allison about her health, and if you two aren't together . . ." She left the sentence hanging, and John picked up the hint.

"Right." He squeezed my good hand and stood up. "I'll check on you later, Lex." Before he could move away I snapped my right fingers to get his attention, then wrote a question on the pad and turned it to face him.

" 'Is someone feeding the herd?' " he read. His face broke into a wide smile. "Yes. We're taking turns with that too. Your dad has a three-inch scratch on his ankle where the gray cat attacked him."

I smiled back around the mouthpiece. That sounded about right. My gray cat, Gus-Gus, hated men for some reason.

John left, and the petite doctor stepped up, fussing with some of the machines near my bed. "I'm Doctor Towne," she told me. "Did I hear correctly that you go by Lex?"

I wrote on the pad. *Yes. Army nickname.* My full name is Allison Alexandra Luther, named for my paternal grandparents, Allison and Alexander. I'd gone by Allie my whole childhood, but a few days into basic training, I'd gone to the barber on post and had all of my long reddish-brown hair buzzed off. I didn't realize at the time that I was setting myself up for a nickname that practically wrote itself.

The doctor just nodded. "Okay, Lex. Are you ready to get that chest tube out?"

Was I ever.

A few unpleasant minutes later, I was sitting up, more or less, though still angled sideways to keep pressure off the stitches on my back. Dr. Towne had given me a big glass of orange juice to sip through a straw. It was supposed to help with the scratchy feeling that the tube had left in my throat.

While I drank, Dr. Towne extracted some X-rays from my file and carried them to the one of those light boxes on the wall to my right. Pinning them up, she pointed. "These are your injuries. You were stabbed five times in the upper back. Three of those wounds went deep into the muscle. We were able to sew them up without a problem, although you'll have some tightness and pain. I'll be recommending physical therapy to help with that."

She pulled that X-ray down and posted up another. "One strike damaged your left lung. Barring complications, it should heal just fine." She pointed to another mark on the X-ray, which I could barely make out. "The last strike was sloppy. Your attacker nicked your left brachiocephalic vein, here, which is why you lost so much blood. We repaired the cut, and gave you quite a bit of blood, but it will take your body some time to stabilize your blood pressure." She shook her head. "Your attacker was apparently *determined* to go for the heart, but the human body is built to protect that organ. If she'd gone for one of the other major arteries instead, she could have killed you." She gave me a wry little smile. "Well, maybe not *you*."

"What does that mean?" I rasped, barely recognizing my own voice.

"Well," Dr. Towne said, looking a little uneasy, "that's the other thing we need to discuss. Your heart wasn't beating when the paramedics arrived. They tried to revive you anyway, which is standard, but frankly, they were surprised when it actually worked."

I nodded. "John told me."

For the first time, the woman's straightforward demeanor faltered, and she looked a little unsure. "Lex," she said gravely, "it wasn't just the one time. Your heart stopped again while they were prepping you, for two minutes. And it stopped *four times* during surgery."

I blinked. That was a lot, even for me. "That happens, though, right?" I asked, my voice an ashy croak. "People die during surgery all the time."

"Not like this," she insisted. "I've never seen anything like it. At one point, the attending surgeon actually called *time of death*, and stopped trying to revive you. They were about to turn off the machines, and suddenly your heart started beating again."

"Oh . . ." I said lamely. What were you supposed to say to something like that? Oops?

The doctor took a deep breath and pressed on. "When you finally stabilized, my attending surgeon called the army and got your records from the hospital in Germany. They were . . . kind of amazing."

I had been airlifted to Germany after I stumbled out of the desert in Iraq, covered in blood. I didn't remember that part, though. And I certainly didn't want to talk about any of it. I mostly just wanted this woman to finish her presentation, so she could leave and I could go back to sleep. "Is there anything else I have to know?" I asked.

Dr. Towne gazed at me, a little wide-eyed at my indifference. I'd heard that some people get really freaked out about being "dead" for a couple of minutes, but it wasn't like it was the first time it had happened to me. "We want to run some tests, maybe do an MRI to figure out why . . . I mean, *how* you managed to recover."

"Is there any indication that my heart's going to stop again?" I asked blandly.

"Well, no, but—"

"Then no more tests," I interrupted her. "That's final." I wasn't going to spend a minute more in the hospital than I absolutely had to. After a moment, Dr. Towne nodded tightly, and I suddenly felt a wave of exhaustion. I felt awful: weak and nauseous and aching despite the painkillers. "Imma sleep now," I mumbled, and was out.

Chapter 3

The next time I opened my eyes, it was just after two o'clock, and my eighteen-month-old niece was doing a little bopping dance on the edge of my bed, her big blue eyes dancing with the secret merriment of babies. I felt something in my heart fill up at the sight of her, looking so happy and unaware. She really was okay.

"Hey, kid," I rasped. The juice and the rest had helped, but my throat still felt like it'd been rubbed with steel wool. My eyes focused in on my mother, who was sitting in the chair next to me, supporting Charlie so the baby could lean against the mattress. She looked exhausted and haggard, which was saying something. Mom was usually one of those women who's always put together, with carefully styled red-black hair and a colorful scarf gracing her neck like a personal token. Everyone who knows her well can read her level of stress by the condition of her clothes and makeup. Today, though, her hair was matted against one side of her head, and she wasn't even wearing powder or mascara. I couldn't remember the last time I'd seen my mother without makeup. *She looks so old*, I thought.

"Hey, Mom," I whispered.

My mother looked up from Charlie, holding my gaze for a long moment before she burst into tears. "Hi, honey," she managed to say. Charlie craned her neck once to check on Grandma's crying, but then turned back to me, blissfully unconcerned. She pounded her hands happily against my sheet, obviously itching to climb up and crawl all over me.

"I'm okay, Mom," I ventured.

"You've got to stop *scaring* me like this," she said through her tears.

"It was for a good cause," I replied weakly, stretching out my right fingers to touch Charlie's hand. She grinned and pounced on my thumb, trying to drag it into her mouth. I'd made the mistake of letting her do that before, though, and I wanted to keep all of my fingers. I pulled them back.

"I know, but . . ." my mother began helplessly, then shook her head, unable to continue. I couldn't blame her. She'd nearly lost me once, then Sam had died, and now I'd put her through another scare.

"Where's Dad?" I asked, trying to change the subject.

She sniffed. "He was here all morning, but he had to go to the office for a couple of hours."

"How's the herd?"

She rolled her eyes. "Ugh. The two yellow dogs got out of the back gate again, but John rounded them up. Oh, and Raja wouldn't let the other cats eat until this morning, which made them just *vicious*."

Raja was my biggest cat, and he fancied himself the lord of the house. "Sounds about right," I said, smiling a little.

"The police want to speak to you as soon as possible," Mom added.

I automatically sat up a little, and immediately regretted it. "Did they find the couple? Or at least figure out who they were?" I asked.

She shook her head. "But they let us take your purse from the store. It's in there." She pointed to a closed closet near the door. "Oh, and Dad and your cousin Paul took your car back to the cabin when they were feeding the herd. The keys are inside on the kitchen counter."

I smiled wider this time. It was good to have family. "Thanks, Mom."

We chatted for a few more minutes about my dad's upcoming sixtieth birthday and my mother's new favorite nail salon, where she wanted to take me when I was out of the hospital. Charlie grew tired of smacking my covers after a while and made a serious effort to climb onto my bed. My mother pulled her off. "We should probably go," she said regretfully. Her eyes were glued to me, like I might evaporate if she looked away. "It's past Charlotte's nap time. Your cousin Jacob is coming to sit with you in a few minutes."

"You guys don't have to do that," I protested. "I'm fine. I don't need babysitters, especially when you all have—"

"Allison Alexandra Luther!" my mother interrupted sternly. Full Christian name. Never a good sign. "You know darn well that that's not how our family does things. Until you get out of intensive care, one of us will always be here during visiting hours." She bent to kiss my forehead, giving Charlie the opening she'd been waiting for to reach down for a fistful of my shoulder-length hair. My mother patiently untangled my hair from her chubby baby fingers and straightened herself up. "I love you," Mom said fiercely. "Get better."

I promised I would.

I managed to stay awake for a full forty-five minutes of Jake's visit. He chatted with me politely, showing me pictures of his daughter on his phone and making quiet jokes about his wife's latest fitness craze without once mentioning the attack or attempted kidnapping. When my eyes started to close, he just kissed my forehead and picked up the remote for the overhead television. Jake was probably the most laid-back of all the cousins: always polite and soft-spoken, quick to smile or to go along with one of Sam's madcap plans when we were kids.

In fact, one of those madcap plans was how I came to acquire the herd. When I came back from the hospital in Germany three years ago, I was in rough shape. My physical recovery had gone well—too well, in fact. The army had never seen anyone recover from what had happened to me, and the doctors who'd treated me in Germany were baffled to the point of suspicion. No one came right out and said I must have been lying about those days in the desert, but I got enough sidelong looks that I wasn't real surprised when they told me I was being honorably discharged.

The first thing I did when I finally returned to Boulder was to have an enormous fight with my parents. I didn't set out to create problems, but my overprotective, endlessly worried parents had just assumed I'd move back in with them and take a job working for my father. They were genuinely shocked when I refused to do either.

Their next offer was to send me to college on their dime, which I also turned down. Finally, they tried just throwing money at me, offering me free access to a trust they would set up for me "until I got on my feet," whatever that meant. I refused that, too. Instead, I couch-hopped at my cousins' houses, took a job at the Depot, and started looking at apartments in one of the few really cheap—and really scuzzy—parts of Boulder. The crappy neighborhood didn't trouble me in the least, mostly because I'd dealt with a hell of a lot worse than a couple of low-grade muggers who might be dumb enough to jump me.

My parents, on the other hand, absolutely lost their shit when they heard about my housing search. Voices were raised, hurtful things were said, and for a moment there it looked like nobody was gonna get anything but coal that Christmas.

It was Sam who finally brokered the peace between us. She and John were living in LA then, but she came back to Boulder for a month when I got out of the hospital, to make sure I was okay. Sam managed to convince our parents that I needed some time and space to myself, at a job that wouldn't cause me any real stress or require me to sit motionless in front of a computer all day. Then she came to me, begging me to accept a compromise: I didn't have to take a dime of our parents' money, but I would allow them to give me, free and clear, the remote three-bedroom "fishing" cabin they barely used anymore.

"Just let them do this for you, Allie," she'd pleaded. "Let them take care of you a little, so they can sleep better at night."

"I'm not in charge of their sleep," I'd told her stubbornly. "And that's not my name anymore."

She'd sighed. "Babe, I am your goddamned twin. You can try to convince everyone else, yourself included, that you're a different person now, but you will always be Allie to me. Now take the fucking cabin and get over yourself."

So I took the cabin.

After a couple of weeks, the family's excitement over my return died down, and everyone went back to their own lives. Sam flew back to LA, but she called me every night, and my parents insisted on weekly visits. Even so, I was only pulling about thirty hours a week at the Flatiron Depot, and I found myself with a lot of free time all of a sudden.

That's when the night terrors started.

I dreamed of my dead friends from the Humvee, the sensation of being dragged through hot sand. I dreamed of the desert, of blistering lips and blood drying on my skin in the hot sun. Each night I woke up screaming, with the taste of sand in my mouth. I switched my work schedule to the night shift, hoping that sleeping in daylight would banish the dreams, but it didn't help. Now it was just lighter outside when I woke up, drenched in sweat, frantic with adrenaline, desperate to save people who were long since dead. I never said anything about the nightmares, but Sam somehow knew. Maybe I sounded tired on the phone, or maybe she had a spy in the family who had noticed the bags under my eyes. At any rate, she tried to get me to talk about it, but I just couldn't go there.

As far back as I could remember, since long before the army, I had felt a darkness around me, a black cloud following me around. Like it was waiting to consume me. Being with my happy-go-lucky sister seemed to push it away when we were kids, and the regimen of the army had done the same. But when I came home from Iraq, the cloud seemed to gain strength, manifesting as the night terrors.

And they kept getting worse, until I was so sleep-deprived that I had a hard time telling the difference between waking and sleeping. Not that I would admit it, of course. Sam knew something was wrong, but no matter how much she cajoled, pleaded, or threatened on the phone, I insisted I was fine. I didn't want her to feel guilty for not being around, and when push came to shove, I could be as stubborn as she was.

So Sam found a work-around. A month after I moved into the cabin, I had just gotten home from my night shift at the Depot when someone knocked on the cabin's front door. I opened it to find my older cousin Jake, with a scruffy black-and-white bulldog mix in his arms. Its head drooped wearily against his red polo shirt, and a long neon-green cast dangled from the dog's right foreleg. "I need a favor," Jake said. He was a veterinarian in nearby Lafayette, and someone had dropped the bulldog mix off at his office after a hit-and-run. "The shelter we usually work with is full," he explained, "and this guy can't stay at the clinic forever. Can you take care of him while I try to find him a home?"

I pulled my robe around my T-shirt and pajama pants and looked doubtfully at the dog. "I'm not really set up for pets," I said lamely. "And I don't know that I'd be any good to him. Can't you take him home?"

"Dani's cat would attack him," Jake said regretfully. Dani was his nine-year-old daughter. "He doesn't need much, just food and someone to help him outside to pee."

I eyed him suspiciously. "Sam put you up to this, didn't she?"

Jake hefted the dog in his arms. "Look, can I just come in and put him down for a second?" he pleaded. "He's getting really heavy."

Of course, I ended up keeping the dog, whom I named Pongo after the father Dalmatian in the Disney movie. Two weeks later, Jake was back with a cat, Raja, and then a cranky, three-legged iguana that I named Mushu, followed by an exceedingly stupid Yorkshire terrier runt I'd had no choice but to call Dopey. Jake brought me all the homeless pets that crossed his path, and within a matter of months my parents' formerly nice cabin had been transformed into a makeshift animal shelter.

To their credit, my parents never said a word about the animal invasion, even when they stopped by to find torn curtains and suspicious stains on the carpets of their former home. Sometimes Jake found the pets' original owners, and sometimes, especially when he brought over cute puppies or kittens, the animals were eventually adopted. Finally I settled on a more or less stable roster of three cats, four dogs, and Mushu, who lived in a cage in his own bedroom so he and the dogs wouldn't try to eat each other. I spent a lot of time taking care of the animals' various ailments, and even more time building a fence around the cabin's backyard so the dogs could run around off-leash. One evening I woke up with Dopey and Pongo sleeping on either side of me and realized that I hadn't had a nightmare in months.

Well played, Sam.

Chapter 4

The next time I opened my eyes, there was a strange man in my hospital room. He had moved the visitor's chair to the foot of the bed, where he was sitting with my chart, reading it intently. He was wearing a dark blue department store suit, not a lab coat. The room was dark, and the clock on the wall read nine-thirty.

"Who're you?" I croaked.

Looking up, the man raised his eyebrows at me. He calmly replaced the chart at the foot of the bed and rose, dragging the visitor's chair back to its place near the head of the bed. He was in his late thirties maybe, tall and slim with pale blond hair, ruddy cheeks, and the kind of translucent Scandinavian skin that would burn instantly in the sun. His face was all interesting angles and cleft chin, creating the overall impression that he should be modeling parkas in an L.L.Bean catalog. The suit was neither particularly nice nor particularly shabby, but I recognized a familiar lump near his armpit—a shoulder holster. I was immediately wary. "Good evening, Miss Luther," the man said, pleasantly enough. "I'm Detective Quinn with Boulder PD."

His hazel eyes pierced mine as he held out his hand, very close to mine so I wouldn't have to work hard to reach it. His handshake was extremely gentle—not weak, exactly, but more like he feared my fingers might crumple to dust. "I'd like to speak to you about the incident at your work."

"Now?" I asked, a little incredulous. I had expected the cops to turn up with questions, particularly since Mom had warned me, but it seemed awfully late. Visiting hours had been over for a while.

Quinn nodded. "As you might imagine, we're very anxious to pursue the couple who kidnapped your niece."

I swallowed, working to get the saliva past my sore throat. "Yes, sir."

"I've seen the security tape, but I'd appreciate it if you would run me through your memories of that night in as much detail as possible," Quinn suggested. Without being asked, he rose and picked up a mug of ice water with a straw from the counter, setting it on the tray table in front of me. "Take your time," he added.

I took him at his word, spending a couple of minutes sipping the water and gathering my thoughts. Then I told him everything, starting from the conversation I'd overheard and ending with the way the man's eyes had seemed to heal even after I'd gouged them. I told him that I thought the couple's names were Victor and Darcy and that they both looked and talked like they were from out of town. I asked him once or twice if the security tape confirmed my story—I really wanted to know if the couples' odd movements had been all in my imagination—but each time Quinn merely waved at me to continue, indicating that he didn't want to taint my memories. He didn't take notes or record the conversation, which seemed a little strange. He just sat and listened, his gaze very solemn and intense. No one came in to interrupt us, not even the nurses.

Quinn nodded when I was through, as though I'd confirmed exactly what he'd expected.

"Do you know why they wanted the baby?" he asked first, raw curiosity bleeding into his voice.

I looked at him questioningly. "I assumed it was just because she's a baby," I said slowly. "Isn't that something people do? Kidnap babies and sell them to people who can't have kids? Or maybe they just wanted to keep her for themselves." I knew there were other, worse things that people could do with stolen children, but I refused to think about them in the context of Charlie.

Quinn studied my face for a moment, and I had the fleeting impression that he knew exactly what those people had wanted with my niece . . . and it was far different from anything I'd suspected. But before I could pursue the thought, he leaned forward and took my good hand. "Lex," he said intently. "I want you to forget everything you remember about the couple. The way they moved, the way he healed. Their names. Forget all of it."

He gave me the same sort of probing look Victor had given me, like I was missing some subtext. At that exact moment I felt something behind my eyes, a subtle *pressure* and a hint of pain. Like the beginning of a headache.

I slid my hand out from under Quinn's and glared at him. "I never told you that I go by Lex," I pointed out. "And how do you expect me to *forget* about this?" It occurred to me that he hadn't shown me any identification. And that the nurses were supposed to take my vitals five minutes ago. "I want to see your badge," I said abruptly.

Looking surprised, Quinn dropped my hand and leaned back in the chair. "Well, damn me twice," he swore. "It's true, then."

My brow furrowed. "What's true?"

Quinn tilted his head to study me, and goose bumps broke out along my forearms. He had that same alien detachment as Victor and Darcy. "You really don't know, do you?" he finally asked.

"I really don't," I said curtly. I have no patience for people who lord their knowledge over others. "But unless you can produce identification, I'd like you to leave. Right now." I reached for the bedside remote that had the nurse's call button. It was six inches away from my right hand, but Quinn managed to beat me to it, even from the other side of the bed. I shook my head, trying to clear it. "These drugs must be *really* good," I mumbled. "Who are you?"

Ignoring me, Quinn held the device out of my reach with one hand. With the other, he dipped into his breast pocket and pulled out a cell phone. He touched the screen to make a call, keeping his eyes on me as he waited for the person on the other end to pick up. "It's Quinn," he said into the receiver. So maybe that *was* his real name. "I think I've got one of yours. Only—funny thing—she doesn't seem to know she's one of yours." Glancing at me, he added, "Allison Alexandra Luther."

He listened for a moment, and I could hear a woman's voice saying something to him. I kept quiet, waiting. He wasn't hurting me—yet—and I was too injured to fight well, anyway. Better to wait until I understood the situation before I made a move.

"How soon can you get to BCH?" Quinn said into the phone, turning his head to glance at the clock on the wall. I couldn't hear her response, but his lips tightened with irritation. "Are you sure you can't come before then?" He listened for another moment. "Okay, okay. Send the kid. But when I say she doesn't know anything, I mean she doesn't know *anything* . . . what? Oh. Stab wounds. In the back."

He hung up the phone and returned it to his pocket.

"Who was that, and what don't I know?" I said coolly.

He looked at me speculatively for a long moment, but he seemed curious rather than dangerous. If he wasn't here to hurt me, why the hell *was* he here? "Quinn?" I asked.

Finally, he sighed heavily, scrubbing the palm of his hand against his cheek. "This isn't my job. You are not part of my job."

"Well," I proposed, "maybe you could start by telling me about your job. You move like a cop, but you're not one, are you?"

He froze, then dropped his hand. "How do you know what a cop moves like?"

"My cousin is with Boulder PD. We have lunch sometimes. So what do you do?"

One side of his mouth turned up in a small smile. "You're very persistent, aren't you?"

"No, I'm very *confused*," I corrected. "And my throat hurts, and I'm trying to decide if I need to get up and beat the shit out of you."

This time he laughed, although I was only half kidding. "I'm not a cop anymore," he admitted. "But I used to be one, in Chicago."

I thought about that. He did have a Midwestern, Scandinavian kind of look. "Are you like some kind of private detective?" I tried. That was the only other thing I could think of that made any sense. Maybe he was tracking the strange couple for another client or something.

"The work I do can be like that sometimes," Quinn said carefully. "You can think of me as a fixer. I work for someone who has a lot of pull in this town, and when that person has a situation that needs to be straightened out, I step in." His voice had gotten a little bitter at the end, like maybe he wasn't an entirely willing participant in his work. Interesting.

"Your boss is a woman, isn't she?"

He examined my face closely. "What makes you say that?"

"You were careful to avoid a singular pronoun right there—you said 'that person' instead of 'he' or 'she,' even though it made your sentence awkward. The majority of people who have pull in Boulder, like in most cities, are male, so saying 'she' would really pare down my list of possibilities. So you avoided the pronoun entirely."

He stared at me. "Now that's interesting," he mused.

I raised an eyebrow. "What, that I know what a pronoun is?" I countered. "No, what's interesting is that you didn't just say 'he.' You don't want me to know who your boss is, but you didn't want to lie to me, either. Why would a fixer need to talk to me?"

He leaned back in his chair, taking my call button with him. "You know, I could sit here and talk semantics all day," he drawled. "Let's go back to the pronoun discussion again, that was fun."

I shook my head slightly. Pain shot up my back, but I'm good at ignoring pain, at least for a while. "No," I retorted, "let's answer Lex's questions so she doesn't start screaming for help."

Quinn tilted his head, studying me again. "He tried to press you. I saw it on the tape."

That brought me up short. "What?"

"Victor, the guy from the Flatiron Depot. He tried to press your mind so you'd back down, but it didn't work. My employer would like to know why."

"What does that mean?" I asked. "Press my mind?"

"It's a mild, short-term form of mind control," he said levelly. "He tried to force your brain into believing you hadn't seen your niece."

"And you tried it on me too, just a few minutes ago." Quinn nodded, unrepentant. I considered that for a moment. I *had* felt something. "Let's say I believe you. How could someone be capable of mind control? Are you guys a government experiment or something?" I had seen movies about super-soldiers. If you got past the ridiculousness, it made sense from a military standpoint. Besides, I knew nothing about technology. For all I knew, super-soldiers were on the horizon.

"No," Quinn said, watching me carefully. "He's a vampire . . . and so am I. And so is my *male* boss."

I laughed in his face.

It hurt my throat, but come on. "You're trying to tell me that you're a vampire, and you live in *Boulder*? What, you discovered that microbrews and hemp taste just as good as blood?"

Quinn shrugged a shoulder, unsurprised by my outburst. "Laugh it up," he said casually. "But I'm pretty sure you're a witch."

Chapter 5

I stopped laughing. "That's ridiculous," I said uncertainly. Not because I believed him, but because it was just such a *weird* thing to say. If you wanted to cover up a crime or convince someone to back off, "you're a witch" doesn't seem like the best place to start.

Quinn sighed again. "Look, I've never been on this side of this conversation, so I have no idea if I'm doing it right. But the only reason you'd be able to resist having your mind pressed is if you already have magic in your blood. That makes you one of three races. You're not a vampire, obviously, and there aren't any werewolves in Colorado anymore. And even if you were, I'd be able to smell it. That means you have to be a witch." He shook his head. "I just don't get how you can have active witchblood and not know it."

I blanched. "What does that mean, active witch blood?"

"I can answer that," said a new voice from the doorway. A shaggy-haired man of about thirty was leaning against the frame. He had olive skin and sharp brown eyes that took in the two of us through rectangular glasses. "Hey, dipshit," he said to Quinn. "You press all the nurses to forget about this room? None of them seemed to know there was a patient in here."

"Something like that," Quinn said, smiling a little. "You made good time."

The newcomer nodded and walked into the room, closing the

door behind him. "Tracy and I were getting a drink a few blocks away. She's gonna walk back to the apartment."

Quinn rose to shake the other man's hand, then turned toward me. "Simon Pellar, meet Allison Luther. She goes by Lex."

I glanced at the thick cord dangling off the bed. Quinn had dropped the call button, and now I had my chance to call for help. But for some reason, I didn't want to. This was all just so odd. It was . . . *interesting*. And since my sister had died, I hadn't found a whole lot of things particularly interesting. Frankly, I'd been in kind of a cocoon for the last ten months.

Besides, Quinn seemed like he knew something about the couple who had come after Charlie.

"Lex," Quinn continued, and my eyes snapped back up to him. "This is Simon, of Clan Pellar. He's generally a hippie ass-hat, but he's also a witch. Like you, only without the amnesia and attention to grammar."

"I don't have amnesia," I retorted, at the same moment that Simon said, "Hey, I like grammar."

I glanced between them, recognizing the easy camaraderie of men who trusted each other. "You guys have worked together before, I take it."

Quinn grinned. "Once or twice," he told me. "Although we hate each other, of course."

"Of course," Simon said with a straight face. "Bloodsucking scum."

"Devil-worshipping mama's boy," Quinn retorted cheerfully.

"You've been saving that," Simon accused. His eyes flicked over to me as he approached the bed. It made me a little nervous, having two strange men in my hospital room while I was incapacitated, but Simon looked harmless. He wore an oversized gray fisherman's sweater and jeans over brown Doc Martens, and he had a canvas messenger bag looped across his body. He shoved his hands in his pockets as he approached, like a little kid looking at a delicate museum exhibit.

"'Luther' like the shoes?" he asked me. I nodded. Luther Shoes was the second-biggest private employer in Boulder, so half the town either worked for my dad or knew someone who did. I gave up trying to hide the connection a long time ago. "Strange," Simon mused. "Luthers have been in town for a while, and I've never heard of you guys having any witchblood."

"I still don't know what that means," I pointed out.

"Sorry. The fact that you have witchblood—one word, by the way—means that one of your ancestors was a full-blooded, extremely powerful conductor of magic," he explained. "The ability to manipulate magic gets passed down through generations, like having blue eyes or being tall. It usually gets watered down over time, though." He gave a little shrug. "Witches who marry witches have more powerful babies than witches who marry humans. You get the idea."

Sam and I had been adopted when we were babies, but I saw no reason to tell either of these men about that, not until I understood what was going on. "Even if I do have . . . that," I began, "—and I seriously doubt it—this is America. The great melting pot. Lots of people must have some witchblood."

Simon shook his head, his hands still in his pockets. "Yes and no. Witchblood children come into their powers around puberty. Then they have a window of time to actually activate that power."

I considered that. "And if you miss the window?"

"Then your magic lies dormant for the rest of your life," he replied. "Probably the majority of people with witchblood never know they have it."

Well, at least that explained what "active" meant. "But if you were one of those," Quinn broke in, "I should have been able to press your mind. No magic, no resistance."

"You're suggesting I 'used magic' during that window," I said skeptically, fighting the urge to make quotation marks with my fingers, which would have hurt. They were very convincing, but the whole thing was just absurd. "That's just stupid. There's no such thing as magic. Or vampires. There's a lady at my job who claims she's a witch, but I'm pretty sure it's just so she can smoke a lot of pot."

Quinn snorted, and Simon gave him an annoyed glare. "It *is* real, Lex," he said gently.

"This has been fun and all," Quinn said, checking his watch, "but if you've got it from here, Simon, I'm gonna take off. Say hey to Tracy for me." He tipped an imaginary hat at me. "It's been interesting, Lex."

Overwhelmed, I just raised a hand in farewell. "Take care, man," Simon said to him. Quinn nodded and headed for the door. "Okay if I sit?" Simon asked me.

I nodded, but before he could say anything else, Quinn's phone rang when he was just a few feet away from the exit. He dug it out of his jacket pocket. "Hello?" he said, reaching for the door handle. Then he froze. "When was this?" Slowly, he spun to look at me, and a chill jolted through me when his eyes met mine.

At that moment I realized that I was starting to *believe* him. Both of them. "Ah, shit," Quinn said into the phone. "Thanks, Luce. I'm on it." He hung up.

"What happened?" Simon asked.

Quinn hesitated for a second, still looking at me. "My 911 dispatcher just intercepted a call from John Wheaton's house," he said soberly. "Wheaton thinks Victor and Darcy are sitting in a car in front of his house." He nodded at me apologetically, then turned and vanished through the doorway.

Chapter 6

The familiar way that Quinn said "Victor and Darcy" made me suspect that he knew exactly who they were and what they wanted. But by the time that thought registered, I was already getting out of the hospital bed—or trying to, anyway. I managed to sort of sit up, but when I went to swing my legs over the side of the bed, the movement sent pain rocketing through my back. Trying to ignore it, I grabbed a tissue from the wheeled table next to me and pulled out my IV, which set off an alarm on one of the machines next to the bed. I clutched the tissue against the spurt of blood on my wrist.

"Jesus," Simon said, shocked. He got up and hovered over me, not wanting to touch me without permission. "You need to lie back down. Quinn can handle this. It's what he does."

I gritted my teeth, panting through them in short bursts as the pain in my back roared in protest. Simon held out his hands like he was spotting me. Which, I suppose, he was. "You have a family, right?" I said through my teeth. Quinn had said he was part of some sort of clan.

"Yeah, so?"

"So John is my brother-in-law, and he's home with my eighteen-month-old niece. You must know why I have to go."

Simon's eyes widened a little, but he didn't back down. "You can't even stand up!" he argued. "How do you think you're going to help them?"

Quinn had said that the 911 operator "intercepted" the call from John's house, which meant the police weren't coming. Quinn was the only thing that stood between that house and Darcy and Victor, assuming that he got there in time. I lifted my head and looked Simon in the eye. "You don't have to help me," I said matter-of-factly. "But you're not gonna stop me."

"You can't just . . . you're not even—" he protested. Then he swallowed and took a breath. "Ah, hell. Wait a minute."

He tore off his messenger bag and threw it onto the empty half of the bed. When he lifted the flap, the bottom of the canvas bag folded out, revealing rows and rows of plastic vials, weird little trinkets, and things that looked like bones, not to mention a bunch of stuff I didn't recognize. It was all held in by little round straps, like a serious artist's set. "What's that?" I said tightly through the pain. "Eye of newt?"

Simon snorted, pulling out two vials. I couldn't see what was inside them, and I wasn't sure I wanted to. "More like a first-aid kit. Quinn told my mom you were stabbed, so I thought I'd bring it along. I'm going to make you a healing charm."

"Will that work?"

"Maybe," Simon hedged. "Magic doesn't usually work on witches, so I'm not sure how much it'll help you"—he tipped the contents of one vial into the other, covered the end with his thumb, and shook it furiously—"but it might. Once it's active, a witch's magic works like breast-feeding: the more you use it, the more of it you have to use. So if you haven't been using it . . ."

"Then I can't be very powerful, and your thingy might not even recognize me as a magic user," I finished for him.

He handed me the vial. The liquid inside was dark and murky and making a sound, like the fizz of carbonation. "You're catching on. Here, drink."

I didn't hesitate. I was desperate to get to John and Charlie, and I would have swallowed an actual eye of newt if it meant getting there faster. I downed the contents, which left a horrible aftertaste in my mouth, like a combination of basil leaves and cherry Nyquil.

"Blech," I said, wincing. "Assuming this whole conversation hasn't been an exercise in bullshit, how long will your spell take?"

"Charm. Should just be a minute or two," Simon answered. "Give it a chance."

I leaned forward *very* carefully, clutching the edges of the bed and hoping I wouldn't pass out. I was dizzy, and it hurt to breathe. Simon was watching me attentively, so I cocked an eyebrow at him. "Breast-feeding?" I managed.

He grinned. "My mom and one of my sisters are doulas. You know what that is?"

"Like a midwife who gives hugs, right?"

Simon chuckled. "Pretty much."

I was about to ask another question when a sharp tingling spread through my torso. At first it was actually kind of pleasant, but it began to burn as it spread toward the knife wounds on my back. I cried out once from the sudden pain, my fists digging into the hospital sheets. I gritted my teeth again. "What's happening?" I hissed.

Simon shrugged apologetically. "The same thing that was going to happen: you're healing. The spell is just speeding it up. Kind of like time-lapse photography."

I couldn't answer. The tingling was spreading down to my jammed fingers, where it turned molten again, and I was way past speaking. Simon reached over and took my good hand, letting me squeeze his. I was a little touched by the gesture—after all, the guy had met me all of fifteen minutes ago. I didn't meet his eyes, but I also didn't let go of his hand.

Minutes passed, and the pain coursing through my body only intensified. I struggled not to cry out again, and involuntary tears leaked out of the corners of my eyes. Simon didn't say a word when I clutched his fingers hard enough to make his knuckles crack. "It's okay," he murmured. "You're gonna be okay, Lex, I promise."

Finally, the pain began to lessen, draining out of my body in increments. "Holy shit," I breathed. It was like the pain was being rinsed away, and my injuries with it. Even my voice sounded more like me. "Yeah, sorry. That's the best healing charm I have, but it's my sister Sybil's magic. It can be . . . abrupt. Kind of like Sybil." He gave my hand a gentle squeeze and let go. "How do you feel?"

"Like I'm just getting over the flu." Experimentally, I sat up straighter on the edge of the bed. My back still ached, but in a tight, manageable kind of way. "But I think I can move around. Let's go."

I jumped to my feet—and Simon caught me as I crumpled to the ground. "Whoa, there, tiger." He smelled like a field of wildflowers, and his sweater was scratchy under my fingers. He propped me back up against the bed. "Why don't you take a moment, and I'll go find you some scrubs to wear."

I looked down at myself and realized I was wearing only a hospital gown. A backless hospital gown. No one had thought I'd be leaving for at least another week or two. "Right. Why don't we do that?"

A few minutes later we were bumping out of the hospital parking lot in Simon's car, some kind of Chevy station-wagon-type thing with an annoyingly low ceiling. "Where am I going?" he asked me.

"Just head toward the airport; John lives in one of those subdivisions off Kings Ridge Boulevard." I dug through my handbag, a small distressed-leather cross-body that had been a present from Sam. I found my cell phone and tried to call John, but after three days the battery was dead.

"Don't worry," Simon reassured me. "That thing about vampires needing to be invited into a house, that's true. So I'm sure your family will be fine."

I considered that for a second. "Then how did they manage to kidnap Charlie out of her crib two nights ago?"

"That's . . ." Simon began, and then he paused, looking perplexed. "That's actually a really good point." He sighed, raking a hand through his shaggy hair. "I don't know how they got in. Gravitational magic—that's what we call the natural tendency for magic to collect in certain places, like a home—isn't very well understood. When we get through this, I can ask my mom about it. She'd know more than I do." He paused for a moment. "Is your sister at the house, too?"

"She died," I said shortly. "Ten months ago."

"I'm sorry." He flew over a speed bump, an act I generally approved of, but the jostling made my back scream, and I let out a grunt of pain before I could stop myself. Simon glanced over at me. "How are you feeling?" he asked, concern in his voice.

"Like my insides are still knitting together."

"Well," Simon said sensibly, "they probably are."

"Still, all things considered, that potion thing was amazing. Why doesn't your sister sell it to hospitals or something?"

Simon was silent long enough for me to look over at him. There was a faraway expression on his face. Finally he said quietly, "Because then people would find out about us. Witches, I mean."

"Would that be so bad?"

"Finding out about witches? Maybe not. But the vampires and the werewolves would cause a panic. And there's been too much tension among the species for one of us to come out and not the rest." He shook his head. "The Old World—that's what we usually call the supernatural side—has existed for as long as it has by staying hidden. The first rule of Fight Club and all that." When I didn't reply, he glanced over. "You never saw that movie?"

"What movie?"

Simon shook his head, smiling a little. "Never mind. Anyway. The Old World doesn't have a single governing body. Instead, it's separated loosely into territories, each with its own rules. But one rule stays the same everywhere: you don't tell humans about the Old World. So I can't give the healing charm to a human—"

"And it doesn't work typically on witches," I finished for him. "That's like a paradox."

"Yes." He shot me a small smile. "I'll admit . . . I was kind of excited to use it."

"But doesn't the fact that it worked mean I'm not actually a witch?" I pointed out.

"Or you could just have a lot of power that you're not using."

I had nothing to say to that, so we rode along in silence for a few minutes. There weren't many people on the streets, and without my asking, Simon was speeding through town. When we reached a red light at a deserted intersection, I told him to run it. There was probably a camera, but I wasn't going to risk Charlie's life over a traffic ticket.

I was trying really hard not to think about John and Charlie being at the mercy of the couple from the Depot. John was assuming the police would show up any second, but nobody else was coming. Fear twisted in my gut, and I took deep breaths.

"There's something you need to know before we go in there," Simon said soberly.

"What?"

He glanced at me, his expression unreadable. "You're technically a witch, we think, so you're allowed to know about the Old World. But you can't *ever* tell humans what we are. Not even your family."

"Why? What happens if I tell?"

"They'll have to be pressed, like Quinn tried to do to you," he warned. "But pressing someone only works if it's done right away. If a human knows about the Old World for more than a day or so, the memory's rooted too deep to be removed."

There was something else in his voice, an aversion, so I pushed him. "And what if that happens?"

He stared straight out over the steering wheel. "They have to die," he said quietly.

"*What?*"

"It's not my rule, okay? It's the one universal Old World law.

Witches have a *tiny* bit of leeway these days—we can tell people we're Wiccan, even use the word 'witch,' but we can never mention the bigger picture or use serious magic in front of people. Humans who can't be pressed are either killed or forced to join up."

"Forced to . . . like, become a witch?"

He shook his head again, his face grim. "Witches are born, not made. Humans who find out have to try to become a vampire or a werewolf."

"Who enforces that rule?" I asked, frustrated. "I thought you said there was no government."

"No governing body," Simon corrected. "But that's for the Old World as a whole. Individual territories are almost all controlled by one faction or another. You're in vampire territory, so the vampires have final say on everything."

"Okay, this is too much information." I exhaled a long, slow breath, my thoughts reeling. "Let's just leave it at 'don't tell anyone.' I can work with that."

He nodded, shooting me a sympathetic look.

John and Charlie lived at the end of a street of very nice single-family houses, the kind where roving packs of neighborhood kids raced from one backyard swing set to the next with no regard for property lines or decorative fences. John's house was the smallest, a little bit down the road from the main grouping, but still part of the neighborhood. I knew he'd chosen it hoping Charlie would grow up with a lot of friends nearby, to help make up for the fact that her family was missing a key member. The house looked fine from the road—no obvious signs of a break-in. Somehow that didn't reassure me.

There were a few cars parked in front of John's house, but they all looked empty to me as we passed. Simon pulled his car over just ahead of them, and I was tugging at the door handle before he'd put it in park. As I pushed open the car door, I finally noticed the autumn chill. It was probably in the low fifties, but the icy wind made it feel colder, especially since I wasn't wearing underwear.

But then I heard Charlie's wails from inside the house, and I forgot all about the weather. The sound lifted my spirits—she was alive and in the house. Simon hurried around the car to join me. I'd taken all of one step toward the house when Quinn appeared next to me.

I managed not to smack him in surprise. "Hey," he said quietly, more to Simon than to me. "I had a feeling you'd show up."

"Where are they?" Simon said in a low voice.

Quinn nodded toward the house. "Wheaton barricaded himself in the back bedroom with the baby. The door must be pretty solid. Darcy keeps throwing herself against it, but she's not any closer to getting in." Quinn frowned for a second, then shrugged. "Must be one hell of a door."

He gestured toward the left side of the yard. "Victor's trying to figure out a way into the room from the outside. He's the bigger threat. I was about to go after him when I heard that piece of shit Chevy you drive. Figured some backup wouldn't hurt." I remembered the size of Victor and figured Quinn's comment was guy-speak for "I'm not quite sure I can take him. Please help."

"Are we sanctioned?" Simon asked. Quinn nodded, then tossed something to him, which he easily caught. It was a stick. *No,* I realized, *that's a wooden stake.* I almost giggled. These guys were acting like Victor and Darcy really were *vampires.* My miraculous recovery was one thing—I could get behind the idea that Simon had some kind of wonder drug—but I still didn't quite buy the whole vampires-are-real business.

On the other hand, I didn't actually care *what* they were. I just wanted to make sure they got the hell away from my family. "You have one of those for me?" I asked in a low voice. Sticks or not, at least they were weapons.

"No," Quinn retorted. "You should hang back."

"Not a chance. I'm going after Darcy while you two take Victor. That door can't hold out forever."

Quinn and Simon exchanged a glance. "She'll kill you, Lex," Simon said softly. "Please, please, just wait here. We'll call you when it's over, and then you can come get your family."

I straightened up, feeling ridiculous in my green scrubs. At least I was feeling better. "Thanks, but I'm not really a 'just wait here' kind of girl."

Simon looked pleadingly at Quinn, who shrugged. "She's a witch problem now," Quinn said cheerfully. "No skin off my nose."

Without waiting for a response, I took off for the house as fast as I could, which turned out to be at a sort of mincing trot. I could feel a pull in my back from the stitches. They would need to come out soon, I realized, but although I felt weak and run down, my condition was worlds better than when I'd woken up in the hospital that morning.

When I reached the stoop, I didn't bother trying to be sneaky. The baby was screaming too loudly for me to hear anything anyway. Instead I just threw open the unlocked front door and beelined toward the first-floor bedroom, the guest room off the kitchen. John was smart—that was the room with the heaviest door and the smallest window. It was where I would have holed up, too.

When I rounded the doorway to the back hall, though, Darcy was nowhere near the guest room door. I froze. Could she have given up? Gone outside to help Victor with Simon and Quinn? Or was she waiting to ambush me? Then Charlie took a deep breath, and in the tiny pause I heard a clinking sound in the kitchen, like someone shaking a piggy bank.

I darted forward, past the locked bedroom door and all the way into the kitchen. The blonde woman from the Depot was standing in my brother-in-law's kitchen, rifling through the junk drawer in the counter island. She had fished out three keys so far and had them lined up on the counter in front of her. *Crap.* I'd known John my whole life, and he would never have a lock in his house without also having the corresponding key. One of those was going to work.

Quietly, I moved to put myself between Darcy and the bedroom door. Apparently satisfied with her find, Darcy collected the keys and started back toward the bedroom, which is when she spotted me.

"Oh, *great*," she yelled, over the sound of Charlie's wails. "The girl with the weird blood. Of course *you're* here."

She took a few steps toward me. "Hey, Darcy." I stalked forward to meet her, which she wasn't expecting. "Rough night? Me too."

She opened her mouth to yell something back, and I slammed my left fist into her nose.

It collapsed with a *very* satisfying wet crunch, and Darcy shrieked with pain, staggering backward, away from the bedroom door. I shook out my hand discreetly, but my own pain wasn't bad. I'd gotten my weight behind the punch. Her eyes went wide with shock as she held her fingers up to her nose, then examined them in disbelief.

That stopped me for a moment and seemed to confirm my suspicion that the vampire thing was bullshit. I'd broken someone's nose before, and Darcy's had felt just like anyone else's. And now she was bleeding like anyone else. Liberally.

Regaining her balance, Darcy swung at me, a clumsy roundhouse that I easily blocked with my right forearm as I jabbed with my left. Same spot. She screamed in pain and frustration and kicked out at me. I turned my body to take the kick in the side. It stung, but no more than any other kick would. No, she wasn't some superpowered creature of the night. She was just a deranged kidnapper. And *that* I could fight.

Encouraged, I launched myself at Darcy, throwing my upper body into her chest and riding her to the ground. I pinned her with a forearm under her throat. Her eyes bulged as she reached for my hair. I slapped her hand down with my free arm. Blood streamed from her nose down her cheeks and into her expensively highlighted hair. "Let me be clear," I said coldly. "I will *always* come for that baby. Always. And if I ever see either you or your boyfriend again, I will not hesitate to break your fucking necks. Do you believe me?"

Darcy made another grab for my hair. I slapped her down again and dug my forearm harder into her neck. Adrenaline churned in my bloodstream. "I said, *do you believe me?*"

Glaring at me, she nodded.

"Why her?" I demanded. "What do you want with Charlie?"

Her cold facade broke, and she let out a surprised laugh, disturbing because it sounded so completely normal. "You don't know?" she asked, genuine amazement in her voice.

There was a shout from outside, and I automatically glanced toward the back door at the other end of the kitchen, half expecting someone to burst through it. In that instant, Darcy wriggled hard enough to free one arm. She grabbed the nearest thing within reach—a plastic baby toy with animals that popped out of little doors—and swung it at my head.

I saw the hit coming and flinched away, managing to soften the blow a little. The hard plastic still crashed into my skull, staggering me enough so that Darcy could throw me off her. She scrambled toward the back door.

When she reached the exit, she turned to look at me, straightening up. My mouth dropped open. Before my eyes, her nose was *healing*: the bleeding stopped, the swelling went down, the bones wriggled into place. All the bruising on her face and arms faded away, and she suddenly *glowed* with life. She opened her mouth and snarled at me, "*This isn't over.*" Then she turned and fled into the night.

Weakened from shock or the hit to my head, I managed to slump against the bedroom door before I collapsed.

What the hell was happening?

Chapter 7

After I caught my breath, I raised my fist to rap on the door behind me. "It's Lex," I yelled over Charlie's cries.

"Lex?" John's voice was baffled.

"Yeah, it's me. You can open the door. She's gone."

After a moment, the heavy wood door popped inward, dumping me over the threshold to the bedroom. "Whoops," I said out loud. Probably should have moved aside. John stared down at me, utterly confused. Charlie hiccupped with surprise, her screams turning to whimpers.

"Hi," I said from the floor, realizing that I might be in mild shock. "Maybe you could help me up."

John slung Charlie onto his hip in a practiced move, then reached his hand down to help me up. I let him pull me to my feet. "What the hell is going on?" John demanded. He didn't get upset very often—I'd probably seen him truly angry three times in all the years we'd known each other—but when he did, his temper was awe-inspiring. "You could barely move your fingers the last time I saw you. How are you here? Why are you wearing scrubs? Who *were* those people?!" By the end he was nearly shouting.

"John," I said softly, "you're scaring the baby."

He looked down at Charlie, whose face had crumpled again. Before she could start crying, he cuddled her to his chest and murmured about getting her a ba-ba. "Come with me," he said to me over the baby's head. "We need to talk."

I followed him into the kitchen, where he pulled an empty bottle out of the cupboard and began to fill it with whole milk from a carton in the fridge. The doorbell rang, and John looked up in alarm. "Hang on," I said, raising a hand. "I think that's for me."

Before John could answer, I trudged back through the house, stepping around an explosion of baby toys that had nothing to do with the break-in, and looked through the peephole. Quinn was standing alone on the front porch. I opened the front door. There was blood spattered over most of his suit jacket, but he wasn't even breathing hard. "Victor?" I asked in a low voice.

Quinn shook his head. "Staked him. Simon's taking care of it. Darcy?"

"I broke her nose, and she ran away," I reported.

He blinked at me. "You broke her nose?" he said incredulously.

I gave a little shrug. "I didn't know what else to do. I wasn't prepared to kill her."

"That's not what I—" Quinn started to say, but he stopped and shook his head. "Look, I need to talk to your brother-in-law."

Automatically, I shifted my weight so I was blocking the doorway. "You're not going to hurt him." It wasn't a question.

"No," he said, his voice firm. "But I may need to press his mind. It won't hurt him, I swear."

I examined his face for a long moment. He looked back at me without flinching, his face open. I didn't want anyone messing around with John's brain . . . but Quinn *had* helped John and Charlie. Maybe he'd earned a bit of trust. "Take off your jacket first," I told him.

Quinn looked down. When he saw the blood, he shucked his suit jacket and casually tossed it behind the bushes near John's front door. He stepped through the doorway and paused, frowning. "What?" I asked.

"I shouldn't have been able to just walk in like that." Quinn answered.

"Lex?" John called from the kitchen. "Who is it?"

"Figure it out later," I told Quinn. He shrugged and followed me through the house to the kitchen.

John was leaning against the counter, a burp rag tossed over his shoulder. He was cradling a much calmer Charlie in his arms as she slurped down her milk. When we came into the room, she tilted her head to check us out without taking the bottle's nipple out of her mouth for a second. She grinned at us from around it. It was adorable, and I felt a familiar stab of grief, a sensation I have all the time when I'm with Charlie. *Sam is missing this.*

"John, this is Quinn," I said, ushering Quinn into the room beside me. "He's the one who told me you needed help."

Quinn didn't offer to shake hands, which was okay because John's hands were full. "Mr. Wheaton," Quinn began, keeping his voice low. "Would you mind if I spoke to you privately for a minute?" John glanced at me, then down at Charlie. "I'm sure Lex can hold the baby," he added reassuringly.

John looked at me again. If it had been anyone else, I doubt he would have relinquished his hold on his daughter. But John had trusted me since before he could shave. I nodded, and he shrugged and started toward us.

When he was still a few feet away, something happened to Quinn. He let out a startled gasp and bent over, trying to turn it into a cough. John paused, uncertain. "You okay?" I whispered to Quinn.

He nodded. "Just . . . swallowed wrong or something."

Shrugging, I walked forward and took Charlie from John. She smiled at me around her bottle again and reached up to grab a strand of my hair. I didn't wear it down very often, especially when I was around my niece, but the scrubs Simon had stolen for me hadn't come with a hair tie.

"Hey, baby-baby," I sang down to her. "Let's go sit on the couch."

I backtracked into the living room, settling myself into a plush armchair. I wanted to keep an eye on the two men, but after the healing and the fight, I was too wobbly to keep standing. I could hear Quinn's voice behind me, speaking in low, soothing tones, and John's familiar voice answering him.

My body may have been exhausted, but my thoughts continued to churn. My mind wouldn't stop cycling through memories from the day, starting with the discovery that I was even still alive. It felt like a day out of someone else's life, or from one of those schlocky horror movies Sam had made me sit through when we were in high school. Vampires and witches and werewolves? It was just too much.

And yet . . . I had run out of other ways to explain what I'd seen.

Charlie had fallen asleep, her little hands relaxing around the empty bottle. It dropped to the floor, rolling away into a pile of toys. I ignored it and raised her limp body to my shoulder, patting her back to coax out a sleepy burp. I kissed her head, snuggling her close. Being near Charlie always soothed me, and after a while my thoughts stopped spinning. Before I knew it, my eyes were drifting closed. Tomorrow I would figure out all of this weirdness, including what Darcy wanted with my niece. For now, though, Charlie was safe. And I was grateful.

Suddenly a quiet voice whispered in my ear, so close that I would have been startled if I'd had the energy. "John thinks you made a miraculous recovery, then came over to help him chase a raccoon out of the house," Quinn said. "I'll stop by the hospital and take care of your sudden departure, but then I'm done. I'm sure you'll be hearing from the witches soon. It was nice knowing you, Allison Luther."

"Don't call me . . ." I mumbled, but he was gone. I let my eyes fall shut and succumbed to sleep.

Chapter 8

I woke up to a tugging, insistent pain on my scalp. It was on the opposite side of my head from where the baby toy had left a lump, but it still kind of hurt.

I opened my eyes. Charlie gurgled up at me, smiling. She was sitting up, facing me, with all of the fingers on one hand tangled firmly into my hair like an anchor line. She tugged joyously, using her leverage to swing back and forth a little on my stomach. "Charlie," I reprimanded gently, but she just grinned wider, showing off her little teeth. She babbled some nonsense at me. I squinted at the clock on the far wall. Ten after six. "At least someone in this family's a morning person," I told her. Usually I was still at work at six, but my sleep schedule seemed to have adjusted back to normal while I was in the hospital. That was going to be a pain in the ass when I returned to work.

I looked around the room. I was still in John's recliner, although at some point he had raised the footrest for me. He'd also draped a polar fleece throw over both of us.

"Good morning," John said, stepping into the doorway. He was blowing on the surface of a coffee mug, and there was a second steaming mug in his other hand.

"Hey," I said groggily, sitting up and lowering the footrest, using one hand to stabilize Charlie in my arms. She wriggled impatiently, and I carefully leaned over to set her down on the floor. She immediately crawled off toward the nearest pile of toys. I nodded at the second cup. "Is that for me, or are things just so bad that you're double-fisting caffeine now?"

John smiled and came over to set the mug on the coffee table next to the armchair. "I was waiting for you to put her down. She's going through a sweeping-mugs-off-the-table phase."

"Mmm," I said, inhaling the scent of hazelnut. "Nice timing." He'd put in a little milk, no sugar, just the way I like it.

"Charlie has me trained. She wakes up at six, so I wake up at six." He glanced up at the clock. "I guess the extra ten minutes of sleep is her concession to last night's adventures."

I glanced at him warily. "Yeah, that was something."

He shook his head in amazement. "I still don't understand how it got in here. Must have left the back door open or something."

"Mmm-hmm," I said noncommittally.

"I'm just glad you got it out of here okay. Aren't raccoons one of those animals that carry rabies? Ugh." He winced. "You sure it didn't scratch you or anything?"

"No raccoon scratches," I said honestly. I took a long sip of the coffee. Part of me couldn't believe this was actually working—John seemed to wholeheartedly believe the story Quinn had fed him. And Charlie was a baby; it wasn't like she'd remember anything. The attack on the house, the 911 call, that frantic drive from the hospital to John's house . . . to him it was like none of it had ever happened. In the early morning light, with my coffee in hand and my friend nearby, it seemed a lot easier to buy John's new version of events than the bit about vampires and witches. I wondered if I could convince myself that the whole thing had been a dream.

I yawned, and the stitches in my back pulled with the movement. I must have winced, because John said worriedly, "Is your back really okay?"

"Yes," I assured him. "I'm fine. Well, not fine, but I'll be fine soon." My head ached, and every part of my body felt unbearably sore. Kind of like the way I felt after the one time Sam had talked me into attending a ninety-minute hot yoga session.

I lifted an arm and tried to scratch my back where the stitches were irritating my skin, but I couldn't reach. John put his coffee down and took a step toward me. "Here, do you need me to—"

"No," I yelped, jumping out of the chair and backing away. John's mouth dropped open, and even Charlie stared at me.

"I'm sorry," I said, keeping my voice calm. "That was an overreaction."

"No, I'm sorry. I thought . . . I mean, it's been so long, and you're like my sister . . . I should have realized it would be awkward." Pacified, Charlie picked up a wooden spoon and began gravely beating it against the side of a toy dump truck like she was getting paid by the hour to do so.

I squeezed my eyes shut. John thought I was afraid of his seeing me naked because we had a fifteen-year-old history. And it wasn't like I could tell him the truth.

I took a deep breath, which is when I realized that my scrubs stank of sweat and dried milk. "Do you have something I could wear home?" I asked.

John hesitated, and I opened my eyes. "I have a box of Sam's stuff in the attic," he began, but I shook my head quickly.

"Just some sweatpants or something would be great."

John got me some of his athletic pants and another long-sleeved Luther Shoes T-shirt, which I took into the bathroom. I made the mistake of glancing in the mirror, and wrinkled my nose at my lanky-haired, red-eyed reflection. I could have been a coed who'd just gotten trashed at a frat party. I've always looked young for my age, at least in the face. In high school John used to call me Babyface when he wanted to tease me, and the guys in my platoon had had a field day with it when I was in the army. I made a face at the mirror and stripped out of the scrubs.

There was a metallic tinkling sound from the floor, and I glanced down. Staples. At least one of the injuries—for some reason I hated thinking of them as stab wounds—had been held shut with staples, and they'd forced themselves out of my skin as it healed. I turned and looked over my shoulder, trying to see my back in the mirror. *Whoa.* One of the wounds, a couple of inches below the army tattoo on my shoulder, was now just an angry pink line. That must have been the stapled one. The others still had the stitches, but the skin had grown together around them, and now it was bright red and irritated. *Great.* I reached back to try to touch one of the injuries, but there was no way I could reach. I sighed. The stitches needed to come out, which meant I'd now have to track down either Simon or Quinn, since I wasn't allowed to tell anyone else what had happened. I'm not particularly shy, but that doesn't mean I enjoy exposing my naked back to a strange man bearing scissors.

I put on the clothes, folding the scrubs to take them with me. Feeling something in the pants pocket, I reached in and pulled out a blank white card, the size and shape of a business card. Nothing was typed on it, but the words *Just in case—Quinn* were handwritten on one side, followed by a phone number. I didn't know when he'd slipped the card into my pocket, but I found myself squeezing it a little to make sure it was real. The edges bit into my fingers.

Well, crap. It hadn't been a dream.

John promised to drop me off on his way to work and went upstairs to get ready. After Sam died, John had decided to take my father up on his offer to come back to Boulder and work at Luther Shoes. He wanted to raise Charlie closer to his mom, and to Sam's family—us. They'd worked out a whole system where my mom took care of Charlie three days a week so John could save on day care.

An hour later, John loaded Charlie's car seat into the backseat of his big 4x4 truck and came over to help me climb into the passenger seat. I could have done it myself, working around the soreness, but I was trying to cover up the extent of my healing, so I made a point to look pained as I got in. It wasn't that much of a stretch.

The ride to the cabin was peacefully quiet, but as soon as John pulled into my driveway we could hear the barking. The herd was awake and in full house-protection mode. John put the truck in park and smiled over at me. "You want us to come in with you?" he asked.

"Nah." I leaned over the backseat and squeezed Charlie's hand. "She's with my mom today, right?" Darcy's parting shot, *This isn't over*, was bouncing around the inside of my sore head.

He nodded. "Then your folks and Elise are coming over for supper tonight," he said. "I'm making chili to thank them for helping with the baby this week. If you're feeling up to it, do you want to come?"

"Thanks," I told him, "but I should probably rest." I kissed my fingers and touched them to Charlie's tufts of dark hair. "Bye, babe," I said, leaning over to kiss the top of her head. "Thanks for the ride, John. See you in a couple days." I had a standing date to babysit on Friday afternoons.

"I'll text that morning to make sure you feel up to it," he suggested. I nodded and started to open the door, but John touched my wrist. "Lex. . ." he began, "I don't know how to—"

"You don't have to thank me," I interrupted him. I tilted my head toward the backseat. "That's Sam's daughter back there. You never have to thank me."

John nodded, his face set. "See you Friday."

I showered right away and slowly pulled on clean sweatpants and a soft flannel button-down, wearing nothing underneath. A bra would only irritate my already-irritated stitches, and my chest wasn't so buxom that I'd miss it much. Then I turned my attention to the herd, who weren't used to being left alone for any real amount of time. Rescue animals don't deal with separation well, and even though my family members had been stopping by, there were demonstrations of the animals' unhappiness all over the house. One of the dogs had defecated in a corner of the basement. There were new, jagged tears the size of cat claws through the screen window in my bedroom. A few lamps and books had gotten knocked around, too, probably by Cody and Chip, inseparable mutts who had been found together and tended to lapse into calamitous chases when bored. I didn't yell at any of them, because I understood. I just cleaned it all up and gave them extra attention.

The movement was hard on all my sore muscles, so at lunchtime I had four Advil and a liter of water with my grilled cheese sandwich. I also remembered to charge my cell phone, finally. I had seventeen voicemails, mostly from my family and the *real* police, who wanted a statement. I wasn't ready to call everyone back yet, so instead I called my store manager, an anxious, heavyset guy who liked to see himself as a generous man of the people, at least until the store owner started breathing down his neck about something. Big Scott—he actually *preferred* that we call him that—seemed excessively worried about my health, and he offered me two weeks off: one paid, one not. I volunteered to return to work the next day, once the stiffness had gone down a bit, but he insisted on the paid week, which was pretty fair of him. And pretty surprising, considering how hard it would be to cover my undesirable 11:00 p.m. to 7:00 a.m. shift. He was probably worried about some kind of a lawsuit.

By then I was getting tired again. My body had done a lot of healing in a short amount of time, so it made sense that it needed extra energy. I went upstairs to the lofted master bedroom and crawled into bed on my stomach.

I expected to pass out immediately, but my thoughts were whirling again. *Witches.* I actually didn't have too much trouble accepting the idea that witches were real. Boulder is a liberal town with a lot of "alternative lifestyles"—my own father was a semi-reformed hippie who'd gone to Woodstock as a kid—and three of the girls in my senior class had claimed to be Wiccan. As far as I could tell, this meant they wore a lot of long skirts and black lipstick and chokers, and watched some movie about teenage witches over and over, but still . . . It wasn't that much of a stretch to consider that some of the people who called themselves witches could actually do some things that others couldn't, like create a medication that could heal me.

It was the other part I was having trouble with. *Vampires.* I didn't read or watch much horror, but even I knew vampires were silly movie monsters, like Frankenstein or the Wolfman. And Quinn had said something about werewolves, too. That was just too ridiculous. How could I possibly take that seriously?

And yet . . . the little voice in my head insisted. Even if I wrote off Victor's eyes healing as a weird blood-loss hallucination, I *knew* I had seen Darcy's nose set itself. And John had truly believed the story about the raccoon, which meant Quinn really *had* done something to his brain. So, like it or not, at least some of what Quinn and Simon had told me had to be true.

But even if vampires were real, what the hell did they want with my niece? Was it possible that whatever was weird about me, this witchblood stuff, had been inherited by Charlie too? I replayed my conversation with Simon in my head. He'd said witchblood was hereditary, that it was passed down within families. But he'd also told me it was dormant until puberty. There would be no reason for someone to kidnap a baby witch. Maybe it had just been a weird coincidence?

My thoughts skipped back to my own alleged connection to magic. My *hereditary* connection. Sam's and my adoption was never a forbidden subject or anything. Every now and then it would come up—when we studied genetics in school, when I had to fill out health forms for the army—but my family rarely talked about it. I rarely even *thought* about it. My parents were my parents. My cousins were my cousins. It was that simple. Oh, sometimes at big family events I would look around at the sea of honey-blond hair and brown eyes—the Luther family trademarks—and feel a tiny sting of displacement, but Sam and I had never been the kind of adopted kids who dreamed of their birth parents, for the simple reason that we knew our birth mother was dead.

When we were teenagers, Sam had once asked our parents where we came from. It was dinnertime, and my parents simultaneously put down their silverware and exchanged a look, like they'd been waiting for the question and had run drills. My mother got up and went down the hall to the fireproof box where they kept all the important documents. While she was gone, my father informed us in a grave, heartfelt voice that our twenty-year-old birth mother had walked into a Denver hospital in the middle of a terrible rainstorm, already well into labor. The doctors put her in a room and did what they could for her, but she died after an emergency C-section, leaving behind fraternal twin girls with no names. An effort was made to find the young woman's family, but it dried up after a few weeks, and we were registered with a social worker. After a few months, we were adopted by the Luthers, a couple who desperately wanted children but couldn't conceive. They were our *parents* in every way that mattered.

Sam and I looked at the birth certificates and newspaper clippings my mother brought back, soaked up the information we found, and promptly forgot about the whole thing. Even later, when Sam went through her teenage rebellion, or when Dad and I fought tooth and claw over my decision to join the army, we weren't the kind of kids to throw "You're not even my real parents!" at Mom and Dad. Sam and I weren't always well behaved, but there was one thing you could say for us: we always knew what we had.

Now, though, I had to look at the whole thing in a different light. If there really was such a thing as witchblood, we must have inherited it from one of our biological parents. Could that have had something to do with why no one had stepped forward to claim us? Had our birth mother been running from something when she stopped at the hospital in Denver? What about our biological father—had the witchblood come from his side? I didn't know a single thing about him.

And I had no desire to, I decided. If Simon was right and I did have some sort of access to magic, I wanted nothing to do with it. I had a good life, with an easy job in my favorite town. I was surrounded by family who loved me, not to mention the herd, and best of all, I could watch Sam's daughter grow up. From what I'd seen so far, getting involved with magic was dangerous . . . and I'd had enough danger for several lifetimes.

After a few minutes I began to doze on my bed, with dogs and cats jumping on and off at intervals as they either checked on me or begged for attention—however you wanted to look at that. At four o'clock I woke with a start, because my unconscious brain had made a connection my conscious mind had somehow missed.

Maybe there *was* someone I could ask.

Chapter 9

I climbed off the big bed as quickly as my sore muscles would allow, heading for the bedroom closet. My army duffel bag was still in the back. I unzipped one of the side compartments and dug out a handful of paper from the trip I'd made to LA ten months ago. I came out with a wad of scribbled notes and addresses, a Xerox of the missing person's paperwork, and a bunch of receipts. Shuffling through the scraps, I finally found what I was looking for: a business card emblazoned with the logo of the Los Angeles Police Department.

When John had called to tell me that Sam was missing, I had immediately made arrangements for the herd, packed up my car, and headed west, unwilling to wait hours for the next available flight to LA. I didn't know the city very well, but Sam was, as she'd said, my goddamned twin. There was no way I wasn't going to go look for her.

I spent two feverish days in Los Angeles trying to retrace Sam's steps and figure out what had happened. At the end of the second day, John got a call from an LAPD detective who broke the news of Sam's death. My sister had been one of the victims of a serial killer named Henry Remus, who'd kidnapped and murdered four women before dying himself. The police didn't expect to recover Sam's body, but there was enough evidence—Sam's blood and the testimony of her surviving friend, who'd also been abducted—to count my sister among the dead.

That wasn't enough for me, though, so I went to see the cop, a homicide detective named Jesse Cruz. He was a pretty good guy, especially considering that I wasn't exactly using my best manners at the time. He patiently went over the evidence with me again and again, and let me talk to Sam's friend. Eventually I was convinced that yes, Sam really was dead.

While we were still talking at the station, though, our conversation was interrupted by a woman in her early twenties, a pretty brunette with bright green eyes who'd called Cruz by his first name. She came skidding into his office, talking fast about something—and then stopped mid-sentence to stare at me. Her face rearranged itself into confusion. "What *are* you?" she'd asked in a bewildered voice.

I glanced at Cruz, who'd stood up as soon as the girl rushed in, but he looked as confused as I felt. I rose uncertainly, taken aback by the question. Not *who* are you. *What* are you.

"I don't . . . I'm Lex."

The girl took a step closer to me. "You're different," she said curiously.

Cruz looked steadily at the girl for a moment, and I could almost see the threads of history and emotion woven between the two of them, some kind of deep trust or love. Then Cruz glanced at me and remembered himself. "Excuse us for a moment, Miss Luther," he said apologetically. Then he stepped between the girl and me and swept her into the hallway.

I sat back down, but before the office door could swing shut, I heard her say, "Jesse, there's something weird about her. She's not human, but . . ."

When he came back a few minutes later, Cruz apologized for the interruption and told me his friend had just come by to drop off some lunch for him. The story rang a little false, but I dismissed the whole thing—my sister had just died, and besides, it was LA. There were weirdos everywhere.

Looking back now, though, after everything that had happened in the last few days, I was suddenly convinced that the girl knew something about me. And considering the obvious closeness between them, Cruz had to know it, too. I picked up the phone and dialed the handwritten number on the back of the card.

The phone went straight to voicemail. "You've reached the cell phone for Jesse Cruz," came his pleasant male voice. "I'll be out of the country until October first. If you'd like to leave a message . . ."

I hung up the phone and opened my old laptop—a hand-me-down from John a few years earlier. Glancing at the business card from Cruz, I sent him a quick email asking him to call me as soon as possible. Before I could close the browser window, a new message popped up in my inbox: "Message Not Received." I clicked on it, my eyes jumping immediately to the line reading, "The employee you've contacted is no longer with the Los Angeles Police Department. If you'd like to reach someone else . . ."

I frowned at the computer, nonplussed. Cruz had quit the force? He'd seemed like a good cop . . . I shook my head and closed the laptop. At any rate, he couldn't exactly help me protect Charlie from Darcy. She would be safe for a few hours, while John had people over—vampire or not, Darcy wasn't stupid enough to storm a house with four adults. That would give me a little more time to figure out how to keep her safe. I grabbed the phone again, called the number on Quinn's card, and left him a voicemail asking him to call me.

When I hung up, I glanced at my bedside table. Four-thirty. I checked the weather on my phone and discovered that the sun would set in about three hours. I had a little time to kill before Quinn would be available. I dropped the phone on the bed, feeling the irritated stitches pull in my back again. Shit. Those stitches needed to come out. Quinn had said Simon would probably contact me, but I didn't want to wait.

Switching back to the computer, I googled Simon Pellar. There was a semi-famous stamp collector with that name, but I seriously doubted the Simon I'd met had been publishing books in 1992. I kept clicking, and to my surprise, a picture of the right Simon came up on the website for UC Boulder. The guy was an associate professor, with an office in the main science building. I thought back to his glasses-and-messenger-bag look. Yeah, I could see that.

I called his office number and was a little surprised when he answered on the first ring.

"Simon Pellar."

"Hey, it's Lex," I said, then added awkwardly, "Um, from last night."

"Hey," Simon said cheerfully. "I was gonna call you later, but it looks like you tracked me down."

I blanched. "What were you going to call me about?"

"You're a witch, Lex," he reminded me. "We need to talk about training you to use your magic."

Oh. That. "I don't want to," I said abruptly, and then immediately felt like a petulant child. "I mean, I have no interest in being a witch. It's nice that I can't be pressed by vampires, but I need to get back to my real life. No offense," I added, feeling like an idiot. No wonder Big Scott thought I gave off a hermit vibe. I couldn't handle a two-minute conversation with non-family.

There was a long pause. "Okay," Simon said slowly. "Is that why you're calling? To tell me you don't want to get involved?"

"Not exactly," I admitted. "I have this other problem . . ." I told him about the stitches in my back.

"Hmm," Simon said thoughtfully. "I forgot about the stitches. Tell you what: give me your address, and I'll call my sister Lily. She did a couple of years of medical school; I'll see if she can stop by."

While I waited, I spent time returning phone calls and texts. My dad had checked in from the office, and two of my aunts had offered to drop off some dinners so I wouldn't have to cook for a few days. Bettina had called twice, and I spent half an hour reassuring her that I was fine, nothing had been her fault, and she'd done a good job by pressing the panic button, even if she couldn't remember doing it. Rather than return the calls I'd gotten from the police department, I phoned Elise directly. My cousin was annoyed that I'd left the hospital without talking to the police, but we arranged for her and the detective in charge of the kidnapping to come and interview me first thing the next morning.

When I was finally finished with the calls, I looked around the cabin for something else to occupy me. I don't usually spend a lot of time sitting still. If I wasn't working or spending time with my family, I was usually outdoors—hiking or mountain climbing or riding my bike. When the weather was bad, I worked out in the little gym I'd set up in the basement. But I was too sore and weak to exercise, so I headed into the living room to my small collection of DVDs.

I was still browsing through them when the dogs suddenly left their various napping stations and swarmed toward the door, barking frantically. "Guys," I yelled tiredly, but they ignored me. We went through this routine several times a day, and it was almost always nothing. The cabin was surrounded by woods on three sides, so there was plenty of wildlife out there. I rolled my eyes and waited it out, silently pitying the cat burglar who thought he could get into my cabin unnoticed.

But instead of dying down, the tenor of the dogs' cries changed from their usual "There may or may not be an animal in the yard!" barks to their "This is not a drill!" barks, finally transitioning into their "Code human! Code human!" barks. I trudged toward the front door, but the doorbell rang before I reached the entryway.

I peeked through the small vertical window in the door, squinting against the twilight. The woman on the other side was a couple of years younger than me, maybe in her late twenties. She was pretty, with warm, dark-brown skin, blue eyes, and small dreadlocks that reached her shoulders. She had on a skintight denim jacket over a floor-length brown silk skirt and dark clogs. A nose ring sparkled in the automatic sensor light on the porch, and a hemp bag big enough to hold an LP record crossed her chest and rested on one hip. She saw me peeking through the window and shouted something, but I couldn't hear her over the clamor from the dogs.

"Guys!" I yelled. The dogs paused long enough to look at me, tails wagging proudly at their security prowess. I sighed and opened the door a few inches, wedging my leg into the crack so the pack wouldn't run out. They crowded around my leg, trying to get a sniff of the newcomer.

"Can I help you?" I asked politely.

"I'm Lily," she said, a little impatient. "Simon's sister?"

"Um. Oh," I said stupidly.

Seeing my embarrassment, the younger woman grinned. "Don't sweat it, we get that all the time," she said cheerfully. "I happen to have inherited more of our dad's genes; he was black. Not in a young Michael Jackson way or anything—Dad would still be black, except he's dead. Can I come in?"

"Sure," I said, a little dazed. My hostess instincts kicked in belatedly, and I remembered to ask if she'd prefer that I put the dogs away. "They'll calm down in a couple of minutes, but some people are bothered . . ." I added.

"I'm good," Lily said, her voice still cheerful. "I like animals."

I backed up, and she expertly squeezed through the door after me, not leaving enough room for the dogs to run out. I held out my hand. "Sorry about them. I'm Lex, it's nice to meet you."

We shook, which made the stitches in my back prickle uncomfortably. "Nice to meet you too," she said. "Simon told me you have some stitches that need to come out?"

"Oh, God, yes. Come on in."

Chapter 10

In the kitchen, Lily began spreading medical scissors, tweezers, and a few other odds and ends on my island counter. We made a bit of small talk about Boulder and the weather, and after a few minutes she took off her jacket, revealing a black ribbed tank top and toned arms that were covered in black patterns from wrist to shoulder. "Wow," I breathed. "Your tattoos are amazing." Each arm was obviously planned as one piece, and instead of separate pictures the swirling ink seemed to suggest a random, always-moving design: part tribal, part Eastern, as if Native American carvings had procreated with Japanese calligraphy. It was only after looking at the tattoos for a few seconds that my eyes started to detect connections in the pattern, although I didn't recognize any of the symbols or structures.

"Oh, thanks." Lily looked fondly down at her arms. "Designed them myself. I used to be a tattoo artist."

"What do they mean?" I asked, then caught myself. "Sorry, that was kind of a rude question."

"It's okay," Lily said, unruffled. "It's a long story, is all. Another time."

"And Simon said you went to med school?" I said tentatively. I wasn't really worried about the stitches—I'd taken my own stitches out before, so I knew it wasn't that hard. I just didn't know what else to talk about.

"Oh. Yeah." She rolled her eyes ruefully, as if med school was just a post-college rite of passage, like backpacking through Europe. "I did two years, but I got sick of not being able to add any magic to what we were doing. I mean, it'd be like you going into war armed with heavy rocks when you could be using guns. Simon told me you were a soldier. I hope that's okay."

"Uh, sure."

She surveyed the counter. "Okay, I think I'm all set up here." Pulling on a pair of surgical gloves, she made a quick motion in the direction of my chest. "Time to sit down and lose the shirt."

"Right," I said, feeling a little awkward. It had been a while since I'd taken my shirt off in front of a stranger, even another woman.

Lily cocked an eyebrow, clearly picking up on my discomfort. "Here, look." Her fingers dropped to the hem of her tank top, pulling it up and exposing smooth brown skin and several more tattoos, not to mention small, firm breasts—she wasn't wearing a bra either. She dropped the shirt back down. "Now we're even."

A laugh escaped from between my lips, and I sat on the stool and started to unbutton my flannel shirt. "I can't believe you just flashed me as an icebreaker."

"It might not be the best precedent to set," Lily said agreeably.

I peeled the flannel off carefully, with Lily helping a little. She handed it to me, and I stuck my arms through the sleeves again, pulling it on backward to cover my front.

Lily let out a low whistle. "Wow," she said admiringly, echoing my tone of voice from earlier. "Your scars are amazing." I felt her touch the thick white line of older scar tissue that bisected my own tattoo, a black design on my shoulder with my unit's shield and the words "US ARMY." "What happened here?" she asked curiously.

"Oh . . . everyone in my squad was getting them," I said, deliberately misinterpreting the question.

When I didn't say anything else, she said quietly, "It's good work." She cleared her throat. "Right. Let's get started on those stitches."

She soaked a cotton ball in iodine and started disinfecting all my fresh injuries from the healed-over stitches. I felt the cold liquid running down my skin and shivered, grateful for the backward shirt. After giving the iodine a second to dry, Lily started at the topmost injury—snipping the stitches with her little scissors and pulling them free with tweezers. "These are either infected or were just about to get infected." I could hear the frown in her voice. "Simon should have taken them out as soon as he gave you Sybil's charm."

"It's not his fa-ault," I protested, stumbling over my words from pain as she tugged at a stitch. "There wasn't any time."

"Still," she grumbled, but good-naturedly now. "My brother thinks he's a goddamned cowboy. A nerdy, overeager, scientist cowboy, which is obviously the worst kind."

I smiled, although she couldn't see it. "Which of you is older?" I said, though I was pretty sure it was Simon.

A snort. "He is. I'm the baby. My sister Morgan is the oldest. The heir apparent, or so she thinks. Then it's Sybil, who tries to keep up by being really tightly wound. Simon and I are more laid-back."

"Still, it sounds like you guys are close."

"I guess. Do you have brothers and sisters?" she asked.

"I have a lot of cousins. We're pretty tight," I said truthfully. If there was one thing I'd learned about small talk in the last year, it was that "dead twin sister" pretty much ruined things for everyone.

"Oh, cousins are the best," Lily said agreeably. "Sibling enough to love you forever, but you never have to worry about them stealing your clothes." She made another careful snip. "I like your earrings, by the way," Lily added. "Is that a griffin?"

"Oh, thanks." I touched one of the little silver studs. I didn't wear earrings often, but when I did, I usually chose this pair, each one a tiny curled-up animal. "Yeah. My cousin Anna gave them to me. She has this weird idea that griffins are my spirit animal," I explained. "She's got a New Age streak, but we've mostly learned to adjust." And at least it wasn't a unicorn.

Somewhere between the second and third line of stitches, the doorbell rang again. It was a sudden, shocking sound, given that the dogs were all still draped on various pieces of furniture when it happened. They hadn't even made it to their first round of barks. I jumped, and Lily poked me hard with the tweezers. All four of the dogs leapt up like they'd been caught sleeping on the job, which was true. "My fault," I called over the sound of barking dogs. "Can you stop for a second?"

Still wearing the backward shirt, I padded through the cabin to the front door, peering through the window again. It was fully dark outside by now, but the automatic sensor light showed Quinn, looking handsome in jeans and a black leather jacket. Was that look a vampire thing?

Using one foot as a stopper, I cracked the door open. The dogs, who had huddled around me, began freaking out in earnest—Cody and Dopey whined and pawed the floor, Pongo barked as loud as he could, and Chip actually began to *howl*. I'd never heard that sound from him before. "Hi," I said over the racket. "You came over."

He nodded, his eyes taking in my backward shirt without any particular reaction. I was getting used to a general lack of readable reactions from Quinn. "The situation has changed a bit on my end. We need to talk, and I try not to discuss anything important over the phone."

"How did you find me?" I asked, eyebrows raised. "I'm not exactly in the phone book."

"From your chart," he explained, practically shouting to be heard over the dogs' racket. I started to open the door, but Pongo, usually the most levelheaded of my crew, let out a vicious growl and lunged at the door. "Oh," Quinn added casually, "dogs generally hate vampires. Some cats, too."

I rolled my eyes. Further proof that dogs are smarter than people. "Of course they do. Hang on."

Closing the front door, I herded all four dogs into the adjacent mudroom, tugging at collars and doing some fancy blocking maneuvers to get them all in at once. As I straightened up, I realized belatedly that I had probably given Quinn a good view of my scarred, naked back through the window—and probably a pretty solid glimpse of my breasts, too. Great. I rolled my eyes as a blush crept up my neck.

When I opened the door, Quinn was standing with his back to the house, pretending to survey the yard in the darkness. He turned when he heard the door open, but very slowly, checking his peripheral vision to make sure I was decent. Oh, yeah. He'd seen my boobs.

"Darcy said that this wasn't over," I blurted, before I could let myself feel any more embarrassment. "She's going to go after Charlie again."

Quinn nodded, his face still unreadable. "I've got two vampires guarding the entrances to your brother-in-law's house, both of them stronger than Darcy. Your niece is definitely safe for the night."

"Thank you," I said, meaning it.

"We still need to talk, though."

I glanced down at my backward shirt. "Simon's sister Lily is here taking my stitches out."

"Can I come in and wait?"

"Sure." I opened the door wider, but Quinn just stood there, cocking an eyebrow at me.

"Oh, right," I said, the blush returning. Apparently it *was* true. "Uh, please come in?" I felt so silly.

As soon as he was inside, I pointed to the kitchen. "After you," I said firmly.

Quinn stepped into the kitchen only a heartbeat ahead of me, so I still saw Lily's face when he entered: a fleeting look of embarrassment, followed by irritation. "Quinn," she said stiffly.

"*Lilith.*" Quinn's voice was equally cool.

"I'll be done in a second," she said. "And then she's all yours."

I immediately decided that whatever was going on between them was none of my business.

Lily went back to work on my stitches, keeping silent now. While he waited, Quinn wandered over to the bookshelves by the entertainment center, perusing the titles with his hands in his pockets. "Damn, that's a lot of kids' movies," he said about my shelf of DVDs.

"Yeah, but they're all good ones," I said, a little defensive. I don't have many movies, and most of them either are animated or were made before 1960. "And I have a lot of cousins with kids. They come over sometimes."

If Quinn heard me, he chose not to respond. "Hey, *The Best Years of Our Lives*," he said, grabbing a movie off the shelf and scanning the back of the case. "I love this movie. Haven't seen it in ages."

"Yeah, it's great."

"I haven't heard of that one," Lily said, gently tugging at another stitch with the tweezers. "What's it about?"

"These three veterans come back from World War II, and they all have trouble adjusting," Quinn told her. "It won a bunch of Oscars."

"Were they in the army, like you?" Lily asked me, her tone casual.

"Different divisions," Quinn answered absently, still examining the back of the box. I realized he must have recognized the shield on my tattoo. Interesting.

As that thought ran through my mind, Quinn looked up and met my eyes, changing the subject. "You have a lot of textbooks here for someone who didn't go to college," he pointed out, gesturing at the bookshelf in the corner.

"Really?" I said innocently. "How many textbooks does someone who went to college have?"

"Not nearly as many as someone who went to medical school," Lily grumbled.

"What about photography school?" Quinn offered, giving her a sly look. "Or education majors? You must have *rooms* full of books."

The witch glared at him sourly. "At least I can read, parasite. Do they even have textbooks at the police academy, or do you have to look at *pictures* of traffic tickets?" She jerked hard with the tweezers.

Ow. "If you're going to piss her off, Quinn, at least wait until she's done with my back," I said, keeping my voice as mild as possible.

Quinn wandered over to stand in front of me, hands in his pockets. "How much longer?" he asked Lily.

"I'm done," she announced, stripping off her gloves. "You should clean the wounds with alcohol at least twice a day," she told me, tossing things back into her hemp bag. "Let them get some air when you can, and I'd forgo a bra for the next couple of days. Call me if it starts hurting or itching again."

"Yes, ma'am," I replied. I got off the stool, turned around, and fixed my shirt with my back to Quinn, holding it shut with my hand. If he wanted to stare at my scarred back for the few seconds it took me to take the shirt off and pull it back on, let him. "I'll walk you out."

"I can find my own way," Lily said sullenly. Then she caught herself and met my eyes. "Um, it was really nice to meet you, Lex. Si said you weren't interested in training, but we should grab a drink sometime. I don't know many people in the Old World outside of my clan. Or *vampires.*" She said the last with exaggerated distaste before shooting a final glare at Quinn and flouncing out. I heard the front door close a moment later.

"What the hell was that about?" I said, turning to face him as I buttoned the shirt.

"Lily and I have this problem where when we're around each other, we accidentally start bickering like . . ." He drifted off as—to my surprise—his gaze brushed down my front, stopping where my flannel shirt still gaped. Annoyed, I stubbornly resisted the impulse to glance down and make sure I was covered. Instead I let out a little whistle, a high note followed by a low one, to get his attention. Quinn met my eyes and looked away, suddenly embarrassed. "Like teenagers," he finished in a mumble. "Sorry, didn't mean to stare."

That took me aback. I had expected him to play innocent, or maybe make some lewd comment, not actually apologize. I was suddenly very aware that there were only a couple of feet between us.

And that he looked like a Scandinavian Indiana Jones in that jacket. I cleared my throat. "You were saying something about the situation changing?"

"Yeah." He looked relieved to be back on sure footing. "My boss wants to meet you."

"Me?" I said, startled. "Why?"

He shot me a "don't be stupid" expression. "Because you're a witch, but you're unaligned with any of the witch clans. He wants to make sure you're not a threat."

I thought that over for a moment. Ideally, I'd like to just try to forget that the Old World existed and go back to my life, but Darcy was still out there, and I wasn't going to be able to relax until I knew my niece was safe. "Well, good," I said, climbing to my feet. "I want to understand what Sid and Nancy wanted with my niece."

Alarm sparked in Quinn's eyes, maybe the biggest reaction I'd seen from him yet. "You can't go storming in there demanding answers, Lex," he warned. "It's very, very important that you show respect."

"You mean like the respect your boss showed for Charlie when he let Victor and Darcy go after her again last night?" I said tartly.

"Technically," Quinn pointed out, his voice cool, "that was my fault. I was supposed to clean up the Depot mess, and I should have spent less time working the police angle and more time looking for them. I just never thought they'd go after the same baby a second time."

"So you thought they'd go after some other baby instead?" I demanded.

"Don't put words into my mouth," Quinn snapped. Then he forced his face into its usual implacable expression. "Look, just come talk to Itachi, and this will all be straightened out, okay?"

"Fine," I retorted. Then I glanced down at myself and sighed. With as much dignity as I could muster, I added, "But I have to change my pants first."

Chapter 11

As it turned out, I had been to Boulder's big vampire hangout at least half a dozen times before.

Like most college towns, Boulder has dozens of coffee shops, but so far as I know only one of them is open all night: a little place called Magic Beans, located on Pine Street, not far from Boulder's pedestrian mall. It had been around since Sam and I were in high school. I'd been in once or twice to get a caffeine fix before my shift at the Depot, but I hadn't noticed anything special about it, except maybe that it was a hell of a lot larger than the average coffee shop in notoriously expensive Boulder. Despite the size and the plum location, though, the prices were pretty comparable to any other coffee shop in town. If I'd bothered to wonder how that worked, I would have figured there was an underground casino in the back room or something. My mind probably wouldn't have made the leap to "secret vampire headquarters." But I guess I'm just naive like that.

Although it was after nine-thirty by the time we pulled up, there were no open parking spots on the street in front of Magic Beans, so Quinn had to find a spot a couple of blocks west. The outside of the building was unremarkable, just a big brick box that was beginning to crumble a little at the corners. "Remember to be respectful," Quinn said uneasily as we approached the building. "You can't go in with guns blazing. You don't want to be on his radar as a threat."

"I don't have a gun, remember?" I said, a little sourly. Quinn had searched me and my purse before letting me get in his car. "And I don't care if I'm on his radar. I care that Charlie *isn't*."

"It might be too late for that," Quinn said ominously, but when I glanced at him he just shook his head. "Come on, let's go in."

Unlike most coffee shops, which are more or less one big room with a cash register planted somewhere, Magic Beans was labyrinthine, a maze of small rooms with tables and chairs scattered around at random. Each room featured art by a different Boulder artist, and each had a door, which you could close if you wanted to have a conversation without disturbing the other customers.

There were fluorescent arrows stuck to the carpet just inside the door, leading first-time visitors through the entry rooms to the coffee counter. The girl behind the cash register was maybe eighteen or nineteen, and she was covered in a pile of bad fashion: several T-shirts and cardigans on top of one another, a handful of cheap costume necklaces, and an enormous baggy skirt that truly looked like it was made from burlap. Her hair was an unattractive bright orange, cut in an unflattering, chin-length bob, and she wore large, square-framed glasses. In most cities, she might have been taken for a homeless person, although everything she wore was perfectly clean. In Boulder, however, she seemed right at home.

"Hi," she said cheerfully as Quinn and I approached the counter. "Welcome to Magic Beans! What can I get started for you guys?"

"Maven," Quinn said matter-of-factly, "We're here to see the boss. He's expecting us."

The young woman—Maven—squinted at him. I realized with a start that underneath the layers of clothes, the odd hair, and the huge glasses, she was strikingly attractive. Sam had been cute, and I had a certain youthful appeal according to some, but this teenager was launch-a-thousand-ships levels of beautiful, even though she was trying to cover it up. It wasn't just her face, I realized, looking at her closely. There was something *inviting* about her. I found myself leaning forward, eager for her response. "Oh, hey, Quinn. Forgot you were coming. He'll see you in the back office," she said pleasantly. "This way, please."

We followed her through another quiet study area and a massive room I hadn't seen before, which was nearly twice the size of the next-largest room at Magic Beans. The floor was polished concrete, and there was a sort of mini-stage set up next to a set of double doors that led outside, judging by the darkness that I could see through the window. "We have poetry readings in here," Maven said, sensing my surprise. "Sometimes even a band. Here you are." In the back right corner of the big room was a tiny office. An Asian man in shirtsleeves and a navy tie was hunched over a desk with neat stacks of papers on it. He looked up as we approached.

"Good evening, Mr. Itachi. This is Allison Luther," Quinn said formally. "She goes by Lex. Lex, this is Mr. Itachi."

The man stood and looked me over. He was a couple of inches taller than my five-five, compact and trim with a very businesslike haircut. His face was intelligent, his movements smooth and efficient.

Dangerous, I thought instantly, though I couldn't pinpoint why.

"I'm pleased to make your acquaintance, Sergeant," he said, extending a hand. I blanched a little at the use of my old rank, but I shrugged it off and held out my hand. Itachi's handshake was firm and quick. "Please, have a seat. Excuse us, Quinn."

If it bothered Quinn to be dismissed, he didn't let it show. He just nodded and stepped out past Maven, who had come into the room behind us. She smiled and closed the door, perching on a chair next to it. I sat on the edge of the visitor's chair across from Itachi's desk. I didn't like the cramped quarters, or the fact that there was a stranger at my back, but I was hoping to get out of there as quickly as possible. "Just Lex, please," I said.

Itachi nodded and gestured to a thick open file on his desk. "I've just been reading up on you. Interesting stuff." He looked down and made a show of lazily turning a page. "Joined the army right out of high school. Two deployments to combat zones. Honorable discharge under . . . odd circumstances." He glanced up, raising his eyebrows. "And you never seem to take advantage of any of Boulder's resources for veterans. You don't walk in the parade, you don't go to the VA or to any support groups." He shook his head, smiling humorlessly. "You didn't want to be a poster child, Sergeant?"

I ignored the question, keeping my face expressionless as my thoughts whirled. I wasn't surprised, necessarily—if vampires really did run the supernatural world in Boulder, they were bound to have access to significant resources. But it took time to cultivate that kind of information, especially when the notoriously close-mouthed US Army was involved. Less than twenty-four hours had passed since Quinn had tried and failed to press my mind. Had they been keeping tabs on me since the attack at the Depot? Or were they just that fast?

When I didn't respond, Itachi turned another page. The next paper in the file was my mug shot. "You've also been arrested twice since you returned to Boulder," he said mildly.

"You have my police records?" I asked before I could help myself. *Damn.* Who *were* these people?

Itachi nodded, his eyes still on the file. "I see that you were in a bar fight a few years ago, shortly after you returned from Iraq." He glanced up, letting a silence brew between us. He was waiting for me to comment.

I clenched my jaw, then painstakingly unclenched it. "Guy wasn't familiar with the concept of no means no."

Itachi flipped the page, revealing another police report. "And you were arrested again just last year, for assaulting a random man on the street."

"It wasn't random," I said, trying to keep my voice calm. "He was kicking the hell out of his dog."

Nodding implacably, Itachi closed the file. "Both times, the victims were convinced to drop the charges after a visit from your father's attorneys."

"I didn't ask for that," I snapped, feeling myself losing control. I had wanted to get a public defender and plead out, but my father insisted on using his lawyers. I finally conceded when he told me he was worried about how my actions would look for the company.

"A lot of veterans have a hard time settling back into civilian life," Itachi said calmly. "But you do seem to carry a lot of anger, Sergeant Luther."

I ignored the formal address. He was either too polite to use my given name or he was baiting me. Either way, I wasn't going to correct him twice.

When I didn't say anything else, he added in a thoughtful tone, "Although of course it makes sense for you to have some residual anger after losing a twin. And so violently, too."

I took a deep breath and made a point of relaxing my muscles. I may have a temper, but I know when I'm being goaded. "You're showing off," I said calmly. "You want me to know that you can get my police file, that you can dig into my personal life. Understood. Now I'd like to move on."

A small smile played at the corners of Itachi's mouth, and for the briefest moment his glance flicked to Maven. "Very well, Sergeant—"

I interrupted him, going on the offensive. "And I would like to know why Victor and Darcy went after my niece," I said firmly. "One time could have been a coincidence. They might have just wanted a baby for . . . some reason." I swallowed, forcing my mind away from that line of thought. "But they came after her a second time. They wanted *this* baby, Charlie, and I'd like to know why."

Itachi's eyebrows raised, and he leaned back in his chair. "And what is this information worth to you?" he said casually, like I'd asked him for a stock tip.

I said, "Am I correct in assuming you didn't order Victor and Darcy to go after my niece?"

For the first time, Itachi looked just the slightest bit uncertain. Again, I saw his eyes flicker toward Maven. Then his expression evened out, and with the same blank-slate detachment I'd seen in Quinn, he said, "That would be correct, yes."

"Then I exposed a discipline problem you didn't know you had," I retorted. "And for services rendered, I'd like some information." Itachi's eyes narrowed, but I wasn't finished. "You *must* be the person to ask, if you really are in charge of all the supernatural crap in Boulder."

"In all of Colorado, actually," Itachi said.

"I wasn't talking to you," I replied. I twisted in my seat to look back at Maven.

The young woman—the vampire—lifted her chin, eyes flashing. She had been leaning casually against the wall next to the office door, but when she straightened up, she didn't look like a spacey barista anymore. When she spoke now, her voice was queenly. "I'm flattered. But I'm here as an advisor only. Itachi is in charge."

I eyed her. She was practically glowing with something: Charisma? Charm? "Like hell," I said.

A surprised smile twitched on her face. "It's true that I have more years than Itachi," she allowed. "But I assure you, he is in charge of the state."

I wasn't sure I believed her—it was strange how Itachi kept glancing at her, and there was some kind of vibe between them I couldn't get a bead on—but I dropped the subject. "If you're an advisor, ma'am, would you mind joining us up here so I don't have to turn to look at you?" *And so I don't have a stranger at my back*, I thought.

"Certainly," Maven said graciously. She stood up and darted to the visitor's chair next to mine. Her shuffling walk had been supplanted by the same lithe, efficient movements I'd seen in all the vampires I'd met so far.

For his part, the leader of the Colorado Old World simply picked up the conversation where it had left off. "So, Sergeant, Quinn tells me that you were unaware of the Old World until you met Darcy and Victor. Is that correct?"

"Yes."

"And yet you survived two encounters with them," Maven mused. "Interesting."

"I had help both times, ma'am," I said plainly. I wasn't trying to be modest, but I also didn't want to claim credit I didn't deserve.

Something about my choice of words seemed to amuse Maven a little, because the corners of her lips turned up just a little. "More than you know," she told me. Her eyes cut over to Itachi, like she was cuing him.

He caught it. "Until a few days ago," he said to me, "I was unaware of your niece. Like you, I initially thought Victor and Darcy had stolen the child for their own needs. It wasn't until Quinn told me about his encounter with her at John Wheaton's house that I understood what she is."

"What is she?"

"Charlotte Wheaton is what's commonly called a null," Maven explained. "A human being who nullifies the magic within a certain space around him- or herself. Of the four creatures that remain in the Old World, nulls are the rarest. I have met several before"—her eyes went unfocused and distant for a moment, then snapped back to mine—"but it has been over a century since the last one."

"Can you elaborate on that definition, please?"

Maven smiled. "Nulls can undo power," she said simply. "When we are physically close to one, our magic disappears. We are human again until we move away."

I considered that for a long moment while the two vampires sat unmoving. My first thought was how ridiculous it sounded—the idea that Charlie, who considered the greatest things in life to be *Sesame Street*, climbable furniture, and personal boxes of raisins, was some kind of traveling magic-free zone? Come on.

But then I thought of how I'd been able to hurt both Victor and Darcy, and the way they'd both healed supernaturally fast when they moved far enough away from my niece. And how they'd been able to get into John's house in the first place. "How close is physically close?" I asked finally.

"Anywhere from a few feet to perhaps ten or fifteen," Maven answered. "The area tends to expand, however, when the null loses control of her emotions."

"When she gets upset," I clarified.

"Yes."

More pieces fell into place. I wanted more time to think about it, to reconsider the distances at the Depot and at John's house, when Charlie was screaming mad, but I wasn't sure how long they would just sit there waiting for me. Already Itachi was looking bored. I decided to accept what they were saying for the moment and spend more time processing it later.

"I guess I can see how it could be valuable to you all to be human again sometimes," I said slowly, "but it hardly seems worth risking an AMBER Alert, especially after Victor and Darcy failed the first time. Why risk so much to kidnap a baby just because she's a null?"

Maven's eyes widened a tiny bit, and I had the immediate impression that I'd made an error. "Lex, being able to neutralize magic isn't just valuable," she said rather patiently. "It's far beyond invaluable for the Old World. Werewolves can stay human during the full moon, and witches, who have no supernatural strength or healing ability, are actually safe from a physical attack by either of the other factions. And vampires, well . . . we can go out in the day."

"There are those of us who would do much worse than risk an AMBER Alert, as you said, to be in the sunlight," Itachi added.

"Oh," I said, feeling stupid.

"To put it another way," Maven continued, in a voice gone soft and cold, "a null can also *get to* anyone in the Old World, regardless of their magical defenses. She could walk right up to me and shoot me in the chest, and I would die. If you managed to find such a person while she's young, and still programmable . . ." She trailed off, letting me fill in the blanks.

Horrible possibilities flashed through my head. Charlie being hurt, being brainwashed. Charlie being taught to hate and kill. "I thought . . . I thought it was a human-trafficking thing," I whispered numbly, fear sending a burst of cold electricity down my spine. Now I felt so much worse than stupid—I felt *helpless*. Charlie was basically the equivalent of free bacon at a dog show, and I was as useless as I was outnumbered. This changed everything.

Maven's eyes narrowed suddenly, and I saw her nostrils flare. A second later, Itachi shifted restlessly. Oh, God. Could they smell my panic? I was suddenly very aware of the fact that I was trapped in a tiny room with two deadly predators, and I worked to push the fear aside. I squared my shoulders and met each of their gazes in turn.

"I want protection for my niece," I said to Itachi. "If you really are in charge of the supernatural world in Colorado, I want you to make sure Charlie is left alone."

Maven tilted her head in thought, an oddly birdlike gesture that reminded me of how Victor had looked at me when he'd been unable to press my mind.

"That is an extremely large request," Itachi said tartly.

"But within your power?"

"Of course." A hint of disdain had crept into his tone.

"You misunderstand," Maven said, acting as Itachi's spokesperson. "It is not a large request because the task is too difficult. Now that Itachi is aware of Charlotte, he can make it clear that she is under his protection. But she is within his enclave, which means she is already his." She lifted a shoulder carelessly. "Why should he care about *your* wishes in respect to something that is already his?"

That shocked me. It hadn't occurred to me that the vampire in charge might already think he *owned* my niece. Everything in me wanted to scream that Charlie wasn't theirs, that my niece would never belong to anyone but herself. That I would kill every vampire in the state before I let one of them touch her. And if Itachi had said those words to me, I might have done exactly that.

But there was something magnetic about this woman. I couldn't explain it, even to myself, but she had a force to her, strong as gravity.

"I suppose the question, Lex," Maven continued, crossing her legs under the burlap-looking skirt, "is, what are you offering?"

"Myself," I said, firmly and immediately.

Chapter 12

Itachi raised a single scoffing eyebrow. "Do you have any experience in making lattes?" he asked sarcastically. I just stared at him levelly. He added in a more subdued tone, "Witches don't work for vampires, any more than foxes work for bears."

Maven glanced at him. "That is historically true, but then again, we don't have the most traditional structure here in Colorado," she pointed out. To me she said, "What do you suggest you could do for us, Lex?"

I swallowed, focusing on my wording. I didn't know much about vampires, but it had occurred to me, of course, that they might be involved in some nasty stuff. *Illegal* stuff. I needed to set my limits clearly without making myself unattractive as an employee. "Security. On call, part time, however you want to do it. The army taught me how to drive a truck, gather intelligence, and look for weapons and for lies. I won't kill anyone or hurt the innocent," I added, "but I could be your daytime Quinn. I'm very motivated, reasonably intelligent, and apparently no one can press my mind."

Itachi stayed silent, waiting for his next cue. Maven was looking at me very speculatively, her fingers now tapping on the file of information Itachi had been reading. "You just got out of one army," she said finally. "What makes you so willing to join another one?"

That took me aback for a moment. Was that really what this was? Another army? There were similarities, I supposed, but the comparison was too strange to really wrap my head around. Then again, I knew that I would do a hell of a lot more than rejoin an army for Charlie.

I started to say just that, but stopped myself. That wasn't what she was really asking me. She didn't care why I wanted to join, she wanted to know why I would *stay*. Why I wouldn't just sell them out to the first person who promised to protect Charlie instead.

"Because I've been part of an army before," I finally said, "I understand concepts like taking orders, chain of command, and working for the greater good. I also know," I went on, "that sometimes protecting the greater good means being the lesser evil."

Maven's eyebrows raised just a fraction, and I knew I'd managed to say the right thing. "Give me your wrist," she commanded.

I started to reach out before I even knew I'd moved, but I caught myself and asked, "Why?"

"We are vampires, Lex," Maven said, not unkindly. "I want to taste your blood. If you work for Mr. Itachi, you'll be expected to make the occasional donation."

I weighed my options, then reluctantly held out my hand. I had no problem with giving blood, and so far we were still well within the "small price to pay for Charlie's safety" arena.

Maven took my hand, turning my wrist to expose the veins. Her fingers were very cool, but not ice-cold like the grave or anything. "I can't press your mind properly," she warned, "but I'm strong enough to press it a little, to help with the pain. Do you want me to do that?"

I shook my head. I'd take pain over mind control any day. Maven nodded and bared her teeth without another word. Her canines looked a little bit sharper than normal, but there was something else off about her teeth, too. Before I could figure out what it was, she was pressing them into my wrist.

To my surprise, they sank through my skin without any resistance. I squeaked as the pain hit, but I managed not to pull my wrist away. She pressed her lips into the wound, forming a seal as my blood spurted into her mouth. I realized dimly that her teeth had looked odd because they were scary sharp—they were roughly rectangular, like any other human's, but razor-edged.

She held out her free hand to Itachi, and he leaned forward, lifting a clean white handkerchief out of his pocket and handing it to her. I looked away. After a few seconds, Maven deftly pulled my wrist away from her mouth, pressing the handkerchief to it at the same time. She tied the handkerchief around my wrist and released me. When she raised her head, there was a luminous smile on her face. "*Well,*" she marveled, shaking her head a little. There was still enough blood in her mouth to stain her teeth red, and I fought the impulse to flinch. "You are just full of surprises, aren't you?"

"What is it?" Itachi asked, suddenly curious.

Maven raised a small hand and dabbed at her lips with one finger. "She certainly has active witchblood," she told him, without taking her eyes off me. Though Itachi looked like he had more questions, he said nothing. I couldn't figure out the distribution of power between the two vampires, but I decided I didn't really need to know until I understood my own situation a little better. Maven could *taste* the magic in my blood?

With everything that was going on, I'd nearly forgotten about Darcy's comment that I had "weird blood." Now it made more sense. I didn't know whether to be intrigued or grossed out by that, so I just pressed the handkerchief into my wrist. It hurt, but although I was pretty sure she'd nicked a vein, the blood wasn't seeping through the delicate white cloth.

"Don't worry, vampire bites clot very quickly," Maven promised. "It won't scar, either."

I nodded. I wasn't really worried about bleeding out. Both vampires were watching me carefully, probably waiting to see if I would freak out. "This is officially the weirdest job interview I've ever had," I muttered.

Maven smiled.

"So?" I asked. "Do we have a deal?"

Itachi's eyes narrowed. "Not so fast," he chided. "There's nothing for you to—"

Ever so gently, Maven laid a hand on Itachi's arm. She leaned over and whispered something into his ear, too softly for me to hear. Itachi's expression didn't change, except for the slightest tightening of his lips. When she was done, he leaned back and nodded.

Maven peered at me through the thick glasses she undoubtedly didn't need. "A probationary period is in order, I think," she said at last. "We want you to help Quinn find out who came after your niece in Itachi's enclave."

"What do you mean?" I asked, startled. "We know it was Victor and Darcy."

"And Darcy is still out there," Itachi countered, his voice sour.

"At any rate," Maven added, "I am inclined to believe someone else sent them to collect your niece. Trying to take Charlotte behind Itachi's back, before he was aware of her—they might have gotten away with that on a technicality, as they say." She smiled without mirth. "But to go after her again, once he was aware of her existence, was a very brazen move."

"And those two were never known for being brazen," Itachi broke in, as though he just wanted to edge his way into the conversation.

Maven nodded her head slightly, agreeing with him. "I'm afraid someone may have . . . motivated them."

"That's it?" I asked, trying not to sound as incredulous as I felt. "You just want me to find out who's after Charlie?" Hell, I was going to do that anyway.

But Maven held up a hand. "In addition to that, we'd like for you to seek counsel from Clan Pellar on how to use your magic."

"My magic?" I echoed dumbly. In my concern over keeping Charlie safe, I had nearly forgotten that I could theoretically do . . . something. Magic, I guess.

Maven arched an eyebrow in a way that suggested this was a deal breaker. "If you are to become our 'daytime Quinn,'" she said, "we want all the use we can get out of you."

I nodded slowly. I didn't want to fuck around with witch powers, but I could learn a couple of spells, or whatever the witches called them, to pacify Maven and Itachi. Maybe I could learn something that would help me protect Charlie. "And then we've got a deal?" I persisted, working to keep my voice light and respectful. I wasn't sure I succeeded.

"These two tasks should determine whether you truly are who and what I suspect," she told me. "If you swear loyalty to us and can prove your value, then we have a deal. We will make sure the Old World stays away from your niece until she turns eighteen, or until you terminate your service, whichever comes first. No one in our enclave will touch her."

I opened my mouth to ask for more time for Charlie, but before I could speak, Itachi said firmly, "That is our *only* offer."

I closed my mouth and nodded tightly. Seventeen years of service, and no guarantee that Charlie would be safe once she was no longer a minor. It wasn't the greatest bargain I'd ever made, but I didn't see a lot of alternatives, short of moving into Charlie's bedroom or trying to convince John to move to Belize. Neither seemed very viable. If I worked for Itachi, at least I could ensure that Charlie got to have a childhood.

"Oh, and Lex?" Maven added. "In the interest of fairness, you should know that if you don't perform to our satisfaction, there is no deal. Itachi will do whatever he wants with the child, and we'll kill you if you interfere."

She said it in a completely reasonable, "just so you know" kind of tone, which somehow made it worse.

"You can try," I said quietly. Itachi chortled with laughter at that, but Maven just smiled, almost sympathetically.

I rose from the chair and held out my hand, with my wrist still encircled by the delicate handkerchief. "I believe we have a deal."

After we shook, Maven called for Quinn. I didn't think anyone would be able to hear through the thick office door, but vampires must have good hearing. He popped his head in, his eyes widening slightly as they took in our new positioning in the room. "Ma'am?" he said to Maven.

"We have a task for you, Quinn." She nodded toward me. "We'd like you and Lex to locate Darcy. Find out if she and Victor were sent by a third party. Then kill her."

A sputter of shock came out of my mouth, and Maven turned her head to look at me. She raised an eyebrow. "This is the Old World, Lex," she said matter-of-factly. "If you truly plan to work for us, you'll need to understand the way we do things. I accept your stipulation against killing, but Quinn has no such condition."

I looked at Quinn, but his face was completely unreadable. Maven continued, "Lex, you'll work with Quinn at night, hunting for Darcy. During the day you'll work with the Pellars to advance your magic. Quinn will set that up for you. Begin tomorrow."

I stepped away from the chair, but paused and looked back at the vampires. "And Charlie?"

"I'll put the word out," she promised. Itachi gave me a polite, dismissive nod.

Feeling a little dazed, I followed Quinn into the hallway, where I stumbled and had to lean against a wall. He stopped a few feet ahead of me and retraced his steps. "You okay?" he asked.

"Fine," I said, working to control my voice. "Just a little light-headed." It wasn't the blood loss. I had bled more while shaving my legs. For some reason leaving Maven's presence felt like moving from strong sunshine into the shade again—not necessarily a bad feeling, but definitely an adjustment.

I suddenly felt very young, and very *naive*. It reminded me of my first deployment to Iraq, where the customs, language, government, and daily risks were so different that it felt like I was on another planet. But now the displacement was happening in my *hometown*. A mile from the hospital where I was born.

Quinn waited patiently until I straightened up again, a question on his face. "Sorry, this is all just happening really fast," I mumbled. "I think I just agreed to go vampire hunting. With a vampire."

"Yeah, well, it's gonna get worse before it gets better," he said frankly. "Most witches are told all about magic by the time they hit puberty. If you're going to tag along with me while I go after Darcy, you're gonna have to pick up a lot of information fast."

I looked up at him. "I've got no love for Darcy," I remarked, "but are you really okay with just killing her? You were a cop."

With exaggerated patience, Quinn took my elbow and propelled me forward, his grip like a concrete cuff on my bicep. When we had passed through two rooms, he leaned over and whispered, "They could still hear you, you know."

"Oh." Oops.

"To answer your question, I don't feel great about it, no. But I don't have a choice," he said, his tone bitter. "Not everyone *volunteered* for a deal with Maven and Itachi."

"What does *that* mean?" I asked, a little hotly. "Do you think I woke up this morning hoping I'd get to feed my blood to a vampire?"

Quinn hesitated. "Sorry," he said after a moment. "I didn't mean you . . . My situation is different, that's all."

"Different how?" I said.

He looked away. "I was sold to them."

My eyes widened. "You were—"

"Come on," he said brusquely, giving me a gentle push. "Let's get you home for some sleep. You have magic lessons tomorrow."

"Oh screw that," I shot back. "You're starting now, right?"

He hesitated. "Well, yeah . . ."

"Then I'm coming with you. What do we do first?"

Quinn sighed, his cool demeanor momentarily ruffled. "You're going to be a pain in my ass, aren't you?"

"Maybe," I told him, and I felt a smile spread across my face. Not a nice smile. "But not nearly as big as I'm about to be in Darcy's."

Chapter 13

One of the many things I'd never bothered to consider in my thirty-one years of life were the logistical problems that came with the care and keeping of vampires.

As I followed Quinn out to his car, a gray Toyota sedan that had probably been purchased for its anonymity, he gave me a rundown of how vampires lived, starting with the fact that they were pretty much dead while the sun was up. "Unfortunately, that leaves us vulnerable," he said, "so vampires keep really great hidey-holes, often underground. Victor and Darcy have a basement apartment not far from campus. We'll go there first, see if we can find any clues about where she might have gone."

A basement apartment? It seemed so . . . ordinary. But then, I guess vampires wouldn't get much access to their food supply by hiding out in Transylvanian castles. Speaking of food supply . . . "How does, um, feeding work?" I asked Quinn. "Is there a way to find her through . . ." I made a helpless gesture, not wanting to say "*who she eats.*"

He shook his head. "Vampires don't need blood every night, and we don't often feed from the same person twice," he informed me. "That's exactly why you find vampires in so many college towns, because of the transient population."

"You just go to the middle of campus and grab somebody?" I asked, incredulous.

Quinn shot me a glare. "We're predators," he stated. "A lion doesn't wade into the middle of a pack of wildebeests and start slashing with its claws. You pick off the edge of the herd, isolate, and feed. Once we learn control, we can exist on very little. The . . . source . . . doesn't even remember it happening."

I decided I didn't need to know more about that right now, and looked out the window. To my surprise, Quinn was driving us into a familiar student neighborhood in South Boulder. I'd spent a little time in that area of SoBo, which was where Sam and John's first apartment had been. When he said "close to campus," he really meant it.

"We're not actually expecting her to *be* there, are we?" I asked.

Quinn shook his head. "Darcy's not that stupid. But I'm hoping we'll find something to point us in the right direction."

"And if we don't?"

"Then we'll talk to the vampire they're pledged to," he said, as if that was a perfectly logical thing to say.

"Pledged?"

"Vampires still have a more or less feudal system of government," he explained. Because it took years for new vamps to learn how to manage finances, create new identities, and control their bloodlust, they always served older vampires for a period of time before striking out on their own. "Most of the time, a new vamp serves his progenitor, the vampire who created him," Quinn said flatly.

"Most of the time?" I asked carefully. I wanted to know more about that "I was sold" comment.

Quinn ignored the question. "When they're done with their service, they pledge a troth," he continued. "Aside from the physiological changes, it's the only bit of magic we really have. A troth is like a formal binding of loyalty. We can't break it." He shook his head a little. "Everyone belongs to someone."

"Like ranks," I said. "A hierarchy of power."

Quinn thought that over for a long moment, then nodded. "Sort of. Younger vampires have to obey not just their own dominus, but any dominus who obeys *him*. So it's more like . . . a lineage of obedience."

"So where did Victor and Darcy fall within the pecking order?"

"They both finished their service a couple of years ago, and they pledged troth to a vampire named Kirby," Quinn explained. "And Kirby belongs to Itachi. Wait, we're here."

He pulled to a stop in front of a perfectly ordinary wood-frame building that had once been a single-family residence. Someone had converted it into two apartments with separate mailboxes, I saw. There was a third mailbox for a basement apartment, along with a dark staircase leading down on the side of the house.

When we got out of the car, Quinn immediately walked around to the Toyota's back bumper, looked around a little, and popped the trunk.

Quinn's trunk was *packed*. The top layer was camp blankets and collapsible chairs, the kind of thing you'd have at a picnic or an outdoor concert. He moved these aside and revealed piles of more sinister supplies, including several power tools and a lidless shoebox full of stakes. I noted with surreal detachment that the shoebox full of stakes had the Luther Shoes logo printed on its side. Quinn pulled out two wooden stakes and handed me one. It was a simple piece of hardwood, about the length of my forearm, machine-sharpened to a rounded point.

"The wooden stake thing is real, huh?" I asked, turning it over in my hand. Frankly, I would rather have had a gun.

"Sort of," Quinn replied. "To kill a vampire, you have to cut off the head or completely destroy the heart. Theoretically you could do that with bullets, if you can get the vampire to hold still, but these"—he held up his wooden stake—"are traditional, which maybe gives them a little bit of magic. More importantly," he added, grinning, "Itachi had them hexed by a witch in Denver. If you can get one in a vampire's heart, the stake will do the rest. We call 'em shredders."

"I thought magic never works against itself," I objected.

"You're thinking too broadly. I can't use my magic against someone else's magic, so I can't turn you or a werewolf into a vampire. But a witch can hex a stake to shred what it touches, and if that's a physical heart . . ." He shrugged. "It doesn't matter if it's a vampire's."

At the bottom of the stairs was a door that looked like solid steel. A whole line of keyholes ran up the side, each one representing a dead bolt.

Quinn leaned his weight back so he could kick in the door. Could vampires break their feet? "Quinn, wait—" I began. To my surprise, though, he struck the side of the door with the hinges. The door burst loose from its frame, although the side with all the locks held. Quinn shook his head. "Typical vampires," he said dismissively. "They invest in a dozen hard-core deadbolts, but it doesn't occur to them to reinforce the hinges. Come on." He pushed on the open side of the door, which caved inward with a screech of metallic protest. Quinn turned and slipped sideways through the twelve-inch crack. I followed. The interior of the room beyond was dark, and I heard the brush of a hand on the wall as Quinn flipped the light switch.

The basement apartment opened straight onto a relatively large living room, with a kitchenette to the right and a dark hallway in the back left corner. It looked like every college apartment I'd ever seen—which, admittedly, wasn't very many. The carpet was worn, the furniture looked pre-owned several times over, and no attempt had been made to tidy up the place or even decorate it—unless you counted the curling poster of Van Gogh's *Vase with Twelve Sunflowers*, and I would have bet money that it had come with the apartment. The whole place smelled like stale body odor and ancient Chinese takeout, which had probably come with the apartment, too.

"Wait here," Quinn told me, and there was a blur of movement toward the back hallway, way too fast for me to follow in the dim light, although I wasn't sure I could have followed it in the middle of a sunny field, either. Before I could even register his disappearance, he was back in the same spot. It was annoying.

"Empty," Quinn said. "As expected." He wandered forward.

"What do we do now?" I asked.

"Search." Quinn looked around, assessing our surroundings. "There are two bedrooms at the end of the hall. You go left; I'll go right. Then we'll work our way back out toward the door. Look for anything that might tell us where she could be: names of friends, receipts from restaurants or hotels, that kind of thing."

I nodded. I'd searched houses before. "Do we have gloves?" I asked. Without comment, Quinn reached into the pocket of his leather jacket, pulled out a pair of surgical gloves, and handed them to me. "Thanks."

The bedroom on the left was small, with a double bed and a nightstand crammed into a corner, and clothes covering the remaining floor space. There was no other furniture, and the tiny doorless closet was the size of a refrigerator. Judging by the posters of naked women and all the men's clothes strewn on the floor, Victor and Darcy had kept separate bedrooms, and this one had been his. The musty, unwashed smell was stronger in here.

Still feeling silly, I pushed my stake through my two front belt loops so I could put on the surgical gloves. Then I used a foot to push around the clothes on the floor, picking up all the pants to search the pockets. After five minutes I had found a few empty packs of cigarettes, some change and crumpled dollar bills, and a handful of receipts for gas stations and seedy bars. I kept the receipts and left the rest.

Moving to the bedside table, I opened the drawers, and was immediately grateful for the surgical gloves. It was full of dog-eared porn magazines and a couple of cheap-looking . . . uh . . . sex enhancement tools. Apparently Victor had suffered from some issues with size or stamina. Or both. Making a face, I clumsily began picking up the magazines, shaking each one out. A handful of subscription cards fluttered to the floor, but nothing useful. I went through the whole pile anyway, and at the very bottom I found my first potential clue: an old snapshot of four people leaning against a red sports car. I peered at the photo. Victor and Darcy were in there, but I didn't recognize the other two men. The group's clothes could have come from any number of eras, but Darcy's haircut was a perfect copy of "the Rachel," the style Jennifer Aniston had made popular in the nineties.

Aside from the glowing good health I'd come to associate with sated vampires, all four of them looked . . . relaxed. Happy. There was a contentedness in their body language that spoke of a long familiarity with each other.

"Find anything?" came Quinn's voice.

I jumped and whirled on him. "Goddammit, Quinn! Stop sneaking up on me!"

He leaned in the doorway, unapologetic. "I'm a vampire, Lex. It's what we do."

I glared at him, but held up the photo. "I found this and a bunch of receipts."

Quinn crossed the room in a flash, taking the photo from me. "This one is Kirby," he said, pointing at the stranger on Victor's left, a muscular, young-looking man with an aquiline nose and thinning black hair. Every vampire I had seen, in person or otherwise, was good-looking, but this one was on the ugly end of attractive. "The other guy I don't know."

"Did *you* find anything?" I asked.

Quinn made a face. "Well, I now know more about Darcy's sex life than I wanted to."

"Right there with you," I said wryly, nodding toward the pile of porn magazines.

"Other than that knowledge, I didn't find much," Quinn went on. "I found a lot of receipts for the coffee shops on campus, which probably means those are Darcy's preferred hunting ground. But I doubt she'd go to one of them if she's on the run."

"You checked the other rooms too?" I asked, eyebrows raised. He nodded. "What about the neighbors?" I asked. "There are what, two floors on top of this one? Do you think any of them were friendly with Victor and Darcy?"

Quinn hesitated for a second, then said, "I doubt it. We don't socialize much with the foundings—that would be the semi-polite term for humans who have no knowledge of the Old World—but I suppose it's worth a shot."

"Let's go."

I followed Quinn back through the musty apartment. Starting at the top of the door, he began unlocking the dead bolts on the inside so we could pull the door all the way open instead of squeezing through past the hinges.

But as the last bolt slid free, there was a tremendous crack and the door *rocketed* inward, sending Quinn back into the living room wall, which his head struck hard enough to leave a dent two inches deep. Before I could even process what had happened, I heard Darcy's voice. "Well, if it isn't the skank with the weird blood, come a-calling," she drawled. "Hello, skank."

Chapter 14

I glanced at Quinn. He was struggling to get to his hands and knees, knocked for a loop. Darcy must have come back while we were in the bedroom, and then waited until Quinn undid the bolts to kick in the door. I turned my attention back to her.

Darcy looked terrible. Her once-perfect hair hung in greasy clumps around her face, and her mad, darting eyes reminded me of one of the animals my cousin Jake had brought me, a cat so feral it eventually had to be put down. She was wearing the same black leather jacket I'd seen at the Flatiron Depot and jeans that had once been very expensive. Now the jacket and jeans were splattered with dark stains, and even in the low light I could tell it was blood, probably from when I'd fought with her at John's house. Had she come back for a change of clothes before she blew town? With an effort, I swallowed my fear and straightened my shoulders, slowly tugging the wooden stake—Quinn's shredder—from my belt loops. "Hey, Darcy. How's the nose?"

Her gleeful expression hardened, and she started moving toward Quinn. "I'll kill you in a second," she tossed at me, like I was next in line at the DMV. She reached Quinn, who was struggling to his feet with the stake clutched in one hand. He looked a little wobbly, and I started toward the two of them without making a conscious decision to do it.

But before I could take more than two steps, Darcy bent down and put one hand under his chin, yanking it up before he could bat her away. Quinn's head snapped back with a crunch that made my stomach roll, and he plummeted to the floor when Darcy released her hold on him.

I stared at Quinn's limp body, stunned. "You killed him," I said stupidly.

Darcy snorted. "Not yet." She picked up the stake that had rolled out of Quinn's hand when he went down and flipped it around in her hand like an Old West gunslinger with a pistol. She straddled Quinn's limp form, and I realized that she was about to stake him.

I couldn't let that happen. I flew forward and tackled her, knocking Darcy off the unconscious vampire.

I drove into her as hard as I could with my shoulder, but Darcy rolled with the impact, gracefully letting my momentum propel her on top of me. When we stopped moving, she laughed at me and splayed herself across my upper body, casually leaning her forearm against my throat to cut off my air supply.

"Stupid bitch," she chortled. My left hand was pinned, so I scrabbled at her with my right, but it was like pushing against a parked semi. I reached for the stake, which had landed a few inches away from my hand, but Darcy just flicked the stake away from my hand, sending it skittering across the floor, looking amused by my efforts. After a moment of watching me struggle, she eased up on my throat by deliberately palming my face, smearing blood-sticky fingers on me as she pushed herself up. When she was sitting on my chest, she reached out and sent a lazy slap across my face.

Stars exploded on the backs of my eyelids, and my stomach's contents threatened to make themselves known. "You are so fucked," she sneered, which more or less echoed my thoughts. "You don't have the baby to protect you anymore. Which means"—she leaned forward, her cool empty breath on my face—"that in a few minutes she won't have you to protect *her*."

Think, Lex. Charlie's life depends on it. Okay, Darcy had inhuman strength and speed, and I couldn't compete with that. But when I'd put out Victor's eyes it had blinded him, at least temporarily. If I could blind her, too . . .

"Here's what we're gonna do," Darcy continued. "Killing you would be fun, but I think it'd be even *more* fun to press you into killing *yourself.* Victor would have liked that." She leaned back and pursed her lips, looking around the apartment. "Let's see. What's a really horrible way to die? Screwdriver through the eye? Setting yourself on fire? Maybe a nice solid self-disembowelment; I like that. Kind of a Shakespearean thing."

I wasn't sure about poking her eyes out with just my fingers, but I had car keys in my pocket. My left hand was pinned next to my thigh, so I started working the key ring out of the pocket. To keep her from noticing, I said, "You can't press me, asshole. Victor couldn't do it, and you're . . . what? *Maybe* half as strong?" I made my voice skeptical.

Darcy's eyes returned to me, narrowing with hate. "Stop wiggling. And don't think you can taunt me into killing you quick. You don't deserve it."

"Oh, I know you can *kill* me," I said flatly. "I'm just a human. But there's no way you have the juice to press me."

Gritting her teeth, Darcy leaned forward and stared into my eyes. Maybe because I was expecting it, I felt that slight pressure again, though it wasn't nearly as strong as when Quinn had done it to me. This didn't even make my head hurt. "Stop wiggling," Darcy said again through clenched teeth.

I played along, relaxing my body as though she'd succeeded. Then something happened that I couldn't explain. I wasn't trying to do it, mostly because I hadn't imagined it was possible, but one moment I was concentrating on Darcy's gaze, trying to gauge if I had any real impulse to do what she asked (I didn't), and the next moment something shifted aside, just for a second, and what had been a one-way street suddenly opened up for two-way traffic. "Get off me," I hissed, and Darcy immediately rose from my chest, standing up and stepping aside.

Then she blinked, and a confused, annoyed expression crossed her face. I scrambled to my feet, but whatever I'd done—a spell, maybe? Could you do those without knowing it?—was over.

"Argh!" Darcy screeched in frustration, shoving me backward. I toppled over a chair, landing hard on my back. "Maybe fun is overrated. You die first." She bared her teeth at me, and I realized she was tensing to leap.

"By the way, Darcy," I said hurriedly, and she paused instinctively. I don't care how many years you've spent killing people—human beings have an innate reflex to let each other have a last word before death. Killing someone in the middle of the sentence leaves a disturbing lack of closure. I know this from experience. "You know he's setting you up to be the patsy, right?"

It was a shot in the dark, but Darcy's resolve flickered, the coiled tension in her body momentarily loosening. "What the hell are you talking about?" she demanded. "You don't know anything about him."

Him. I snorted derisively, pushing the bluff. "Maven does."

She stepped closer, glaring. "What? What does Maven know?"

We were maybe two feet apart at this point, with Quinn's motionless body behind her. I had to try to do whatever I'd done before that got her off me. I stared into her eyes again, but nothing happened. Before, Darcy had been the one to open the connection between us; I had no idea how to do it myself.

A memory flashed through my mind. Sam and I were about six, playing with a long cardboard tube left over from a roll of Christmas wrapping paper. We stood at either end of the tube, each with an eye raised to it like it was a spyglass, giggling as we "spied" each other. I remembered the way Sam's eye had looked through that tube; like there was nothing else in the world, just Sam centered in a small circle of light at the end of a long tunnel of darkness.

I pictured two cardboard tubes, put them against my eyes, and looked straight into Darcy's. Something stirred along the sides of my vision.

Then nothing happened.

"You don't know anything," Darcy said smugly, her fists uncurling. She bared her teeth again, tensing to strike.

No, Lex, Sam's voice said in my head, *you couldn't put the tube right up against your eye, or it'd be too dark. You had to leave a little space to let the light in.*

I visualized the tubes again, now with a little bit of space between us. The space served as a buffer, letting me stay who I was, out of Darcy's head. The tingling started along the sides of my vision again and I pushed harder, concentrating on the connection.

Slowly, millimeter by millimeter, Darcy's face slackened, her lips parting as her jaw dropped open the tiniest bit. Excitement swirled through me so quickly that I almost lost the connection. I had her. *Thanks, Sam.*

Wait, now what? What the hell was I doing?

"Touch your nose," I said softly. It was the first thing that popped into my head. Darcy's right index finger came up and rested on the tip of the nose I'd broken a couple of days ago.

"Good," I said. Whatever I was doing made her follow directions, but could I use it like a lie detector? "Tell me what you were planning to do with Charlotte Wheaton," I commanded, feeling sweat break out on my forehead. The connection was difficult to maintain, like holding yourself halfway through a pull-up.

"Our senior was bringing her to the merchant," Darcy answered tonelessly. "Then the merchant was supposed to get her to her new . . . parents."

The way she said "parents," as though it was the closest term she knew to describe something awful, made my blood go cold. "Your senior?" I repeated in confusion. "Like your boss?"

That must not have been the right wording, because Darcy blinked several times, and I felt my control slipping. Gasping with the effort, I blurted, "Tell me who told you to take Charlotte Wheaton!"

I pushed as hard as I could on the connection, and Darcy began, "Our orders . . ."

And then the tip of a wooden stake popped out of her chest. The link between us broke, and I felt myself tumbling through the cardboard tubes into darkness.

Chapter 15

I woke up in the car, the lights of Boulder flashing intermittently over my face.

I sat up fast, looking around. I was in the passenger seat of Quinn's Toyota. My neck was stiff from where it had been leaning awkwardly against the door, and I wasn't wearing a seat belt. Quinn was driving, his face grim.

"What happened?" I asked.

"You fainted."

"I did not," I said crossly. "Fainting is for preteen girls and those really weird goats. I do *not* faint."

For the first time Quinn looked over at me, his eyes rolling. "Okay, then. You abruptly lost consciousness, without any outside force affecting you in any way."

"That's better." I arched my back, trying to stretch the kinks in my neck. "What happened? Where's Darcy?"

Quinn jerked his head to indicate something over his right shoulder. "She's in the back."

I twisted in my seat, seeing a too-small bundle underneath a shabby gray blanket. I leaned over and lifted a corner of the cloth.

"I wouldn't do that," Quinn began, but it was too late. I saw the corpse, wrapped in two layers of clear plastic.

"Oh, wow," I said softly. We were still in the city, and there was just enough light from the streetlamps for me to study Darcy's body. It still had the blonde hair and the bloodied black jacket, which was somehow a whole lot creepier than if she'd been dressed in trailing bandages like a movie mummy. Because that's what the rest of Darcy's body looked like. It was desiccated to the point that I couldn't even tell if there was any skin left on it, or if I was looking at a skeleton.

I'd seen dead bodies when I was with the army—too many of them. But those had all been reasonably fresh corpses, still in the process of decay and rot. Darcy's corpse didn't look like she'd died an hour ago, that was for sure. I looked back at Quinn, raising an eyebrow. "Jesus, how long was I out?"

Quinn let out a surprised laugh. "Our bodies do that when we die. Magic is connected to life; that's what it prefers. When a vampire dies, the magic sort of abandons them, and the body returns to whatever condition it would have been in if the person had never become a vampire."

I scrunched my face, thinking again of the horror movies Sam had made me watch when we were teenagers. "I thought vampires turned into dust."

He shrugged. "Only the really, really old ones do that. Darcy was turned maybe thirty years ago, so she's not that far along yet. Still a skeleton," he added, almost cheerfully.

"Oh."

The head with its bare skull seemed to be staring at me every time we passed a streetlight, so I flipped the blanket back over it and turned around in my seat again, buckling my seat belt. "Aren't you worried about getting pulled over or something?"

He shook his head. "I checked all the lights already, and I'm driving at exactly the speed limit. Anyway, if I got pulled over, I'd just press the cop to forget me."

I considered that for a moment. "So what do we do now?"

"Now we need to ditch the body," he replied, his tone careful. I saw him glance at me out of the corner of his eye and understood that my response in this moment was important. I could ask him to drop me off before he got rid of Darcy's body, and he might even agree. I had to admit, the idea was tempting: It was late, my body still ached, and the dogs would start tearing up the cabin pretty soon if I didn't let them out.

But I was the one who'd begged to work for vampires, and the one who'd insisted on helping Quinn tonight. I had asked for this. And if I tried to pick and choose which parts of Quinn's job to do with him, it wouldn't speak well of my willingness to be a team player.

Besides, it wasn't like we were burying an innocent, or even a human. I'm not a fan of killing by any means, but Darcy had come after Charlie, which was one offense I could never forgive. And she would have killed Quinn and me both if things had gone a little differently. I wasn't going to shed any tears for her.

"Okay," I said finally.

We drove in silence for a while after that. I knew this was my chance to ask some questions about the supernatural crap I had suddenly become a part of, but I just didn't have the stomach for any more information right then. Instead, I fought to think about something that didn't involve bodies or bloodshed. Each time I tried, though, my thoughts returned to Charlie. It was aggravating.

Quinn drove us through the outskirts of the city and into the mountains, the darkness deepening until there was nothing to see that wasn't in the car's headlights. The night was overcast and quiet, and after a while a chill crept into the car. I reached over and turned on the heater.

"Sorry," Quinn said. "I don't really get cold. I mean, I do, but it takes a lot." His voice had taken on a shade of awkwardness.

"Yeah?" I said, stretching my legs out in front of me to get my toes closer to the heater. "That must be nice."

"Listen, Lex," he said, clearly uncomfortable. "I wanted to thank you."

I turned my head to look at him, but his eyes were fixed on the road. "For what?"

"For sticking around when I was unconscious. Not letting Darcy . . . you know."

He still didn't look at me, and I realized that Quinn was embarrassed. He was supposed to be the vampires' enforcer, and he'd let himself get benched by a psycho wielding only a front door. In front of me, the newbie human. "It never occurred to me to leave," I said honestly, turning my head to look out the window so he could have a little privacy. Vampires could get embarrassed. What a weird concept.

After a couple more miles' worth of silence, Quinn asked, "Did Darcy say anything while I was out?"

I considered that. "She said they were taking Charlie to some kind of middleman or dealer, who would hang onto her until someone else was ready to act. A 'senior.' I assumed that meant whoever she was working for." I didn't mention the weird link I'd created between us. Until I knew exactly what I'd done, and whether I could do it again, it didn't seem like a good thing to share.

"She used that word, 'senior'?" Quinn's voice had taken on interest.

"Yeah, why? What does it mean?"

He shrugged. "Pretty much what you said—someone she considers a boss, a superior. It might even just be a vampire who's a lot older than her—'senior' is a term of respect."

"Could she have meant the vampire she's pledged to . . . Kirby, right?"

I couldn't see Quinn's face very well at the moment, but I could practically hear the wheels turning in his head as he considered this. "Not necessarily, but it's possible," he said finally.

"Or maybe it's the vampire *Kirby's* pledged to," I pointed out. "Itachi."

To his credit, Quinn didn't immediately leap to his master's defense. He took a moment to consider it. "I honestly don't think Itachi is responsible," he said at last, and I realized that for the first time since I'd met him, he sounded completely human. For just a moment I caught a glimpse of what Quinn must have been like as a cop in Chicago . . . and as a regular man. He had a calmness, a centeredness, as if he considered everything thoroughly before acting. Then the glimpse was gone, and the unreadable Quinn had returned. "By Old World rules, he already owns your niece," he said, still talking about Itachi. "There's no reason for him to try and steal the kid away from himself."

I couldn't really argue with that. "Okay, but we do know that Maven was right; Victor and Darcy were working for someone," I said aloud. "Only Darcy was our best lead to finding out who that was, and we just killed her." I felt my fingers clench into fists.

"Don't worry," Quinn reassured me. "Tomorrow night we'll go talk to Kirby."

I glanced at the clock. "It's only midnight. Why wait?"

The side of Quinn's mouth turned up. "Have you heard the expression 'Don't shit where you eat?'"

Apparently, disposing of bodies happened often enough for Quinn to have a regular body dump site. Unfortunately, it was two hours outside of Boulder.

We drove into Rocky Mountain National Park for nearly ninety minutes. When we finally pulled off the highway, Quinn followed a few dimly lit streets before turning onto a completely dark, unmarked dirt road that led deeper into the park. Wherever we were going, it was a very specific destination. "How did you guys pick this place?" I asked, shaking my head a little. When it came to the middle of nowhere, there were an awful lot of places to choose from in Colorado.

"It has a certain . . . cachet," Quinn said dryly. The dirt road dead-ended, and he pulled the Toyota to a stop. He got out and popped the trunk, pulling a heavy-duty flashlight out of the tightly packed space. He handed it to me. "I can see pretty well in the dark," he explained, "so you can hold the light."

He gathered Darcy's body out of the backseat, still wrapped in both the plastic and the blanket, and then I followed him along a path across the scrubby mountain desert. We left that path within minutes, but even in the rough terrain Quinn strode along gracefully, at a pace that most speed walkers would admire. I had to struggle to keep up with him, partly because my body was still stiff, but mostly because I had to pick my way along with the flashlight, stepping around scrubby plants, fist-sized rocks, and prairie dog holes. I was used to hiking, even right here in the park, but Quinn's speed was making me feel like a clumsy tourist—and he had to carry the awkward bundle of skeleton with him.

We kept hiking for almost forty-five minutes, until we reached a broad expanse of land next to the mountain. The place didn't look like it'd seen a human in decades, if ever. Suddenly I had to work hard not to get spooked. This was mountain country, but the emptiness and isolation reminded me too much of Iraq for comfort. I moved my light up toward the backs of Quinn's legs, to remind myself that I wasn't alone.

Finally, we saw a sign of human civilization—an enormous, decrepit sign that read *KEEP OUT. NO TRESPASERS.* The writing was in fading red paint on weather-beaten wood, and as my light played over it, I realized the sign was nailed to some kind of door that seemed to lead right into the mountain. It was secured with a huge, rusted padlock that looked older than I was.

"Speak, friend, and enter," I murmured under my breath.

"Oh, *that* movie you've seen?" Quinn tossed over his shoulder.

"I read the books," I told him. "When I was a kid."

Other than the still-reddish paint, time and Colorado dirt had turned everything in sight more or less the same rusty brown color, and it took me a moment to realize that the heavy door was the entrance to one of Colorado's many abandoned mines. This must have predated the park. Quinn went right up to the entrance, ignoring the padlock. I trained my light on the door while he set the bundled body on the ground and reached for the sign. I'm not sure what I was expecting—maybe another display of vampire strength—but Quinn just dug his fingers into the sides of the giant sign and tugged on it. The heavy sign immediately came away in his hands, leaving a neat hole big enough to step through.

I laughed. "Clever."

Quinn shrugged. "Keeps out the riffraff. There's a mine shaft in there that goes down a hundred feet. That's where we're dumping her." He paused and wheeled around, as if something had just occurred to him. "You claustrophobic?" he demanded.

"Uh . . ." I wouldn't say I was *afraid* of enclosed spaces, exactly, but like many soldiers who'd served time inside a giant tin can with a metaphorical target painted on it, I didn't exactly enjoy them. The cramped office in Magic Beans was about as small as I could easily handle. I didn't want to tell Quinn that, though.

Quinn stepped closer to me, giving me an appraising look. "I can take it in by myself," he said levelly.

I shook my head. "I'm fine," I said through gritted teeth.

His gaze didn't leave my face. "You're not fine," Quinn decided. "Hang on a second."

In a blur of movement, he and the bundle disappeared through the hole before I could say another word. "Dammit, Quinn!" I stepped up to the hole and leaned in, pointing my flashlight in either direction. Just a long, low hallway on either side. "Shit," I said, with feeling. No way was I going in there without knowing which way he'd gone.

I drew back and noticed that the clouds had parted, revealing enough starlight for me to see an outcropping of rock a few feet away from the mine entrance. I went and sat down. There was nothing to do now but wait, and—

Before I could even finish the thought, Quinn was back, popping out through the hole as nonchalantly as if we'd been playing hide-and-seek. *Damn*, I thought. How fast *were* these people?

"See? Just took a second," Quinn dismissed. "Let's go."

On the hike back to the car, I said angrily, "I would have gone in with you, you know. I could have handled it."

Quinn didn't answer until we were twenty feet or so down the path. Then he mumbled, "I was in the Gulf War. The first one."

"You fought in Desert Storm?" I said, surprised.

He shrugged. "I was eighteen, kind of naive and stupid. Served two years in the infantry so I could go kick some ass." The wry smile that followed was the most human expression I'd seen on him yet. "Seems like a hundred years ago, now. I remember riding around in the Humvees, though."

"Yeah." My body was warm from the hike, but I shivered anyway.

"You do a lot of patrols?" Quinn asked.

"Yeah."

Most people stopped asking questions at that point, but Quinn pushed on. "Any explosions?"

"Four," I said shortly. The scars on my back twinged as I remembered. "The last sent me home."

I saw him nod. "PTSD?"

"No." It had been a near thing, but I'd technically escaped the diagnosis that plagued so many American soldiers returning home from war. I credited Sam for that. Sam and some damned convenient memory loss about my last two days in Iraq.

"I had it," Quinn said abruptly. "PTSD, night terrors, claustrophobia, the whole thing. Embarrassing, back then."

"You got treatment?" I asked, curious despite myself.

Quinn shrugged. "Nah. Just time. I can still remember those night terrors, though."

We walked on in a slightly more companionable silence, all the way back to the Toyota. I realized, for the first time, that with vampire speed Quinn could have probably made the whole hike in a quarter of the time it had taken both of us.

The drive back to Boulder was mostly uneventful. I began to doze after forty-five minutes, then started awake when I heard Quinn's voice float over from the driver's side. "You're really serious about working for him, aren't you?"

"I'm really serious about Charlie," I said quietly. "And I don't know of any other way to keep her safe other than to back the horse I think will win."

Quinn was quiet as he digested this. I got the impression that he had as many questions for me as I did for him, but neither of us were showing any more cards tonight.

Chapter 16

At seven-thirty the next morning, two hours after I'd finally collapsed in my bed, my cell phone began to shriek.

Dopey and Pongo were in bed with me, but neither of them stirred at the angry little machine vibrating on my nightstand. I was tempted to follow their example, but I reluctantly reached over and grabbed the stupid phone, answering without bothering to look at the caller display.

"'Hate you," I mumbled, by way of greeting.

"Hey, Lex!" said a familiar cheerful voice. "It's Lily." When I didn't answer right away, she added, "Lily Pellar?"

"Yes." I managed to pull myself up until I was more or less sitting. Dopey woke up and looked at me with vacant good cheer, part of her tongue sticking out between her teeth. "What's going on?"

"My mother spoke to Itachi last night. I understand the vampires want you to undergo training after all."

"Uh, yeah."

"Cool. Simon has classes today, so I'll be leading your training session."

I yawned. The conversation wasn't quite interesting enough to keep my eyes open. "Uh-huh."

"We can do it at my mother's farm. It's kind of Witch Central in Boulder, so you should know where it is, anyway. I'll text you the address. Just wear something comfortable. Come by in, say, an hour."

That got my attention. "Wait, *what?*"

She'd already hung up.

I set an alarm for eight-fifteen and went back to sleep. It wouldn't leave me enough time to shower, but at eight-thirty in the morning Lily Pellar could deal with however I smelled.

Unfortunately for me, the dogs flipped out at eight, going on a full-out barking spree. Dopey and Pongo launched themselves off the bed, and I peeled my eyes open for just long enough to throw a pillow at the bedroom door, shutting it behind them. If they wanted to bark at rabbits through the living room window, they could damn well stay out there.

A moment later, however, the doorbell rang. "Nooooooo," I groaned. Had Lily decided to come pick me up? What kind of monster *did* this sort of thing to a person?

But when I got to the door and waded through the herd of barking dogs and curious cats, it wasn't Lily on the doorstep. The cops. I'd completely forgotten that I'd agreed to give my statement this morning. Stepping away from the little window in the door, I looked down at myself. I had managed to strip out of my dusty clothes the night before, exchanging them for an oversized army T-shirt and underpants. My auburn hair was alternately plastered to my face and poking up in different directions, and my fingernails were encrusted with dirt. Great.

I opened the door a crack, leaning around the frame to greet my cousin Elise and . . . oh, shit, Detective Keller. "Sorry, guys, I was just getting dressed," I said apologetically, gesturing helplessly to indicate that I was sans pants. Keller craned his head a little, trying to see what I had going on beneath the T-shirt. Enjoy the gray cotton panties, asshole. "I'll be right with you. Elise, give me a second to get to the bedroom, then come on in. You know where the coffee is."

My cousin opened her mouth to respond, but I had already shut the door and was hightailing it for the bedroom. I turned off the alarm clock and started yanking open dresser drawers, snatching the first pair of jeans and T-shirt I saw. "Son of a bitch," I swore to myself. Of *course* it was Keller.

Boulder isn't big enough to have a designated homicide-robbery division. Instead, there are about twenty detectives who investigate anything from sexual assault to bank robbery to kidnapped pets. With so few spots, it's difficult for regular patrol cops to get promoted—Elise had been trying for years—and Detective Neal Keller was the kind of guy who loved to lord his power over the cops he outranked. I'd lived in Boulder my whole life, and I knew that most of the city's police were good people doing tough jobs. Keller, though, was a first-class dick.

Unfortunately, thanks to a combination of bad luck and worse timing, he was also the cop who had arrested me *both* times I'd gotten in trouble. Had they sent Keller today to try to rattle me? No, that was too paranoid for Boulder PD. He had probably just been the only detective available at the moment.

Still.

As soon as I was dressed, I texted Lily to warn her that I'd be late. Then I ran a brush through my hair, scrubbed my fingernails in the master bathroom, and went to face the cops.

When I padded into the kitchen, tying my hair in a tight ponytail as I walked, Keller was sitting at the island counter looking around the open dining/living room area while Elise made coffee across from him. She had shut the dogs into the mudroom, and I could hear their muffled, indignant barks at the way their friend Elise had treated them. I reminded myself to walk slow and look weak and stiff. After less than four hours of sleep and a hell of a week, it wasn't hard.

I blew out a breath and said, "Sorry about that, Detective, Elise. Must have overslept a little. I'm on some pretty strong painkillers."

I nodded toward my pharmacy bottle of Vicodin, which I'd conveniently left on the kitchen counter by my water glass.

Neither cop looked at the amber cylinder, which meant they'd already spotted it. "No worries," Elise said, then shut up when she caught Keller glaring at her. She straightened, smoothing down the front of her uniform. Elise had the Luther brown eyes and honey-blonde hair, which was set off nicely against her dark patrol uniform. She was attractive rather than pretty, her unremarkable features enhanced by that healthy, relaxed-by-outdoor-sports look that was shared by a lot of people in Boulder. Hell, I probably had that same look when I wasn't up to my eyebrows in supernatural bullshit and stab wounds.

"Your cousin is only here as a courtesy to your family," Keller growled at me. He was in his late forties, balding, with a perpetually tight expression and suspicious eyes. He had on a forgettable suit that reminded me a lot of the one Quinn had worn to my hospital room. Had that really only been a few days ago? "I'll be asking the questions, and you'll direct your responses to me."

His tone was unnecessarily nasty, and I was suddenly certain that my father had made a call to the department and demanded that Elise be allowed to join the interview. My father had a way of inserting himself into my life, and it wouldn't be the first time he'd strong-armed the department into pulling Keller away from me.

No wonder the detective was pissed. I suppressed a sigh. Thanks, Dad. "Of course, Detective Keller. Elise, let me get that coffee."

She shooed me away. "You sit and rest. I know where the cups are."

I shot my cousin a grateful look and gingerly took a seat on one of the four stools. Still eyeing me, Keller sat down two stools away from me. "What can I tell you, Detective?"

Keller set a small digital recorder on the counter between us. "Start by running through the whole night, in your words," he ordered.

So I walked them through it, starting with setting up the soda display. I told them everything, minus Victor and Darcy's names and the weird things I'd seen them do—healing, recovering from blows, moving fast. Hopefully the security tape hadn't caught that, but even if it had, I'm sure Quinn would have handled it. After all, he'd seen the footage.

Keller made me stop and go back several times, tossing in oddly specific questions like which brands of soda I'd used for the display and the *exact* words I'd yelled to Bettina. I knew he had to test my story, but by the fourth time I'd gone back over the same part, I was ready to reach over and punch him.

I forced myself to calm down. The best way to get rid of Keller was to answer all of his questions politely and professionally, and not give him the satisfaction of getting to me. I wasn't some lost, angry drunk anymore.

Well, I *definitely* wasn't drunk, anyway.

When he was finally satisfied, Keller asked, "And you have *no* idea who would want to harm your brother-in-law or his family?" He sounded skeptical.

"No, of course not," I lied. "I figured it was some kind of kidnapping thing, some couple that wanted a baby."

"Kidnapping, yeah. You know, we saw the security tape."

I glanced at Elise, but she was just sipping her coffee, her eyes giving away nothing. "Okay . . ." I said to Keller.

"Something went wrong with the feed—a couple of times there were some blurs or static, stuff the tech guy couldn't really explain," he went on. "Had to be done by someone who knew the system."

Or maybe vampires somehow had an effect on technology? Interesting thought. Keller paused in case I wanted to jump in with more information, but I just waited him out. "What we did see, though, it looked like you clocked that guy pretty good with the jar of baby food."

"Yeah, I guess," I said warily. Where was he going with this?

"I picked up one of those jars when I was at the store," Keller went on. "Thick glass. It should have left a goddamned dent in his head, pardon my French."

There was a hint of accusation in his voice. I knew better than to rise to it, but I was tired and distracted, and I heard myself saying weakly, "Maybe I didn't hit him as hard as I thought."

If I hadn't been watching, I might have missed the flicker of triumph that passed across Keller's face and was gone. "You trained in combat, right? In the service?"

"Yes."

"So maybe you pulled your shot a little bit," he suggested, soft and dangerous.

I stared at him. It took a long moment for his meaning to sink in. "You can't possibly think I was in on this," I burst out. "I got *stabbed*!"

"You look like you're moving around okay," Keller observed.

"Wha— why on *earth* would I kidnap my own niece!" I said, working hard to keep from raising my voice. "I adore that kid!"

"Maybe a little too much," Keller suggested, his voice floating carelessly over the rim of his coffee cup. "Maybe you figured she'd be better off with you."

I was about to explode, but luckily, at that exact moment I glanced at Elise. Anyone who didn't know her as well as I did wouldn't have been able to interpret her expression, but I understood: *He's just poking at you. Calm down.* I took a deep breath, focused on my cousin's face, and reminded myself that Elise hated working with Keller. She'd sucked it up to come support me. I needed to trust her.

I blew out the breath. "Do you have any other questions for me, Detective?" I asked as pleasantly as I could.

Keller's eyes narrowed. "Not for today. We're not dropping this, though."

"Glad to hear it," I said evenly. "Have you identified the couple who kidnapped Charlie?"

Now his face scrunched into a full-out scowl. "Not yet, but it's only a matter—"

"Then it sounds like you have a lot to do. Please don't let me keep you," I said, standing up stiffly. "If you have further questions, just call my attorney. I'm sure you still have his number." I held out my arm, gesturing for Keller to walk in front of me.

He was obviously unhappy, but there wasn't much he could do. When his back was turned, Elise shot me a grin and a thumbs-up. *Call you later,* she mouthed. I nodded, still feigning bravado. If Keller actually did start bothering my lawyer, though, I was going to have to start turning tricks to pay for his services.

When they were gone, I called Lily Pellar. "How'd it go with the cops?" she said immediately.

"Fine, I think." I paused. "But I don't suppose I have time for a nap before witch class?"

She laughed. "Sorry, Lex, but I have plans this afternoon."

I sighed. "Okay. I'll see you in a few."

"Cool. Oh, and Lex?" she added.

"Yeah?"

"My mom reads auras, so don't be surprised if she says something kind of weird when you first get here."

Uh, okay. I suppose it couldn't be any weirder than *Hey, let's go vampire hunting.* "Roger that."

Chapter 17

It was a beautiful, crisp fall morning, and the good people of Boulder were enjoying it. I drove past several herds of cyclists and almost as many solo runners. It made me resent my car, wishing I could be enjoying the weather with the rest of the town. But Simon's mother's farm was fifteen miles away, and it would take too long to bike out there.

Pellar Farms took up a huge swath of land that tapered to a point at two intersecting county highways. Having lived in Boulder all my civilian life, I was expecting a sloppy hippie commune, but the hand-carved wooden sign next to the intersection was neat and professional, with the farm's website displayed on the bottom in black reflective paint. The main building was a sprawling two-story residence. Next to the house was a small farm stand where crops were sold "right off the vine," and several outbuildings, including a decrepit barn, several sheds, and an open-air building that was probably used for canning. I could see signs of activity out in the field: people bent over rows of plants, a small tractor running. It was peaceful and idyllic, but give me a sprawl of mountain forest and a dirt bike any day. Peaceful and idyllic isn't in my gene pool.

As I parked on the L-shaped gravel driveway near the main building, I noticed Lily Pellar standing near the house, chatting with an older Caucasian woman who was crouching down to tend a cluster of violet-blue geraniums. Today Lily was wearing a cream-colored lace tank top that set off her tattoos, paired with skintight purple leggings with six inches of shiny silver zipper at the ankle. I could never have pulled off that ensemble, but she looked like a pop star on her way to the recording studio.

She turned when she heard my car, reaching a hand up to shade her eyes, and the woman beside her rose to her feet. She was tall, with thick rangy limbs and the kind of heavy-not-fat bulk that came from a lot of hard work and a lot of good food. Her pewter hair hung down her back in an impressively complicated fishtail braid. She wore khaki capri pants, gardening clogs, and a button-down purple linen top, and there was a big smear of zinc oxide on her nose. She looked like she would easily fit in at my mother's book club.

The two of them started toward me as I climbed out of the car. "Hey, Lex," Lily called. "This is my mom, Hazel Pellar. Mom, this is . . ."

Her voice trailed off as we both stared at her mother. The other woman's welcoming smile had wilted away as I got closer, replaced by a look of total revulsion. She darted forward, moving between me and her adult daughter. "Get away from my house," she hissed at me.

I felt the strangest sensation, as if all the wind on the planet was suddenly rushing past me toward the older woman. Behind her, Lily's mouth dropped open. I leaned my head to the side so I could look at her over her mom's shoulder. "Lily? Is that what you meant by 'kind of weird?'"

"No," Lily said carefully. "This is a little weird even for her." She circled around to face her mother and gently took Hazel's hand. "Mom, what's the matter?"

"Don't you see it?" she demanded, still staring at me. "Can't you see the color?"

Lily looked at me speculatively, then closed her eyes for a second, frowning in concentration. She opened her eyes and looked at me again, her face twisting into a puzzled expression. "Huh." To me, she said, "Lex, your aura's black."

I looked at her blankly. "So?"

"I've never seen black before," she said conversationally, as though she'd just learned I had a gold tooth or a giant mole on my back.

"She's a black witch," Hazel Pellar whispered.

Lily visibly paled, her warm brown skin turning momentarily sallow. "Well, that explains some things," she said shakily. "Changes some things, too, I guess."

"I don't know what that means," I said, trying to rein in my temper. I took a step closer to the two of them. "And I'm getting pretty goddamned sick of—"

I barely registered Hazel flicking her wrist before I went flying backward through the air, the back of my head striking my car with a dull thump.

Chapter 18

When I came to, I was lying on a sofa, my head pillowed on something that felt an awful lot like a bag of crushed ice. No, the pellets were too perfectly round. Definitely frozen peas. I glanced around and discovered I was in a living room, presumably at the Pellar house. From behind the sofa, I could hear voices arguing in hushed tones.

". . . exactly what I'm saying," came Hazel's voice. "Black means *death*, Lily. That woman has death in her blood."

"You're actually *scared* of her?" Lily said incredulously. "My mother the great witch overlord is scared of a trainee?"

"You're damned right I am," the other woman snapped. "And don't call me that."

"Mom, she has no idea what she is. She obviously needs help, and by our own laws, we're bound to aid another witch," Lily argued.

"And even if we weren't"—this from a third, male voice. Simon was here, too. When had he arrived?—"The order to train her comes directly from Maven. Our hands are tied."

Hazel sighed audibly. "You don't get it, kids. I know neither of you are great with auras, but hers isn't just black. It's . . . opaque. She has *serious* bloodlines." There was actual *awe* in her voice, and I felt a chill race along my skin. Maybe it was just the frozen peas. "If what she told you is true, and she really doesn't use her magic, then she is as close to a purebred as any witch I've ever seen."

There was a long moment of loaded silence before Lily finally spoke. "You always said there were families who breed for magic," she pointed out. "Maybe she comes from one of those."

"She must. But the idea that a line of black witches could even survive that long, much less retain this much power . . ." She trailed off, and I could practically hear her shaking her head. "It's terrifying, Lil. Whatever that young woman is, it's terrifying."

I glanced around the room, looking for an exit. I needed to get out of here. Fast. Judging by the fact that she'd thrown me eight feet through the air with a flick of her wrist, Hazel Pellar was powerful. And now she was calling *me* terrifying. I didn't really understand what was going on, but I could see the writing on the wall.

I just couldn't see a way out. The inside of the farmhouse was surprisingly modern, or maybe I had just subconsciously expected a lot of spiderwebs and a cauldron. But I was in a wide living room with a flat screen TV hanging on the wall, lavender canvas-covered furniture, and a lot of windows. But no external door.

Unfortunately, my movement made the bag behind my head crinkle. Suddenly Simon's face popped into view over the back of the sofa. I gasped.

"Hey, Lex," he said pleasantly. "Sorry, didn't mean to startle you."

I sat up, the back of my head aching. The living room had an open floor plan that connected into the kitchen, where I could see Lily and Hazel sitting at a long counter with ceramic mugs in front of them. "Where's my bag?" I said brusquely. "I'll get out of your hair."

"Hang on," Lily said, hopping off her stool. "You hit your head pretty hard. I think it's just a bump, but I need to check you for a concussion."

She grabbed a small but professional-looking medical kit off the counter and hurried into the living room. Hazel didn't move from her seat.

"Mom?" Simon said in a sweet voice, as Lily went past him. "Isn't there something you'd like to say to Lex?"

Hazel glared at her son. "Don't patronize me, Simon Aleister Pellar." Her gaze shifted toward me. "My children tell me you're unaware of your abilities," she said stiffly. "I apologize for throwing you. I just . . . reacted."

"There, was that so hard?" Lily said teasingly. She had perched next to me on the sofa and was shining a dim flashlight into my eyes.

Hazel sighed, a bit of the hostility leaching out of her shoulders. "Don't mind my kids. They got in trouble a hundred times for using that particular hex when they were in high school. They're very much enjoying the turnabout."

"*Yeah*, we are," Lily said happily. She clicked off the little flashlight and held up one hand. "Your pupils are reacting fine. How many fingers do you see?"

"Seven." Lily made a suspicious face at me. "Okay, three."

"What's your full name?"

"Allison Alexandra Luther," I recited.

"What's the last thing you remember?"

"Your mother throwing me into my car," I said grimly. My head ached again, and I'd just gotten it to stop aching from the *last* time I'd been hurt. Unbelievable.

"We used to call it the catapult," Lily said conspiratorially. She turned her head to look at Simon, who had backed up and was leaning in the wide doorway between the kitchen and living room. Probably to stay between me and his mother. "I think she's fine."

"Good," Hazel said, climbing to her feet. She didn't sound particularly pleased. "I'm going outside to get some air. And finish the geraniums." She marched toward a screen door behind her.

After we heard the door slam shut, there was a long moment of silence while Simon picked up one of the mugs on the counter and took a leisurely sip. Then he calmly put the mug down again and said offhandedly, "So, that went well."

I snorted. "I really am sorry," he added, sounding sincere. "Mom's under a lot of pressure from the clan right now. She was raised with a lot of traditions that are becoming . . . unfashionable."

"When did you get here?" I asked Simon. "How long was I out?"

"Just a few minutes," he assured me. "I was on my way here anyway, to pick up a bag of veggies for the faculty lounge." He glanced at something over my head, and I followed his gaze to a clock on the wall.

"What's a black witch?" I asked quickly, before he could make an excuse and leave. I wanted all the allies I could muster. *Which means*, I realized, *that I already consider Simon an ally*. Huh.

Lily put her flashlight back in the little medical kit, then crossed her arms under her breasts as if she were chilled. "The *polite* term is boundary witch," she informed me. "The majority of people with active witchblood are trades witches, meaning they can manipulate magic to do a little bit of everything. Some trades witches, like most of Clan Pellar, also have a religious aspect to their magic. They're usually referred to as hedge witches. You've heard of Wicca?"

"Sure."

Lily raised one hand in a "there you go" gesture. For a second I thought I saw her tattoos writhing on her forearm, and I wondered if I didn't have a concussion after all. "My mother is our leader. We celebrate Wiccan holidays, we have certain traditions and rituals, and we *believe*," she said, cutting her eyes briefly toward her mother's vacant seat at the counter, "that every creature has a right to free will, and that anything we put out into the world will eventually return to us threefold."

"Which is why we use very little aggressive magic," Simon put in. He came over and sat in the lavender armchair adjacent to the couch, so I had a Pellar on either side of me. Now that the two of them were close to each other, I could see the resemblances—the angles of their cheekbones, the shapes of their noses, even their eyebrows. It was just their skin color that varied. "I've never seen Mom freak out on someone like that."

Lily shook her head. "Me either . . . but we're getting off track. The point is that we can manipulate magic in a variety of ways, as long as we stick to our code and our traditions. But there are also witches who are born with . . . *specialties*. Passed down through their bloodline."

"What kind of specialties?" I asked warily.

Simon jumped in. "It can be anything: a knack for finding the lost, a certain gift with one of the four elements, maybe the ability to nudge the weather in a certain direction."

"Like a talent," I said tiredly. I just wanted to go home and climb into bed, where I could hopefully forget the last week had ever happened. Instead, I was playing student. "Being good at languages or music or something."

"Kind of," Lily agreed. "But there's one very rare specialty that's considered a curse rather than a gift." Stretching out one black high-heeled boot, she traced a line in the nap of the carpet with her toe and tapped a foot on one side of the line. "There's the land of the living," she began, and then tapped her foot on the other side. "And the land of the dead."

"Boundary witches access magic that crosses the line," Simon finished.

There was a collision in my thoughts. "Oh," I said softly. I met Simon's eyes. "It's true, then . . . I can't die?"

"You *died*?" Lily said incredulously. "When was this?"

"I was stabbed by a vampire a few nights ago," I told her. "My heart stopped. Um . . . a few times."

She nodded thoughtfully. "Your soul tried to cross the line, and your magic wouldn't let it pass. Was that the only time?"

"No. Three years ago, in Iraq. And," I said, remembering suddenly, "when I was thirteen. I drowned while I was whitewater rafting. But that happens to lots of people. My friend gave me CPR,

I thought . . . everyone thought that's what brought me back . . ."
I realized I was babbling and snapped my mouth shut. John. John
had given me CPR. I hadn't thought about that moment in ages.

Lily and Simon exchanged a meaningful look. "What?" I said,
looking between them.

"That solves one mystery, anyway," Lily offered.

I looked at Simon. "It was the magic," he explained. "Your
friend didn't bring you back. When you died that first time, it woke
your magic."

I felt my eyes go big as his meaning sunk in. At the hospital
Simon had said you had to use magic within a window of time,
around puberty, in order for it to become active. A sour taste filled
my mouth as I remembered all that river water.

As if he could read my mind, Simon got up and poured me a
mug of something warm and greenish. Tea. Gratefully, I picked it
up and took a sip. It was flavored with berries, or maybe pomegran-
ate, and only a little bit warmer than room temperature. I drank
anyway, ignoring the bitterness, trying to gather my thoughts.

"Your mom said I have death in my blood," I said finally. "Like
I was the goddamned Grim Reaper or something."

The siblings exchanged another look, a shorthand communica-
tion, and I felt a sudden pang of grief for Sam. I would never have
that again. "We really are sorry about that," Simon told me. "Mom
just panicked a little. There aren't many boundary witch bloodlines
anymore, and most of the remaining ones have let their blood go
dormant on purpose."

"That's seen as . . . you know, the responsible thing to do," Lily
said apologetically. "The powers are too dangerous, too visible."

Seeing my confusion, Simon added, "She means they're hard
to hide."

"*What* powers?" I asked, getting frustrated again. "I mean, I get
that not being able to die is a big deal, but how am I dangerous to
anyone else?"

Lily glanced at her brother. "This is more your area of expertise, Si." To me, she added, "Our mom doesn't know, but he's been studying the evolution of magic. As a"—she lifted her fingers to make air quotes—"side project."

Simon made a face at his sister. "You make it sound like I took up scrapbooking or something." He shrugged and lowered his voice. "Look, the truth is . . . I don't know much about boundary witches. I've never met an active one. But my broad understanding is that you specialize in anything that deals with the line between life and death."

Seeing that that had cleared up absolutely nothing for me, Lily mused, "Well, you'll probably be able to sense magic. Most of us can, of course, because it's the force of creation, of life. But it's also a force of death, I guess."

"Okay . . ."

"And if you really are as powerful as Mom suspects, you might be able to communicate with remnants," Simon said thoughtfully. "Spirits that, for whatever reason, don't cross the line when they die."

"That's . . . you're talking about *ghosts*," I said stupidly. "Like . . . *ghosts*."

He nodded, apparently oblivious to how absurd he sounded. "You'll also age much more slowly than foundings or other witches," he continued, "because your cells will be reluctant to die. That's probably the real reason why your face looks so young."

"So there's a plus," Lily said, giving me a small smile.

"Oh, also, boundary witches have a special affinity for vampires," Simon added. Beside me, Lily made an "oh, yeah" face.

"What does that mean, affinity?" I said, feeling lost.

"Remember the rule that magic doesn't work against itself? Well, vampire bodies are dead, reanimated by magic. They were supposed to cross the line, but they didn't."

My eyes immediately darted to Lily, who seemed accustomed to translating for her brother. "You can press 'em, Lex," Lily said cheerfully. "Turnabout is fair play, and all that."

"Oh." At least that explained what I'd done to Darcy the night before. "And that's why she wanted me," I said to myself. To the Pellars, I added, "Maven, I mean. That must be why she wanted Itachi to hire me." And maybe why I'd felt such a head rush in her presence.

Simon and Lily exchanged another look, though I couldn't interpret this one. "Okay," I said slowly, my thoughts dragging through corn syrup. "A few days ago, I was a register monkey at an all-night convenience store. Today it turns out I can't die, I age slowly, I might be able to talk to fucking *ghosts*, pardon my language, and I can press vampires." I shook my head. It was just too surreal.

Then an image flashed in my mind: Hazel Pellar standing between me and her kid, a look of determined hatred on her face. You don't look at someone like that just because they can press vampires. "There's something you're not telling me," I said, looking up so I could gauge their reactions. "Why does your mom hate boundary witches so much?"

Lily looked away, fiddling with a couple of silver rings on her fingers. Simon said softly, "It's a . . . historical thing, Lex. During the Middle Ages, boundary witches . . . did some things."

I raised an eyebrow. "So did the Christians," I countered. "But nobody gets tossed at a car for going to Sunday school."

Lily gave a little snort, but she still avoided meeting my eyes. Simon heaved a sigh. "Don't freak out," he said reluctantly. "But, theoretically . . . you can raise the dead."

Chapter 19

I freaked out. Well, actually I burst out laughing, but it had an edge of hysteria that I couldn't control.

"In theory, any really, really powerful witch could raise the dead," Lily said over the sound of my laughter, as though that might help me understand. "But trades witches would need a full coven and a shit-ton of mandragora in order to do death magics. Even then, it'd be dangerous for us."

I stopped laughing. "Manda-whata?" I asked, feeling helplessly lost.

"It's an herb for death magics," Simon explained. "Not important right now."

"Death magics," I echoed, suddenly dazed. "Magic for death."

"Uh-oh," Lily said, raising her eyebrows at her brother. "I think you broke her, Si."

He ignored her. "Look, Lex, the short version? Boundary witches have been hated and feared since the Inquisition. They did some stuff back then, and they ended up being seen by many people as an . . . accident of nature and magic, like an . . ." He winced, looking apologetic. "An abomination."

I looked between the two of them. Simon was clearly uncomfortable, and Lily was still having trouble making eye contact with me. But neither of them seemed afraid of me. "You two seem to be handling it okay."

"Well, Simon's a scientist," Lily answered, giving a little shrug. "And I have a particularly liberal outlook when it comes to marginalized minority groups." She wrinkled her nose wryly, and I realized she was referring to her skin tone. "But most witches, especially the ones from our mother's generation, see it differently."

"Mom doesn't think you're going to murder us right now or anything," Simon offered. "She's just afraid that if we teach you how to use your power, you'll . . . well, use it. And grow more powerful."

"Like breast-feeding," I said absently. I shook my head, trying to ground myself. In the army, I'd been to briefings where we had to process a lot of information very quickly. Either I was out of the habit, or the bump on my head was a lot worse than Lily had thought.

"Okay, fine. I can get more of the history later. For now, though, what do we do? Maven wants me trained, and your mom wants me banished from the state."

Part of me was hoping they'd say they couldn't train me, that I'd have to go home and find another way to keep Charlie safe. I didn't want to be a witch, and certainly not one with death in her blood. I just wanted to go home, maybe go for a bike ride, and then watch something with Gregory Peck saving the world from corruption and tyranny.

But both of the Pellars suddenly looked very sober. "We have to train her," Lily said to her brother. "We can't let Mom renege on the deal. It could start a war, Si."

Simon gave her a long, speculative look, then nodded. "I don't remember her actually forbidding us from training her," he said to the ceiling. "We'll really just be carrying out her wishes, by keeping her deal with Itachi." His gaze flicked back to Lily. "If I cancel my class," he began, "can we divide and conquer?"

She made a sour face. "I hope you don't mean—"

"I'll start working with Lex; you start working on Mom." Lily was obviously about to protest, so Simon added, "Come on, Lil, you're the baby—and her favorite. You know she'll listen to you."

"How come I'm only her favorite when my older siblings want something?" Lily complained, but I could tell by the look on her face that she was going to acquiesce. She let out a frustrated grunt. "Ugh, fine. Just go out to the barn or something so you're not right in her face."

Lily went out the back door to run interference with their mother, who had progressed to the geraniums behind the house. Simon led me out the sliding glass door, across the wooden porch, and along the driveway toward the old barn I'd seen when I drove up. I felt his eyes on me most of the way. "You okay?" he asked when we were nearing the barn.

I shook my head. "Not even close."

He shot me a sympathetic look and slid open the enormous wooden door, motioning for me to step past. Inside, I paused for a second so my eyes could adjust to the dimness. There was a fenced-off concrete walkway cutting straight through the barn, which was otherwise divided into a quartet of large stalls, each big enough to comfortably house six to eight cows. The barn was deserted now, but I could tell that at one point there had been actual cows here—the air still smelled faintly of stale manure, and there were pockets of griminess where years of caked-on dirt and cow feed had left permanent stains on the furnishings. Despite the barn's obvious age, everything was well cared for, with swept concrete floors and signs that the fences were hosed off regularly.

"There used to be a few dairy cows here, but when my mom took over the farm she switched to agriculture only," Simon explained. He led me to the center of the building, where a decidedly rickety-looking wooden ladder led up to a plain square hole cut into the wooden ceiling. "This way," he urged, and without waiting to see if I'd follow, Simon hopped onto the ladder and began climbing, disappearing through the hole. I didn't like the idea of following him into a room I couldn't see, but I swallowed my discomfort and began climbing after him.

I had to squint as I rose into the hayloft, because sun poured into the space from several open-air windows, bathing it in warm light that sparkled from particles of hay dust in the air. The loft was filled with neat stacks of hay bales that formed a sort of loose amphitheater—the stacks were highest near the walls tapering down to the middle of the loft, which had a wide area with no hay at all. When I stood up, Simon flipped a trapdoor closed, concealing the ladder we'd climbed beneath a plain square of wood with a ring in it. Then he climbed onto one of the midsize stacks of hay, four bales high, on the opposite side of the room. "Pick a stack and climb on," he said, gesturing to the room.

"Is this like a psychological test?" I said suspiciously. "The size of the stack of hay I pick indicates the size of my affinity with magic or something?"

Simon laughed, a surprised, carefree sound. "Not that I know of. They're just more comfortable than the wooden floor."

Still a little skeptical, I chose a stack that was as tall as his, but against the opposite wall, so we were about ten feet apart, four feet off the floor. The hay sticking out of the top bale felt sharp and prickly, even through my jeans, but I could ignore it. "What are we doing up here?"

Simon shrugged. "It's a good place for early lessons. It's quiet, nobody ever comes up here, and with the trapdoor closed it's fairly hard to get hurt, as long as nobody accidentally starts a fire." He nodded toward the wall behind me, and I turned my head to see two massive fire extinguishers bolted into the wooden support. "We've got that set up just in case."

"Nice," I said, turning to face him again. "What do you want me to do?"

He folded his legs. "Sit crisscross applesauce, as my sister says, and let your hands relax where you want them. Then close your eyes." He left his hands resting against his legs and shut his own eyes, providing an example. "Before anything else, I'm going to teach you how to sense magic."

I mimicked his relaxed posture, letting my eyelids fall. I was still tired, so it wasn't hard.

We stayed that way for about ten heartbeats, and then I became aware of a conscious desire to fidget. I wanted to move my legs, my arms, to climb the bales of hay and stack them in a pile that I couldn't reach the top of. I wanted to stick my head out the open window and look around the farm, maybe do some pull-ups on the wooden ladder. My limbs wanted to *move*.

"Lex . . ." Simon began, and I popped open my eyes.

"Yeah?" I followed his eyes downward, and saw that my leg was jiggling. "Oh, sorry."

"You don't hold still much, do you?" he asked with a wry smile.

"Of course I do," I said defensively. "In the car, in the shower, when I watch movies. All the time."

"Uh-huh. Is that what you do for fun, watch movies?"

I shrugged. "Once in a while. When the weather's bad, or when I get sick."

"And the rest of the time?"

I blew out a breath. "I like being outdoors. I run and bike. Box a little. Mmm . . . hiking, rock climbing. I'm on an intramural softball team in the summer." Intramural softball: my big nod to socialization.

"Hmm," he said, as if I'd just revealed some great secret. "Let's try again."

I closed my eyes again, this time making sure I wasn't jiggling my knee.

"Okay. Now I want you to focus on your breathing," he said calmly. "Picture the air going into your lungs, traveling all the way down your limbs to your toes and back out again. Feel the breath as it passes through each part of you."

It was a lot harder than it sounds. Concentrating on my breath for a moment was easy, but keeping my focus on it and not letting in any other thoughts was nearly impossible. I kept trying, although it felt like trying to dam a stream with just my hands. Finally my breathing settled into a regular, slow pace as I visualized each breath.

"Good," Simon murmured. "Now extend your senses and feel the temperature of the room, the air on your skin."

"Extend my senses? What does that even mean?" I grumbled, keeping my eyes closed.

"Have you ever had a minor injury or a headache?" Simon asked, his voice still low and soothing. "And you take some ibuprofen or aspirin to make the pain go away?"

"Of course. I did it this morning."

"Well, a few minutes after you take the medicine, you focus on the place in your body where the pain was, and you sort of *listen* to that spot, to see if the pain's gone yet. You sense it out, for lack of a better phrase."

"Okay . . ."

"Now do that with your skin. Sense what your skin is feeling, and then extend those senses farther to feel the air in the room."

That made more sense to me, and I tried to do as he asked. But after a few seconds I lost my focus, and images began to click through my brain—a slide show of my life, mostly my life in the army. I'd seen it many times before. When I'd first gotten home, I'd seen it every time I blinked.

Abruptly, I opened my eyes and scrambled off the bale of hay. I stalked across the open floor to another stack and climbed on, not pausing until I reached the open window above the top bale. I leaned out and took a deep breath. When I turned around, Simon hadn't moved except to open his eyes. He was watching me calmly. "What are we doing?" I demanded. "This can't be magic."

"Technically, this is meditation," Simon said easily. "I needed to know how well you could concentrate."

I looked away. "Not very well."

"Then we'll try something else," he said levelly. "Sit down, please."

Reluctantly, I abandoned the breeze and returned to my original seat.

"This time, I just want you to listen," Simon coaxed. "Close your eyes and make a list of everything you hear."

Okay, that I could do. I strained to hear something. There was the sound of an engine in the distance, maybe a tractor or a riding lawnmower. I could hear a few bird calls through the open window, too. And something else. Off in the corner, I heard the tiniest rustle of hay. "I think you have mice," I said, my eyes still closed.

"We do."

"Is that what you wanted me to listen for?" I asked, trying to keep the impatience out of my voice. *What do you want me to do?* This was for Charlie, after all. He just needed to name something and I'd do it.

"Sort of. Concentrate on the mice, the same way you concentrated on your body. Focus on the sound."

So I closed my eyes again and concentrated on the corner of the room where I'd heard the hay move. With great effort, I tried to focus my attention on that spot.

Just as my concentration started to slip, I felt something: a tiny living spark, smaller than a grain of rice. There was a sort of color to it—a pretty, glowing blue. I let out a tiny gasp and opened my eyes, losing it.

Simon was looking right at me, and I knew that however different our talents might be, he could feel it too. "What *was* that?" I asked wondrously.

He gave me a small smile. "You were sensing magic. Some people call it the soul, or the spark of life. People perceive it differently—your brain finds a way to interpret it that makes sense to you. For me magic is . . . mmm . . . sort of a density in the air. Lily envisions a third eye she can switch on and off. Whatever works for you. Can you do it again?"

I closed my eyes again and extended my senses, as Simon had instructed. This time it was easier to find the spark, because I knew what I was looking for. I concentrated on it, on the blue almost-glow that emitted from the mouse. In Iraq I'd looked through thermal imaging goggles a few times; this felt a lot like that. A sea of darkness interrupted by a bright flash of warmth.

"It's like heat-sensing goggles," I said softly, without opening my eyes.

"Good," Simon encouraged. "Now push out farther. Find the rest of them."

I tried to extend the area of my senses, but it got spread too thin, and I lost the first spark. I went back to it and started again, thinking again of the heat-sensing goggles. This time, instead of concentrating on the first spark and expanding in all directions, I *moved* it, like a flashlight beam in the dark. I pointed the beam of my attention toward the same spot and tried to push past it. I found that first rice grain of life again, then another behind it. And another.

A moment later my beam reached the back of the loft and abruptly flared and expanded. Suddenly there was a huge flash of magic, blinding in its radiance. My eyes flew open, and I lost my grip on the beam.

"That was me," Simon said calmly. "You sensed my life force."

"You could *feel* that?"

He shook his head, bemused. "No, just a logical guess."

I shook my head, standing up and hopping off the bale of hay so I could pace across the expanse of clear wooden floor. I was totally unnerved. "I don't like this. I don't think . . . Mice are one thing, but I shouldn't be able to *feel* other people's life forces. It's . . . invasive."

"It didn't feel invasive, though, did it?" Simon asked mildly.

I paused, considering. "No," I admitted. "It felt . . . fantastic." I went back to pacing, but I could feel his eyes on me.

"Let's do it again," he suggested.

So we did. For the next two hours, I concentrated on the sparks of life in the barn. Simon taught me how to ignore the blaze of his own soul and focus on the mice, until I knew that there were exactly twelve of them in the barn, six were babies, and their nest was seven inches left of the exact intersection of the two walls, underneath the hay. With my eyes closed, I "felt" them inside my head, each mouse represented as a tiny speck that sort of glowed softly, moving as the mouse moved. It was eerie. And completely fascinating.

After two hours my stomach growled, and I opened my eyes to see Simon checking his watch. "We need to wrap this up soon," he told me, a little regretful. I remembered that it was Friday, and some people actually had to work regular jobs today.

I nodded. I was a little tired, but exhilarated. "That's amazing," I said happily. "When you guys talked about learning magic I thought I was going to have to memorize Latin or something." I could see how being able to sense life could be useful, especially in a combat-type situation.

But Simon smiled ruefully. "Technically," he pointed out, "you're not actually *doing* any magic yet. I've just been helping you sense the magic that's out there for you to manipulate."

My glee dissipated a bit. "Right," I said.

"I want to do one more thing before we call it a day," he said, and his voice was suddenly . . . grim. He leaned forward so he could reach into his back pocket and pulled out a leather gardening glove. "Hang on a second," he told me. I watched him get up and go over to the bale of hay above the mice's nest, flipping it forward like you'd flip a stone to dig up earthworms. There was a quick rustle of movement and a bit of squeaking as he leaned over and rummaged through the hay.

"Simon?" I said uncertainly. "What . . ."

He straightened up then, the hand with the glove holding one of the little white field mice by the tail. "What are you doing?" I said warily.

"Shh, it's okay," Simon reassured me. He sat down on the hay bale across from me, still holding the mouse. I glowered at him, suddenly afraid he was going to drop it in my hair like an eighth grader. But he settled into his seat, holding up one palm in the universal gesture of "I'm not going to hurt you," and finally I relaxed.

But I shouldn't have.

"I just want you to focus on its spark of life, please," Simon coaxed, and I closed my eyes and obeyed. Now that I understood how to extend my senses, I found the mouse's spark right away.

"Focus on it," Simon said softly. I did, concentrating on the tiny blue glow. *It was so little*, I marveled. And Simon's glow was so much bigger, but it was brighter, too. Maybe humans had more of a soul than mice? That would—

Abruptly, I heard a tiny *snap*, and the blue spark of life I'd been focusing on flickered out. No, wait, it was still there . . . but the bright blue glow had been replaced by a sickly, yellowish-brown, gaseous mass.

And then the gas started to drift toward me, like an airborne toxin.

Chapter 20

My focus broke.

My eyes flew open, and I bolted off the hay bale, scrambling backward until my shoulder blades hit a wall. There was no toxin in the air, not that I could see, anyway. Just Simon sitting there with a guilty look on his face and a dead mouse in his hand.

"No!" I shouted. In an instant I dove forward, tackling him to the ground. That was the plan, anyway, but when I was within a hairsbreadth of touching Simon, he calmly held up his free hand, his lips moving inaudibly—and I glanced off him.

Wait, *what*?

I stood up and swung a left roundhouse at his cheekbone, the fury pushing my limbs long before I had the chance to think. Again, he held up a hand, muttering, and I seemed to slide right off into the air near it.

"Sergeant Luther, *calm down*!" Simon barked, and I froze, a decade of instincts stirring back to life in my nerve endings. I managed a slow step backward, my hands still bunched into fists. I could feel the tension forming a U from the ends of my left-hand fingers across my shoulders and down to my other fist, but I couldn't seem to let go of it. I could hear my breathing, heavy in the quiet hayloft. "Why?" I demanded.

"First of all, let's keep in mind that it's a *mouse*," Simon pointed out, his voice a little heated now. "There are three cats and four kittens on this farm, so this little guy's days were numbered no matter what."

I didn't move. "Second," he continued. "Stop and assess how you feel right now."

That took me aback for a second, and I obeyed him without thinking. How did I feel? I felt . . . exhilarated. Fulfilled. The darkness that surrounded me had been channeled into something for a moment there, and it was like I had a purpose again, for the first time since I'd been kicked out of the army. I felt . . . powerful.

"I want to do it again," I whispered in answer. All the fight went out of me, and I hunched back to my bale of hay. "What's happening to me?"

"It's okay," Simon reassured me, but I didn't feel very reassured. "Come on, let's get out of here. Go for a walk."

I nodded numbly, and he flipped open the trapdoor.

We didn't speak on the way out of the barn, or as we walked down the driveway. At some point, Simon must have gotten rid of the dead mouse, but I didn't see what he did with it and I didn't care. The only thing I could really think about was how close I was to my car.

I wanted to go *home*. I wanted to send gravel flying in the air as I flew out of that driveway and never looked back. I wanted to grab John and Charlie and evacuate them out of the state, forget that I had ever heard the words "boundary witch" or "magic" or "null." Just start over somewhere else and live a normal life, leaving all my darkness behind.

It would never work, though. I'd given Maven and Itachi my word, and they would never let me grab Charlie and waltz out of there. They'd force me back, if only to make a point about not defying them. And besides, I had roots in Boulder, deep ones. If we ran, Charlie and John might be safe, but I had a couple dozen more family members in this town that the vampires could go after. I'd seen the file they had on me. There was no way it didn't include all my aunts and uncles and cousins, not to mention my parents. Hell, my dad was the president of Luther Shoes. They could walk right into his office.

No, I had to stay. I had to get control of this. I would just need to be stronger, that was all.

That was all.

We were a few hundred feet down the road when Simon finally spoke again. "These are potatoes, which you probably know," he said casually, nodding at the field on our left. "Onions on the other side of the road, and we have a lot of tomatoes, too. All in all, we've got about four hundred acres. That's small for Colorado, but it would be pretty big in the smaller states."

"A farm boy, huh?" I said lightly, grateful for the change in subject. "And a witch. And a college professor."

"*Associate* professor," he corrected, grinning.

"What do you teach?" I asked. "No wait, let me guess: Occult Studies? Myth and Mythology? History of Witchcraft? No, that wouldn't be in the science building . . . or *would* it?"

He laughed again. "Evolutionary Biology. That part is all me, but there's actually a long history of witches being farmers. It's one of the few professions where we can use our gifts and still stay under the radar." He shrugged modestly. "Our crops just do a little better than some."

"Do you live here, at the farmhouse?" I asked. "You keep saying 'we' and 'our.'"

"Not really. I've got an apartment in town, near CU," he told me. "But I grew up here, and I still stay over weekends sometimes, help when I can." He flashed a grin, his teeth flashing in the late-morning sunlight. "There's not a lot of testosterone around here, so I think my brothers-in-law appreciate it when I turn up. Two of them work the farm pretty much full-time."

We walked on for a while, Simon letting me have some space. I wasn't sure if he had suggested the walk because he knew the activity would make me feel better, or if it was just a coincidence, but I appreciated the exercise anyway. My head cleared up when I was moving. "You said your sisters were witches, too," I said finally. "Are your brothers-in-law?"

"Nah. Statistically, almost all witches are female," he said cheerfully. "Men who inherit the magic gene are few and far between. Sybil's husband, Oliver, is from an old witch family; he just doesn't have witchblood. Morgan's husband, Tony, is human, so we're not allowed to talk about vampires or werewolves in front of him. He knows that my whole family are practicing Wiccans, but we downplay the actual magic part." He shrugged. "Tony thinks the Pellars have the equivalent of a really green thumb."

"Hmm." I tried to imagine telling my parents I was a witch. My live-and-let-live dad would do his best to ignore it; he would assume I was going through a weird fad. My mother would be so grateful that I was interested in something, she'd probably offer to be a witch with me. "What about your girlfriend?" I asked Simon. "Is she a witch, too?"

He glanced over at me, surprised. "How did you know I have a girlfriend?"

"In the hospital," I said promptly. "Quinn told you to say hi to Tracy, who had gone home ahead of you. None of your sisters are named Tracy, and you're not wearing a wedding ring." I shrugged. "Ergo, Tracy is your girlfriend."

He gave me a sly half grin. "Tracy could be my boyfriend," he pointed out.

"No," I said firmly, "You said 'she' in the hospital."

He gave me a surprised look. "Good memory. Yes, she's a witch. She's been in our clan since we were kids."

"High school sweethearts?" I asked, making sure my voice didn't come out all wistful.

"College," he said. "We complement each other well."

That didn't exactly sound like the basis for a thriving romance, but then again, what did I know? Maybe it worked for them. "What about you?" Simon asked. "Do you have someone?"

"No," I said. "Most of the guys I meet are half-drunk college kids who come into the store to buy condoms at two a.m. Before that . . . I had a couple of casual relationships in the army, but nothing to write home about. Literally."

He chuckled and pushed his glasses up on his nose with one hand. "Listen, about Quinn . . ."

I looked at him uncertainly, a little thrown by the segue. He wasn't about to ask if I was interested in Quinn romantically, was he? I mean, it hadn't escaped my attention that the guy was great-looking, of course. And, okay, it had certainly been a long time since I'd . . . let's say, gone on a date. But Quinn was a vampire. A *vampire*.

Happily, Simon just said, "I heard you were helping him figure out who went after your niece. We didn't really get a chance to talk about it before, what with my mom and all, but how is that going?"

So I filled him in on the case—what little we knew, anyway. "He's picking me up tonight and we're going to talk to Darcy's . . . um, I don't know the terminology, but the vampire she was sworn to," I finished.

As we turned and walked back toward the house, Simon said hesitatingly, "Just . . . be careful, okay? Around Quinn, I mean."

I paused, forcing him to stop and turn too. "I thought Quinn was your friend," I said, eyebrows raised.

Simon shrugged. "He sort of is, to my eternal surprise. And I would trust the guy with my life . . . as long as keeping me alive was in Itachi's best interests."

I digested that for a moment, then resumed walking. "Vampires aren't like us, Lex," he said eventually. "You make your choices based on what's best for you and the people you love. So do I. But

Quinn has to do what's best for vampires. Specifically, the one he works for. He doesn't have a choice."

Lily and Hazel were nowhere to be seen when we got back to the main house, and I realized that neither of them had been out front when we left for our walk, either. Simon must have noticed this when I did, because he dug out his phone from a pocket and looked at the screen, squinting against the sunshine. "Lily texted," he informed me. "She's taking Mom into town to run errands, maybe catch a movie. Lily's really great at helping Mom get her mind off . . . you know." He gave me an embarrassed smile.

"Her problems?" I volunteered. "Such as the perversion of nature who's suddenly appeared in her life?"

"Ehhh . . ." Simon tilted one hand back and forth. "She doesn't think you're a perversion of *nature*, so much as a perversion of *magic*," he offered helpfully.

I lightly kicked the back of his knee as he walked, making him topple forward. He managed to right himself without falling on his face. "I may have been *slightly* deserving of that," he said loftily. Then his face turned serious. "Listen, Lex, I'll call you tomorrow after I talk to Lily, and we'll work out a schedule for lessons. But there's one other thing you need to know today." He gave me a complicated look, part sadness and part awe. "Now that you've used your magic a couple of times, it's going to grow."

"So . . . ?" I prompted.

"So, you should know that until you learn to channel it properly"—I thought of the flashlight beam of awareness I'd directed at the mouse, and how damned hard it had been to keep it going—"you're not going to have control of it. Magic is tied to emotions," he explained, "You know how you can channel your feelings into doing something constructive or destructive? The same is true of magic."

I wasn't particularly good at channeling my emotions, but I didn't say that. "Got it."

Simon hesitated. "In the meantime . . . you'll feel things really hard."

I shrugged. What else was new?

"And," he added with some urgency, "I wouldn't try to press any vampires."

But that was, like, the coolest thing I could do. "Why not?"

He shook his head. "You're gonna be a little unstable for a few weeks while your magic settles in. Which makes it a lot more likely that you'll slip up, giving a vampire a chance to gain control of you instead. And if they figure out you tried to press them . . ." He shook his head. "They *really* wouldn't like that."

Chapter 21

On the way back into Boulder, I grabbed a veggie sub from a chain place, driving with one hand so I could inhale it in the car. I was back at my cabin by mid-afternoon. My whole body was exhausted from the night of body disposal and the day of magic lessons, but I wasn't ready for sleep yet. I was in terrible need of a reality check—and so were the animals. Shelter pets tend to thrive on routines, and I'd been doing nothing but breaking ours for the last week.

So instead of a nap I went straight to the backyard and threw a tennis ball for a while, enjoying the fall sunshine and the infectious excitement of the dogs. Only Cody and Chip, both retriever mixes, actually *fetched* the ball, mind you—Pongo found toys uninteresting but enjoyed snuffling along the edges of the fence, and Dopey was simply too stupid to grasp the concept of bringing something back. Once in a while she would follow Cody and Chip for the first ten feet as they chased the ball, then scamper back to me, expecting praise for her accomplishments. I just laughed and complied.

After about an hour I went inside and took a long, hot shower, taking the time to shave my legs and pluck my eyebrows. Then I pulled on my nicest jeans and paired them with a camisole—I still wasn't supposed to wear a bra—covered by a nice long-sleeved knit top. I brushed my hair out in the mirror and nodded to myself. This was another Sam strategy—she always insisted that the key to feeling better inside was looking better on the outside. It had always sounded stupid and vaguely sexist to me—especially since I'd spent so many years trying *not* to look attractive—but I still appreciated the sentiment.

I realized that I suddenly, *desperately* missed my sister. She was the only one I could talk to about . . . well, I wouldn't say "stuff like this," because finding out that I had a magical connection to the forces of death isn't the kind of thing that happens every day. But Sam was always the one person who accepted me in every way. Besides, she was my twin. She would've had the same witchblood.

I wondered, not for the first time, if that could have saved her life. Would she still have died if her magic had been active, too? Probably not. But then again, in order for her magic to have become active, she would have had to die when we were teenagers. This was all too messed up to contemplate.

At four-thirty I left the house for my regular Friday date. Okay, well, "date" might have been pushing it, but it was probably the closest I got these days.

After Sam died and John came back to Boulder to work at Luther Shoes, my parents worried about him constantly. A twenty-nine-year-old widower who spent every moment either working for his father-in-law or taking care of his baby daughter? They decided he was in desperate need of some fun, and since they were still worried about me, too, they concocted a brilliant plan: all of a sudden, John's whole division started going to happy hour at one of the Boulder bars every Friday after work. There was some sort of trivia game on Fridays, and John was involuntarily drafted into the Luther Shoes employee team. And since Friday was my regular day off, and I didn't tend to socialize with any bipeds, I was recruited to babysit Charlie every Friday evening.

John and I put up a token protest, of course—it's grating, having your parents manipulate your social life at thirty—but we both had to admit the plan was a good one. I loved spending time with my niece, and having a regular date to see her gave me something to look forward to each week. And John, whether or not he was willing to admit it, could use the distraction of a weekly evening out with someone who was able to say more than six words.

John had texted that morning and offered to stay home from trivia night this week, since he thought I was still recuperating, but I'd insisted he go out with his friends. I wanted the time with my niece. I missed her—and besides, until Quinn and I figured out who had sent Darcy and Victor after Charlie, I'd feel better with her in my sight.

So at five o'clock sharp, I pulled up to my parents' great big house in Mapleton to collect my niece.

I opened the door just a crack at first, since Charlie had a habit of playing right on the other side of the door. When I was sure it was safe, I pushed the door all the way open. My mother was sitting on the steps leading to the second floor, keeping an eye on Charlie as she practiced climbing the stairs. When she saw me, Charlie squealed and her whole face broke open in a grin. "Hey, Mom," I said. "Hi, Charlie!"

My niece waved and looked down to study her feet, uncertain how to get herself down to me. "Oh, no, you don't," my mother said, scooping Charlie into her arms. "Gramma will take you." She carried Charlie down the steps, and when I held out my hands, the toddler dove for them. I laughed and cuddled her to my chest, planting kisses on her cheeks. "You're sure you're up for this?" my mother said anxiously, watching my movements. "What did the doctor say about your back? Are you supposed to lift things?"

"As a matter of fact," I said, smiling at my niece, who was now patting both of my cheeks enthusiastically, "I got a clean bill of health."

"Really?" my mother said, brightening a little. She was wearing khaki pants and a flowery blouse. She had to forgo jewelry and scarves while she babysat, but she was in full makeup, and her short hair was coiffed perfectly. Charlie, on the other hand, was wearing simple baby jeans and a long-sleeved onesie that was splattered with dried applesauce. "But it seemed so serious the other night! Did you consult with your surgeon?"

"No, Ma," I said, still making faces at my niece. "I've got a new friend, she's a doctor. She took my stitches out and said everything looks great." Okay, that was a slight revision of the actual events, not to mention a plumping of Lily's credentials, but if it made my mother feel better . . .

"Oh, that's wonderful," she gushed, beaming. "I'm so glad you're spending time with friends. And you just look so much better," she added as an afterthought.

That was my mom: she was happier to hear I had a friend than she was about my good health. "Diaper bag?" I asked.

Bag and niece in hand, I said good-bye. I drove Charlie over to John's house, let myself in with my key, and got us set up in the kitchen with some sliced lunch meat, sliced strawberries, and sliced mozzarella cheese. You have to do a lot of slicing with a toddler, I'd discovered. In the back of my mind I'd been a little worried that Charlie would have some kind of lasting trauma from her kidnapping, but to my relief she seemed like her normal baby self: a graham cracker addict who waved at strangers and clapped every time someone said, "Yay!"

After I fed Charlie, we read some board books and I sang her "Little Bunny Foo Foo" about three times, and then it was time for her to go to bed. "Goodnight, Charlie-bug," I said softly as I put her in her crib. "Love you."

Back in the living room, I felt exhausted all of a sudden, and sort of depressed, like someone had turned off the sunshine. I sat down in John's recliner and, for the second time in the past three days, drifted off to sleep there.

I dreamed of my sister.

No big surprise, really—I had just spent the last two hours with her daughter, after all. In the dream, Sam and I were about ten, and our parents had taken us to the Bobolink trailhead for the day. At first, I didn't know if it was an actual memory or just a composite, a piecing together of dozens of similar days. Either way, John was there, too—by the time we were seven, he spent more time at our house than his own.

My dad had taken John on a bird-watching trail, since he was the only one of us kids with the patience for staring at tiny animals as they flew around. My mom was getting lunch ready at a picnic table, and Sam and I were climbing on an outcropping of rocks, trying to make our way down what seemed like a long line of them without falling off. I went first, out of habit and necessity. From the time we were born, I was Sam's guardian. I was bigger and more sure-footed, not to mention more cautious than clumsy, imp-ish Sam. So our hands were linked, and I would place one Luther hiking boot on the next boulder—they *seemed* like boulders to us, anyway—before putting my weight on it. Then I would move aside and let Sam hop on.

In the dream, she followed me along the path until we ran out of rocks. "I'll lead the way back," she said mischievously, and dropped my hand. Then she abruptly took off skipping, heading back the way we had come at a speed that scared me. "Slow down!" I yelled after her, but Sam either didn't hear me or didn't want to stop. Even at ten, she would do *anything* for me or John, so long as it wasn't taking care of herself.

I followed her as fast as I could, my eyes on the rocks in front of me, but Sam was faster, and I lost sight of her quickly. Soon I reached the end of the rocky outcropping, but I still didn't see my sister anywhere. I ran through the short tangle of trees and across the clearing to the picnic table where my mother was setting out plastic silverware. "Where's Sam?" I asked her, panting.

My mother looked up in surprise. "I thought she was with you?"

My dad and John returned from the bird-watching trail, and they hadn't seen Sam, either. She was just gone. We began to search, our calls for Sam growing more and more frantic by the moment. I felt the desperate, crushing panic of knowing that I had failed my sister.

"Allie. *Allie!*" There was something warm on my hand. I opened my eyes and saw John kneeling in front of me, his fingers resting on mine. He was wearing a black button-down, untucked, over a white T-shirt, and his usual denim jacket. He'd just walked in the door. "You were calling for Sam." His dark eyes were concerned.

I took a deep breath to tell him I was fine, it was just a dream— but I realized if I opened my mouth I was going to burst into tears. I clenched my jaw and shook my head a little, trying for a rueful smile, but John knew me too well. He gave my hands a sharp tug, pulling me forward and into his arms. It surprised me, but after a moment I threw my arms around his neck and held on for dear life, letting myself have the hug. He smelled like detergent and his house, that particular scent that places get through the unique combination of their contents. Sam had smelled the exact same way. When Charlie was born, it had just added to the scent a little, giving it a note of baby wipes and diaper ointment.

"I dreamed about that time in the park," I whispered, when I was sure of my voice. "We lost her, remember?"

"She'd just gone back to the car to get her book," John reminded me, his lips in my hair. He relaxed his grip, expecting me to pull away, but I wasn't ready to look him in the eyes yet, so I hung on. He let me. "She was fine, Allie."

"Don't call me Allie," I mumbled.

John released me and leaned back on his heels, and I suddenly realized that I had slid off the chair and was kneeling beside him. He pushed the hair out of my eyes with one hand, hooking it behind my ear. "Why not?" he asked.

I blinked in surprise. My family had asked me the same question a hundred times when I'd come home from Iraq. I'd just said I was used to Lex now, and I preferred it. This was the first time John had questioned the name. "Sam always thought it was to punish yourself, because you lived and your friends died," he said quietly. "She was wrong." Maybe it was the dream, or maybe I was still partly asleep, but I told him the truth. "It's because Allie died, too."

John just nodded, his eyes probing mine. Twenty-five years stretched between us in that look, two and a half decades of love and grief and missed chances. I focused on the clock behind his head. Five to eight. "Oh, shit!" I cried, jumping up. "I have to be somewhere."

"We should talk—" John began, but I grabbed my hoodie off the couch and skirted around him.

"Gotta run."

Chapter 22

On the way back to my cabin I took several deep breaths, trying to clear the scent of John's house from my mind.

John had been my first crush, from the moment he gave me CPR on a little beach along the Arkansas River, saving my life—or so I'd thought at the time, anyway. I'd carried that stupid, hormone-fueled torch for years. Then the towers at the World Trade Center fell, and the course of my life changed.

Sam supported my decision to join the army, but the rest of my family was disappointed and worried. My father, who'd spent much of his young adulthood protesting the Vietnam War, begged me to stay home, but eventually even he became resigned to my enlistment. It was John, of all people, who couldn't stop fighting my decision. He couldn't understand why I would want to leave Boulder for the army, why I thought it was my duty to help protect our country. We argued all throughout the summer after senior year, about the war, about politics, about patriotism. He said I was too smart for the army, I said that was a bullshit elitist attitude, and after circling around and around the issue for three months, he'd finally declared his feelings for me.

We spent one night together, at my parent's cabin, which was now my home. And then we said good-bye, neither of us able to accept the other's position.

John and Sam both matriculated at CU that fall, and I was deployed shortly thereafter. By the time I came home between my two tours, we had all moved on. John and Sam were dating, and I had a couple of relationships with fellow soldiers under my belt. More importantly, I was a different person. Harder, and sadder, and more determined than ever to be a soldier. I'd spent my whole childhood protecting Sam; as an adult I'd finally found a way to protect something bigger than one person, bigger than a million people. Okay, Sam and John's relationship stung a little, but for the most part my thoughts were on the other side of the world, with my fellow soldiers. I had a different life.

Sam and I drifted apart, though that had more to do with me being on the other side of the planet than it did with her dating my high school crush. When I eventually came home from the hospital in Germany, Sam re-emerged as a crucial part of my life, and John went where Sam went. Simple enough. I was so damaged then, the black cloud ever-present in my thoughts, that I barely felt any connection to the teenaged Allie who had loved John. I didn't know that girl anymore, and I was genuinely glad that Sam and John had found happiness together.

But now Sam was gone, and John and I were both alone, both without her. I saw him all the time, of course, especially once I started babysitting on Fridays. But I'd kept a distance between us, mostly out of fear. There was just something very seductive about the last person in the world who knows you to the core . . . and cares for you anyway.

As I pulled into my driveway I shook my head, pushing the old hurt away. It had been well over a decade since John and I had spent our one night together. Everything was different now. I was some kind of witch, apparently, and Charlie was a null, and . . . wait. I frowned.

Headlights flashed in my rearview mirror. It was eight o'clock exactly, and Quinn had arrived to pick me up. I got out of my car, and climbed straight into his sedan. "It can't be a coincidence," I said after I'd flung myself into the passenger seat.

"And hello to you, too," Quinn said evenly. He was wearing jeans and his leather jacket, with a white button-down shirt underneath. "What can't be a coincidence?"

"Charlie being a null, and me being a witch," I told him. "You said boundary witches were rare, and nulls even rarer. So how is it possible that the two of us are related, and we both have these . . . identities?"

Quinn frowned as he put the car in reverse and began backing out of the driveway. "I don't know much about probability," he allowed, "but it does seem unlikely."

"There has to be a connection."

He shrugged. "You should talk to Simon about it."

"Why Simon?"

Quinn looked over at me. "He's an evolutionary biologist. He studies this kind of thing."

"Oh. Right." I had forgotten all about Simon's day job in my quest to understand his other work. "I don't think he knows about Charlie being a null," I admitted. "I'm not sure I should tell him."

I glanced at Quinn, but his face gave away nothing. When it became obvious that I was waiting for a response, he sighed and said, "You might be right. The more people who know about your niece—"

"The more people there will be who want her for something," I finished. I nodded. "And although I mostly trust Simon, I don't know about . . . the rest of Clan Pellar."

A sly half grin appeared on Quinn's face, but his voice was nonchalant as he said, "Speaking of which, how did it go with Mama Pellar?"

"Oh, fantastic," I said sarcastically. "We're best friends now. I'm going to her house tomorrow so she can braid my hair."

The grin erupted on his face. "That bad, huh?"

"I take it you know what I am," I said.

Quinn nodded. "Maven told me when I called to report in last night." He shrugged. "For what it's worth, I didn't know about boundary witches, either."

"You still could have warned me," I pointed out. "Before I went to the Pellars' place."

"I'm not your girlfriend, Lex," Quinn said frankly. "If you can't handle Hazel Pellar *disliking* you, how can I count on you to help me protect my boss?"

I hated to admit it, but he had a point there. "So you're saying," I grumbled, "that I'll never be a good henchman if I can't suck it up?"

Quinn laughed out loud, sounding surprised again. I got the feeling he didn't laugh a lot.

"Tell me about Kirby," I prompted.

The smile dropped off Quinn's face as quickly as it had appeared. "Kirby is bad news," he said shortly.

I waved my hand to indicate that he should continue. Quinn sighed. "Look, when Maven and Itachi moved to Colorado, the vampires who came with them spread out over the state's bigger cities. I don't know why Maven and Itachi decided to stay in Boulder, but when they did, Itachi forced a few vampires to move with them. All of the vampires in town are either new, like me, or . . . *problematic*."

"What does that mean, 'problematic?'"

"It's a 'keep your enemies close' kind of thing," Quinn explained. "Most of the vampires who live in Boulder fucked up somewhere along the way. Including Kirby."

"What did he do?"

"He was pimping female vampires out to humans."

I contemplated that for a moment. "Like, literally pimping? Not a metaphor?" Quinn nodded. "So Itachi is against illegal behavior?"

He started to answer, then reconsidered. "I don't think Itachi has a problem with prostitution in general," he finally said. "But Kirby was also pressing the johns' minds to think they'd gotten laid when they hadn't. They were paying for nothing."

I snorted. "Sounds like they kind of deserved it."

"Maybe," Quinn allowed. "But it was only a matter of time before one of them realized he hadn't actually gotten laid and decided to start some shit with Kirby or one of the girls. Part of Itachi's job as dominus is to stop problems like that before they happen."

"Dominus? You said that before. I don't know what it means."

"Remember when I said vampires have a feudal system of government, at least in this state?" Quinn said. "'Dominus' is the Latin word for the upper class of vampires."

"What class are you?"

"Villani," he said shortly. "The servant class."

"How many classes are there?"

"Technically just the two. New vampires are all villani. Once you're strong enough to start making your own baby vampires or strike out on your own, you become a dominus. Some vampires never leave the villani class, though."

"Huh." I thought that over for a moment. "You said 'technically,'" I pointed out. "'Technically' there are only two classes."

Quinn hesitated. "I'm not sure how much I'm supposed to tell you," he admitted. "At any rate, all you need to know is that Kirby outclasses me, but I'm here on Itachi's orders. And Itachi is Kirby's sworn dominus."

I thought about pushing him further, but there really wasn't much point. Frankly, I was surprised he had come right out and admitted he couldn't tell me. "So Kirby has to answer your questions, but he doesn't have to be nice about it," I summed up.

"Exactly."

We turned onto College Ave, and I got my first glimpse of the Sigma Pi fraternity house. Kirby, Quinn explained, was an honest-to-goodness frat boy.

The frat house was a monstrous building, with several wings and a long, semi-circular sidewalk that was mostly covered by illegally parked Jeeps, Audi wagons, and fancy SUVs, all of them much nicer than my ten-year-old Outback. Boulder is a town full of rich kids, which I couldn't get too smarmy about. Technically, I'd been one of them.

Young frat-boy stereotypes were busily unloading crates and plastic shopping bags from the vehicles. *It's Friday night*, I remembered. They were throwing a party.

"How is this even possible?" I wondered. "I mean, he can't go to classes, right? Does he even drink beer?"

"Technically, we can eat or drink anything," Quinn said wryly, "but we can't digest anything but blood, so we have to throw it up afterwards." He shrugged. "Kirby doesn't live in the house, and the other fraternity brothers think he takes all his classes at night and online because he has a part-time job."

I was flabbergasted. "That sounds ridiculously complicated. And temporary. I mean, if he's not aging . . ."

"He's about five years into his Van Wilder bit now," Quinn told me, parking his sedan behind the last station wagon in the line. "He can only keep this up for another year or two, but that's long enough to annoy the hell out of Itachi, which I think is the whole point."

"Oh. Revenge for breaking up Kirby's prostitution ring?"

"I would avoid using the word 'revenge,'" Quinn said carefully. "Feuds can start when you throw around words like that. I would call it 'acting out a little.' But yes, Kirby was annoyed that he had to move to Boulder, so he got himself accepted to CU so he could force a time limit on his stay here. He'll eventually have to 'graduate,' and he's hoping Itachi will feel it necessary to send Kirby somewhere else."

"Oh." I thought about all that for a few seconds. "Who's Van Wilder?"

We walked past the sea of cars to the line of brick archways that formed the entrance to the house. Quinn reached out and snagged the shoulder of the nearest brother, a short, big-eared freshman holding the beer tap he'd obviously been sent to fetch from one of the cars. "I'm looking for Kirby," he said to the kid. "He around?"

The kid swallowed nervously a few times, looking from Quinn to me and back, and then blurted out, "Kirby not seen, have I," and darted into the building.

Quinn and I exchanged a glance. "Let me try," I suggested. Quinn made a little "after you" gesture. I saw another young-looking kid carrying a garbage-bag-sized sack of chips and a trough of dip. He was tall and broad-shouldered, with a great bushy beard and dark hair covering his arms and hands. I stepped into his path. "Excuse me, I'm looking for Kirby," I said, polite but firm.

In a perfect imitation of the first guy, the kid looked nervously back and forth between us, then gave a tiny nod and opened his mouth. Instead of speaking, he just let out a warbling cry, halfway between a roar and a bird call. He, too, ran into the house.

I shrugged at Quinn. "All things considered, that was not a terrible Chewbacca impression," he said thoughtfully.

"Should we keep trying?" I asked. "Or just go in?"

"I can't go in without an invitation," he reminded me. "From someone who lives here."

"Oh. Right."

An older kid came hurrying through the same archway that the hairy boy had entered, heading straight toward us. It took me a moment to recognize him as the other guy in Darcy's picture. I tilted my head toward him so Quinn would look, too. "Yeah, that's him," he muttered under his breath.

Kirby was built like a wrestler: short and muscular, with a "don't start with me or I'll flatten you" expression that eased up a little when he saw Quinn. He still had that aquiline nose, but he must have done something to disguise the prematurely thinning dark hair I'd seen in Darcy's photo, because now it looked thick and lustrous.

"Sorry about that, guys," he said in a relaxed, jovial tone that didn't match his hard-ass appearance. "The pledges are only allowed to speak in the manner of the movie characters we've chosen for them. I see you've met Chewbacca." He shook his head happily. "Kid's not going to have an easy time picking up girls tonight, let me tell you." In a quieter voice, he added, "Shake my hand and smile, Quinn, people are watching." Quinn reached out and shook, plastering on a warm smile to match the one Kirby was displaying. Then the frat-boy vampire looked at me, his eyes running up and down me in an *interested* manner that made me want to cross my arms over my chest. I resisted the urge. If he'd been an ordinary punk college kid, I would have said something, but the guy could probably bench press my Outback. "Who're you?" he asked me.

"Kirby, this is Lex. Lex, Kirby. She's being considered for a job with Itachi," Quinn said succinctly. "Did you hear about Victor and Darcy?"

Kirby's eyes narrowed. "Not here," he muttered. In a conversational voice, he added, "Sure, you're almost there. Walk to the corner with me, and I'll point out the street."

The three of us trooped to the edge of the semi-circular sidewalk, where Kirby pointed down the road, pretending to give us directions. "Yes, I heard that they're dead," he said quietly. "And I know they had it coming. I had no idea they were planning to try to kidnap a founding baby." A doubtful expression crossed his face, and he corrected himself. "Well, a null baby, I guess. Itachi put the word out that she's protected now."

I'd believed Maven and Itachi when they'd promised to protect my niece, but it was nice to have the independent confirmation. I cut my eyes to Quinn, letting him take the lead. "They both pledged troth to you," he said, his voice as low as Kirby's.

The other vampire nodded. "I made Victor myself. Took Darcy on when she came to Boulder a couple of years ago and started rooming with Victor."

"And who are you pledged to?" I broke in, just in case Quinn was wrong about the chain of command.

Kirby's fake-friendly expression wavered as his eyes narrowed at me. "Itachi, same as him," he retorted, tilting his head at Quinn. Kirby's eyes were on me, and he didn't see the little flicker on Quinn's face as he said this. I filed that away for later.

"How often did you see the two of them?" Quinn asked.

Smiling again—just a friendly college kid chatting with some out-of-towners—Kirby shrugged. "I'd check in with them once or twice a month, or they'd check in with me. And before you ask, no, they never mentioned doing any side work, and they weren't showing off a sudden influx of cash or bragging about a new job. We would meet somewhere, they'd tell me everything was fine, I'd remind them of the rules, and we'd split."

Quinn pulled the photo out of his pocket. "Is this you?"

Kirby's glance was quick and careless, his face revealing nothing. "You know it is."

"Who's the fourth person?"

The friendly, open expression Kirby had been forcing suddenly faded. "That's Nolan. He's one of the Denver vampires." He gave Quinn a quick glance. "I haven't seen him since the purge."

Quinn asked a few more questions after that, but Kirby really didn't seem to know anything more about Victor and Darcy's plans. "Look, I gotta get back to the party before this looks any more suspicious," he said, his face still cheerful. "Good luck and all. If anyone asks between here and the car, you two are trying to visit your nephew at Tau Kappa." Without waiting to see Quinn's response, Kirby turned on his heel and disappeared into the throng of people near the house's archway.

Quinn shot an annoyed look at Kirby's back and started toward his car. "Come on."

A DJ had set up giant speakers and a table while we were talking to Kirby, and as Quinn and I walked back to the car, "The Fallen" by Franz Ferdinand came pulsing out of the speakers. It seemed pretty appropriate.

Back in the car, I asked, "How is it possible that Itachi put that guy in charge of two other vampires?"

Quinn tilted his head to the side as he thought that over. "It's just kind of . . . how they do things," he said at last. "I can't really think of a comparison, except maybe Alcoholics Anonymous."

I chortled. "Sorry, what?"

"Sponsors," he said, completely serious. "In AA you have a sponsor, and you also become a sponsor. The whole thing is this big system so you learn responsibility."

"That sounds ridiculously stupid," I argued. "What's to stop Kirby from turning all his vampires against his boss?"

"Because Itachi is the only vampire in Colorado who can officially sanction kills," he said shortly. "Kirby might enjoy needling Itachi, but he knows exactly how far he can push him. Trust me, Kirby's dominus responsibilities are the one thing he takes seriously."

He was staring through the windshield, where we could just barely see Kirby standing in a loose circle with four of his frat brothers. As we watched, Kirby put Chewbacca in a headlock and started laughing.

"I don't think he was involved," Quinn said finally, mostly to himself. "Kidnapping a baby so you can train her the way you want, to do the things you want to do—that's a long-view move. I don't know Kirby all that well, but I just don't think he's a long-view kind of guy. I could see him knocking over a liquor store, sure, but kidnapping a baby?"

"He could have been the . . . you know, the fence," I offered, uncertain of the terminology. "The middleman for another buyer."

Quinn shook his head again. "Kirby's got plenty of money. That whole prostitution thing, which was a hell of a risk, was just for his own amusement. And selling a baby isn't particularly amusing, nor is the kind of heat that would have come down on him if he'd gotten away with your niece."

In front of us, Kirby had finally released poor Chewbacca and was telling the throng of brothers a story with great enthusiasm, waving his hands around to emphasize the point. The other frat boys were hanging on his every word, watching Kirby with the fervor of cult members. "I agree," I said finally. "It doesn't seem like his style. But do you think he knows something he's not telling us?" I wished we had gotten Kirby alone so I could have tried the mind-pressing thing again; I was way too new at it to experiment in front of a big crowd of college kids.

Quinn shrugged and started the car. "If he does, we're not going to find out tonight," he said pragmatically.

"Denver next?" I asked.

"Denver next."

Chapter 23

Boulder is only about thirty miles northwest of Colorado's capital and biggest city, and in perfect traffic you can make it there in forty minutes. But since plenty of people work in Boulder but live in the much less expensive Denver area, there were a lot of commuters. The traffic was far from perfect by the time we began the trek south.

Quinn called Itachi on the way and got an address for Nolan. When he hung up, I asked, "Did he tell you anything else about the guy?"

He shook his head. "Not really. I've heard a little about him, though. He was a big player during the purge."

"I don't know what that means," I said irritably. I was getting really tired of playing catch-up. Every time I thought I had a decent grasp of the Old World, someone started talking in made-up terms.

Quinn tapped his fingers on the steering wheel, his face expressionless as ever. Finally, he said, "Remember I told you there are no werewolves in Colorado?"

"When I was in the hospital, yeah."

"Well, this whole state used to be werewolf paradise, with a pack in most of the bigger cities. Then one of the alphas, Trask, decided to take over *all* the packs." Quinn eyed me. "You ever met a wild dog? Or a pack of wild dogs?"

Some unpleasant images from Iraq flashed in my head before I could push them aside. "Unfortunately."

"Trask turned his people into that, or gave it his best shot, anyway." Quinn's voice was perfectly level, his voice betraying no emotion at all. He might as well have been describing the history of deforestation. "Of course, a few of the wolves tried to stand up to Trask. He killed them, too."

I stared at him. "Someone had to have noticed."

Quinn lifted a disinterested shoulder. "They did, but the Old World is like the Wild West. You stake your claim on a patch of land, and you do your best to defend it. As long as Trask wasn't drawing enough attention to alert the foundings to our presence, no one wanted to challenge him. He was too strong."

"Someone must have stepped in," I objected. I didn't like bullies, and I *really* didn't like the kind that got away with killing people.

"The witches did—sort of," Quinn confirmed. "When Trask was on his rampage, three of Colorado's big clans got caught in the crossfire. One of their leaders decided something had to be done."

"Hazel," I whispered.

Quinn nodded. "Hazel went to the oldest, most powerful vampire in the United States, and she begged for help."

"Itachi?"

A brief, amused smile graced Quinn's face. "Maven is the one with the serious power. Hazel went to her." It was the most unguarded thing he'd said yet, and I saw him glance over at me, unsure if he'd overstepped. I made my face neutral. "Anyway. There's a whole long story, but basically the witches cut a deal: if Maven killed Trask and forced all the werewolves out of the state, Hazel and her clans would swear total loyalty to the vampires for a period of twenty years."

I remembered the way Hazel had reacted when Simon explained that Maven wanted me trained. "And Maven really did it."

"Yes," Quinn said. "This was thirteen years ago, before my time. All I really know is that she summoned every vampire who'd sworn troth to her—and believe me, the girl's lived long enough to collect quite a few allies. She promised them a place in her new enclave if they fought for her. Itachi became her second-in-command, and he called in all of his vampires, too, including Nolan."

"Jesus, it sounds like a war," I said in awe. "How the hell did they keep it quiet?"

Quinn shrugged. "Like I said, it was before my time, but Maven's been covering up murders for hundreds of years. Anyway, when it was over, most of the regular vampires who helped ended up in Denver or Colorado Springs, including Nolan."

I considered that for a few minutes. Something about the dynamic between Maven and Itachi felt off to me, and I said so.

"Maven . . . doesn't want to lead," Quinn explained after a moment's hesitation. "I'm not sure why, exactly. Something to do with her history. She has serious power, but no interest in being in charge of a territory. Itachi, on the other hand, doesn't have as much juice, but he's plenty ambitious. So he leads and she kind of . . ."

"Acts as his muscle?" I suggested.

He smiled. "Something like that."

I thought that over for a few minutes. I couldn't really see Maven, the teenaged bag lady with the orange hair, as the equivalent of a four-star general. Then again, she *had* seemed much more powerful than any of the other vampires I'd met. "How old *is* Maven?" I wondered aloud.

"I'm not really sure," he admitted. "But from things she's said, I'd guess Middle Ages." His expression turned grave, and I got the message: *don't piss her off.*

I would sure as hell try.

We headed into southwestern Denver, and a little over an hour after we left Boulder, Quinn pulled into the parking lot of a swanky condo building in the Cherry Creek neighborhood. It was a mostly residential area, with lots of cul-de-sacs and big single-family houses that probably cost more than I'd earn in two lifetimes at the Flatiron Depot. Nolan lived in a lone condo park in which six or seven buildings were clustered around a small central area, where there was probably a pool and a walking path. We circled the enormous square parking lot a few times until we found a sign for units 8 to 12.

The inside of the building had the same restrained sense of wealth as the outside, like this was a place for people who had plenty of money but no desire to flaunt it. In the lobby, Quinn pushed the button for Nolan's unit a few times, getting no response. He glanced over his shoulder at me, and I shrugged. This was his show. I was just the on-the-job trainee. Quinn sighed and glanced around, then planted his feet and tugged *hard* at the handle of the interior door. It cracked open with a terrible metallic crunch.

Nolan's condo was on the basement level. We found the stairs, which led us past a small gym and a sauna before depositing us in front of the door of unit 12. Quinn knocked, waited for a moment, then knocked again. "Nolan?" he called, his voice authoritative.

"He's probably just out," I reasoned. "Getting, um, food." I still hadn't completely wrapped my head around the idea of vampires existing on blood they drank from regular people.

"Probably," Quinn said, but he looked up and down the hall again. When he was sure no one was coming, he got down on his hands and knees and put his face right next to the crack of the door. Then he *sniffed* in long, deep inhalations that held no embarrassment or self-consciousness.

I tensed. Of the few vampires I'd met, Quinn seemed the most human. But moments like this one reminded me that I wasn't dealing with an ordinary man. I heard Simon's voice in my head. *Vampires aren't like us, Lex.*

I thought of the horror in Hazel Pellar's eyes when she looked at me. Then again, I wasn't much like "us" either, was I?

Finally Quinn straightened up, looking put out. "What?" I asked.

"Blood," Quinn said shortly. "Too much blood." He took a closer look at the door, which was far less secure than Victor and Darcy's door had been. There was a single dead bolt and an ordinary knob lock. "From now on, I'm bringing lock picks everywhere we go," he grumbled. Before I could respond, he leaned back and kicked the door so fast that I could barely follow the motion of his leg. The door shot open, and I heard the knob crunch into the plaster wall behind it. I raised my eyebrows at Quinn. "What is it with you and doors?" I asked. He gave me a sheepish look and stepped forward, flicking a light switch on his right.

My first thought was that whoever had killed Nolan had made no effort to hide his body. The dead vampire's skeleton was sitting three feet away from the door, wearing jeans and a blue T-shirt. The clothes puddled around the skeleton, which was situated on top of a large red stain. I was so busy looking at all that bright red blood that it took me a moment to realize there was no skull attached to the body.

"Lex," Quinn said impatiently, and I registered that it was at least the second time he'd said my name. "You need to come in and close the door."

"Right," I said stupidly, stepping all the way in and shoving the door closed behind me. It didn't latch, but it stayed more or less shut. "Where's his head?" My voice came out sounding like a little kid's, and I swallowed.

"Here." Quinn had wandered into a small kitchenette on our left, just behind the counter. "It rolled."

"Right." I shook off the shock—I'd seen much worse, just not this *weird*—and moved closer to the body. "Do we think it's Nolan?" I asked.

Quinn came over to the skeleton, studied it for a second, and then squatted down near the left arm. I tried not to flinch as he gently picked up the skeleton's hand, which snapped loose in his fingers despite the care he took. There was something shiny on the wrist, which slid off the forearm bone into Quinn's hand. He studied the fancy-looking watch for a moment and tossed it to me. "It's him."

I caught it and, seeing an inscription on the back, read it aloud. "For N, my greatest soldier, a token of my thanks. —I." I looked up at Quinn. "This could have been planted on the body," I pointed out. "Nolan might have killed someone else to fake his death."

Quinn shook his head. "Look around. This wasn't a fight. Besides the big pool, there are only a few drops of blood on the carpet, and none on the walls. Nolan let someone else come in, someone he trusted enough to turn his back. That's how he died." He jumped up and circled the body to stand behind me, gently taking my shoulders and positioning me just inside the door. "You're Nolan. While your back is turned"—he swung an imaginary dagger—"I take a swing and lop off your head, which isn't as easy as they make it look in the movies, by the way. You pretty much need vampire strength. Anyway, this happened fast, just inside the door. You wouldn't stop to put a watch on someone before chopping off their head."

"It could have been put on the body afterward," I pointed out, although we both knew I was just playing devil's advocate.

Quinn was shaking his head before I'd finished the sentence. "That thing is brittle as shit—pardon my language." He nodded at the watch in my hand. "The clasp on the watch is complicated. No way you could get it on the skeleton without snapping off its hand."

"Gross," I said. "But okay, I agree that it's probably Nolan." I glanced around. I'd never seen an actual beheading, but I'd seen arterial spray before. Quinn was right. There wasn't enough blood. "But that doesn't explain why the blood is in one neat puddle like that. If his head was cut off, shouldn't it have spurted everywhere?"

"Yes," Quinn said absently. "But I don't think he bled at all." Before I could ask what that meant, he abruptly reached forward and flipped the skeleton over.

I jumped, half expecting it to roll the extra two feet and bump into my ankles. But it just lay there on its back, allowing me to see the empty plastic bag that had been beneath it.

"A blood bag," Quinn said. He got up and went over to the fridge, beckoning me to follow. I stepped carefully over the body and joined him.

He opened the fridge door, exposing neat rows of deep red IV bags. "Most of us drink live, but Maven has a private donation center set up for anyone who wants it, or for those of us who aren't great at pressing foundings," Quinn told me. "The bag was still was in his hand when he answered the door, which confirms it was a vampire." Before I could ask, he added, "If it'd been a human, Nolan wouldn't have still had the blood bag in his hand."

Okay. "What do we do now?" I asked.

Quinn looked straight at me, his gaze so intense that I flinched. "Nolan being dead . . . it complicates things," he said frankly. He dug into his pocket and pulled out a cell phone. "I gotta make a call, and then we'll take a quick look around."

Quinn, as it turned out, wasn't responsible for doing the vampire dirty work in Denver— they had their own person for that. After placing the call, he grabbed a wooden chair from the small table in the living room and used it to prop the door shut. "We don't have a lot of time," he said, "so search fast." He looked around. "Why don't you start in the living room? I'll head for the back bedroom, and we'll meet in the middle."

So for the second time in two days, I found myself searching a vampire's quarters for clues. Nolan's place was the opposite of Darcy and Victor's filthy college apartment: the condo was tidy and sparsely decorated, with simple, comfortable furniture and lots of neutral colors. There weren't even a lot of places to search. I had only gotten as far as flipping through the stack of reading material on Nolan's side table—fishing magazines, an invitation to a condo association meeting, some junk mail—before Quinn called for me.

I followed his voice to the little bedroom at the end of the hall. I rounded the door frame, and right in the center of the otherwise empty room I saw a big pile of brand-new baby gear, still packed in bags and boxes. There was a high chair, a Pack 'n Play, an economy-sized box of diapers, a changing pad, and two bags bearing the logo of a popular kids' clothing store. I reached into the clothing bag and pulled out a package of onesies, size eighteen months. An involuntary shiver shook me where I stood.

"This is where they were bringing Charlie," I whispered.

Chapter 24

Quinn just nodded, his face expressionless. I tried to focus on the logic, the chain of events, before I lost myself in *what could have happened*. "Victor and Darcy picked up Charlie," I said slowly. "They realized they'd forgotten to bring any diapers from John's house . . . and maybe they didn't know Nolan already had some here. So they stopped at the Flatiron Depot to grab a package before leaving Boulder." I looked around the room. "This wasn't her final destination, though. Darcy said their senior was going to take Charlie to the 'merchant,' which I figured meant middleman."

"That makes sense," Quinn agreed. "They'd want to get her out of Itachi's enclave as quick as possible. Besides, if the plan was for Charlie to stay here, Nolan would have set all this stuff up. My guess is that he was storing it here, maybe overnight, and was planning to hand it off with the baby."

"But who killed Nolan? It wasn't Victor or Darcy. That puddle of blood is bright red. He was killed tonight, probably while we were talking to Kirby." So not Kirby, either.

"Well, we know there's a fourth player in the kidnapping," Quinn said. "The person who wanted Charlie. Whoever it is doesn't want to make another grab for her right now, not while Itachi and Maven are watching her. But Nolan was a loose thread."

"Meanwhile, we're looking for the kidnapper," I finished. "It was only a matter of time before we found Nolan, and whoever did this knew it." I gritted my teeth, fighting down the urge to punch something. "We must have missed this guy by *minutes*."

Quinn checked his watch. "Speaking of which, we need to get going."

"What? Are you serious?" My voice came out harsher than I'd intended, and frustration was turning my stomach. Quinn and I were at a dead end, and we both knew it. I just wasn't ready to admit it yet. "We've barely looked around."

"The Denver crew's gonna be here any second," the vampire explained.

"But we don't *know* anything," I protested. "We haven't searched enough—"

"There's not going to be anything else here, Lex," Quinn insisted. "Nolan was a pro. He was too careful to leave evidence of who he was working for, and even if he *had* made a mistake, the killer would have found it first."

I pointed at the stack of baby supplies. "Then why didn't the killer take this stuff?"

"Because," Quinn said patiently, like I was a particularly dim-witted child, "he—or she—wanted us to find it."

I shook my head, confused. "Why would he want us to find it?"

"Because he's done, at least for now." Quinn nodded at the baby stuff. "He didn't move it to a new location, he didn't smuggle Nolan out of state to keep him away from Itachi's investigation. We're supposed to find this and know that he's done. It's over, Lex."

I stared at him, incredulous. "*Over* over? Are you suggesting that we just stop looking for whoever *kidnapped* my niece?"

There was a knock on the front door, and Quinn grimaced. "Can we agree that there's not going to be anything else in here, and move this conversation outside?"

I allowed Quinn to lead me down the hall and back to the entryway, where we let in two vampires dressed in jeans and CU sweatshirts. The woman looked to be about my age, with a blonde ponytail tied high on her head and a gigantic tote bag in lieu of a purse. The man seemed a few years younger, with an earring and shaggy hair that curled past his ears. They looked like any normal couple on their way home from a football game, except for their unreadable expressions and the easy, fluid way they moved. Quinn didn't introduce us; he just gave the vampires a tight nod as we edged past them toward the door. They returned the nod in perfect, eerie unison, and I was careful not to touch them as we went by.

Back at the car, Quinn started for the driver's door, then glanced over his shoulder at my face and stopped. "What do you mean, it's over?" I demanded. "We're not done. *I'm* not done. Someone killed Nolan, and whoever did it was in on Charlie's kidnapping." I glared at him, my hands balled into fists. There were people talking and laughing at the far end of the lot, and Quinn stepped very close to me before answering.

"I'll talk to Maven and Itachi," he said quietly. "But I know exactly what they're going to say." A bitter expression crossed his face. "'Sometimes the cost of secrecy is not knowing the whole truth.' Three of the four players are dead, and the fourth player is walking away. That will be good enough for them."

"But there are other threads to pull," I said through gritted teeth. "Itachi has contacts with the police, right? Maybe he can get into Nolan's financials and find out who paid for the baby stuff. Or we can go back to Kirby and push harder. Victor and Darcy's neighbors, we never did get to talk to them, and maybe they—"

"*Stop*, Lex," Quinn interrupted. "This guy killed a high-ranking vampire, a frickin' general in Itachi's army. You don't think he'll have covered the rest of his bases? And if we go poking around at Nolan's bank or Darcy's building, we may end up accidentally pointing him at people who really don't know anything. We've been outmaneuvered. We're done."

"And where does this leave me?" I demanded. "I was supposed to help you find and stop this guy. It was my goddamned field test.

If I don't get this position with Itachi, he's not going to leave Charlie alone." My voice broke on Charlie's name, and I hated how weak that sounded.

"I'll tell them you did good work," he promised. "I'll make sure he and Maven know this wasn't your fault."

"That's not good enough," I sputtered.

Quinn studied my face for a moment. I don't know what he saw there, but he closed even more of the distance between us, until we were close enough for him to whisper. "Do you need to hit me?" he said.

My eyes widened. "What?"

"You're shaking," he said matter-of-factly. I looked down at my fists. Sure enough, there was a visible tremor. Glancing around, Quinn quickly reached out and grabbed my hands, stilling them.

I reacted without thinking, jerking my hands back and snapping them out to shove Quinn *hard* into the side of the car. He hit it with an audible thump but didn't react. The voices at the other end of the lot went quiet.

Quinn just leaned there, his eyes probing mine. "Feel better?" he asked, his voice still low. "I meant it, you know. You can hit me if you want. You might break your hand, but if it you think it'll help, I won't stop you."

Balling up my fists, I spun on my heel and paced a few feet away, my body thrumming with unspent anger. When I was sure I wasn't actually going to hit him, I turned and stalked back. He had straightened up, but was still leaning against the car, motionless. I just stared at him, seething. I'd struggled with anger since I'd gotten out of the army, but something different was happening now. It felt like rage was rolling through every part of my body, seeping out from my chest down into my legs and fingers, pushing out against the inside of my skin. *You'll feel things harder*, Simon had told me. I felt like I was going to explode.

Quinn's nostrils flared suddenly, and he glanced down. "Lex," he said softly, genuine concern in his voice. I followed his eyes down to my left hand, which he took gently, turning it over and uncurling my fingers. There were four thin trickles of blood trailing from my palm. I'd clenched my fist hard enough to draw blood. "Oh," I said lamely. "Does that—"

Quinn dropped my hand and jerked away from me. His pupils had dilated, and he turned his head, avoiding my eyes. "Christ . . . did Simon say anything about your magic growing?"

"Yeah, I guess . . . why?"

"I can smell it in your blood," he whispered, his face clouding over. "It's . . . it's like it's singing to me."

I shrunk back from him. *An affinity for vampires.* You got that right, Simon. Apparently death magic was coursing through my veins, and that affinity worked both ways. Great.

Quinn reached into his pocket and pulled out the car keys, holding them out and staring at them. "You should probably drive yourself back to Boulder. I'll catch a bus or something. Please, Lex, I . . . I don't want to hurt you."

His gaze flicked toward my face for an instant, vulnerable and begging, and I forgot my anger. Quinn's eyes were full of pain, some sort of raw wound that hadn't healed, that probably never would.

He had hurt someone, once.

Compassion surged inside me. I looked around quickly, but I didn't have a tissue or anything, and my purse was still locked in the car. Without thinking, I peeled off my long-sleeved shirt and wound it around my hand as tightly as I could. Then I checked Quinn's face. "Better?"

He nodded and dropped his arm, his relief evident. "Thank you."

"Who did you hurt?" I said abruptly. I'd meant it in a supportive way, like *I'm here if you need to talk*, but I was out of practice with talking about real things, and it came out all wrong.

He met my eyes, pain still raw on his face. "My wife," he said softly. He shuddered. Actually *shuddered*, although I seriously doubted that vampires needed to react physically to emotional stimuli. It was so . . . human.

"Quinn . . ." I whispered. "It's okay. You're not going to hurt me." I reached up with my right hand and touched his cheek, leaning into him. He bowed his head, and I touched my forehead to his. Neither of us moved, and I felt something stir in me, something I'd put to sleep a long time ago. Quinn's hands wrapped around my waist, and he pulled my body forward, which drew my mouth closer to his . . .

"Hey, dude, you gonna give her your jacket or what?"

Quinn and I jerked apart. The voice had come from a laughing girl of about twenty-five, who was tottering past us on spiky heels, heading toward the apartment building. She was on the arm of a dumb-looking jock of a guy, all muscles and gold chain necklaces, and he gave my chest a frank stare as they went by. I was suddenly very aware that a) it was all of forty degrees outside, and b) I was wearing a soft jersey camisole Sam had gotten me for Christmas and no bra.

I shivered, still clutching the shirt around my hand, hugging it in to my chest to cover my erect nipples. It didn't do much to hide my embarrassment, though. I'd almost just *kissed* him, for God's sake. I couldn't trust myself, couldn't trust that whatever I was feeling for Quinn wasn't the result of my swelling connection to magic. I took a deep, shuddering breath.

Quinn mumbled something and shrugged out of his leather jacket, leaning forward to wrap it around me. "Thatta boy," the party girl called over her shoulder. "Whoops." She wobbled on her heels and for a second I thought she was gonna go down, but the jock caught her, sending Quinn a wink. "Have a good night," he yelled.

"Take me home," I muttered to Quinn.

Quinn insisted that I couldn't come along to talk to Maven and Itachi. We argued about it for most of the trip back from Denver, but he was adamant. He thought I was too emotional about the whole thing to deal with them directly, but he promised to call me after his conversation and fill me in.

But he didn't call me that night. At sunrise, I went to bed, now worried that Maven or Itachi had decided to punish Quinn for what they might have seen as his failure to catch Charlie's kidnapper. I meant to nap for just a couple of hours, but was awoken by the ringing of my phone a little after seven I'd been asleep for more than twelve hours. I grabbed my cell and saw Quinn's number in the display.

"Hello?" I said cautiously.

"It's me." Quinn sounded fine, and I felt a momentary sense of relief before I remembered to be irritated with him. "Sorry I didn't call last night."

"What happened?"

"Hang on a second." There was a pause, and I heard the sound of a door closing. Then another. Then a third. "I'm at Magic Beans," he explained. "Just trying to get some privacy."

"What did they say?" I said, more insistent this time. "Can we keep looking for the kidnapper?"

"No," he said heavily. "I was right. They agreed that three out of the four is good enough for now."

I kicked at a pillow in frustration, sending it flying off the bed. Dopey looked up from her spot beside me, bewildered. "Shit."

"I know. If it helps, though, your niece is now considered permanently under Itachi's protection."

"What about me?"

He paused. "I swear, I told them you did a good job."

"But?" I prompted.

"But . . . they want to think about it a little more. They're vampires, so 'we need to think about it' could mean for a night or a month. Meanwhile, no one's gonna touch Charlie."

I flopped back against the remaining pillow. "*They* can touch her," I said coldly. It wasn't enough for Charlie to be safe from every monster but two. I wanted her to grow up safe, period.

"The kid is what? A year and a half?" Quinn pointed out. "They've got no use for the baby until she's at least talking. You just need to be patient."

Be patient. Yeah, right. Maybe if I went and talked to them myself . . .

But Quinn sensed exactly what I was thinking. "Lex," he sighed, and I thought I heard actual concern in his voice. "Seriously, this isn't the time to run over here and make your case. Their whole concern is that you're too close to this . . . and that you'll be too emotional and unpredictable while your magic comes in."

"You *told* them about that?" It was stupid to feel betrayed, but I did.

"I had to," he said, his voice thick with regret.

I didn't trust myself to answer him. Simon had warned me that Quinn's first loyalty would be to other vampires, and I'd let myself believe he was on my side. What an idiot.

"Look, just . . . keep up the magic lessons," he said when I didn't speak. "Do anything you can think of to make yourself more valuable to them, especially Maven. I think she likes the idea of a boundary witch working for them. She's just not sure about you personally. Don't do anything to scare her off."

"Fine," I said shortly. "I can do that."

Well, I could try.

Chapter 25

I'd missed a call from Simon while I was sleeping on Saturday. I called him back, and we arranged another training session for the following week. That Sunday I went back to work at the Flatiron Depot. Big Scott had scheduled a second manager for my first night back, so I ended up having a nice, quiet shift restocking the shelves and working on inventory. At break time, I ate two pieces of the "Welcome Back" cake Big Scott had bought from the nearest Safeway, and by the time I returned to work Monday night, all the cake was gone and everything was back to normal. I found it surprisingly comforting to be at work, where I always knew what to do and nobody threw around made-up words for mythological happenings. A couple of nights later I even worked with Bettina, who still seemed confused as hell about what had happened the night Charlie was taken. I figured out pretty quickly that it was best not to mention it.

The following Friday I took care of Charlie like always, and the next night my parents took me out to dinner "just to catch up." My mother spent most of the time talking about my father's upcoming sixtieth birthday party, and I pretended that I'd never forgotten about it. The Luthers had a big family dinner every few weeks to celebrate all the birthdays that month—there were too many of us for individual celebrations—but this was going to be different. It was the first major family event since Sam's death, and my mother was determined that it would be a Big Deal. There's not much of a

Who's Who in Boulder, but what little "high society" we did have would all be there.

A little more time passed, and with the exception of spending a few afternoons a week with the Pellars, my life actually started getting back to normal. My extended family slowly toned down their hand-wringing after what they'd perceived as a garden-variety kidnapping attempt, if there is such a thing. I went hiking with my cousin Anna, babysat for my other cousin Brie, and went to the shooting range with Elise. She gave me the good news that the police had decided I was no longer an official suspect.

"Even Keller?" I asked skeptically.

She made a face. "Okay, he still thinks it was you, but then he probably thinks you're behind every bad thing that happens in Boulder."

"He's like the Sheriff Teasle to my John Rambo," I grumbled, but I couldn't entirely blame the guy, either.

When I wasn't spending time with my family or the herd or at work, I kept to myself, which was exactly the way I liked it.

But although days, and then weeks, slipped by with no word from the vampires and nothing remarkable happening in Charlie's life, there was still a part of me that just couldn't relax. Mostly it was because I'd started having these dreams. They were tangled, patchy things, wisps of conversation layered under snatches of dread and the occasional bolt of pure panic. I would wake up disoriented and confused, with Sam's face in my mind and the vague sensation that I needed to be with Charlie *right now*. There were usually three or four members of the herd staring at me when I woke up, with resigned expressions on their faces that said their mistress had finally lost it.

Now that I was back on my regular work schedule, I was sleeping from midmorning to late afternoon, and the dreams haunted me more often than not. After one terrible week during which I had the dreams every "night," I started the habit of driving over to John's house around sunset, when he usually put Charlie to bed. I would park a few houses down and watch the house, like I was on a stakeout in one of those generic cop shows. His neighborhood housed a lot of professors who came and went at odd hours, but if anyone ever noticed me, they didn't seem troubled by it. I still felt like a creep or, at the very least, an idiot, but I couldn't seem to stop.

During these vigils, I thought a lot about my dead sister, wondering for the thousandth time what she would think of all this. I thought about John, whom I'd been careful to avoid seeing alone. And, to my surprise, I thought about Quinn, especially the moment when he'd begged me not to let him hurt me.

Each time when I finally left to let the dogs out before my eleven o'clock shift, I would feel the dread and panic start to bleed back into my mood.

One Thursday night in mid-October, I was sitting in my car outside John's, munching on a bag of barbecue chips and waiting for him to get home with the baby so I could get my hit of Charlie-is-safe relief. It was nearly eight, so I figured he'd probably gone to my parents' or his mom's house for dinner and would be back any minute.

There was a sudden knock on the passenger window. I jumped in my seat, and looked over to see Quinn waving at me with a little smirk on his face. We hadn't spoken since the night he'd called to tell me the vampires weren't sure about me. Part of me still hadn't forgiven him for dropping the case . . . or for telling Itachi and Maven that I was unstable.

Even if it was true.

I sighed and unlocked the door, watching as he climbed into the car. To my horror, I realized that I was actually kind of glad to see him. Between the way he'd tattled on me and Simon's warning about vampires' motives, I wanted to loathe his undead guts. But there was also a part of me that found him very . . . comfortable to be around.

"Is it absolutely necessary for you to scare the shit out of me every time we meet?" I demanded.

"Hey, Lex," he said, ignoring the question. "How's tricks?" He glanced around the car. I keep it fairly neat, but there were a few empty containers from fountain sodas and chips that I hadn't gotten to yet. "I see you've developed an exciting new interest in stalking."

"Is there news from Itachi?" I asked fervently. "Did they make a decision about me?"

He shook his head. "No, sorry. The coffee shop gets really busy this time of year—midterms—and there's been a bit of trouble with one of the Colorado Springs vampires. I think they've put the whole situation with your niece on the back burner. Charlie's still protected," he added hastily. "Just not a priority right now."

I didn't bother saying that Charlie was always a priority to *me*. Quinn already knew. "Then why are you here?" I asked coolly.

He gave a little shrug. "Just checking in. I hear you've been keeping up with the magic lessons. How did you get Mama Pellar's permission?"

I smiled wryly. Three afternoons a week, Simon or Lily came over to the cabin to teach me magic. Whenever I asked about Hazel's thoughts on my training, though, they inevitably changed the subject. "I don't actually know," I admitted. "I'm not one hundred percent sure she even knows." I got the sense that Simon and Lily had told Hazel that it was better to have me on their side than for me to be an unknown quantity, but they were too polite to tell me that.

Quinn nodded impassively. "How are the lessons going?"

I automatically opened my mouth to answer but caught myself just in time, turning in my seat to fully face Quinn. John's street was well lit, and the vampire was looking at me with calm curiosity. "Who's asking?" I said bluntly.

A flicker of surprise crossed his features, either because he didn't expect me to see through him, or because I'd hurt his feelings. If I hadn't seen the look on his face when my palm had started bleeding, I wouldn't even know whether he *had* feelings. "Just me, Lex," he said quietly. "I promise."

"The lessons have been fine," I said. Then I sighed, relenting. "Okay, not that fine. I'm learning more about what I can do—Simon geeks out about it on a regular basis—and it turns out I've got plenty of juice. But so far I'm a filter, not a focus."

Quinn nodded again. "You can pull the magic through you," he translated, "but you can't push it where you want it to go?"

"Something like that." I gave him a brief rundown of my training. For most of the sessions, we would go out behind my small backyard and stand near the fence that formed a border with the forest just beyond my cabin. Whichever Pellar was helping me would have me sense out the life in the forest. I had gotten good at visualizing myself putting on night-vision goggles and then filtering my vision until I caught the glowing sparks of mice, squirrels, and rabbits. I started to understand the sizes and shapes, although that wasn't precisely the right word, of the different creatures.

When Lily was my teacher, the practice would be laid-back and exploratory: she was big on improvisation, letting the lessons go wherever they took us. Eventually she started working with me on tethering down my emotions so my magic wouldn't flare up and overwhelm me anymore. Simon, on the other hand, was much more organized and regimented. He actually brought a clipboard out to the backyard with us, using it to take notes on my capabilities. I'd made him swear he wouldn't kill anything just for my education again, so his big thing was to have me practice turning on my magical plane mindset over and over again until it became second nature. When I got good at switching it on and off quickly, we started working on concentration, making sure I could hold the thermal-imaging mindset without getting easily distracted. Which usually meant trying to do it while Simon tossed pinecones at my face.

One day, during a Simon practice, I had a breakthrough. We were working on expanding and contracting the beam of my scrutiny, so I would concentrate on a space about twelve feet by twelve feet, and then narrow my focus down to a single small nest of field mice within that square before repeating the process. That afternoon practice had run long, and the sky had started to darken while we were still working. As I was concentrating on the mice, there was a sudden rustle of feathers and air, and I felt the larger spark of an owl swoop down onto my mice, snatching one of them up.

As the mouse died, its spark didn't just fade out—it *changed* into that same sickly, yellowish-brown, concentrated mist that had drifted toward me from the dead mouse in the hayloft. And I had a realization.

"As it turns out," I told Quinn now, "I've been feeling these sort of sparks of life, but they're more than just little blips on my radar. They're *containers* for the death-essence. Or at least that's how my brain interprets it."

Quinn considered that for a long moment, then asked, "What happened to the essence when the mouse died?"

I shivered. "It drifted toward me. It was . . . attracted to me."

"Wow," Quinn said, impressed. "You really do have death in your blood."

After that epiphany, if I really concentrated during my practices, I could actually *feel* the death-essence within each blue buzz of life. After all, the potential for death is in all living things. I didn't say that to the undead vampire beside me, though.

"Can you do the same stuff that the other witches do?" Quinn said idly. "Protection spells and healing and whatnot?"

"No," I admitted. Simon had tried to teach me a very simple charm to clean something. I'd seen him use it on an old grill behind the cabin, forcing the dust and grime off it in one small, potent burst of magic. Then he'd reached down and picked up a fistful of dry dirt, depositing it on top of the grill. I hadn't been able to clean off a speck. "Apparently, if it doesn't have to do with death, I can't access it."

"What about your niece?" he pressed. "Did you ever ask Simon about a connection between nulls and boundary witches?"

I eyed him suspiciously. "What is this, a quilting bee?" I retorted. "Do you really expect me to believe you tracked me down just to play catch-up?"

A long moment ticked by with Quinn's face frozen on neutral. "Yes, I asked," I muttered.

"What did he say?"

"He's looking into it," I said tiredly. This particular subject had been an ongoing source of disappointment for me. "Apparently there aren't many witches who study the scientific or historical connections between different types of magic, or if there are, they don't talk to each other. Simon's been doing research, but he said it isn't easy to find records of nulls, and the ones that he's found show no particular connection to boundary witches."

"What about the other way around?" Quinn asked. "Has he found boundary witches who have connections to nulls?"

I shook my head. "That's even harder, apparently. Nobody's wanted to admit to being a boundary witch since the Inquisition." Not that I could really blame them.

"You could ask Maven," Quinn pointed out. "She's known a few nulls."

I considered that for a moment, then shook my head. "Maybe after Simon exhausts all his options. Right now I'm still trying to get her and Itachi to see me as a useful employee. I'm not sure asking for favors is the right way to go about it."

We sat there in silence for a few more minutes, staring at John's house. "What exactly is your plan with this?" Quinn said eventually. "You're hoping the bad guy makes a run at her during the three hours a day you happen to be watching?"

I thought of the dreams I'd been having. "It's not that," I told him stiffly. "It's just that these are the only three hours of the day when I've been getting any peace." He opened his mouth to respond, but before he could say anything, I added tartly, "See, some of us actually have a hard time letting a murderous kidnapper get away with it."

Quinn didn't meet my eyes, just stared straight ahead out the windshield. His jaw tensed and untensed, as if he was trying to decide whether or not to speak. Finally he sighed and reached into the breast pocket of his leather jacket. He pulled out a wad of paper and tossed it to me.

"What's this?" I clicked on the car's reading light and unfolded the bundle, scanning the top few lines. "Phone records?"

He nodded. "For Victor, Darcy, Kirby, and Nolan. Those weren't easy to get, by the way. Vampires almost exclusively use prepaid cell phones."

"You pressed some people," I summarized. I looked down at the list of numbers, but nothing jumped out. "Is there anything here?"

"Not really. They all mostly called each other, like a closed loop. And Itachi and Magic Beans. Kirby contacted his fraternity brothers, of course. Darcy called a few clothing stores."

I let my hands rest in my lap and stared at Quinn. "Do Maven and Itachi know you're doing this?"

He shook his head. "And I could get in a lot of trouble if they found out. Technically, neither one ordered me *not* to pursue the case, but if they knew I was following up on my own, they'd probably be pissed."

"Then why do it?" I asked.

He finally turned his head to stare at me, his cool eyes assessing mine. "Oh," I said stupidly. "You did this for me."

"Some of us have a hard time letting a murderous kidnapper get away with it," he said, throwing my own words back at me.

At that moment John's hybrid car finally pulled into the driveway, and with a breath of relief I watched as my brother-in-law stepped out of it, wearing his denim jacket, and opened the back door to pull out Charlie's car seat. I caught a glimpse of the familiar tuft of dark hair as he swung the car seat around the door. John reached back into the car and pulled out something else, too, and I found myself leaning forward a little as I tried to make it out: a wide, thin package on a hanger.

"It's a tux," Quinn mused. His night vision was no doubt a hell of a lot better than mine. "Huh. He doesn't really seem like a tux kind of guy."

I rolled my eyes. "It's for my dad's sixtieth birthday party," I explained. "My mom had the bizarre idea that black tie would be fun. So now all the Luther Shoes employees who are going have to run out and rent tuxedos, the poor bastards."

Quinn's mouth quirked. "I take it you're not a fan of formalwear."

"I'm a fan of comfort, durability, and movement," I said archly. "Not sequins."

"But you're going to the ball anyway?"

"I have to." My mom was going all-out for this stupid thing, even though my dad, as a general rule, didn't like fuss. When I'd suggested that I would be better off manning the kids' room—most parties have a kids' table, but in this case Mom had actually hired a nanny service to take care of the guests' kids so everyone could enjoy the party—she'd put her foot down and said I was to be charming, polite, and engaged. Apparently I had used up all the sympathy points I'd had left over from my multiple stab wounds. "And don't call it a ball. It's a friggin' birthday party."

"Where is it?"

I flushed and muttered, "The Glenn Miller Ballroom."

Quinn's face broke out into a grin, and I swatted him.

Chapter 26

The next day was a cool, overcast Friday, and Simon came over in the early afternoon so we could do my magic lesson before I had to go babysit Charlie. The dogs announced his presence at one o'clock, and I went outside to meet him, figuring I could avoid his having to deal with the herd. When I stepped out, though, Simon was already halfway to the front door. He usually wore khakis or jeans and a button-down shirt to our practices, the kind of outfit a young professor would wear to class, but today he had on threadbare green cargo pants and a quilted vest over a long-sleeved hoodie with paint on the sleeves. I was immediately suspicious, especially when I noticed that his outfit included a pair of galoshes.

"Simon?" I said warily. "Why are you wearing that?" As I stepped off the porch, I caught sight of his station wagon in the driveway. "And why is there a goddamned *canoe* tied to the top of your car?"

"We're going to canoe out into the lake," he said, his voice obnoxiously cheerful, "to see if you can sense life underwater."

I glared at him. I don't like large bodies of water. Oh, I'm fine in bathtubs and the occasional swimming pool, but anytime there's wild, natural water under me, I have a tendency to freak out. Let's just say there was a reason I joined the army instead of the navy.

My dislike of water extends to a serious discomfort with boating, since I actually fell out of a boat the first time I died. "Not a chance," I informed him, folding my arms across my chest.

"Look, you need a new location, Lex," he argued. "We've been doing the woods for weeks, and it's too easy for you now. It's time for a new challenge."

"Yeah, your lips are moving, but all I hear is 'Lex, I want to do an experiment on you,'" I grumbled, not moving an inch toward the boat. "I'm a boundary witch, Simon, not a magical guinea pig."

"It's not that, I promise," he cajoled. "But I know Lily's been helping you work on controlling your emotions. And fear is a really strong emotion. You need to learn how to focus despite it."

Shit. I really wished that wasn't such a good argument. But when I was in the army, we rarely dealt with one problem at a time under ideal conditions. Instead, my unit was usually facing several different obstacles at once, in 110-degree heat. And the army trained us with that in mind. I had to admit, this didn't seem much different—if I ever did get into a situation where I would need to use magic to protect Charlie, I would probably be terrified.

So I went and got my own galoshes, muttering under my breath about mad scientists, and begrudgingly got into the car.

I guided Simon down the scrubby access road toward what Sam and I used to fondly refer to as "the lake." I'm still not sure if it had an actual name, or if it was just considered an offshoot of the nearby Sawhill Ponds. It was a tiny, green patch of water—Sam and I could swim across it by the time we were ten—and when we were kids, my dad and some of the neighbors had pitched in to stock it with fish. Then my dad got too busy with Luther Shoes to fish much, and I hadn't been to the lake in years. For obvious reasons.

It was just as I remembered—green water, tiny rocky beach. If anything, it seemed even smaller. But it suddenly struck me as menacing. When Simon opened up the back of the station wagon, I grabbed myself a life jacket, tugging the straps and snapping the buckles very carefully. I looked up when he laughed. "Jeez, Lex, you look like you're preparing for the firing squad. I promise we'll stay shallow. And look, the lake is calm."

I eyed the murky water, which seemed menacing against the overcast skies. It was true that it wasn't moving much—the breeze wasn't nearly strong enough to create anything approaching waves—but I couldn't shake the feeling that the water was my enemy. What bothered me was that I couldn't see what was going on underneath the surface. Admittedly, I probably wouldn't run into a whirlpool here, but there could be giant rocks or long tendrils of seaweed just waiting to latch onto us and trap us underwater.

Still, I forced myself to follow Simon, helping him drag the small fiberglass canoe into the shallows. It felt way too light, practically fragile, and I had to choke down my misgivings as we climbed inside. Simon paddled out, not commenting on how hard I was clutching the sides of the canoe, until we were about thirty or so feet from the shore. "Is this far enough?" I asked him through clenched teeth.

"Sure." He laid his paddle on the floor of the canoe, alongside our feet, and let the boat drift. "Okay, turn on your mindset," he instructed. This was his preferred term for the meditative state of mind that I perceived as thermal-imaging goggles. I had to admit, "mindset" was a lot easier to say.

I closed my eyes and obeyed. Well, I tried to. But every time I visualized putting on my thermal-imaging goggles, the rocking of the canoe would suddenly unnerve me and I'd lose my grip. I took a few deep breaths, trying to relax my body, and tried again. Nothing. I opened my eyes and glowered at Simon. "You just *had* to bring a canoe," I said accusingly. "It couldn't be a nice flat-bottomed rowboat, could it?"

He just smiled benignly. "Try again," he encouraged. "There's no rush."

I harrumphed and closed my eyes again. This time I didn't try to drop straight into my tunnel-vision frame of mind. Remembering our first lesson, I tried concentrating on what I could hear around me: birds, some chirpy bugs, the slight ruffle of the breeze through the trees near the shoreline. I took a deep breath, letting myself relax. Forcing myself to remember that it was okay.

I took a slow, calm breath. And just like that, I could switch into my mindset. "Got it," I murmured.

"Good. Now extend it *down*."

I felt myself frowning. I had never tried that before, because I'd always been on the ground. Carefully, without opening my eyes, I did as he asked.

The first spark was straight under my feet, maybe six inches below the canoe. I assumed it was a fish—the area residents were probably still stocking the pond—but unlike with most of the aboveground animals I'd detected, I couldn't crack open my eyes to confirm what I was feeling. The second spark was a few inches from the first one, loitering near the drifting canoe's bow, unaware of its occupants.

"Now go farther, Lex," Simon said softly.

I nodded at him without looking, and began to widen the beam of my focus. Five sparks. Eight. Thirteen. My God, that one was big. Were all of them fish? Maybe some crayfish? Wait, no, crayfish were only in running water, right? Then what were they, snails? Leeches? I shuddered, my breath coming faster. I *hated* leeches.

"Lex . . ." Simon said soothingly. "It's okay. Pull back. Turn it off."

I barely heard him. Thirty sparks of life, and that was in maybe a ten-foot radius. What if I extended it farther? Could I? Sure, it seemed possible, but it might be a bad idea.

Unfortunately, as my brain was still putting that together, I had already done it, pushing my senses out thirty, fifty feet. Oh, *no*. There were so many sparks now, too many for me to count. Just then something bumped the bottom of the canoe near my feet—a large fish, probably, but I squeaked in fear. What if it was a big rock? What if the canoe tipped and we fell in?

Panicking, I reacted defensively. My intention was to break my mindset, like I always did when I was overwhelmed, but without meaning to I sort of *tugged* on it, gathering it back to me. It resisted, like it was stuck on something, so I began to pull in earnest, as though there was an enormous net under the surface of the water and I was holding the edges, reeling it in—

"*Lex*," Simon was shouting. I felt a sprinkle of water, not more than a handful, spatter on my face. My mindset finally broke, and my eyes flew open, my breath coming hard and fast as I stared at the horrified look on Simon's face. He wiped his wet hand on the knee of his pants, looking at me with awe and regret and maybe . . . fear. Why was *he* so freaked out? I was the one who was having the panic attack. Although I actually didn't feel nervous anymore, which was strange. Instead, I felt . . . fantastic.

I was panting so hard that it took me a few seconds to hear it: the *blurp, blurp, blurp* from the surface of the water. My thoughts frozen, I tilted my head carefully—I wouldn't risk falling in—to see over the side of the canoe. My eyes flew to the source of another *blurp*, and I watched as the pale white belly of a dead fish popped to the surface, squishing into a space between two other bellies. I gasped, but it was too late to protect myself—my tunnel vision widened, and I finally saw it: dead fish after dead fish, bubbling to the surface in a gruesome landscape all around the canoe, the sight broken up by the occasional frog or slimy black leech.

I had pulled the death-essence right out of them. *Hundreds* of them.

Chapter 27

I don't remember getting back to the shore. Simon must have paddled us both in. His voice was buzzing at me, but I wasn't registering a word he said. I was flying high, my brain tumbling in cartwheels inside my skull. The second the canoe hit dirt, I leaped out and took off in a dead run, leaving my galoshes behind when they fell off. I didn't mind. Bare feet were easier, anyway.

It was half a mile back to the cabin, and I had never run so fast in my life. I felt superb. My arms and legs pumped, hurtling me along the sandy shoulder of the little unmarked road, and I felt like I could run all the way to the state line. I could run forever.

I didn't slow down until I was a few feet away from my front door. Then I skidded to a sloppy halt, bumping my hip into the doorknob. If it hurt, I didn't feel it. I grinned at the door for no reason, breathing only a little bit hard. Feeling a sudden twinge of pain, I glanced down at my feet. My breath caught in my throat.

The tops of my feet were grimy, with streaks of dark red. That didn't make sense: the lake water wasn't red, it was green. Confused, I put a hand on the door for balance and leaned sideways to check out the bottom of my left foot.

It was covered in oozing red lines that dripped right onto the porch. Still not understanding, I glanced back the way I had come. Red footprints traced my path down the driveway and onto the porch. That was the first moment I realized it was blood.

And the high crashed down around me, letting in the agonizing pain of my sliced-up feet. I screamed. From inside the cabin, the dogs barked and howled in sympathy.

Ten minutes later, I was sitting on the counter in the mudroom with my legs in the utility sink next to me, sobbing as I rinsed off my feet. Simon had been pounding on the door for most of that time, even rattling the doorknob to test the dead bolt, but I had no intention of opening the door to him or anyone else. Probably ever again. Eventually, he took the hint, and the knocking stopped. I was left alone with my thoughts and my bloody feet.

The army teaches you to handle panic, of course. There are a number of big training sessions focused solely on that, and I'd done okay when faced with scary situations in Iraq. But this was different. As I ran the cold water over my feet, trying to clear the blood long enough to see the actual cut, my thoughts tumbled around in a babbling craze, because the scary thing in question hadn't come from an insurgent or a raid or even the barrel of a gun. It had come from *within me*. I had pulled the life out of those fish, which was bad enough, but then I had *used* it to fuel my body and ignore pain.

I turned the water off, trying to see the cuts on my feet before the blood obscured them again. I'd gotten all the dirt and lake slime off, but there were dozens of small cuts on each foot. Most of them were superficial, but there were two on my left foot and one on my right that looked deep. I was trying to decide whether any of them needed stitches, but between the blood and the tears that continued to course down my face, I couldn't *fucking see them*. I blew out a shaky breath, frustrated.

Then a terrible thought crossed my mind. I'd felt high, juiced after pulling the life out of those fish. Like a junkie who'd finally gotten a fix. But what was making me high, *exactly*? I had a sudden suspicion.

I pointed at my left foot and murmured the words Simon had taught me, the simple little charm that cleaned an object for you.

As I said the words, I moved my finger downward, pointing into the sink because that's where I wanted the mess to go.

There was a spark of atmosphere in the mudroom, like the pressure right before a thunderstorm, and then every single piece of dirt, blood, pet hair, and dust in the entire room flew into the sink, immediately followed by all the dirty laundry on the floor, the odds and ends I'd taken out of my pockets before putting clothes in the wash, a few pieces of jewelry I'd taken off in the mudroom and forgotten about, and so on. A hailstorm of stuff flew past me to get to the sink, and I almost fell off the counter.

It didn't stop until the sink was full. I righted my balance and froze, looking around the room. It was spotless. Literally. There wasn't a speck of dust on the small window ledge, a place I had never cleaned in the three years I'd lived in this cabin. Even the sink fixtures were clean. Mary Poppins, eat your heart out. "A filter, not a focus," I whispered.

The dogs were barking, scrabbling their claws against the wooden door of the mudroom. Looking back at the sink, I pulled my feet out from under the piles of stuff and examined them. The wounds were bleeding again, and it was still hard to take a good look at them. At first I thought the whole exercise had been basically futile, but then I realized that other than the new blood, my feet were flawlessly clean. *That's probably good for fighting infection, right?* I thought woozily.

"Okay. I'm gonna need some help after all," I announced to the pile of clothes. I leaned back a little and dug into the pocket of my jeans. Miraculously, my cell phone was still there, having survived the epic footrace back to the cabin. With shaking fingers I scrolled through my contacts to find Lily's number.

"This is not good," she said half an hour later as she examined the soles of my feet. I was still on the counter in the mudroom, where

I had set down a few layers of paper towels to staunch the blood that was still oozing sluggishly from my wounds. Aside from not wanting to get blood on the carpets in the rest of the house, the mudroom seemed like the cleanest place for me to wait for Lily. I was leaning way back on the long counter so I could point my toes to the ceiling while she examined my injuries. Her face was about five inches away from my feet, which ordinarily would have embarrassed me, but there was no way in hell my feet smelled bad just then. They were practically gleaming, they were so clean.

Lily finally tore her eyes away and looked up at my face. "I can stop the bleeding, but you're right, the three bad gashes need a couple of stitches each. Or . . ." She trailed off.

"Or . . . ?" I prompted.

Lily winced. "I could Super Glue them," she said reluctantly. Seeing the disbelieving look on my face, she added defensively, "Hey, it's what surgeons do to arthroscopic entry wounds. It'll sting like a bitch, though, and you'll still need to stay off them for at least a day."

"Sold." After my misadventures with the stab wounds, I was a fan of any plan that didn't involve getting more frickin' stitches.

Lily got out her first-aid kit, retrieving the biggest tube of glue I'd ever seen. I looked away, focusing on the ultra-clean ceiling tiles. Agreeing to having my cuts glued shut was one thing, but I wasn't quite ready to watch it happen.

"So," Lily said as she worked. "I got the strangest call from Simon on the way here."

I flinched, struggling not to shift my feet, but didn't answer. "It seems that he's with some colleagues from CU," she continued, "convincing them that a lake full of dead fish is the result of low oxygen levels in the water."

I considered that for a moment. As excuses go, it wasn't bad. I didn't know anything about water oxygen levels, but I remembered something on the news a while back about a bunch of fish dying from the same thing in Southern California. "Are they buying it?" I asked.

"The deoxygenated water thing? So far. The trick is convincing them that they shouldn't bother with autopsies or water samples. He may have to stall them until dark, then get Quinn to press them." I snuck a glance at Lily, but she was totally focused on my injuries. Today her dreadlocks were tied back with an aquamarine scarf, and she had on a black off-the-shoulder shirt that reminded me of the top that Sandy changes into at the end of *Grease*.

"There," she said after a few more minutes, leaning back and looking at my feet with satisfaction. She pulled a roll of white gauze out of her kit and started to carefully wrap it all the way around my foot. "Do you want to tell me what happened?" she asked casually, her tone in direct contrast to the care she was taking with my foot.

"I'm assuming Simon already told you."

"About the lake, yes." She cut the gauze with a small pair of scissors, taped it in place, and started to wrap it around the other foot. "But he didn't have too many details about your bloody run through the country or why this room"—she glanced around"— suddenly looks like Mr. Clean's personal workshop."

She started to slowly pack up her supplies, giving me time to gather my thoughts. I sighed and sat up straight, swinging my wrapped feet to dangle them off the edge of the counter. "I pulled out their sparks," I said quietly. "The fish, I mean. But their death-essence didn't just go into the air or back into nature or whatever. It went into *me*." I remembered once again the way that first mouse's death-essence had looked as it drifted toward me. I shuddered. Now we knew I could pull it into me.

She looked at me thoughtfully. "And it felt good?"

I nodded. "It was incredible," I admitted. "It was the best high. I ran and ran, which helped take the edge off it. But I still had more." I gestured at the room.

Lily looked around. "So you decided to practice the cleaning spell?"

"Not exactly." I leaned forward to bury my face in my hands. "I was just trying to clean my feet," I said softly.

I felt Lily's momentary stillness as she absorbed that, and then she boosted herself up on the counter next to me. "Well . . . we knew your powers were strong. And they've only been growing," she said haltingly. "You couldn't get regular magic to work, but it sounds like when you absorbed some of this essence, you could suddenly do a witch charm. Interesting."

I lifted my face to look at her. "I'm like a goddamned vampire, Lily. I can suck the life out of things. That's too much power. It's too *big*."

She shrugged. "We knew that magic and creation and life are all kind of the same thing. But maybe death is part of it, too. You stored up these animals' essence and converted it into magic. Could you do the cleaning spell again right now?"

I considered that for a second. "I don't think so. I feel . . . depleted. Like the high's worn off."

She nodded. "So there you go. You used up the magic, the essence, you took from the fish. Now you're out again."

"That's the stupidest thing I've ever heard," I muttered. "I'm not going to kill living creatures just to clean off my feet. I'm a vegetarian, for crying out loud."

Lily gave me a rueful smile. "So we'll teach you a few defensive spells," she suggested. "Serious, save-your-life stuff, so you can save yourself if you get backed in a corner. That'd be worth killing a few fish, right?"

"Maybe," I said doubtfully. What if there weren't any slimy lake fish available? What if I was forced to use someone's pets? I thought of the herd and tried not to shudder.

"Plus, there's the whole thing where you can't die," she pointed out. "That continues to kick ass. And you can sense the life in a given area, which could be vital someday."

I shook my head, unconvinced. "It just doesn't seem like enough."

"For what?"

To make it worth being a freak? I thought. But I was smart enough not to say that in front of a representative of Clan Pellar. "To make me attractive as an employee," I explained instead. It was still true. "So that Itachi will agree to leave Charlie alone."

That was, after all, the whole reason why I was doing any of this. If I wasn't still hoping to make a deal with Itachi for Charlie's childhood, I would have promised never to say anything about the Old World and forgotten I'd ever known any of these people. Well, the vampires, anyway.

As soon as I thought that, my whole body went cold with fear. "Lily . . . we have to keep this between us. Itachi *can't* know that I can use animal death-essence to fuel magic."

Her eyes narrowed as she thought through the implications. "You think he'll force you to start sacrificing things," she concluded. "Pets and stuff."

I shuddered. "That would be bad enough, but no. I'm afraid he'll force me to sacrifice people."

Lily went still. "Do you think that would work? That you could pull the death-essence from humans?"

I looked her in the eye. "I am never, ever going to find out."

Chapter 28

After Lily left, I hobbled out to the living room, trying to keep my weight on the edges of my feet without rolling my ankles, and collapsed on the couch. Within thirty seconds, two dogs and a cat had piled onto my lap. "Hey, guys," I said with a laugh. "Are you trying to tell me something?"

Petting the animals with one hand, I called John at his office to beg off babysitting Charlie that night. I hated to do it, but as much as I loved the kid I could hardly chase her around when I wasn't supposed to walk. More importantly, I didn't want my mom or anyone else to know I'd been injured again. So I told my brother-in-law that I thought I might be coming down with a cold and didn't want to give it to Charlie.

After I talked to John, I called my mother to let her know about the change in plans. Luckily, she was too distracted with last-minute party preparations to question me closely. I was just hoping my feet would heal enough in the next twenty-four hours for me to still go. I was their only child now. It wouldn't be right to miss the party.

"Okay, hon," she said absently. "Hang on a second." She half covered the phone to holler out a question about centerpieces to someone else in the room. Then she was back. "You picked up your dress from the dry cleaner's, right?" she demanded, suddenly *very* focused on me. "And the shoes from your dad's office?"

"Yes and yes," I said, grateful that I'd had the presence of mind to run errands that morning before my magic lesson. "Shoes and dress. Check."

"What about jewelry?" my mom inquired. "I have some lovely pieces that would complement your gown—"

"No, thanks," I broke in quickly, before she could start listing every necklace she owned. "I'm covered, Mom, I promise. Is there anything you need help with?"

"No, you take a day and rest that cold. I'll send one of your cousins over with some chicken soup and cough drops so you'll be good as new before the party."

"That's not really how colds work, Mom."

"It is now."

I listened to her chatter on about party preparations for a few more minutes; then she added, "Oh, before you hang up, honey, your Aunt Violet happened to ask me who you're bringing as your plus-one. Is it that young man from . . . um . . . your job?"

I rolled my eyes. I occasionally palled around with a couple of the male Depot employees, although less since I'd stopped going to bars. It wasn't a romantic thing; I just missed having camaraderie with a group of guys, like I'd had in the army. But I'd once made the mistake of bringing one of them to a family barbecue. I knew he was coming as my friend, *he* knew he was coming as my friend, but of course my whole family had assumed we were on the brink of getting married and having babies. "No, Mom," I said now. "He's seven years younger than me. I think he's dating a sorority girl from Topeka."

"Oh, that's nice," she said vaguely, but I didn't miss the relief in her voice. "Who are you bringing, then?"

"Um, no one, Mom," I said uncomfortably. "I don't have a plus-one." I hadn't sent a formal RSVP to the party—why would I, when I was the one helping my mom update the guest list?—and I had just assumed they'd realize I wouldn't be bringing anyone. I'd thought I only needed to mention a plus-one if I *was* bringing a plus-one. Apparently I'd had that backward.

There was a silence on her end, which stretched on for long enough for me to attempt to fill it myself. "I'm sorry, I guess I didn't think it was that important whether I brought a date to my dad's birthday party."

She sighed. "It's not that, honey, it's just . . . we're doing this for your dad, you know, because he does so much for the family. He's been talking about you girls a lot lately, and I know he worries about you." I found myself nodding along with her, which was stupid for a couple of reasons. "It'd just be nice if he could see you happy and dating, even if he's not the love of your life. Maybe a guy friend?"

I knew she was manipulating me, but I couldn't really fault her for it. My dad was the cornerstone of our whole family, and it wasn't like she was asking for the moon. "I'll ask around, okay? If I can find someone, I'll bring him. But no promises."

"Thank you, sweetie." The gratitude in her voice made me grimace.

When I was off the phone, I leaned back on the couch, idly scratching Pongo's wrinkled bulldog cheeks. Who the hell could I ask? I immediately thought of John, but that would be a mistake. My family knew that we were friendly, even friends, but showing up at this thing on his arm would come off as a Statement.

But if not John, then who? I didn't really have a social life outside of work and my extended family. All my coworkers were either married or college-aged, and going with one of my male cousins would only make my pathetic dating situation more pronounced. Simon would probably be willing to come as a friend, but he had a long-term girlfriend, which made me feel awkward about asking. The guys I knew from summer softball were all married. I wondered if I could get away with bringing Lily. She'd probably get a kick out of it, but it would start a whole bunch of rumors. I didn't mind being thought of as a lesbian, really, but I wasn't comfortable lying if my parents asked me outright, which they undoubtedly would. And that led me right back to where I'd started.

Stop stalling, Lex. I knew what to do, of course. Even as I told myself it was a stupid, halfway crazy idea, my fingers were already typing away on my phone, checking what time the sun would set the next night.

Then I called Quinn.

"So you're asking me to be . . . what, your arm candy?" he said once I'd explained the situation. He sounded amused, but in a remote way, like he wasn't yet invested in the conversation, much less the actual event.

"Pretty much, yeah." I fidgeted, embarrassed, but I didn't know what I could say to make the situation less awkward or my case any stronger.

"Isn't your family going to think that we're dating?"

"I'll tell them we're just friends," I offered.

There was a beat of silence. "*Are* we friends?" he said in a low voice. "Is that what we are?"

I thought about that for a moment. I was never going to have Quinn over to watch a movie or help me move my couch. He was never going to drive me to the airport or come rock climbing with me. But he had kept investigating Charlie's kidnapper after being told to stop, and he'd done that for me. That wasn't the same as choosing me over his boss, but it was something. Maybe friendship. "Don't you think we could be?" I said.

"Yes, but I'm . . . drawn to you," he said reluctantly, in the same tone you'd use for "yes, but . . . you have crippling body odor."

"Well, I think you're supposed to be," I offered. "Death in my blood, remember?"

There was another moment of silence, this one much longer. Then I sighed into the phone. "Look, Quinn, I promise I'm not going to try to take advantage of you. I pretty much just need a warm body to convince my parents I'm not a hermit. Uh . . . you know what I mean," I added hastily, as I realized "warm body" might not necessarily apply to Quinn. "It's a favor, like being a date to someone's cousin's wedding."

"Well . . ." Quinn said slowly, and he trailed off for so long I thought he was scrabbling for an excuse to say no. But then he admitted, in a shamed voice, "I do kind of like to dance."

Chapter 29

At three o'clock the next afternoon, a cadre of my female cousins descended upon my house.

My feet were much improved, but I was trying to stay off them as much as possible in order to pass for healthy at the party. So instead of going for a hike, I was in the basement lifting weights and listening to NPR in bike shorts and a yoga top. Then I heard the dogs flip out. A moment later the doorbell rang.

Grabbing a towel, I went up the steps and down the hallway as gingerly as I could and peeked through the front window. There stood my cousins Elise, Brie, and Anna, and Jake's wife Cara, all with mischievous smiles and armfuls of clothing. Expensive-looking clothing, so I herded the dogs into the still alarmingly clean mudroom. Maybe they would normal it up a little.

I opened the front door with my eyebrows raised. "Surprise," they chorused. Anna even did jazz hands.

"It's not my birthday," I said.

Anna, who was twenty-six and a grad student at CU, stuck out her tongue at me. "We're getting ready for your dad's party here," she explained. "Your mom and my mom's idea."

Yep, that sounded like my mom. Making sure I was involved. I eyed their armfuls of clothes and makeup cases. "Isn't that kind of a lot of work for you guys?"

"Your dad's bribing us," Cara said shyly. "He's sending a limo."

Brie shot me an evil grin. She was thirty-seven, the oldest of our generation, a dentist with two sons and a perpetually harried expression. "Plus, the men have to get all the kids ready," she said.

Shaking my head, I opened the door wide. "Well, come on in." I was smiling despite myself.

The four of them trooped inside, chattering about who was watching Brie's and Cara's kids and what they were going to wear. Elise, the last one through, paused in the doorway and whispered, "I think Aunt Christy was afraid you'd be sad, you know, without Sam."

I nodded. "And afraid I'd decide to just stay home?"

Elise smiled ruefully. "You know your mom."

"I heard Lex has a daaaate," Anna teased over her shoulder. "Who's the guy?"

"Or *girl*," Elise said, fake offended. Anna grabbed a throw pillow off the couch and chucked it at her. Elise batted it aside with a stagy karate chop.

I shrugged. "Just a friend."

Cara, who was nearly as soft-spoken as her husband, asked, "Where'd you meet him?"

Oops. I couldn't sound too enthusiastic about Quinn—or like I was working hard *not* to sound enthusiastic—or my whole family would think I was in love. "He was on my softball team over the summer," I told them. "He's a nice guy. We go hiking once in a while." Well, we'd gone on one long hike together, anyway. I just wasn't going to mention the body-disposal portion of the evening.

I jumped in the shower and spent fifteen minutes blow-drying my hair so that Cara, an actual hair stylist, could pin it up in big curlers. Then I made everyone some coffee and sat at the counter, listening to stories about Brie's sons and Cara's daughter Dani and Anna's history professor and a hilariously drunk guy whom Elise had arrested after he walked through a plate-glass window at McDonald's. I didn't talk much, but I laughed and asked questions, my heart warmed by the familiar patter of my family.

Their lives had been dramatically unlike mine since long before I found out I was a witch. When I was a soldier, shotgunning energy drinks, patting down Iraqi women for bombs, and saying prayers every time I got in a Humvee, I couldn't believe I'd ever had a life that revolved around a big, sloppy, loving, exuberant family. And when I was with them, it was hard to believe I'd ever buzz-cut my hair and challenged the guys under my command to pull-up contests. But by the time I came home between tours, I'd realized both roles were an integral part of me—the soldier *and* the scion.

When I'd come home from the hospital in Germany after my second tour, it was harder to remember how to be in the family, how I was supposed to talk and react and smile in front of the people who loved me. Even now there were days when I felt like I was still adjusting to being back, after three years in Boulder. But without my family, I knew a big part of me would have died.

Well. Bigger part.

When my hair was done, I sat down at the counter and swiped on some mascara and lipstick, figuring that was good enough. But Anna gave me a long-suffering sigh and made me sit back down at the counter. She proceeded to put about thirty different substances on my face, only about half of which I recognized. When she finally put the cap back on the last tube, she blew gently on my face—"to get the extra powder off"—and pronounced me done. I went into the bedroom to put on my dress.

There was a stranger in my room. I jerked, backpedaling a step before I realized I was looking at my own reflection. Anna's makeup had transformed me from my usual youthful-steely look into something softer and more . . . glamorous. Wide, shining curls framed my face in a curtain that dipped over one eye. I shook my head in amazement, watching the curls bounce. "Not too shabby, guys!" I yelled. Or rather, the stranger in my mirror yelled.

At six-thirty, the limousine arrived for my cousins. I tried to bid them good-bye, since Quinn wasn't picking me up until seven, but they unanimously decided to wait for my date to show up so they could give him the once-over. "You guys, this isn't the prom," I reminded them. "I don't need a chaperone."

Elise snorted around one of the apple slices I'd put out for us to munch on. "That's for sure," she said, her mouth full. "I've seen you shoot, woman."

My other cousins tittered. "And you'll see him at the party," I added. "You can meet him then." I made a shooing motion, but none of them left their perches around the room. In their long gowns and sculpted hairdos, they looked like the world's most belligerent bridesmaids.

"Oh, we'll all be busy with husbands and family stuff then," Brie argued. "Come on, Lex. We'll give him the eyeball, make sure he knows you've got backup." She tilted her head to give me a pointed, lazy-eyed stare. I laughed. It was nice to see Brie have a chance to be goofy.

When the doorbell rang at seven, Elise, Brie, Anna, and Cara exchanged wide-eyed looks of glee. They began to get up, but I jumped to my feet first. Mostly because I hadn't put on my shoes yet. Shoes still kind of hurt just then. "Stay!" I ordered them. In unison, all four of them raised their right arms and saluted, giggling hysterically. I rolled my eyes as I padded briskly down the hall, my skirt swishing at my calves. The dogs were barking madly, but that happened so frequently I barely registered it anymore. I pulled the door halfway open and saw Quinn.

He wore a black tuxedo with a long black tie that was on the thin side. His hands were in his pants pockets, and for a breathless moment I just . . . looked at him. He quirked a private smile at me, giving me a once-over. My dress was made of deep emerald satin, with a simple high-cut halter neckline that showed off the lean muscles in my arms and shoulders but covered most of the scars on my back, including the new ones. The full skirt flared out from a fitted waist, swirling as I walked. Anna, who'd picked it out, had decided the simple gown needed a little something extra, so she'd added a wide metal belt of braided silver links that sat at my waist. We stood there gazing at each other for a long moment, and I felt heat creep up my chest, flushing my cheeks under the makeup.

Then I heard my cousins giggling behind me and remembered myself. "Mr. Bond, I presume?" I said, cocking an eyebrow.

Quinn gave me a small smile. "Does that make you Miss Moneypenny?"

I shrugged a bare shoulder. "I've been called worse."

The giggling intensified, and Quinn raised his brow inquisitively. "My cousins," I explained. "They'd like to meet you."

A flare of discomfort crossed Quinn's face. "It's okay. I can make this really easy," I reassured him. Without checking behind me, I banged the door wide open—exposing the four of them, who were huddled in the hallway. "Cousins, this is Quinn. Quinn, some of my cousins." Before any of them could speak, I grabbed my peep-toe heels and my silver clutch from the hall table, stepped across the threshold, and swung the door shut behind me. "Shall we?" I asked innocently.

Quinn grinned at me.

Chapter 30

My parents, both CU graduates, had a thing about the Glenn Miller Ballroom, which is located in the University Memorial Center on campus. They'd been holding major events there for years: most of the cousins, including Sam, had had their wedding receptions in that room. My parents had hosted a big thirtieth-anniversary bash there a few years back, and before I managed to talk them out of it, Mom had even wanted to host a welcome-back reception for me there when I got out of the service. With one thing and another, I'd been coming to this specific venue for most of my life.

But I'd never seen it look like this.

Through a combination of lighting and decor, the whole room seemed to be done in warm fall tones, which perfectly complemented the harvest-red centerpieces. The centerpieces, in turn, perfectly matched the cummerbunds on the members of the seven-piece orchestra that was playing on the short raised stage. Starlight gleamed faintly through the skylights, and the whole effect was magical, like we'd walked into an autumn garden party for fairies. Quinn whistled. "You gotta hand it to my mom," I observed as Quinn and I stepped into the enormous room. For the first time in my life, I was almost glad to be wearing heels—the shoes put a different kind of pressure on my feet, keeping my weight off the worst of the cuts. "She knows how to throw a shindig."

Quinn gave me a sidelong look. "Shindig?"

"Hootenanny?"

The corners of his lips turned up. "I'd lean more toward 'soiree.'"

"Nah, that's playing right into her hand," I said, but fondly. I pointed left, to where my parents were standing in a loose receiving line. "Come on, let's get introductions over with."

We joined the line, where several of my parents' friends and extended family members were already waiting. I started introducing Quinn around as my friend from softball, which everyone seemed to accept, although my Aunt Violet and my cousin Paul both sent me knowing winks, like "friend from softball" was some dirty sex position. Which, I supposed, was possible.

We got to the front of the line, and my mom waved us over. She was wearing a sparkly gold dress with a jewel-cut collar, looking radiant and a little self-satisfied as she basked in the glow of the party's success, whispering occasional comments in my dad's ear. My father is not a particularly handsome man, especially because he refuses to lose the short white ponytail that's the last vestige of his hippie childhood, but he certainly looked dashing in his tuxedo. He had a particular stoic expression I recognized from my high school graduation and Sam's wedding photos. It meant "I'm playing it cool, but secretly I am doing a proud happy dance."

I smiled and kissed his cheek. "Happy birthday, Dad," I said, then turned to gesture at Quinn. "This is my friend Quinn. Quinn, these are my parents, Christy and Richard Luther."

Quinn extended a hand, which my dad shook heartily. "Nice to meet you, sir," Quinn said politely. To my mother, he added, "This is a beautiful party, ma'am."

"You're so sweet," my mother responded, beaming. She touched the back of her hair. "I hope you two are having a good time."

Quinn assured her that we were, and she leaned forward to ask him a question about what he did for a living. While she was distracted, I leaned forward and said conspiratorially to my dad, "How are you holding up?"

He grinned at me. "Your mother went way overboard, you know," he said in a voice that was fighting not to sound exuberant. "It's just a birthday. I don't need all"—he gestured helplessly at his tux, the ballroom, the decorations—"this trouble."

"You deserve it though, Dad," I said, pecking his cheek again. "I'm so proud of you."

And I was. A decade before Sam and I were born, my dad and his brother had started designing vegan shoes as a sort of hobby. Nobody was more surprised than they were when the business took off. Now you could buy a pair of Luther Shoes in Paraguay.

"I'm proud of you too, baby," my dad said, lifting his arm to give me a one-sided dad hug. He glanced at Quinn. "Glad you're doing better."

Quinn and I moved on, letting the flow of people lead us toward the dance floor. I was thinking about my dad's words. *Was I doing better?* I was a frickin' witch. I had access to magic that no one should be able to touch.

Without looking at me, Quinn took my hand and tucked it into his arm. I smiled faintly. At the same time, it was nice to have purpose again, even if that purpose went no deeper than turning myself into a valuable asset so I could do scut work for a vampire. Maybe Quinn and I wouldn't be able to find the person behind Charlie's kidnapping, but I would keep training with the Pellars. I would learn a couple of really solid defensive spells, like Lily had suggested. And I would protect Sam's daughter, whatever it cost me personally. I set my jaw.

"You okay?" Quinn said, sensing the shift in my mood. I nodded, hoping the gesture would help clear my head. "Dance?" he asked. I nodded again.

The band was playing jaunty dance songs, like you hear at wedding receptions, mixed in with a bit of swing music. Incredibly appropriate for the Glenn Miller Ballroom. As we stepped toward the dance floor, they swung into a snazzy rendition of "Dream a

Little Dream of Me." Quinn held out his hand, and I let him pull me toward his chest.

I couldn't remember the last time I'd danced with a partner, if you didn't count my cousin's kids standing on my toes as I shuffled them around. My parents had paid for dance lessons when I was a kid, mostly because Sam liked them. I was the athlete, but she thought tutus were the coolest, so we'd kept up with the lessons for nearly six years. I could tell that Quinn's movements were technically perfect, but he was keeping his body just the tiniest bit rigid, like he was afraid to relax. I bit down a smile.

"What?" he asked, with a slight raise of his eyebrows. "Did I step on your toes?"

"No, no," I reassured him. "You're good. Very . . . proficient." I hesitated for a second, then added, "Thank you for coming tonight. It means a lot to me."

He nodded, his eyes searching mine for something. Then we resumed dancing, but Quinn seemed preoccupied. "What is it?" I asked, as the band began the first chorus of Billie Holiday's "Solitude." We had automatically slowed down for the song, and my cheek brushed his as I craned my head back to see his face.

Quinn gave me a little shake of his head. "I shouldn't be here," he murmured. "I shouldn't be doing this with you."

I stopped dancing. "Then go," I said in a whisper. "My dad already saw us together. Go if you need to."

Quinn stared at me, his eyes searching mine with an intensity that took me aback. I lifted my chin and looked right back at him. Heat sparked between us, and Quinn broke first, looking away. His arm around my waist tightened as he drew me back in. "That's not what I meant," he said.

We danced through the song, not speaking. The tension grew unbearable, so I started babbling. "When I was a teenager, Sam and I watched *Ferris Bueller's Day Off*," I said. "You ever see that movie?"

Looking surprised, he nodded. "It was Sam's favorite," I continued. "There's this line, when Ferris is talking about his friend—he says he's wound so tight that if you stuck a lump of coal up his ass, in two weeks you'd have a diamond."

Quinn's lips quirked up. "You're saying I'm like Cameron?"

"Maybe a little . . . Were you like this as a human?"

He led me through a careful spin. Very controlled. "No," he said, leaving it at that.

I thought about his voice from the night before. *Are we friends?* I still had friends from the army. None of them were geographically close, but we communicated now and then, because we could only talk to each other about certain things. The ones who had spouses often said they were afraid to go near them. To get close again.

Quinn had hurt his wife.

The melancholy song ended, and without really discussing it we both turned and headed toward the side of the room, moving off the dance floor. It wasn't until we reached the refreshment table at the far end of the room that I realized I'd been holding Quinn's hand the whole way. We let go and I grabbed a bottle of water, gulping down half of it. Then I leaned against the wall, a little tired from the dancing.

Quinn watched me, obviously waiting to speak until I was finished. "Lex," he began, "this isn't a good idea."

I raised my eyebrows. "Us being friends?"

He nodded. "Or anything along those lines."

I put the cap back on the bottle, twisted it tight, and set it down on the table, considering my words. "I'm not afraid of you, Quinn," I finally said.

"You should be."

I rolled my eyes. "Why, exactly? Because you can press me? Nope, wait, you can't. Can't make me do anything I don't want to do. Because you're physically stronger than me?" I shrugged. "I spent a decade serving with guys who were bigger and stronger than me, and I managed to survive."

"Presumably, they weren't trying to drink your blood," Quinn said, his voice strained.

I felt my expression harden. "No, but some of them wanted other things from me, and I held my own. Always." Quinn shook his head a little, unconvinced. "Is this because of what happened in the parking lot?" I asked, a little more gently. "Because you liked how my blood smelled?"

He nodded. The song ended, and the band moved seamlessly into "I Want a Little Sugar in My Bowl." Great song.

"You had the chance to attack me when I was bleeding," I reminded Quinn, keeping my voice low. "You didn't."

"But I *wanted* to," he said, his voice husky. "I haven't wanted anything that much since I turned."

I reached up, putting one hand on his cheek. I moved just a little bit closer, putting my mouth right next to his ear to make sure no one overheard me. "I will not ever let you hurt me," I whispered to him. "Don't worry so much." I leaned back so I could see his face. "Do you understand?"

I saw the relief break out over his face. "Yes, sir," he whispered back.

Chapter 31

Quinn and I danced for a few more songs, and then I noticed that two of the servers, young women in their early twenties, were waving at him. "Ex-girlfriends?" I asked.

He let out a short bark of surprised laughter. "They're baristas at Magic Beans," he explained. The girls each grabbed one side of a full keg, heaving it toward the bar at the opposite end of the ballroom. "I should probably help them with that," Quinn remarked. "And then I might say hi to the couple in the corner, they're regulars. You'll be okay for a minute?"

"Of course." While Quinn was gone, I looked around for my cousins and realized they were all occupied: dancing with their spouses and laughing, enjoying this rare opportunity to dress up and go out. They all looked so happy and grown-up. I smiled. For the first time I sort of appreciated my mother's decision to make the party black tie. It was like looking at the most beautiful version of everyone.

Grief is a funny thing. I hadn't even been thinking about Sam, not really, but suddenly I was hit by a tidal wave of longing for my sister. I wanted her to *be* here, smiling and laughing and teasing my father. She'd be dancing like an idiot, a gorgeous gown swishing around her as she did silly, unselfconscious dance moves with John, drawing him out, making everyone crack up. God, I missed her.

As if reading my thoughts, the music suddenly faded into silence, and I glanced toward the raised platform where the band sat. Most of the members of the band were stepping off for a break, but as they shuffled offstage they left behind a pianist and a guitar player. The guitarist paused for a moment, pushing hair behind her ears. Then she closed her eyes and began playing the simple, haunting chords to a song I recognized instantly.

"Unchained Melody" gets a lot of scorn for being cheesy, but you don't become one of the most popular love songs in the history of recorded music by accident. *Ghost* had already been out for over a decade by the time I was in high school, but that song was still the theme of my high school prom when I was a junior.

It also happened to be Sam's favorite goddamned song in the world.

I felt my eyes well with tears. I looked up and there was John, his unruly hair tamed down with gel, his tuxedo just the slightest bit ill-fitting. I smiled. He held out a hand wordlessly, and I took it, allowing him to pull me in for a dance.

"I miss her, too," he whispered. "Your mom asked them to play it, in her honor."

I nodded, suddenly choked up.

"Do you remember," he said into my ear, "when Sam decided to see how many times she could play this song in a row before your dad flipped out?"

I let out a startled laugh. "Oh, God, I had forgotten about that. Was that during the infamous college road trip?" I felt, rather than saw, his nod. "Poor Dad. He still thought he could talk me out of the army by showing me some fabulous college that would sweep me off my feet."

"He was so *sure* you'd like Berkeley, if we could just make it there. And Sam decided she needed to break his spirit on the first day." There was a smile in his voice that I found myself echoing.

"Hey, it was her favorite song." I shrugged good-naturedly. "What're you gonna do?" My poor, ex-hippie father was usually the more patient of our two parents, but a man could only take so much "Unchained Melody" in a row before losing it. "How far did we make it?" I asked. "I can't remember."

John lifted his hand, leading me through an effortless twirl. "Salt Lake City," he said when I returned to him.

I smiled. "Sam saved us all some time. Even if I hadn't joined the service, I would never have gone to Berkeley."

John's smile faded, and he pulled me close again so I wouldn't see his expression. "Because Sam didn't get into Berkeley," he said matter-of-factly.

I shrugged. "But you did," John pressed. "And Stanford. And USC."

I felt my expression harden. "What's your point?"

He looked away. The last chorus was beginning, and we would walk away soon. But for some reason it was important to me to understand. "It was so long ago, John. We were kids. What does it matter now that I wouldn't have gone to a certain school if I had gone to school at all?"

He sighed. "I'm just . . . I don't think you give yourself enough credit. You never have. When we were kids, you acted like the sun rose and fell on Sam's say-so, when *you* were the one who could have done anything with your life."

I stopped dancing then, not caring who noticed us. "You can't exactly tell me she wasn't special, John. She was your *wife*." I really hoped the words *you chose her over me* weren't as obvious to him as they felt in my head.

"Of course she was special. Of course I loved her. But I just never understood why you decided to write this goddamned narrative," he said, frustration buzzing in his voice, "that Sam had value and you didn't."

"I never—"

"When Sam was alive, you made your whole life about protecting her," John insisted. "Sometimes I wondered if you decided to join the army, to protect the country, just because Sam was in it."

"Come on, even I'm not that codependent," I said, trying to make my voice light.

"And now that she's dead," he continued, like he hadn't heard me, "you're making your life all about remembering her. Grieving for her. It's been almost a year, Allie."

"That's pretty fucking rich, coming from you," I retorted. "Not exactly back out on the dating scene, are you?"

He hesitated, and something congealed in my stomach. "Actually, I just started seeing someone," he said finally.

We both went still. The song ended.

"Oh," I said lamely.

"It's getting late," John said. "I should probably get Charlie home."

I nodded, discreetly wiping under my eyes to protect my mascara. "I'll walk with you, so I can give her a kiss."

He started through the crowd, and I trailed after him. After only two steps, though, I felt someone's gaze on me. I glanced up and met Quinn's eyes. He nodded me on with his usual implacable expression; he'd heard where I was going. Which meant he'd also heard everything we'd said before that. I blushed. Whatever ground I'd gained with Quinn would be gone now. One step forward, two steps back. Story of my life.

I followed John silently through the doorway and into the east ballroom, which my mom had rented for the kids. It was like a junior version of my dad's birthday ball. There were kid-friendly finger foods and a small set of speakers playing age-appropriate music. The room was full of laughing, screaming, running boys and girls, the descendants of all the Luther Shoes employees, and I took a second to privately admire the soundproofing that had kept this cacophony out of the main ballroom. I waved to Jake's twelve-year-old daughter Dani, who was tucked into a corner with an iPad on her knees. Brie's sons were there too, but they were involved in an elaborate chase game with some bigger kids, so I didn't interrupt.

There was a cordoned-off area for the kids under age two, with a couple of small plastic slides and some baby toys tossed about. No Charlie, though. I trailed John as he headed toward the employee in the baby area, a young woman in her twenties wearing a pink polo shirt that had the words *Go and Play Child Care* embroidered on the back. "Hey, I'm looking for Charlotte Wheaton," John said politely. "Is she off getting a diaper change or something?"

The girl, who had a round face, acne, and the blissful look of someone who truly loves kids, gave John a puzzled smile. "Nobody's getting changed, but let me check the clipboard," she said brightly, hoisting a toddler higher on her hip and leading us toward a podium that was stashed against the wall, out of the way of the gallivanting kids. There was a clipboard on top. The girl paged through it. "You signed the waiver, right?" she said absently. John confirmed that he had. "Oh, right here," she chirped, pointing to a name on the third page. "Charlotte Wheaton, goes by Charlie? I don't remember her, but"—her cheerful voice faltered—"um, it says she was already checked out, just a few minutes ago."

"By who?" John demanded.

The round-faced girl looked up at him with a hesitant smile. "Um . . . her father. John Wheaton."

Chapter 32

"*I'm* John Wheaton," John said, his voice a terrible alloy of anger and fear.

The girl's face bleached to a pale white. "I . . . I don't know what could have happened," she stammered. "I don't remember seeing her. Karen?" she called, waving over one of the other two workers. "Do you recall signing out Charlotte Wheaton?"

"Eighteen months old," John supplied.

Karen's face was as blank as the first girl's. Instinctively, I spun on my heel and hurried over to Dani, bending down to tug the earbuds out of her ears. "Dani, did you see someone take Charlie?" I demanded.

She blinked at me, pushing her round glasses higher on her face. "Yeah, that guy came and got her," she said. "I was trying to help Peter get Chris down the slide, but I figured he was the babysitter . . ."

"John!" I yelled, startling him out of his heated conversation with the attendants. "I need you to get Quinn *right now!*"

"Who?" he said, confused and worried. "We need Elise, we gotta call the cops—"

"John," I said, pouring as much patience into my voice as I could manage, "I can go after her, but I need Quinn right now. Please."

He looked at me for the length of a heartbeat, then nodded, trusting me. He raced out of the room. I turned back to Dani, crouching down so our faces were level. "Honey, I need to know what he looked like."

"Did I mess up?" Dani asked, her voice edged with fear. "Should I have gone to get Uncle John?"

I smoothed down her hair. "No, baby, you did just fine. Do you remember anything about how he looked?"

"He was like in college," she volunteered. "Um, dark hair. I don't remember what he was wearing but he was kind of . . . big?" She let go of the iPad and spread her arms, holding them away from her body. "Lots of muscles."

Oh, *shit*. "Did he have a funny hooked nose?" I asked, miming a bump over my nose with one finger. "Like this?"

She nodded, her face relaxing a little as she realized I knew him.

"How long ago?" I said urgently, having to concentrate to keep from squeezing her arms.

"Like, two minutes. Did—"

John and Quinn ran in, John starting to panic in earnest. "John, I need you to stay calm and keep this quiet," I said. "I can get her back, but we can't—"

"You must be joking," he interrupted. "We gotta call the police right now, time is everything—"

I met Quinn's eyes. The vampire didn't look confused or upset; he just gave me a calm, what-do-you-want-me-to-do look. "It was Kirby, and it just happened," I said, ignoring John. "There's no time. I'm going after him."

He nodded. "I'll press them and join you in a second."

I winced, but he was right. If we let John make a big fuss and call the police, Itachi would throw his resources into containment rather than an investigation. "Tell him she's spending the night at my house," I said grimly. "He'll be okay with that."

John started to yell at me, and Dani burst into tears, but I couldn't worry about any of that.

I was already running.

Holding the front of my dress, I raced down the stairs at neck-breaking speed, skidding down the last few steps so fast I had to catch myself on the wall. I raced out of the stairwell and burst outside, looking wildly to my left and right. At first I figured he must have used a car for his getaway, but would he have gone for the southeast lot or the southwest one? I took a few steps southwest and realized that traffic was jammed up around the building. The fickle autumn weather had decided on a breath of warmth, and people were everywhere. Between the party and all the regular Saturday night events on campus, a car wouldn't have been a very dependable way to get anywhere. He would probably have fled on foot, at least at first.

But that didn't tell me anything about where he would have *gone*, goddammit. I turned in a slow circle, peering around the campus, hoping for a flash of movement, for the sight of someone running. There were plenty of people around, but I didn't see Kirby, or anything else suspicious. I grabbed at my hair, ready to scream. *The frat house*, I thought suddenly. Would he have gone there to get his car? No, it wasn't too far, but he would have had to take busy Broadway to get there, which would make it too likely that he'd run into people who knew him.

The smart thing to do, I decided, would have been to park a block or so away from the UMC, someplace out of the immediate traffic but easily accessible by foot. And if he was planning to get on Highway 36 toward Denver . . .

Grabbing the bottom of my dress again, I turned and sprinted southeast toward Macky Auditorium, ignoring the renewed surge of pain from my feet. There was a huge lot on the other side of the auditorium, with easy access to the highway and not much visibility. That was where I'd park, if I were stealing a kid.

I tried to figure out how many seconds I'd lost while I was considering my options. Thirty? Sixty? I ran harder, trying to make it up. The heels were making it hard to move, but my only other option was to take them off, and that's how I'd hurt my feet in the first place. So I pelted down the sidewalk as fast as I could, ignoring the joggers and strolling couples who stared and murmured as I raced by, my emerald skirt flying behind me like a banner. I put everything I had into forward movement, well aware that if my shoe caught the asphalt wrong I was done. I wondered why my shoes felt wet, then realized that my cuts had reopened.

I ran across Euclid Ave, weaving through traffic, disregarding the honks and curses. I hit the grass in front of Macky—

And recognized the wall of muscle twenty feet in front of me. Kirby was strolling along the green lawn abutting the music building, wearing something strapped to his back. I skidded to a stop, but it was too late—he'd heard the crazy woman pounding along the sidewalk in heels and, like everyone else on the lawn, he had turned to look at me.

There was a long, frozen moment when I registered that he was wearing a BabyBjörn with my niece inside, her eyes wide and unfrightened, looking around the lawn with mild interest. She was okay.

And then she was turned away from me, as Kirby moved to run.

I chased him, but I was much too slow. "Stop him!" I screamed desperately to the students loitering on the lawn. "That's not his kid!"

Several of them stood up, and two male professors in their forties began to halfheartedly chase after Kirby, who started running full-out. The gap between us began to widen, and I knew I was seconds away from losing Charlie. "No!" I howled, and without thinking I pulled on my mindset again, trying to target Kirby and pull the goddamned motherfucking undead *life* out of him . . .

I'd forgotten about what Charlie could do.

Kirby ran out of sight, completely protected from me by my niece's power. I kept going for another moment, screaming, knowing it was useless, and then the two professors in front of me dropped to the ground like stones in a pond.

Then the group of students on the lawn nearest them. Then a jogger. Then two dog-walkers.

I was watching them in horror when my foot caught a tree root. I went flying through the air, crashing down hard on my right shoulder. I screeched with pain as it dislocated. By the time I managed to struggle to my feet and look around, every single person on the wide Macky lawn had collapsed on the grass.

The wave of stolen magic hit me, and I lost consciousness.

Chapter 33

I opened my eyes to darkness. For a moment I wondered dully if I'd blinded myself with the magic. It didn't matter, really. I'd lost Charlie, and I'd killed a couple dozen people with my fucking mind. I'd stolen their life force—and for what? I'd been so sure that everything would be fine if I could just catch Kirby . . . and then I'd lost him. By morning Charlie was going to be in another state.

I had failed to save her, just like I'd failed to save her mother.

Very slowly, the room around me came into focus, and I realized with a dim sense of relief that I wasn't blind—I was dreaming. I was sitting on the edge of my twin bed in the bedroom Sam and I had shared at our parent's house, the one we had insisted on sharing even though the new house had plenty of space. I looked around the room fondly. There was Sam's mussed bed, looking like she'd just jumped out of it. There was the stuffed bear she'd slept with since we were three, and I recognized the stack of novels on my nightstand as being from my AP English class.

Then I frowned. Something felt off. I dreamed about my sister all the time, but this felt different. I wasn't usually so conscious of being asleep, for one thing, and everything was too . . . *detailed*. My dreams were usually fuzzy and content-oriented—I would dream about this or that event, real or imaginary, and that's all I would remember later.

But this time I saw all the minutiae—what I was wearing (jeans and a plain Luther Shoes T-shirt), the names on the posters on our walls, the piles of clothes, clean and dirty, on Sam's side of the room. It even *smelled* like the obnoxious floral air fresheners my mom had liked to use throughout the house when we were kids. Had I ever had a dream with *smells* before? This was too weird.

"*Finally*, Allie," said a voice from in front of me. "It took you long enough."

I looked up. There was Sam, sitting cross-legged on her own twin bed across from me, though it had been empty just a second ago. She was wearing the same outfit I'd last seen her in: black leggings, ballet flats, and a drapey turquoise top that hid her postpartum baby pooch. My sister had been small-framed, with a brunette pixie cut and big blue eyes that were identical to mine. People had rarely guessed we were twins, and sisters, but if you looked closely, our eyes gave it away.

"Sammy?" I said in a small voice. I began to stand up, but she shook her head, motioning for me to stay where I was.

"Sorry, babe, but you can't hug me. It doesn't work like that."

I looked around for a moment and then sat back on my bed, folding my legs to mirror her. This was how we'd had a thousand conversations in high school, back when Sam and I were making plans to room together at college. Before 9/11, before I'd decided that being a soldier was my destiny.

"Usually when I dream about you, we get to hug," I pointed out.

"You're not dreaming, Allie," she told me seriously.

I snorted. "Of course I am. I'm talking to my dead sister."

Sam just raised one eyebrow at me, waiting for me to put it together.

"I'm talking to my dead sister," I repeated. "Are you saying that this is real? *You're* real?"

She nodded. "I'm me, or what's left of me." Then she put on a low, dramatic voice. "*I* am the *soul* of Samantha Wheaton!" A goofy grin broke out on her face.

I stared back, not believing. This was just another dream—more vivid and heartbreaking than usual, maybe, but still a dream. Wasn't it?

Sam arched a single eyebrow at me, a trick she'd always been much better at than I was. "Allie, you know for a fact now that vampires are real, and you've personally died and come back several times. How is this any weirder than that?"

"Because I want it to be true," I whispered.

She rolled her eyes. "Fine, I'll prove it. I'm gonna tell you something you don't know. You can't dream about things you don't know." Her eyes searched the air above my head for a moment; then she brightened. "Dad's fifty-fifth birthday, when you were in Iraq," she said to me. "Brie and I got drunk on champagne and threw up in the bushes behind Mom and Dad's house. You can check the story with her."

"That's . . ." I shook my head. I believed her. "If it's true, how did we . . . do this?"

She shrugged. "You tell me, Allie. You called. I just picked up the phone."

"I miss you so much," I said, my voice quavering. "I'm so sorry I wasn't there when he killed you."

Sam rolled her eyes again. "You've gotta get over that, babe."

"Get over what? Your *death*?"

Her face softened. "Get over the idea that you could have done something. Why do you think I sent you the dream of that time in the park? You could only do so much to keep me safe, Allie. At some point I was gonna be the person I was gonna be." I must have looked unconvinced, because she huffed out a sigh. "Look, I chose to live in LA. I chose to go out that night. Even if you'd been *with* me, you probably couldn't have prevented it."

"You've been sending me dreams?" I said stupidly. "You can do that?" Sam nodded. I thought of all the dreams I'd been having since Quinn had officially dropped the case. "What does that mean?"

"It means your access to magic is getting stronger, babe," she said gently. "You're communicating across the line."

"You know about magic?"

"I didn't when I was alive, no. But I do now." She cocked her head to the side for a second, as if she were listening to someone I couldn't hear. Her face darkened. "But I'm not supposed to talk about that."

"Sounds like you have a lot of rules."

Sam scrunched her face at me. "And you know I do *so* well with those. I'm trying to be good, though, so we can talk."

I just shook my head, too bewildered to even know where to start. "I don't know what to say. I . . . I lost her, Sam. I lost Charlie." My eyes filled with tears. "I was so stupid."

"Hey, hey," Sam said hurriedly. "Don't cry. She's not lost yet. You're going to find her."

"I can't." I drew my knees up, hugging them in front of me. "I'm too dangerous to go anywhere near her right now, Sammy. I killed all those people. I can't control myself."

Sam sighed and scooted to the edge of her bed, leaning forward and resting her elbows on her knees. She looked straight into my eyes. "Allison," she said quietly. "Listen to me carefully. There is *no one* else, do you understand? The police can't help, and the vampires only care about damage control. You are *the only one* who can help my baby."

I sniffed, shaking my head. "I don't know how. She could be anywhere by now."

"Then you get your people together," Sam said, "and figure it out." She tilted her head again, pausing. Then she cursed. "I have to go. Babe, you've got to find my daughter. So *get up*."

I did, or at least I tried to. I struggled for only a second before the pain in my shoulder and feet broke over me, making me writhe. A cool hand touched my face, brushed my sweat-stuck hair away from my eyes. "Lex?"

I went still. The man's voice was so soft, so worried, that it took me a moment to place it. Quinn. I opened my eyes. I was lying on a couch, and he was crouched on the floor next to me. We were in some sort of darkened room. I recognized the carpeting and color scheme from Macky Auditorium. My eyes went wide as I remembered what had happened.

"Oh, God! Did I—all those people—"

"Alive," Quinn said firmly. He hesitated for a second, then added, "But unconscious. The EMTs I talked to said they should be fine . . . probably." In response to my questioning look, he added, "I pressed some of the cops into thinking it was a gas leak. Not my best story, but it will hold until Itachi can get some more vampires here to help."

I struggled to sit up. Quinn must have popped my shoulder back in place while I was out, but the room still spun around me. When I tried to squint at a wall clock, the walls spun, too. At first I thought it was the pain, but pain didn't make you feel drunk. I felt like I was about to burst from the forces swirling inside me. I lay back down. "What's wrong with me?"

He shook his head. "I'm not sure," he said softly. "Your pupils are dilated almost to the edge of the irises. I called Lily and Simon, but there's a clan assembly tonight. Nobody's answering."

"How long was I out?"

"Two hours." He frowned. "I was starting to get worried."

I tried to sit up again, but the room wasn't any more cooperative this time around. Quinn laid a hand on my arm, trying to still me. "Lex, I don't think you should—"

"He took Charlie," I said, panting. "Help me, please."

Quinn hesitated for one more second, then nodded. He draped my left arm around his shoulder and stood me up, supporting me around the waist with his right arm. For a moment I helped him as much I as I could; then I remembered that he was a vampire and let my body sag against him so I could focus my energy on thinking.

"Where exactly are we going?" Quinn murmured to me.

"You said the witches are getting together tonight?" He nodded. I smiled grimly, or at least I think I did.

"Well, I'm a witch, right? Let's go get introduced."

Chapter 34

We made our way out of the building that way, with Quinn supporting me as I staggered forward. Then he grunted with annoyance and abruptly reached down to scoop up my legs, clasping me to his chest. My dress had torn a little when I'd fallen, but I still felt like I was on the cover of a goddamned romance novel, getting carried around in my formal gown. It would have been embarrassing as hell if I'd had the energy to give a shit.

Neither of us said anything as he hauled me to his car, but I caught Quinn glancing down at my feet a few times, and I realized he could smell the blood that had seeped out of my reopened wounds, gluing my shoes to my feet. Gross. It was sticky and uncomfortable, but I figured it might be even worse for Quinn if I took the shoes off, so I just tried to ignore it.

The edges of my vision seemed to blur and twitch. Now that my body was in motion, the scenery rushing past me, I was having trouble keeping my eyes focused on one thing, so I closed them. My skin felt like it was about to explode. "Quinn," I whispered. "It's getting worse. Hurry."

He tore down the country roads, arriving at the Pellar farm in about half the time it should have taken. When Quinn finally put the car in park, I braced myself against the dashboard and squinted. A few different sets of headlights were backing away from the farmhouse, so I figured the meeting had to be breaking up. That was probably for the best.

Quinn took one of the spots that had just been vacated, blocking in a red minivan. He came around and opened my car door. I managed to unbuckle my seat belt before he scooped me up again. "I can walk," I said woozily, but neither of us really believed me.

There were a few voices moving in our direction, chatting and laughing. The voices kept stopping when they got close to us. I ignored all of that and closed my eyes so I didn't have to try to interpret any more images with my addled brain.

Later—a minute? Ten minutes?—I heard Quinn call out Lily's name. I lifted my head again. We were in a big, open clearing behind the farmhouse, and there were candles everywhere. I couldn't understand how the flames were staying lit . . . or why the air above them was so shiny. "Pretty," I murmured.

"What happened to her?" said Lily, who was right next to my head now. Or at least her voice was.

I jumped in Quinn's arms. "Hey, Lil," I said drunkenly. "The lights are super pretty."

Lily looked at me hard. "*Simon!*" she shouted, without looking away from me.

Simon moved away from a group of people and jogged over. "You better set her down," he told Quinn. There was concern in his voice, real concern, and I squinted hard at him.

"You sound sad, Simon," I told him. There was someone hovering at his shoulder, a pretty Asian woman with jet-black hair cut to frame her face. "Ooh!" I said happily. "Simon's lady love! Simon says you're a witch, too." I giggled. "Heh. 'Simon says.'"

"She's getting worse, I think," Quinn said over my head. "She was coherent when she first woke up, but she's losing it."

He started telling them about Charlie, and I tuned out, not wanting to let them kill my buzz. At some point Quinn put my legs down, but his arms were still the only things keeping me upright. Lily began touching me, but that was okay. I'd seen her boobs, so we had real trust.

Then Simon reached a thumb up and lifted my eyelid, shining a penlight in my eye. "Hey!" I complained. "Not cool, Simon!" I tried to karate-chop him away, but my arms weren't working quite like I wanted. I sighed and endured his examination of my other eye. There was some more discussion, and when I tuned in again Simon was saying, "I've never seen anything like this." There was a frown in his voice.

"I have," announced an annoyed, steel-cut voice.

Suddenly Hazel fucking Pellar was in my line of sight, moving her son aside to peer at my face. She put her hands on my cheeks, probing my skin. I could feel energy pass between us, but I didn't know if it started from her or me. "She's magic-drunk," she said matter-of-factly. "Witches aren't meant to hold this much magic inside. We're conductors, not car batteries. She needs to ground it."

There was an uneasy silence, and I saw Hazel look back and forth between her two children. "What?" she demanded.

"That could be a problem," Lily said sheepishly. There was a pause; then she added, "We've only taught her one spell, and she overdid it."

At the same time Simon chimed in: "She can't manage regular spells yet."

There was a terrible silence. "But you should see her sense out life?" Lily offered in a small voice. I started snickering, which probably didn't help.

"You two *swore* to me," Hazel exploded, "that you were just trying to teach her control! Not teach her everything *but* control."

That made me mad. "Hey! That's not fair," I said, glaring at Hazel. Or trying to, anyway—her image kept flickering around like one of those jumping spiders. "They've been *helping* me, working their asses off and donating time that I'm sure they'd rather spend doing a million other things instead of—"

"*Lex*," Quinn interrupted. I paused. The hair on my arms was standing on end, and there was an electric charge in the air, like when I'd done that spell in the mudroom. Hazel was watching me with narrowed eyes, and I dimly realized that whatever she'd thought of me before today, I'd just made it a lot worse. I whimpered.

"She's too powerful," Hazel snapped. "I warned you about this—"

"*Please*," I broke in. "I have to save my niece. Please. Whatever's going on, I have to save her tonight. Please, she's a null, and this vampire took her—"

Hazel drew in a sharp breath. "Your niece is a *null*?"

She said something to Simon and Lily for a minute, and they answered, but I barely heard what they said. "Do you guys hear kind of a buzzing?" I wondered aloud.

I got distracted for a while, listening to the buzz, and then Quinn's voice was whispering in my ear. "Lex, honey," he said, "There's too much magic in you. It's too much for your body."

I could hear the thread of worry in his voice. I turned to look at him, and for a second I thought I could even see it. I raised my hand to run a finger along it, but instead I touched his face, experimentally running my finger over his lips, tracing a line across his cheek to his ear. "Do you like me?" I asked idly.

Amusement sparked in his eyes. "Much to my chagrin," he said solemnly. "But I need you to listen. Lily thinks she knows a way to get the magic out, but it's going to hurt."

"What happens if she doesn't?" I asked, immediately proud of my competence.

"We don't know," Quinn told me. "You could die, or you could hurt someone."

"Do it," I said. He said something else after that, but I didn't hear it because the buzzing was back, bigger, like a wave that had chased the smaller wave that came before it. "What?" I yelled.

The second time I half heard him and half read his lips, until finally I understood what he was trying to tell me.

"I'm gonna have to hold you down."

Chapter 35

I would never remember much of the next few hours, except the pain.

Lily needed me to lie on my stomach with my arms stretched in front of me. I held still as long as I could, but then the pain was too much. I began to struggle and then fight them outright. It was just in my nature.

Eventually, Quinn had to lie down on my back to hold me with his body weight, but even he couldn't keep *all* of me from moving, and for a few seconds it looked like I was going to hurt Lily very badly. Then Hazel, of all people, lay down on the ground in front of me and took my hands. She looked straight into my eyes without fear, and I obeyed her order to be still.

Then finally the pain was gone, and it was like gravity had suddenly been restored to the world. Up was up, down was down, and I was me again. For a second the relief was so great I almost blacked out. I think I maybe did lose consciousness briefly, because when I opened my eyes I was lying on my side in the field, not touching anyone. I curled inward, enjoying the feel of the cool grass on my skin. Then I realized that the pain in my shoulder was gone. I wiggled my feet experimentally. They also felt fine.

I sat up without incident and looked down at my dress. The skirt was in tatters and one strap was ripped off, but the upper half was still more or less intact. "Quinn?" I said, squinting against the dim light. The only light in the field emanated from the candles, which I now realized were encased in long vertical tubes of glass, to protect them from the wind.

"I'm here," came his voice from behind me.

I turned around and saw him sitting in the grass, peering at me over the screen of a cell phone. "Where is everyone?" I asked. "Did I hurt someone?" A new thought occurred to me. "Was it all a dream?"

He smiled briefly. "No and no. Hazel thought it might be best to give you a little space, and Lily needed to rest for a while. It took a lot out of her, but she'll be fine."

"What took a lot out of her?" I asked, puzzled.

I saw a strange look come over his face, mostly thanks to the glow from his phone. "You don't remember what she did?"

"No . . ."

"Look at your arms," he instructed.

I held out my arms and tried to look. There was some sort of marking covering my forearms, stretching down over my wrists and almost into my palms. "What is it?" I asked.

"Here." Quinn tapped something on his phone's screen, then scooted across the grass and held it up to my arms. The light from the phone flared, and for the first time I could make out the swirling black ink that crawled up my arms.

"You guys tattooed me?" I said in amazement. It was a hell of a lot of tattooing. "Why?"

"To pull the power out," Simon called. I looked up, and when my eyes adjusted to the dimness again, I could see him hurrying across the lawn toward us. A flashlight beam bounced along in front of him.

"Lily's tattoos," I remembered. "She said they were a long story."

Simon nodded. He knelt down in front of me and gently took my hand, flipping it over to inspect the tattoos with his flashlight. "They look good."

In the better light, I could see they weren't just swirling patterns—my arms were a mirror image of each other, and together they formed an emblem. "A griffin," I said, looking up at Simon in wonder. I was wearing the little griffin earring studs at that moment, which seemed like an unbelievable coincidence.

He smiled. "She's been working on the designs pretty much since we met you, but she wasn't sure it was a good idea." He shrugged.

"What do they do?"

Simon answered, "Think of them like . . . a funnel. They'll let you channel magic through your hands. That should help with the problem you've been having."

"A filter, not a focus," Quinn reminded me softly.

"Oh," I said. "Not that I'm not grateful, but why do this now?"

"We had to get the magic out of you," Simon explained. He gestured at my arms. "The only way to construct something like this on a witch is by using the witch's own power. Lily's tattoos took her a couple of years to complete, using a little bit of power each time. Yours drew all the power out at once, more or less."

"They're not even bleeding," I said, examining them.

"True." He smiled at me. "You should be feeling better in general, because of transferring so much magic. I can explain, but it'd take a while, and I know you're in a hurry."

"Charlie," I said suddenly. I looked at Quinn. "What time is it?"

"Two a.m.," he said matter-of-factly. Two in the morning wasn't exactly late for him.

Then again, it wasn't late for me, either. I stood up. "We've got to—" I wobbled, a little unsteady. "Where do we go?"

Quinn shook his head. "That's a good question." He held up his phone. "Itachi and Maven have their vampires watching the highways, all the major roads out of the state. Kirby tried to pass into Wyoming two hours ago. They turned him around, but he got away."

"Was Charlie in the car?" I asked.

Quinn shrugged. "Our people only saw the top of a car seat, but presumably."

It made me oddly relieved that Charlie was in a car seat. It was kind of stupid, since I knew Kirby could still do any number of horrible things to her, but at least if they got into a fender bender she'd be fine. "Okay." I paced a few feet away, thinking. My shoes still felt sticky and disgusting, but I could handle that. I paused and turned back to Quinn. "What time does the sun rise?" I asked. "Seven? Quarter after?"

He nodded. "About that."

"Then we've got five hours before he tries to leave the state again," I concluded.

It was Simon who said, "How do you figure?"

"Charlie," Quinn said, understanding dawning on his face.

I nodded. "Kirby's got a null with him, so he can go out in the sun. His smartest move is to wait until dawn, when all the vampires guarding the border will have to go to ground. Then he can sashay right out of Colorado."

"If they cross the state line," Quinn said quietly. "Itachi and Maven can't help. She'll disappear."

I nodded and resumed my pacing. "How do we find them?" I glanced at Simon. "You said something once about using spells to find things?"

He shook his head. "We'd need something of Kirby's, preferably hair or fingernails. But even then it's unlikely the magic would work."

"Because he's also magic?"

Simon nodded. "That, and because he's with a null. I'm not sure anyone could find a null."

"Shit." I paced to the edge of the candlelight, then back. It was getting downright cold out here, and I longed to go inside the farmhouse, which was now glowing with light. But I wasn't ready to face all those people—the ones who'd had to hold me down while I screamed.

I needed to focus on the problem at hand. I needed a plan. "Back to the plan," I muttered. What was Victor and Darcy's original plan for Charlie? They were going to take her to Nolan's house.

Nolan was then going to take her to a middleman—Kirby?—who would take her out of state. Like links in a chain, presumably to avoid accountability. Each person would only have the baby for a few hours, so they wouldn't appear suspicious.

I stopped pacing and turned back to the two men, who were watching me. Simon looked a little bemused, which was kind of fair. I probably looked ridiculous, with the ruined dress and my hair and makeup smeared everywhere. Quinn's expression looked as implacable as ever at first glance, but I was getting better at reading the subtleties. He was watching me intently, looking for an opening to jump in and help.

"Was Kirby always in on the plan?" I said to him. "We were both so sure he wasn't involved after we spoke to him at the fraternity."

He shook his head. "I've been thinking about that. I could be wrong, but I believe Kirby was recruited later, after the attempt with Victor and Darcy failed."

"You don't think he could be the middleman?" I asked. "The 'merchant' who was supposed to get Charlie from Nolan?"

Quinn shook his head, but Simon visibly jumped. "Wait, say that again," he urged.

I raised an eyebrow, but said, "Darcy told me that she and Victor were taking Charlie to their senior—Nolan—who was taking her to the merchant. The merchant would place Charlie with new . . . well, she used the word 'parents,' but it felt like she meant something more insidious."

Simon closed the space between us in three steps and took my arm. "You're positive she used the word 'merchant'?" he said.

"Yeah, why?"

Simon looked from me to Quinn, then back at me. "Because the Merchant isn't just a middleman. He's a witch."

Chapter 36

Quinn made a call to update the vampires. While he did that, Simon and I started toward the house. I was moving okay on my own, but I noticed he was keeping one hand hovering behind my back, ready to catch me in case I toppled. "Who is this guy?" I asked. "The Merchant?"

"His name is Billy Atwood. He's a shitkicker witch just east of Gainesville who fancies himself an outlaw," Simon explained, his voice sour. "He's the last in the Atwood line of witches, at least around here. As far as I can tell, he doesn't even have much power, but he thinks he deserves to be a badass. He started calling himself the Merchant when he began dealing."

"Drugs?" I asked.

Simon nodded. "Drugs, guns, stolen valuables. He's so unbelievably small-time, though, that nobody particularly cares. Atwood's the only drug lord I've ever heard of who has to keep up a day job. He's a freelance welder."

"He sounds like an asshole. Why the hell would vampires be working with him?" I wondered.

Simon's expression turned thoughtful. "He's hungry, for one thing. Always striving for upward mobility. And he has no scruples. If someone promised him enough money, he'd be happy to kidnap a baby. He'd probably see it as his chance to graduate to a better class of badass."

"Plus he's a fall guy," I said, remembering the links in the chain. As evidence goes, it was thin, but the more I thought about it, the more convinced I was that Kirby had gone back to the Merchant's to hide out until daylight. He would want to stay away from the other vampires—it was too likely that they would tattle to Itachi if he went to them—and since we hadn't found the Merchant during the first go-round, there was no reason for Kirby to think we'd find him now. No one knew that Darcy had mentioned the word "merchant" to me, and if she hadn't, we would never have thought to look for a witch.

Quinn caught up with us, walking on my opposite side. "We're sanctioned," he said grimly. "Kirby *and* this Merchant, if necessary."

Simon held up a hand. "Whoa. Atwood is a piece of shit, but he's a *witch* piece of shit. Our problem. I'm coming with you, and I'll take care of him."

Quinn opened his mouth to protest, but I held up my hand. "Stop. Simon comes, and we'll fight about it in the car." I looked down at the remains of my dress and my blood-soaked shoes. To Simon, I added, "Does Lily keep any clothes here? And maybe some sneakers?"

Ten minutes later I met the two of them at Quinn's car, wearing Lily's black leggings, ribbed white tank top, and black motorcycle jacket, which strained at the arms—I had more muscle than its owner. Lily didn't have any sneakers at the farmhouse, but Hazel had reluctantly handed over a pair of crimson Keens that were a size too big for me. They didn't do much for the rest of the outfit, but at that point I was willing to take anything as long as it wasn't sticky or high-heeled.

I had longed for a shower, but settled for rinsing the dried blood off my feet in the bathroom sink and splashing water on my face to get rid of the smeared makeup. I slicked back my hair with water to keep it out of my face. My shoes and dress had gone straight into the bathroom garbage. Hopefully none of the borrowed clothes would suffer the same fate. The leather jacket alone probably cost two weeks' pay at the Depot.

Lily had looked drawn and exhausted, but she'd promised she would be fine. When I tried to thank her and Hazel, they just waved me on. "Get that null back," Hazel said, her expression grim. "You're going to need her."

Gainesville was a minuscule town about fifteen miles north of Boulder, near the entrance to Rocky Mountain National Park. The population was something like a thousand people, which meant they had a few bars, a single gas station, and not a whole lot else. Gainesville was a town you drove through on the way to a music festival in Lyons, not a place where anyone actually chose to stop.

And yet here we were, leaving for Gainesville. "Weapons?" I asked Quinn before we got in.

He nodded. "Everything we need is in the trunk," he promised.

Quinn drove while I sat shotgun. Simon and Quinn spent the first third of the drive fighting over which of them had the responsibility to kill Billy Atwood, if it came down to it. I ignored the argument. I didn't care what happened to Atwood. All I cared about was making Charlie safe.

They finally agreed to play it by ear, which they frankly should have thought of to begin with, and as the argument wound down I turned to look at Simon in the backseat. "What's the layout of the property?" I asked. "Where will this guy be keeping her?"

"Billy lives in what's left of the Atwood farm," Simon explained. "It's not a working farm like ours. It's basically just a small house and an old barn he uses for welding projects."

"Where would he keep Charlie?" I asked. "The house?"

Simon looked uneasy. "You gotta understand, I've only been to check on this guy twice to make sure he wasn't abusing magic. And both times he was working out in the barn when I got there. I've never even been in the house."

"Well, you're all we've got," I said firmly. "So take a guess: house or barn?"

"Hopefully the house," he said. "He usually keeps the stuff he fences in the barn, but the place is like something out of a horror movie: the whole building is packed wall to wall with welding gear and junk, all of it with sharp edges and covered in rust. It's a tetanus outbreak waiting to happen."

"That seems idiotic," I said. "What if a neighbor kid wanders in?"

Simon shrugged. "It's dangerous, yeah, but it acts as its own security system. Nobody wants to look through that death trap to find the valuables he hides in there. It's crammed so full of metal edges that it's impossible to move from one wall to the other unless you know the place. I don't think Atwood even bothers closing the barn door at night."

"That is literally the worst environment I can imagine for an eighteen-month-old," I said. Panic clawed up my rib cage as I involuntarily pictured Charlie toddling around in a room like that. "He wouldn't keep her in there, would he?"

"Probably not," Simon said. "But like I said, I don't know the layout of the house at all."

"Then we go in and search blind," Quinn said. "Tell us anything you do know about the house or the layout of the farm. Anything at all."

Simon considered that for a moment. "There's a driveway that runs north-south. The barn is on the west side of the driveway, and the house is on the east side. It's small, maybe three bedrooms or so, two stories. Probably built early in the twentieth century." His brow furrowed. "Come to think of it, the barn's tall enough for a second story, too, although I don't remember seeing a hayloft." He shrugged. "I was too busy trying not to slice off my elbows, frankly."

We were going in without much intel, but we didn't have a choice. All that mattered was stopping Kirby before he could get Charlie out of the state.

But would that actually make my niece safe?

"Quinn," I said, "Something else to consider . . . If you're right, and Kirby was brought into this thing later . . ."

Understanding flashed in his eyes. "Then there's still someone else pulling the strings," he finished with a frown. "That's not good. He or she might decide to oversee this thing in person."

Shit. Quinn had guns and shredders in the car, but what if they weren't enough? What if we were up against someone who'd be prepared for those things? I turned to look at Simon again. "How stable am I?" I asked. When he just blinked at me, I rolled my hand in the air. "You told me last month not to press any vampires because my magic was too unstable. Kind of a lot has happened since then." Simon chortled at the understatement.

Before he could answer, Quinn broke in. "*What* did you just say?" He looked at Simon in his rearview mirror. "Did she just say she can press vampires?"

It was kind of funny, hearing so much shock in his voice, but I kept my focus on Simon.

"In *theory*," he said hesitantly, "the tattoos should stabilize you."

"But?" I prompted.

He shrugged. "You know the deal. Boundary witches are unpredictable. And you've got more access to raw magic than anyone I've ever met."

I tilted my head, thinking it over. "I'm gonna take that as a 'stable enough,'" I decided.

Quinn was still looking back and forth between me and his mirror. "You can press vampires?" he repeated. "Why didn't you tell me? Have you ever pressed me?" There was an edge of anger in his voice. "Seriously, Lex, did you?"

"See?" Simon pointed out. "They *really* don't like that you can do that."

I eventually persuaded Quinn that I hadn't pressed him, and we kept going straight north on Highway 36. Then Simon had Quinn go left on Ute Highway instead of heading straight into the town of Gainesville. We were in a very rural part of the county, with darkness unbroken except for the occasional single spotlight above a barn or house. The ground was all scrubby brush out here, which made it seem more like ranch country than farm country, but what the hell did I know about that?

Finally, Simon told Quinn to pull over and cut the lights. He complied, and we were suddenly sitting in near-total darkness, the brushwood around us lit only by the stars. "The Atwood place is a little less than a mile down this road," Simon said in a low voice. "I think we should leave the car here and hike up. We may actually have a shot at the element of surprise if Kirby stays close enough to Charlie."

Quinn popped the back latch, and we all got out of the car and walked around toward the tepid glow of the trunk light. I'd seen the top two layers of Quinn's stash—camping gear covering up power tools and shredders—but now he shoved all of that aside and grasped the little hook to open the spare tire well.

There was no spare tire. Instead, the space had been slightly enlarged and packed with a small but excellent assortment of fire-arms. "Help yourself," Quinn said casually, as though he was shar-ing a bag of M&Ms. I recognized an 8-gauge shotgun, which couldn't have been legal, and a TAR-21 assault rifle, which was gor-geous but which I couldn't shoot lefthanded. I admired a Desert Eagle handgun, but it was way too big for my hand. Then I realized I was standing around playing Goldilocks and the three guns, and told myself to stop geeking out.

"Yessss," I hissed as I spotted a semiautomatic Beretta M9, exactly like the one I'd used in the service. I grabbed the Beretta, two spare magazines, and a Mossberg 590 pump shotgun on a strap, slinging it over my head in a move as familiar as brushing my teeth. Then I reached for a handful of shredders. As I did, Simon frowned at them.

"You should know that if you take those stakes close to your niece, they might not work afterwards."

"Why not?" I asked doubtfully, examining the point of one of the stakes.

"Oh, they'll still go *into* a vampire's heart," Simon promised, giving Quinn a little sidelong glance. "But I'm not sure how the spell on them will react to being near a null. It might short out, which will make it almost impossible to actually kill a vampire with one—unless, of course, you can get him to hold really still."

I remembered Quinn explaining that you had to either remove or practically mince a vampire's heart in order to kill it. "Okay, but they're still safer to use around a baby than one of the guns," I pointed out grimly. "Remember when you guys are shooting that any ricochets could go into my niece. Don't fire unless you're positive you'll hit your target."

They both nodded, sobered.

I helped myself to a simple fast-draw holster that had already been conveniently attached to a belt. The belt was so long that it ended up hanging low on my hips like I was an Old West gunslinger, but as long as it didn't pull my pants down, I couldn't care less. I was getting into that state of mind I remembered from the army: quiet, alert, and still . . . until I needed to snap into movement.

Quinn took only a bunch of shredders and a handgun I didn't recognize. Simon looked grimly at the weapons cache for a long moment, but then just grabbed some shredders, tucking them into the breast pocket of his army-style jacket. I wondered if I'd freaked him out by bringing up the idea that a ricochet could accidentally hit Charlie, but I shrugged off the concern. If he was really worried about controlling his shots, he shouldn't have a gun.

All three of us took penlights from the top stash of supplies, and then Quinn closed the trunk. We left the Toyota and headed for the farm as quietly as possible. Simon had suggested that we curve around the driveway and approach from the east, so that we would come up on the back of the farmhouse. Quinn, who had vampire reflexes and night sight, took the lead, and Simon and I followed as closely as possible, walking blind through the countryside.

Quinn moved silently through the undergrowth, and I wasn't much louder, having spent a good deal of time sneaking around with guns. Simon, however, was a disaster in the stealth department: his shoes kept catching on weeds, and the stakes clanked around in his jacket. He tried clutching one hand to his chest to keep them still, but that threw off his balance just enough to make him stumble more. I fought not to snap at him, reminding myself that he wasn't a soldier or a vampire. His work with the clan probably didn't require too much experience with covert operations. After a quarter mile or so I switched places with him so he could follow Quinn more closely, and that helped a little.

Finally Quinn slowed to a stop, and ahead of us I could see a small farmhouse with a couple of lights on, including one outdoor security light above the back screen door. Back in the car, we'd decided on a strategy. The house would likely have two entrances, a front door and a back one, and some windows on the second story that a vampire could get in and out of easily. As we drew closer to the house, I made eye contact with the men, touched my watch, and nodded. In my head, I began to silently count as we split off: Simon to the back door, me around to the front. Quinn would wait until we were in position and then take a running leap onto the lower part of the roof, so he could duck in through a second-story window. It was a risk—if Charlie happened to be close to wherever he landed, there was a possibility that he'd fall back down, maybe find himself with a broken leg or two. But Quinn had assured us that if that *did* happen, he'd heal fast enough to be back in the fight within a few minutes.

I slipped around the side of the house, noting the gravel driveway just beyond it. I could only make out the edge of the driveway in the spill of light from the house, but there was another light on above the barn, a plain, unpainted wooden structure. Simon had been right—the main door, a massive piece of wood that had to be slid back and forth, stood open, a yawning, sinister black hole in the structure. Unlike the Pellars' cheerful red barn, this one was slightly dilapidated, like years of heavy snowfall had caved in parts of the roof and no one had cared enough to fix it. I kept an eye on the barn, just in case Kirby was hiding out there after all.

I made it to the door of the house just as my count hit fifty, and pulled the M9 out of the fast-draw holster. I counted off another ten seconds, and at the one-minute mark, I reared back and kicked in the cheap front door.

Chapter 37

The door flew inward with a tremendous crash, echoed by another crash deeper inside, as Simon burst through the back door. Quinn would be on the second story, but his entrance was silent—he must have found an unlocked window.

With the M9 in hand, I moved through a short, shabby entryway and to the right, into a living room where a single standing lamp emitted a wan yellow glow.

The room was small and looked like a museum diorama of the seventies, furnished with just an old dusty sofa sleeper and an even older armchair made out of material that looked like burlap. The only modern touch was an enormous flat-screen TV hanging on the wall, which said a lot about Atwood's priorities. I passed through the room and entered an empty kitchen, with fixtures of a similar age and quality as the living room furniture. Then I found myself in a small dining room. I saw movement in the opposite doorway and tensed my finger on the Beretta's trigger.

Simon moved through the doorway, a stake in his left hand, the fingers of his right hand stretched out in front of him. The gesture reminded me of the day in his hayloft when he'd used the shielding spell on me, and I realized he was preparing some kind of offensive spell. I lowered the Beretta and nodded at him. "Stairs back this way," he said in a whisper so low it was almost silent. He jerked his head back the way he'd come, and I nodded and followed him.

Quinn was waiting for us at the bottom of the steps.

"The house is empty," he said in an undertone.

My chest tightened with disappointment. "What about a basement?" I asked.

Quinn gestured behind me, and I turned my head and saw a door. "I checked there, too," he said. "I didn't see any other buildings when we arrived, so if they're here, they've gotta be in that barn."

I winced, remembering Simon's description of the building where tetanus goes to die. "Then we've lost the element of surprise."

"Probably."

I blew out a breath and turned to Simon. "How many entrances to the barn?"

The entryway where we were standing wasn't lit, but there was enough light spilling down from the stairs for me to make out his look of concentration. "Four," he said at last. "Aside from the big front door there are three more, one in the middle of each side." He shrugged. "The gable's boarded up, so there's no entrance through the hayloft."

I met Quinn's eyes. "The hayloft," I said, and he nodded in agreement. "Is it like yours?" I asked Simon.

He shook his head. "In our barn the hayloft extends the whole length of the building. This one is small, maybe . . . mmm . . . twelve, fifteen feet wide, at the west end of the barn."

"How do you get up there?" I asked, checking my watch. We'd been in the house for about three minutes, which was forever in an assault scenario. We needed to keep moving, but we couldn't go in completely blind, either.

"There's no permanent ladder," Simon answered me. "He must keep one on the first level somewhere, and he only props it up when he needs to get up there for something." He glanced at Quinn. "Like in *The Ring*," he added.

Quinn tilted his head in acknowledgment, although I had no idea what he was talking about. It didn't matter, though, because the way he described it, the hayloft would be the perfect place to hide something you didn't want found.

"I think we have to assume she's up there," I told the two men. "Here's what I think we should do."

The three of us went straight through the house's front door—at this point speed was more important than trying to be sneaky—but fanned out as soon as we were outside, so we'd make a more difficult target.

"As soon as we're close enough, you need to sense out the life in the barn," Simon had told me before we left.

"What? No, you should do it." I wasn't in any hurry to use magic again, tattoos or not.

"You're stronger than I am," Simon said simply. "And you have a wider range."

I did? "Simon . . ." I began uneasily, but he broke in.

"You can do this, Lex," he encouraged. "It's just sensing out life. You could do this in your sleep."

There was no time to argue with him. I swallowed my excuses and bobbed my head.

Once we were in the yard, Quinn broke off to the right. He would go around back and try to get into the barn through the boarded-up gable on the second story, much like he'd done at the farmhouse, but he'd wait for Simon's signal before trying to break in. Simon and I darted to the left, where an enormous propane tank stood a few feet southeast of the barn's gaping front door. I just prayed that Kirby and Atwood weren't stupid enough to shoot the tank.

The most immediate problem was going to be light—there was a fairly bright spotlight attached to the front of the barn, which was probably on some kind of automatic timer, but there were no lights on inside. That gave Kirby a distinct advantage over Simon and me: if we used the flashlights inside the barn we'd be sitting ducks, but if we tried to go without them, we'd cut ourselves on the welding equipment. We had to get the lights on inside the barn before doing anything else.

We crouched in the shadows, and then Simon nodded to me. I took a deep breath and closed my eyes, visualizing myself putting on thermal imaging goggles. Now I was sort of glad that Simon had made me practice turning my mindset on and off under any circumstances, including when I was terrified. Eyes closed, I pushed my senses toward the barn. I'd been worried the tattoos would limit me, but Simon had reassured me that they would only affect the way I manipulated magic, not the way I sensed it out. Right away, I felt a huge pulse of essence at the southern wall, the one nearest us. It was about midway down the barn's side, probably next to the door. I hadn't felt a vampire in my senses yet, but I figured it would be different from a human, and this felt human. "Atwood's by the southern door," I murmured to Simon.

"I feel him, too, but that's as far as I can go. Push farther," he directed.

So I did. I felt the next presence at the far end of the barn, probably by the west door. This one felt . . . *interesting*. Simon had told me that my brain interpreted the magic in a way I could understand, and for whatever reason it usually made sparks of life blue. But this spark was a deep, wormy red. It was a different magic from the magic of creation I saw in humans and animals, or from the yellowish death-essence that drifted out of them when they died. A darker magic. "Vampire," I breathed. To Simon, I said, "Kirby's at the west door."

I felt, rather than saw, his nod. "Let's go," he whispered, starting to stretch upward.

"Wait," I said, reaching out to grab his arm. Something was wrong: Tactically, west and south weren't the right places to guard, not if my niece was in the hayloft. And Charlie was a baby—even if she was restrained in a crib or a car seat, wouldn't they want someone to be with her? My eyes were still closed, and I pushed my magic harder, feeling past where I'd felt Kirby.

"Oh, shit," I hissed. "There are more of them."

Simon crouched back down. "Humans or vampires?"

"Human . . . there's another human at the north door. Atwood or somebody else. And that's gotta be Quinn, on the northwest corner of the building . . ." I opened my eyes, frowning. "There's a big blank area in the middle, I can't seem to feel—" Then I got it, and my heart tripped with excitement. "Charlie!"

"So we have at least one extra human, and an unknown number of people in the hayloft with Charlie. What do you want to do?" Simon asked.

"Stick to the plan," I told him firmly.

He hesitated for just a moment, trying to read my eyes in the shadows, but then nodded. "Go," I said softly.

Simon took off to the right, around the front of the propane tank. I followed just far enough to watch him march right up to the barn's gaping east door, the one closest to us. He stood to one side of the doorway, for a moment, mumbling something. Then he spun on his heel, waving a hand into the barn.

What followed was the loudest crash I'd ever heard. It seemed to go on forever, a cacophony of metallic screeching and clanking as metal bits big and small slammed into each other. "Anybody home?" Simon yelled. I grinned. Okay, so maybe it wasn't a signal so much as a distraction. As he reached into the barn, groping for a light switch, I took off around the left side of the propane tank, the Beretta in my hands.

As I was still approaching the barn, Simon must have found the switch, because a beam of light suddenly shot out of the window in the south door, revealing the silhouette of a tall, broad-shouldered man guarding the door. Caught in the light, he began to move toward me. I cocked the Beretta, pointing it at his center. "Don't move," I ordered, but the shadow kept coming. When he was a few feet away, I saw that he was quite young, with a bushy beard and a long, wicked-looking piece of metal pipe in one hand. And I realized that I knew him.

"Chewbacca?" I said, confused. Why would a freshman pledge from CU be here? "What are you—"

But he didn't even slow down. I couldn't shoot the kid, not until I was sure what team he was on, but the pipe came swinging toward my head like it was a T-ball. I ducked under it, but the kid was fast for his size. He turned around and started toward me again, and as the light caught him, I saw that his eyes were dazed and cloudy. Shit. He'd been pressed. I *definitely* couldn't shoot him.

But that didn't make his attack any less real. Chewbacca raised the pipe again in an overhead swing, intending to smash the top of my head. I lurched backward, just barely managing to get out of range before the pipe came whistling down. When it hit the ground in front of me I stomped one foot on it, leaned forward and punched the kid square in the nose with my right hand.

He dropped his hold on the pipe and straightened, looking disoriented. "Chewbacca?" I said hopefully, in case the blow had reversed Kirby's press, but the kid just gave a little shake of his head and started toward me again. I heard a gunshot echo from the far side of the barn. Shit, I didn't have time for this. I put the Beretta in its holster and dropped to the ground, kicking my left foot out as fast as I could and sweeping Chewbacca's legs out from under him. He went down on his ass *hard*, and I picked up the pipe, wound up, and smacked him on the side of the head, praying I'd used the right amount of force to knock him out but not kill him. He folded to the ground, and I sprinted toward the west side of the barn, where I'd last felt the vampire.

Chapter 38

I had the gun ready as I rounded the southwest corner of the barn, but there was no one on that side of the structure. Light was spilling out through the open door, though, and I hopped a decaying paddock fence and raced toward the entryway. I stopped to peek around the rotting wooden door frame.

And had to take a second look.

Simon had warned us, but the inside of the barn was still grotesquely fascinating. Atwood had filled the whole space with makeshift tables built of sawhorses, covered by flat, wall-sized pieces of steel. They were placed at random, so there were no neat rows through the building. Then he'd covered every inch of every surface, including the barn floor, with grimy junk. I recognized bits and pieces of engines, rusted coffee cans filled with nails and screwdrivers, blades for everything from forklifts to lawnmowers. There were larger pieces of metal shoved in there, too, and I didn't recognize most of these: parts from semi trucks, maybe?

Every bit of it was covered in layers of grease and rust, and Simon was right—everything was sharp. It would have taken me half an hour to walk from one wall to the other—except that Simon had blown an aisle through the very center of the goddamned barn. There was a two-foot-wide path running the length of the space, from where I was standing now to the east door where he'd come in.

I grinned. Well, that explained the clanging.

Cautiously, I stepped into the barn, my gun tracking along with my sight as I took in the mess. The hayloft was directly above me, about ten feet up, forming a partial overhang like a theater balcony. And in the center of the makeshift aisle, right below the edge of the hayloft, there was a pacifier. It had to have been dropped or kicked off the edge *after* Simon created the aisle. I took in a sharp breath, wanting to dance with relief. Charlie was *here*.

But I was suddenly very aware of the fact that, despite all the noise, she hadn't started crying. Why wasn't she fussing? I took a cautious step forward, into the aisle, but before I could see the edge of the balcony, I heard two quick gunshots from the north side of the barn.

Shit. I longed to check on my niece, but first I needed to help the others. I spun and flew back out of the door I'd come through. I started to round the corner, but my training kicked in and I jerked to a halt at the northwest corner, peeking around the side of the building.

There was a frickin' brawl unfolding on the lawn. No, *two* brawls. Ten feet in front of me, Kirby had Quinn pinned to the ground and was trying to wrestle a shredder out of his hand. Fifteen feet beyond that, Simon was struggling with a shorter man holding a handgun. He'd managed to point the guy's arm straight into the air, and the shooter had pulled the trigger several times.

Of the two of them Quinn seemed to be in greater danger, so as I walked forward I raised the Beretta and fired two shots directly into Kirby's stupid thick skull.

That got everyone's attention.

Simon and the kid—as I got closer I saw his protruding ears and recognized him as poor Yoda, the other pledge—froze for a moment, staring at me. Kirby swayed back, which gave Quinn a chance to wriggle out from under him. Now Kirby was kneeling, blood pouring from his temple, but even as I circled him the bleeding slowed and then stopped. I stared, fascinated. The bullets hadn't actually gone through his skull. Did vampires have harder bones than regular humans? Maybe if I used a bigger caliber next time—

Out of the corner of my eye I saw Simon snatch the gun from Yoda and club him on the back of the head. By then I was face-to-face with Kirby, who gave me a woozy leer as he began to push himself off the ground. I holstered the Beretta, swung the shotgun up, and fired into Kirby's chest from two feet away, the gun pointed directly at his heart.

Kirby froze in place, his features gone temporarily slack as his vampire healing powers rushed to keep up with his wounds. That was exactly what I wanted. I dropped the rifle and got even closer—Quinn yelled something at me, but I didn't hear it—and looked straight into his eyes. *Shit,* I thought, *I should have practiced this.*

I breathed in and out slowly, trusting Quinn to help Simon, trusting Simon to keep Quinn from interrupting me. I tuned them out and focused on nothing but Kirby's eyes. It was surprisingly easy. I'd been practicing my mindset for almost a month now.

When I was sure I could handle it, I opened up a connection between us. I'm not sure how I did it, exactly, I sort of just . . . willed it into existence, and it was there. I pushed my concentration into it—and nothing happened.

Kirby began to blink and stir.

Without my thinking about it, my body did exactly the right thing. I raised my hands and placed them on either side of Kirby's face, funneling my power into him. And I *pushed.*

It was too much. I knew the second I'd done it. I wasn't used to the tattoos focusing my magic like that, and I'd used more force than I needed to. Kirby whimpered, his mind threatening to break.

I backed off slowly, carefully, so I wouldn't give him mental whiplash. Finally, I found a balanced amount of power and asked him the question, even though I was pretty sure I knew the answer.

"Where is Charlie?"

"In the hayloft," Kirby said, his voice flat and dreamy at the same time.

"Is Atwood with her?"

"Yes."

"Is she hurt?" My voice hardened, and he paused for a long moment. Finally he answered, "We gave her a drug to make her sleep, but she's not injured."

I gritted my teeth at that, but forced myself to calm down. Drugging babies was horrible, but I needed to concentrate on the fact that she was safe. And finish this.

"Besides you, how many people are involved?" I asked. I wasn't leaving any room for error this time. We were getting every last fucker who'd been involved in this kidnapping.

"One," Kirby said, in that same slightly dreamy monotone I'd heard from Darcy.

Good. "Who?" I demanded. "Who sent you after Charlie?"

"Itachi," Kirby said. "It's his operation."

Itachi.

My mind raced, scrambling to understand. That explained why Kirby had felt it was okay to steal my niece while she was under vampire protection, but according to the vampires, she already belonged to Itachi. Why would he want to steal something he already had?

Then the full implication hit me. If Itachi was behind this, no vampire in Colorado could be trusted. They were all sworn to him, so he could order any one of them to steal Charlie, right? Even—

At that instant, the world dropped out from under me.

For a second I thought I'd been shot, or tackled to the ground, but then Simon's face was floating in front of mine. "Lex," he was calling, and I realized I'd simply crumpled into the grass. In front of me, Kirby was lying prone on his stomach, his head facing straight up, a grisly, lifeless expression on his face. Quinn stood over his body. He'd snapped Kirby's neck, severing the connection between us and nearly breaking my mind.

As I watched him drive a shredder deep into Kirby's back, I wondered vaguely what it would have looked like if I'd been sensing out life when that happened. Wiping his hands on his jeans, Quinn straightened up, watching me with hooded eyes.

"Quinn?" I said in a small, distant voice. "Why did you do that?"

"I didn't know how long you could hold him," he said guardedly. "And I figured you must be done by now. What did he say?"

I glanced from him to Simon, who was looking at me with wide eyes. A few feet beyond him, Yoda was lying unconscious in the grass. "You guys didn't hear it?" That was impossible—they'd been standing no more than a few feet away.

"You weren't talking out loud, Lex," Simon said. When I just stared at him stupidly, he repeated, "You pressed him without speaking."

I automatically looked down at my hands, at the griffins tattooed on my arms and wrists. *Figure it out later, Lex.* My eyes focused on Quinn again. "So what did he say?" he asked impatiently, looming over me. "Who's behind all of this?"

I didn't think about it, didn't even consider it, or I probably would have realized the futility. But I acted on instinct, and in a fraction of a second I'd snapped up the Beretta and pointed it at Quinn's heart.

"Itachi," I whispered.

Quinn's gun was tucked in his belt—I guess vampires didn't need to worry about shooting themselves in the leg—and I knew he was faster than me, but he made no move to reach for it. "Lex," he began, speaking in a reasonable tone that bordered on patronizing.

"Simon," I interrupted, not looking away from Quinn, "do you remember what you said during my first magic lesson? About Quinn?"

"That I trusted him with my life," came Simon's quiet voice, "as long as me being alive was in Itachi's best interests."

Quinn just looked at me, his face pleading. "Lex," he tried again, but I shook my head tightly.

"You snapped Kirby's neck awfully fast," I growled. "And you staked Darcy, too, just as she was telling me who she worked for."

"I didn't know that," Quinn said.

He began to move now, ever so slowly. He lowered himself onto one knee, then the other. He slowly raised his hands to the top of his head and laced his fingers, keeping his eyes on mine the whole time. "You told me you trusted me," he said softly.

"I've been wrong before," I replied grimly, keeping the Beretta pointed at his heart. The muzzle had begun to tremble, just a little. It wasn't a particularly heavy gun, but I still wasn't going to be able to hold it up much longer without it wobbling. I was going to need to make a decision.

"Then press me," Quinn suggested. "Press me and ask me the question."

I hesitated, then shook my head. I couldn't focus the magic without putting my hands on him, and I couldn't risk putting the gun down. It might not be the greatest weapon against a vampire, but it was a whole lot faster than scrambling to get out one of the shredders. "I can't do that right now."

He nodded, his fingers still laced on his head. "I'm not sworn to Itachi, Lex," he said, his voice quiet.

"Bullshit," I blurted. "You work for him directly. You called him from the Pellar farm, probably to tell him we'd be here. To *warn* him. Why the hell would I believe you?" I said, my voice trembling. I *wanted* to believe him. I wanted it to be true so badly I felt tears prickling my eyes. But I'd been to war, and I'd seen some of the things people could do to each other. I was many things, but I was no longer naive.

"I called Maven. I swear it," Quinn said huskily. "I swear on the life of my wife and the lives of my children, I have never pledged troth to Itachi. I am sworn to *Maven*. I am her agent. I'm her . . ." He trailed off for just a moment, like he was searching for the right words. "Her inside man."

I suddenly flashed back to the night when we'd questioned Kirby outside the frat house. Kirby had said that he and Quinn were both sworn to Itachi. Hadn't Quinn reacted to that, just a little? Not knowing what to think anymore, I began to lower the gun, opening my mouth to ask a follow-up question. But as soon as the weapon moved away from his chest, Quinn leapt at me.

Chapter 39

Several things happened at once.

I started pulling the trigger, and I hit Quinn in the stomach and the leg before he soared over me—and straight into Chewbacca, who had snuck up behind me with the length of pipe. The frat boy roared as Quinn tackled him and rode him to the ground. By the time Chewbacca's back hit the grass, Quinn had sunk his teeth into the kid's neck.

I just watched, stunned, as Quinn fed off the boy. I hadn't seen Quinn in action before, but he was powerful, savage. It was nothing like the polite, delicate wrist feeding I'd given Maven.

"Quinn," I said after a moment. "That's enough. He's done."

For a moment I didn't think he would listen, but then the vampire detached himself from Chewbacca with a snarl, forcing himself upright. The boy's body slumped to the ground, but I could see his eyelids fluttering. He was alive.

Quinn turned to glare at me, defiance in his eyes and blood smeared around his mouth. My gaze dropped to his wounds. Vampires had hard skeletons, I was discovering, but I'd shot him in the gut and the meat of his thigh, and his wounds were healing more slowly than Kirby's shots to the temple had. His clothes were saturated, and he was still bleeding. I looked back up and met his gaze without flinching.

It probably should have bothered me, seeing him feed on the

kid. I was dimly aware that I was supposed to be appalled, but all I felt was . . . tired. And relieved. If Quinn really had been working for Itachi, there'd be no reason for him to save my life.

"Do you believe me now?" he demanded, wiping his mouth with the back of his hand.

"Yes," I said simply. I nodded at Chewbacca. "Can you press him?"

Quinn grunted in affirmation and turned back to the kid, who was sitting up now, one hand pressed to his neck. Quinn crouched awkwardly in front of him, keeping his wounded leg straight. "What's your name?" he commanded.

"Brian."

"Look at me, Brian." The kid complied, eyes huge with shock. "You will stop trying to hurt people. You will go home and forget everything you saw here tonight." For the first time, I could actually *hear* the pressure in his voice, and I wondered if it was the tattoos or if I'd just gotten stronger. "All you will remember is that you and your brothers were messing around out in the country, and you fell on an old barbecue fork. Do you understand?"

Brian nodded, looking a little dazed, and Quinn backed off.

There was another crash from the barn behind me, and I met Quinn's eyes. "Simon," I said, and we turned and sprinted toward the doorway.

In the barn, Simon was lying half on and half off one of the make-shift steel tables, breathing shallowly.

Without discussing it, Quinn walked backward down the aisle, his gun pointed up at the hayloft, while I rushed to Simon's side. Blood had soaked through his jacket, and I could see puncture wounds where he'd landed on something that had sliced through the fabric and into some skin. There was broken glass scattered next to his body, and I couldn't tell how much more was under him. Or inside him. "Simon!" I said, frantic. "How bad is it?"

Simon just stared up at the barn ceiling, blinking. "Fucking booby trap," he mumbled. "Didn't think . . . he had it in him."

"Hey!" I snapped, smacking his cheek a little, and his eyes rolled toward me. "How bad are you hurt?"

"Fell on . . . old lanterns . . ." He winced, but I knew that wasn't his only injury. I glanced down and spotted half of a ladder. I cursed as I leaned down to look at it. Atwood had sawn the rungs partway through the middle, and Simon, who had been expecting a *magical* attack, hadn't even noticed. He'd tried to run up there after my niece. Just like I'd asked.

"Simon?" I said again, even though his eyes had gone distant. There was no response.

"Oooh-ee, girlie, you are in *trouble!*" came a whoop from above me. I backed a few steps away from Simon so I could see the edge of the balcony.

A sixtyish man in jeans and a faded flannel shirt crouched at the edge, a gleeful expression on his leathery face. "That is a Pellar right there. You'd best rush him to a hospital before he bleeds out." He flashed crooked yellow teeth at me, and I pointed my gun at his face.

The older man just tsked at me. "Wouldn't do that, girlie," he drawled, carefully tilting his body sideways. His right hand, which I'd thought he was leaning on, was actually holding a gun that was pointed behind him. I stood on tiptoes to see past the witch. About four feet from his back stood a dark-gray Pack 'n Play, its sides spotless and its plastic edges gleaming. It was the only thing in the entire barn that looked new.

"You might hit the wee one." Atwood said smugly. Then he added, "And if you don't, I will."

I glanced at Quinn, but he was right next to me, so his position wasn't any better. We were at a stalemate.

"Kirby's dead," I called up to the older man. "What exactly is your plan now?"

He chewed the inside of his cheek for a long moment, considering it. "As I see it, y'all are screwed," he said at last. "When Kirby doesn't call, Itachi will send reinforcements here to get the kid. Maybe he'll even come himself."

"What makes you think Itachi's involved?" Quinn asked coolly.

Atwood snorted. "I'm not as dumb as them Pellars think I am. I know who Kirby's been talking to on the phone."

"He might just hang you out to dry," I pointed out. "Leave you here to take the fall."

"He might," Atwood allowed. "But I've got the prize." He smirked at us. "Now, if you wait and fight, the kid could get killed. If you touch me, the kid will *absolutely* get killed." His eyes narrowed. "But if you walk away, she'll go off and live with some nice folks who'll raise her."

I winced. The Beretta was getting heavy again, and I was at the limit of my nerves. "You got any ideas?" I said to Quinn out of the side of my mouth.

He gave a tiny shake of his head. "Ordinarily I'd jump up there, but without knowing how far her aura extends . . ." he murmured.

Seeing us talking, Atwood said, "So? What's it gonna be? You really wanna start a gunfight when I've got mine pointed at the kid?"

I took a long, long look at him and the Pack 'n Play, judging the distance between them. *Help me out here, Sam.* Could I really take risks with Charlie's life? Was that what my sister would want?

"Lex," Quinn whispered to me, "Simon's heart just stopped."

For an instant, I froze. Then I put the Beretta in the holster and nodded at Quinn to follow my lead. He tucked his .45 into his belt behind him. "Okay," I said. "You win."

A dubious look crossed Atwood's features, but I didn't pause long enough to watch. "Let's get out of here before Itachi shows up,"

I said to Quinn, already moving toward the barn door under the hayloft. "The shitkicker can clean up his own mess."

Quinn looked genuinely surprised, but he followed my lead, trusting me. I crossed under the edge of the hayloft and waited for him. Then I reached out and snagged the .45 from his belt, raised it straight in the air—and fired two shots up into the old wood beneath Billy Atwood.

There was a clatter and a muffled thump. I set the pistol down on the closest table and stepped back so that I was just under the edge of the hayloft. "Boost me up," I said urgently.

Quinn just stared at me in shock. "Quinn!" I yelled, and he snapped to comply, forming a stirrup with his hands. I put one of Hazel Pellar's crimson Keens into his hands and he lifted me straight up, putting a little restrained bounce into his movement. I hit the edge of the hayloft with my stomach and held on.

Atwood was lying on the loft floor, shock frozen on his face. I quickly assessed his wounds as I was clambering up onto the floor beside him. It looked like one bullet had gone up through his foot and grazed his forehead. The other had entered through his buttock and gone up into his gut. I had no idea what it was doing in there, but whatever it was had been enough to force him to drop the pistol—I was guessing a spinal injury. "Thank you, Sam," I muttered under my breath.

Kicking the gun away from Atwood's twitching hand, I hurried over to the portable crib, starving for a glimpse of my niece. I peered into the shadows of the loft—

And there she was. My breath caught in my throat, and I fell to my knees next to her, leaning on the edge of the crib. Charlie was on her back in the Pack 'n Play, still wearing the lavender jersey dress John had put on her for the party. I leaned over and hovered my fingers in front of her nose. "Charlie? Baby?" I said. She didn't stir, but her breath was warm and steady on my fingertips. She was perfect.

I wanted nothing more than to scoop her up and rock her in my lap, but I couldn't, not yet. "Quinn!" I yelled. "Stand back, okay?"

Without waiting for his response, I dropped to the floor and kicked Billy Atwood, once, twice, until his body slid off the hayloft. He'd lost consciousness by then, but I would have done it regardless.

"Put him next to Simon!" I ordered. I scooted to the edge of the hayloft, rolled onto my stomach, and lowered myself until I was hanging off the edge by my hands. Then I bent my knees and made the four-foot drop to the barn floor.

Quinn lifted Atwood up, letting him thump down on the steel table next to Simon. "I need you to call an ambulance for Simon, but then stay quiet, okay?" I said grimly. Without waiting for Quinn's nod, I imagined my goggles, closed my eyes, and *focused*.

The first thing I noticed was Quinn. His vampire essence blazed in my radar, a bright, tempting red flare. With an effort, I pushed it away and concentrated on the blue, human sparks of Simon and Atwood.

Only Simon didn't have one.

My gut clenched in fear and desperation, but I forced it down, focusing on Atwood. His blue spark was faint, and I could already see it beginning to dissipate, with the sickly yellowish-brown essence rising to the surface.

I reached in and *pulled*. There was probably a better way to do this, I knew—some sort of ceremony or something—but I had no idea what it was. I had no idea what I was *doing*, really. I was just operating on instinct and hope and the frantic desire not to let my friend die. Or at least, not to let him stay dead. So I imagined my hands were like a net or a fan, and I waved Atwood's essence toward me, not daring to hope.

Later, I would compare it to the scene in *The Little Mermaid* where Ursula pulls the mermaid's voice out of her throat with phantom hands. Instinctively I herded Atwood's essence through the air with cupped palms. It was hard to keep it together, keep it contained once it was released from the witch's body, but my focus was absolute. I drove the essence toward Simon's chest, redirecting it into his heart.

And then I covered his heart with both hands, my tattoos writhing on my arms, and held the essence inside my friend, refusing to let it leave him again.

I don't know how long I stayed there, locked in my mindset like a trance. Eventually the paramedics came, and Quinn had to pull me off Simon by force. I lashed out at him for a moment, beating at him with my fists and feet, and then I returned to my senses as the last bit of my power and energy seeped out of me. I went limp in his arms, and for the third time that day he reached down and scooped me up.

He must have fetched the car and changed his bloody clothes while the ambulance was on the way, because he was wearing clean jeans and a soft, faded T-shirt that tickled my cheek as he carried me outside. This time I was too weak to be annoyed.

Quinn put me in the front seat of the car before disappearing back into the barn for a few minutes. I zoned out, not quite asleep, not quite awake, feeling like I'd run a marathon and then followed it up with two hours of hot yoga and a sedative. I saw the ambulance pull away, sirens screaming, but couldn't muster any feeling about it. I'd done the best I could.

A few more minutes went by, and then the passenger door opened again. Quinn ducked in and thrust a warm bundle into my arms. Charlie! With effort, I managed to lift my arms enough to hold her, inhaling the scent of tear-free shampoo and John's house. I wanted to talk to her, to murmur assurances that both of us would be okay, but I didn't have the energy. She was still unconscious anyway.

Charlie was going to have to sit in my lap, since we didn't have a car seat. Kirby had used one, but there was no sign of his vehicle at Atwood's property, and we didn't want to stick around and look. Quinn told me he had called the cops and told them the truth, more or less: that Atwood was a small-time fence who'd decided to branch out into kidnapping and selling attractive babies to childless couples. It would probably be an issue that there were no actual kidnapped babies on the premises, but Quinn was pretty confident that the cops doing the search would find all sorts of other stolen goods, as well as the baby supplies Atwood had used for Charlie.

Quinn drove carefully back into town, heading straight to John's house. It was after four when he pulled his car into the driveway and turned off the engine, his eyes trained on me. He looked as tired as I felt, and I realized that he was close enough to Charlie to be human.

He wasn't the only one she was affecting. I was still tired, but after twenty minutes of holding a null, I no longer felt like I was about to collapse into a puddle of ooze. I found my voice. "Tell me about working for Maven," I said, shifting Charlie to the crook of my right arm.

Quinn frowned through the windshield for a moment. "She trusts Itachi," he said after a moment of silence. "She believes he is loyal to her. But she's also aware of how . . . *thirsty* he is for power. So just in case, she keeps a handful of vampires who are sworn to *her* scattered throughout the state. And when I was traded to the two of them, she found out I had a gift for pressing people and a background as a cop"—he shrugged—"so she claimed me for hers."

"How did you feel about that?" I asked.

"I was glad." He smiled ruefully. "Well, no, I was bitter and angry and heartbroken, but after I got a little distance from my death, I ended up being grateful that I belonged to her instead of him."

I nodded. "You could have told me."

"I wasn't supposed to tell anyone," he said, looking uncomfortable. "Least of all . . ."

"Least of all an unstable boundary witch who'd swear loyalty to anyone who'd protect her niece?" I said archly.

Quinn sighed, a very human sound. He *was* human, I reminded myself, hugging Charlie close.

"What are we going to do?" I asked. "We have to tell her, right?"

"I'll tell her," he said, nodding. "She'll decide what to do with Itachi."

"I'm coming with you," I said.

He looked at me, squinting a little in the light from the car's dashboard. "I think you should stay with your niece," he said at last. "It could get . . . confrontational."

"That's exactly why I should come," I argued.

"It's not that," he said. "If something happens and Itachi gets away . . . he might decide to make one final run at her before he skips town."

I considered that for a moment. By "if something happens," I understood him to mean "if Itachi kills Maven and me." I didn't have much hope against Itachi under those circumstances, but as last lines of defense go, I was better than nothing.

"Okay," I agreed reluctantly. "But I don't love the idea of you going in there alone."

"I'll be fine." Quinn hesitated for just a moment, glancing at the house in front of us. "Charlie's dad, John . . . Are you in love with him?"

I blinked, taken aback by the bluntness of the question. Then I took another moment to really consider my answer. "No," I said at last. "A long time ago I was, but I was just a kid then."

Quinn watched me carefully. "At the party, you two seemed . . . complicated."

I nodded. "John was my first love, yeah, but he was Sam's last. He'll always be family, but I don't want to be with him." I shook my head. "I just sort of wish he wouldn't be with anyone else, either. Because that would mean that Sam's really gone."

Quinn studied my face for a second, then leaned over the baby's head and pressed his lips to mine in a warm, gentle kiss, maybe the sweetest I'd ever gotten. I kissed him back, my left fingers rising to twist themselves in his shirt.

It was a little awkward with the baby in my arms, but that was okay. This kiss wasn't about sex; we weren't going to go any further right now. It was more like . . . a declaration. He cupped my face in his hands, gently nudging my nose with his own as we pulled apart. We smiled at each other.

Affinity for the dead, indeed.

Quinn said he would call me as soon as it was over, and this time I made him promise. Then I crept to the front door, used the hidden key to open it, and slipped inside with Charlie. I snuck through the silent house and put her in her crib. There were still a few things I would need to explain—why I brought her home early, how I got her here without a car seat, et cetera—but I would figure something out.

Before I got too tired, I dug my phone out of the pocket of the leather jacket and called Lily's cell to check on Simon. He was in surgery. "They think he's going to pull through," she reported. "They just can't figure out how he managed to lose that much blood and still hang on for so long."

I smiled without mirth. "I know the feeling."

There was a long, uncomfortable pause from Lily. Then she asked, "Lex . . . what exactly did you do to him? You know he's going to ask."

I considered the best way to answer, and finally said, "Just call me when he wakes up, and I'll come explain it in person." Lily promised to give him the message, and we hung up. I wasn't looking forward to that conversation. But it suddenly seemed more important than ever for me to understand everything I could about boundary witches, and Simon was my best resource.

I needed to stay until sunrise, and John's couch was studded with half-embedded baby toys, so I wound up sprawled in the same armchair where I'd slept the night after checking myself out of the hospital. I was exhausted, and it was no wonder: over the last twelve hours I'd almost killed a crowd of people, gotten drunk on magic, been heavily tattooed with a funneling spell I still didn't understand, watched my friend die, and brought him back to life. Oh, and I'd been on a desperate search for my baby niece the whole time.

But now Charlie was safe, I'd done right by Sam. I wondered sleepily if I should advise John to get a dog, or at least a security system. Could vampires get around security systems? Probably. Could they get around giant dogs? I'd have to ask Quinn.

My phone began to vibrate ten minutes later while I was still staring into space. I fumbled with the screen and managed to answer it on the third ring. "Quinn?" I whispered. "Are you okay?"

"Sort of," he said, his voice heavy. "But Maven needs you at Magic Beans."

"Now?" I glanced at the clock. It was a little after five, and I couldn't remember ever feeling this tired before. "What about Charlie? Is Itachi—"

"Trust me, Charlie's safe," he said. There was a mechanical tone in his voice that suggested there were other people listening in. And it didn't take a great leap of the imagination to assume they probably drank blood and could hear both sides of our conversation.

"I'm on my way," I said.

Chapter 40

John kept his car keys in a bowl near the back door. I traded them for a hastily written note and pulled the quiet hybrid out into the night. Maybe it was just leftover adrenaline from the day's events, but as I drove through the empty, darkened streets of Boulder, I couldn't push back the feeling that something was very wrong. I kept remembering the coldness in Quinn's voice—it had felt like a mask for something else. Fear? Worry? For the first time, the possibility occurred to me that maybe Maven just didn't believe him. No, that didn't make sense. He was sworn to her, and he was low on the food chain, so he couldn't lie to her, right? This had to be something else.

When I got to Magic Beans, I barely threw John's car into park before I ran toward the door, still in my borrowed clothes. But the front entrance was locked. There was a sign stuck in the glass: "Closed For Inventory. Reopening Sunday." I circled around to the door at the back of the building that led to the big, auditorium-like room. It was locked, too, but it opened as soon as I rattled the knob.

Quinn's head poked out.

"What's going on?" I panted.

"You can come in," he said. His voice was cool, but his eyes were shooting me a meaningful look. The only problem was that I wasn't sure of his meaning. I narrowed my eyes in confusion, and he mouthed, "Be calm." As I nodded, he added, "Maven needs to speak to you right away."

He stepped back, swinging the door wide, and I followed him into the building.

The room was full of people . . . or, rather, vampires. Dozens of them, all of them standing still on the concrete floor, watching me enter. I blinked in surprise. They ranged in age from teens to maybe early fifties, and there were a whole bunch of races and economic classes represented. They appeared to have nothing at all in common, but there was something just . . . *creepy* about them. It took me a second to realize that none of them were moving.

I don't just mean they weren't walking around—I mean they weren't *moving*, at all. People stand around all the time, but they shift their weight, look around, check watches and cell phones. They fidget. But every single person in the room was perfectly still, except for the occasional blink to keep their eyeballs lubricated. I swallowed, trying to banish my fear.

"Hello, Lex," came Maven's pleasant, perfectly even voice from my right. I turned my head and saw her standing on the small raised stage, dressed in a shapeless hemp dress and ankle-high boots. Itachi stood at her right elbow, a little behind her. The body language was obvious: she was in charge of this situation. "Thank you for coming. There has been a lot of excitement in Boulder this evening, not to mention a flurry of rumors. I thought it prudent to clear the air."

I nodded wordlessly, and Maven gestured for me to come toward her. Quinn, who was already at the front of the crowded floor space, gave me a slight nod. I took a deep breath, squared my shoulders, and went to her.

Maven smiled warmly. Unlike Quinn or Itachi, she seemed to be very comfortable with tossing around human expressions and body language, which for some reason unnerved me. She rested a hand on my shoulder, and I managed not to flinch. "Everyone," she called out in a "Can I have your attention" sort of way, which seemed ridiculous given that they were all frozen. "This is Allison Luther, but she prefers the nickname Lex. You may have heard a few rumors about her in the last month. It's true. We have a boundary witch among us."

I expected some reaction from the crowd, but they all remained silent, every eye trained on Maven. "Lex," she began, turning to face me. "Most of these vampires are aware of your involvement in tonight's events on campus, but I don't think many of them realize what a boundary witch can actually do. I thought a demonstration was in order."

I didn't understand. My eyes flickered to Quinn, but he had his game face on, giving me nothing. Sensing my confusion, Maven took a tiny step back, revealing Itachi on her other side. "Perhaps you'd like to ask Itachi a few questions," she suggested.

My stomach plummeted through the floor as I finally got it. She wanted me to press him, the de facto leader of the entire state, in front of dozens of vampires who didn't know that I could do it.

I stared at her, horrified. "This is what you wanted, isn't it?" Maven said. "To show me what you could do?"

From the corner of my eye, I saw Quinn take a single step toward me. He caught himself when Maven sent him a sharp look. Conflict warred in his eyes, and I tried not to wince. If Maven hadn't noticed that Quinn and I cared about each other, she would figure it out any second. I stepped forward. "Of course," I said. Turning to Itachi, I raised my hands, my tattooed arms still mostly covered by Lily's jacket. "May I?" I asked.

Itachi, for his part, looked . . . well, baffled, but with gravitas, like Lawrence Olivier struggling to comprehend a dirty limerick. He obviously didn't know that boundary witches could press vampires, or he would have torn my throat out on the spot. Instead, he was letting the scene play out, confident that none of us had any evidence on him.

Which we didn't, I realized. It was our word against his—everyone else who'd been involved with the kidnapping was dead.

Emboldened, I placed my hands on either side of his head, making sure the tips of my tattoos made contact with his skin.

It took a long time—or at least, that's how it seemed to me. I don't know if it was exhaustion, or if Itachi was simply more powerful than either Darcy or Kirby, but opening the connection between us felt like trying to start a sputtering old lawn mower. He opened his mouth twice, probably to ask what the fuck I was doing, but before he could speak, I felt the connection finally lock into place. He had time for a quick expression of absolute shock before his face went slack.

"Tell me who sent Kirby after Charlotte Wheaton tonight," I said, careful to use my actual voice.

He fought me for a second, trying to push back, but it was too late by then. He was mine. "I did," he replied. The room had been silent before; somehow it seemed to become even *more* silent.

"What did you intend to do with her?"

"Raise her," he said woodenly. "To worship and fear me."

Images of Charlie in servitude flooded my brain, either from my imagination or Itachi's, and the connection between us almost broke. "Tell me your long-term plan for Charlotte Wheaton," I commanded, once I'd regained control.

"I want to train her to kill Maven," he said, his voice dreamy.

Now, finally, the crowd did react. Whispers flowed through the group on the floor, but I ignored the sound, clinging to my focus. "Why?" I asked, adding a little extra pressure.

Itachi hesitated for a second—not because I'd lost the connection, but because he couldn't find the words. "Because . . . because she is more powerful than I am," he said. "I knew I needed a new weapon to take and keep control."

The whispers increased, and I could feel a tremor running through my hands. I was pushing my body hard. "Maven?" I murmured.

She laid a hand on my shoulder. "That is enough."

Sighing with relief, I released the connection between Itachi and me, my mind closing off like shutters on a window. Itachi blinked rapidly, his eyes darting to Maven. He tensed and opened his mouth to speak—

And she reached into his chest and pulled out his goddamned heart.

It happened so quickly. I heard the snap of his ribs, and his blood sprayed over me and those closest to the stage. But it only lasted a second before there was a crackle of magic, like barometric pressure, and his body began to wither and fade, so quickly it was hard for my eyes to comprehend. Within seconds it had collapsed into a pile of sinewy bone. Maven, meanwhile, just calmly contemplated the *heart* in her hand as it shriveled into a knotty bit of . . . well, it looked like jerky for a minute before it disintegrated into dust. Distastefully, she brushed her hands off on her ugly dress.

I glanced at the crowd. Every single vampire, including Quinn, looked completely flabbergasted. It would have been funny, really, if their stares of disbelief and fear had been directed only at Maven. But no, many of them were giving me the same look.

"That was my own fault," Maven announced grandly, gesturing at the bundle of Itachi's remains. "I grew too complacent, it seems. Allowed too much to pass. There will be some changes in Colorado in the immediate future." She gestured at me, and this time I did flinch a little, my arms going up to protect my chest. "Lex works for me now. She will never press any of you without my express permission," she added, a warning for me in her voice. "But please treat her with the same courtesy and respect you show Quinn." She made a show of checking her watch. "There will be much more, of course, but the sunrise is not long off, and I know many of you have traveled far tonight. Please feel free to use my own accommodations," she said sweetly.

When they realized they'd been dismissed, the vampires began to shuffle off, looking decidedly uncertain of themselves . . . for vampires. Maven moved into the crowd to coordinate everyone's daytime resting places, while I stood where I was, frozen in shock.

Quinn sidled up to me. "What just happened?" I asked, my voice no louder than a whisper.

He took my elbow and, after exchanging a glance with Maven, led me across the room and into the tiny office where I'd first met Maven and Itachi. I collapsed into one of the visitors' chairs. Quinn came over and knelt on the floor beside it, touching my face, my hands, checking on me. "I'm okay," I mumbled.

"You need rest," he said. "You've been through a lot."

"Do we have to clean up that body?" I wondered aloud.

He glanced over his shoulder. "We have a . . . daytime hiding place. It can go there for today, and we'll take care of it tonight. We need to figure out the logistics for your new job anyway."

"What just happened?" I repeated, my brain on autopilot. "Did we win?"

He sighed. "Yes and no. Itachi's gone, and you got the job, which means Charlie will be left alone. But Maven has also outed you to every vampire in the state. They'll be afraid of you now, which means they'll want you dead."

"Then why did she tell them? She could have forced Itachi to confess by herself."

"Yes, but this way, she's tied your fate to hers," Quinn said, his words oddly formal. "You're under her protection now, just like Charlie is. As long as you have Maven behind you, everything will be fine. If anything happens to her, the other vampires will kill you." I gave him a wry look. I wasn't the type who needed things sugarcoated, but jeez. "Like it or not, Lex," he said gently, as if needing to make sure I understood, "you work for the vampires now."

A giggle escaped my lips, surprising us both.

"What?" he asked, giving me a small smile.

"Hazel is going to be *pissed.*"

Epilogue

When I finally drifted to sleep that morning, showered and clean, two dogs and a cat draped around me on the bed, I dreamed of Sam. Or I guess you could say I called her.

Our old bedroom came into view more slowly this time, my mind struggling to form the meeting room where our essences could talk. Finally, though, the haze cleared away, and there was my sister, sitting cross-legged on her bed with a wide grin on her face.

"Thank you for saving Charlie," she said. "I wish I could hug you, babe."

"It's okay, Sammy."

"Now, when you wake up," she instructed, "you should get John to take her to the doctor, just to make sure whatever they gave her wore off."

I smiled, a little sadly. My sister had been such a naturally gifted mom, yet she'd had so little time to actually *be* that person. "I will."

"And be careful," she warned me. "With the vampires, I mean. They're going to push you, push what you're willing to do." She hesitated for a moment, then grinned again. "Although that Quinn fella, he's pretty easy on the eyes, huh?"

"Exactly how much of my life can you see up there?" I asked, feeling a little scandalized.

She waved a hand. "You know I can't tell you that." She fidgeted for a moment, biting at a fingernail, and then added, "Speaking of things I can't tell you . . . there's something you deserve to know about now, but I'm not supposed to say anything."

I arched an eyebrow at my twin. "Be more cryptic, Samantha."

"I know, I know. It's just that there's a lot I'm not allowed to say." She hesitated, as if struggling with her wording. "Just . . . ask Jesse Cruz how I really died."

And just like that, she blinked away.

Acknowledgments

Starting a new series can be a lot of work, and *Boundary Crossed* wouldn't have made it into your hands without plenty of help. My eternal gratitude goes out to the beta team: my beta anchor (betanchor? There's a combo in there somewhere) Elizabeth Kraft and my fellow urban fantasy author Steve McHugh—not to mention Brieta Bejin and Matt Ventimiglia, who gave me lots of advice on the lovely city of Boulder, and Denise Grover Swank, who tossed in some last-minute "chemistry" advice (wink wink nudge nudge).

My special thanks also to Sybil Ward, a former US soldier who did a wonderful job keeping an eye on how I portrayed Lex's state of mind. For more background on US soldiers in Iraq and how they handle coming home, I also highly recommend David Finkel's wonderful nonfiction works *The Good Soldiers* and *Thank You for Your Service*. Although I can never personally comprehend what it was like to fight in Iraq during the war, I credit Mr. Finkel's books with helping me get as close to understanding as I can.

Of course, this page wouldn't be complete without sending my gratitude to the 47North team, especially Britt Rogers, who will be running the world any minute now, and Angela Polidoro, who was always quick with brilliant advice.

Last but so far from least, thank you to my family, especially my husband, sisters, parents, and—you know what, just all of you. You are instrumental in keeping me sane and reasonably productive, without which I would never have Lena, Scarlett, Sashi, and now Lex. I love you guys.

An Excerpt From
Melissa F. Olson's
Dead Spots

Prologue

Jared loved trees.

His little sister was the better climber, to his disgust, but at twelve, she lacked Jared's reverence for the trees, his respect. Emily would shimmy up, crow her victory, and skitter down again, laughing and breathless. It was Jared who loved to sit and listen to the wind, to find the perfect nook and watch the leaves move.

After their mother died, Jared and Emily took to the trees, escaping their house each hot summer night to sneak into the park at the end of their block. They stayed as late as they could to avoid having to hear their father cry and hiccup into his Jim Beam. Sometimes he brought women home—cheap, disposable women with acrylic nails and vacant eyes—and this was too much, too far. It was better in the park, where they could climb the trees. After the sun set, the mothers packed up their children and the joggers ran home. A listless park employee came to chain and lock the gate, and Jared could pretend they were out of the city and truly alone. Emily curled up at the bottom of a tree to read a book in the harsh streetlight, brushing at the ants. Jared would nestle into the branches above, humming so his sister wouldn't be afraid.

One night at the end of September, Emily fell asleep, and Jared could listen to the wind and the quiet all by himself. He squinted at the branches, trying to see shapes and patterns, and wished again that the LA smog didn't cover all the stars, that he could just pick up and go somewhere clear. Somewhere with trees. He was supposed to have his learner's permit by now, but his father couldn't sober up enough to help him get it. Jared thought about his mother, who hadn't been a saint but had tried hard, and his father, who was so weak and pitiful that Jared already felt as though he himself were the adult. He was turning this thought over in his head as he too drifted off to sleep.

When Jared opened his eyes, hours had gone by, and he almost fell out of the tree in his shock. He opened his mouth to yell for Emily, but closed it again when he heard the voices below. He squinted downward but couldn't make out the figures surrounding the tree. Had they been discovered? How much trouble would they get in? Jared suddenly had a child's impulse to hide, to leave Emily to take the blame, but after a quick flash of guilt, he began to creep slowly toward the lower branches. He relaxed an inch when he made out the two ordinary-looking young people talking to his sister. Just checking on her, probably. Before he could call down, though, one of them moved suddenly, and Jared heard Emily's scream, shattering the air. He suddenly couldn't move, couldn't go help, even as he saw the second figure join the first: gently, reverently, biting down into Emily's neck.

Chapter 1

At 2:00 a.m., Eli's ceiling fan made a sluggish *whug-whug-whug* noise and stopped moving. I know because I was staring at it.

It had been an unusually warm September in Los Angeles, and the temperature in Eli's bedroom had to be pushing eighty. I threw off the sheets and muttered something along the lines of "stupid fan," which made Eli stir beside me, rolling over and throwing an arm across my waist. He smelled like the sea, from surfing, and in the weak light from the streetlamps outside the window, his deep tan glowed against my pale skin. He nuzzled into my hair, and I was saved from having to awkwardly disentangle when my cell phone started playing a muted rendition of "Black Magic Woman." Work. Thank God. I gently lifted Eli's arm and rolled out of the bed, hurrying over to my jeans, which had somehow gotten thrown over the mirror on top of his dresser. Huh. Luckily, my cell phone had clung to the pocket, and I grabbed it and flipped it open. Yes, my phone still flips. It is also not smart.

Kirsten's voice was cheerful and apologetic, as usual, directing me to a vacant house in Calabasas where a young realtor and her two friends had been playing with love spells. I picked up the men's wallet I keep in my front pocket and pulled on the jeans and purple top I'd worn to the bar. Then I grabbed my keys and my knee-high boots and tiptoed out. I didn't leave a note. He would figure it out when I got to the door, anyway.

Whenever I'm not around, Eli has to go back to being a werewolf.

I hadn't felt drunk when I followed Eli's pickup truck back to his place, but it still took me a few tries to find my van, which I guess is what happens when you drive after two glasses of whiskey. On the way to Calabasas, I used the stoplights to put on my boots and pull back the tangled mass of my long near-black hair. Even in LA, the streets were nearly deserted, and I had that creepy sensation that city people get when there's no one around, like maybe everyone else in the world has died or left without your knowledge. Before I had to go too far into that pleasant line of thinking, though, the lady in my GPS announced that I'd arrived at my destination.

I pulled into the driveway of a raincloud-gray McMansion, and the witches—I use that term loosely—opened the garage door and waved for me to pull the van right in. They were nearly identical: all blonde, all scared, and all wearing some slight variation of light, sleeveless sweaters and what my mother used to call slacks. I would not have been able to pick them out of a lineup.

"Ms. Bernard?" said the blonde on the right, stepping forward. "I'm Sarah-Ann Harris. Thank you so much for coming."

"Not a problem," I said briskly. I slid open the van's side door and grabbed my work duffel. "Tell me what's happening."

Sarah-Ann Harris glanced at her two friends, who looked away. "Um, well, we were trying this spell, you know, because Hillary's boyfriend keeps cheating, and we wanted him to fall in love with her alone for forever?" She headed into the house, walking backward like a tour guide, and I followed her, with the generic blondes trailing behind us like a limp parade. Because they're such a diverse collection of talents, I never know what I'm going to get on any given witch case, but the silent line of expensive highlights was a little unnerving. "There was this sacrifice part—"

"Chicken or dove?" I interrupted.

"Um, dove. But then we couldn't go through with killing it because Ashley's in PETA." she babbled. Hillary and Ashley? Seriously? Worst witch names ever.

"And we were gonna just set it free, and then something happened . . ."

We rounded a corner, entering a spacious dining/living area with no furniture. I eyed the polished hardwood floors first and decided I didn't need to bother with surgical booties. At the far end, glass double doors opened onto a three-seasons porch where I could see candles and books spread on the floor. As we came closer, I spotted a panicked little gray dove hopping frantically about in the doorway, and it took me a second to figure out what the big deal was. "Is its *head* on backward?" That was a new one, even for me.

"Yeah, um, I'm not sure what happened. We think maybe the pages got stuck in the spell book? And we did some kind of healing spell instead, only it didn't heal?" Sarah-Ann said. "So, like, if you go near it, the dove's head will go back, right?" She looked like she was about to cry. God.

"No," I said grimly. I strode across the room, my boot heels striking the polished wooden floors like a timpani drum, dropped my bag, and bent down to pick up the terrified little thing. It cuddled into my chest for a moment, looking at my face with its backward-facing eyes. I took a deep breath and snapped its neck with my other hand. Ick. But at least its head was now facing the correct direction. When I looked up, Sarah-Ann and the clones were staring at me like I'd just stabbed a preschooler.

"But," Sarah-Ann said in the reasonable, patronizing voice of a woman who's used to getting the window booth, "we called for you. Kirsten said to call when something went wrong, and we did."

I crouched in front of my duffel and retrieved a ziplock baggie the size of a shoebox, talking as I worked. "Ongoing spells undo themselves around me, and you couldn't perform any kind of magic within about ten feet of me. But the dove wasn't really under a spell anymore, it was physically changed." With the little body secured in the ziplock and the ziplock stowed in my bag, I turned back to the women, handing each of them one of Kirsten's cards. "Sarah-Ann,

I know you have this number, but here it is again, just in case. Kirsten will be expecting each of you to call her tomorrow morning to discuss what happened tonight. If she asks her questions and is satisfied with your answers, that'll be the end of the matter. Do not make her track you down."

They each nodded at me, frightened, and I took another deep breath, trying to stay professional. "Now, will there be anything else? Do you guys need help clearing up your spell materials?" They shook their heads in unison, still looking stunned, and I gave them a nod in return. "Then I'll see myself out. Have a good evening." I turned on my heel and marched out to the van, putting the little dead bird in the freezer compartment in the back. In the morning, I'd take it to Artie, my furnace guy. If it had been a human body, I'd have gone right away, but a dead dove wasn't worth sneaking onto his property at 3:00 a.m.

Back in the van, I leaned my head against the steering wheel for a second. It irritated me that they had expected me to fix the dove, or maybe it just irritated me that I couldn't. I'm a null, which means I can cancel out magic within a radius, but I have limits, too. As I sat up and turned the ignition, my cell phone rang again, and I checked the caller ID. Dashiell. Great. A vampire was just what my night needed. I flipped it open. "Bernard."

"Scarlett," Dashiell began, drawing out the *a* as usual. "There is a situation in La Brea Park. I will meet you at the entrance in fifteen minutes."

"Uh, okay. I'm in Calabasas now, on a Kirsten case, but I'll be there as fast—" I realized that I was talking to myself and shut the phone, glancing at the clock. *Shit.* Even with no traffic on the freeway, there was no way I could get to the entrance of La Brea Park in fifteen minutes; it was impossible. And Dashiell was coming himself, in person? He might be the most powerful creature in Los Angeles, but like most vampires, Dashiell stays the hell away from me if at all possible, not wanting to age even a few minutes.

It had to be really bad.

I briefly considered speeding, but only in that way you think about something you know you'll never do. That's one of the rules: don't get pulled over. My van is checked weekly to make sure all the lights are working and the gas and oil tanks are filled, and it undergoes a full inspection and detailing twice a year. If the cops pulled me over right now, all they would find was a dead dove, but even that would be bad. I had no idea whether they'd be able to figure out that I'd broken its neck backward, but even something small like that could get the rumor snowball rolling, or at best, tarnish my reputation with the supernatural community. In my business, there's no such thing as an overreaction.

I drove south on the 405 highway as fast as I dared, three miles over the speed limit, but I was still another fifteen minutes late to meet Dashiell. La Brea Park closes at sunset, so the actual entrance driving to get into the park was chained and locked. As I pulled up to the gate, he materialized out of the shadows, a fortyish-looking vampire in impeccable black pants and a deep-green cashmere T-shirt. His dark-brown hair was a little mussed, and his blandly handsome face looked dangerously angry. I was definitely in trouble.

I parked the van at the curb and rolled my window down, turning the engine off. Dash took a few steps toward me, but stayed well out of my ten-foot radius.

"You are late," he stage-whispered. "Our situation has grown more complicated."

No point in groveling. "I'm sorry. Tell me what's happening."

"I got a text message from a private number and came to see for myself," he said shortly. "There are three bodies ahead; they have been torn apart. There is blood, so I do not think it was the vampires. Perhaps one of Will's people." Vampires, as a rule, don't waste blood. Will is the head of the local werewolf pack. The werewolves in Los Angeles occasionally run around in the parks that close at sunset. LA is one of the rare cities where the Old World creatures share territory more or less in peace, though when push comes to shove, Dashiell is in charge. Witches and werewolves aren't immortal, after all. It's an uneasy peace, darkened by preceding centuries of tension, and it works best when everyone sticks to their own kind. Usually the vampires take care of vampire business, and the wolves take care of wolf business, but there is some overlap, especially when the perpetrator is unknown.

"What's the complication?"

"A jogger ran through here two minutes ago, and she saw the bodies. You have only a few minutes before the police arrive." He pointed toward a nearby clump of trees. "Go." And just like that, he vanished.

I grabbed my duffel and sprinted toward the trees, fumbling to pull out a flashlight as I went. In cases where there's a time crunch, you have to prioritize, and priority one would be the bodies. There would still be evidence without bodies, but the police couldn't do much with a few bloodstains outdoors in a public park. I raced through the trees, trying to avoid roots and rocks, and stopped dead a quarter mile in, where I found a small clearing that had been painted red.

Melissa F. Olson's *Dead Spots*—also set in
the Old World universe—is available now
from 47North. *Boundary Lines*, the
Boundary Crossed sequel, releases Fall 2015.

About the Author

Photo © 2013 Elizabeth Kraft

Melissa F. Olson was raised in Chippewa Falls, Wisconsin, and studied film and literature at the University of Southern California in Los Angeles. After a brief stint in the Hollywood studio system, Melissa moved to Madison, Wisconsin, where she eventually acquired a master's degree from the University of Wisconsin–Milwaukee, a husband, a mortgage, a teaching gig, two kids, and two comically oversized dogs, not at all in that order. Learn more about Melissa, her work, and her dog at www.MelissaFOlson.com.